The Book of Mischief

Also by Steve Stern

Isaac and the Undertaker's Daughter
The Moon & Ruben Shein
Lazar Malkin Enters Heaven
Harry Kaplan's Adventures Under Ground
A Plague of Dreamers
The Wedding Jester
The Angel of Forgetfulness
The North of God
The Frozen Rabbi

For Children

Mickey and the Golem
Hershel and the Beast

The Book of Mischief

NEW AND SELECTED STORIES

Steve Stern

Graywolf Press

This publication is made possible in part by a grant provided by the Minnesota State Arts Board, through an appropriation by the Minnesota State Legislature from the Minnesota general fund and its arts and cultural heritage fund with money from the vote of the people of Minnesota on November 4, 2008, and a grant from the Wells Fargo Foundation Minnesota. Significant support has also been provided by the National Endowment for the Arts; Target; the McKnight Foundation; and other generous contributions from foundations, corporations, and individuals. To these organizations and individuals we offer our heartfelt thanks.

Published by Graywolf Press
250 Third Avenue North, Suite 600
Minneapolis, Minnesota 55401

www.graywolfpress.org

Published in the United States of America

Printed in Canada

ISBN 978-1-55597-621-7

2 4 6 8 9 7 5 3 1
First Graywolf Printing, 2012

Library of Congress Control Number: 2012936222

Cover design: Christa Schoenbrodt, Studio Haus

Cover art: *Prague Skyline* by David Wicks, www.wicksart.com.
Photo of acrobat Henry Wheaton, SHOW Circus Studio,
by Addam Hagerup, www.addamidiom.com.

For Sabrina again, and again

Contents

The Book of Mischief

I

NORTH MAIN STREET, MEMPHIS

The Tale of a Kite

It's safe to say that we Jews of North Main Street are a progressive people. I don't mean to suggest we have any patience with freethinkers, like that crowd down at Thompson's Café; tolerant within limits, we're quick to let subversive elements know where they stand. Observant (within reason), we keep the Sabbath after our fashion, though the Saturday competition won't allow us to close our stores. We keep the holidays faithfully, and are regular in attending our modest little synagogue on Market Square. But we're foremost an enterprising bunch, proud of our contribution to the local economy. Even our secondhand shops contain up-to-date inventories, such as stylish automobile capes for the ladies, astrakhan overcoats for gentlemen—and our jewelers, tailors, and watchmakers are famous all over town. Boss Crump and his heelers, who gave us a dispensation to stay open on Sundays, have declared more than once in our presence, "Our sheenies are good sheenies!" So you can imagine how it unsettles us to hear that Rabbi Shmelke, head of that gang of fanatics over on Auction Street, has begun to fly.

We see him strolling by the river, if you can call it strolling. Because the old man, brittle as a dead leaf, doesn't so much walk as permit himself to be dragged by disciples at either elbow. A mournful soul on a stick, that's Rabbi Shmelke; comes a big wind and his bones will be scattered to powder. His eyes above his foggy pince-nez are a rheumy residue in an otherwise parchment face, his beard (Ostrow calls it his "lunatic fringe") an ashen broom gnawed by mice. Living mostly on air and the strained generosity of in-laws, his followers are not much more presentable. Recently transplanted from Shpink, some godforsaken Old World backwater that no doubt sent them packing, Shmelke and his band of crackpots are a royal embarrassment to our community.

We citizens of Hebrew extraction set great store by our friendly relations with our gentile neighbors. One thing we don't need is religious zealots poisoning the peaceable atmosphere. They're an eyesore and a liability,

Shmelke's crew, a threat to our good name, seizing every least excuse to make a spectacle. They pray conspicuously in questionable attire, dance with their holy books in the street, their doddering leader, if he speaks at all, talking in riddles. No wonder we judge him to be frankly insane.

It's my own son, Ziggy the *kaddish*, who first brings me word of Shmelke's alleged levitation. Then it's a measure of his excitement that, in reporting what he's seen, he also reveals he's skipped Hebrew school to see it. This fact is as troubling to me as his claims for the Shpinker's airborne faculty, which I naturally discount. He's always been a good boy, Ziggy, quiet and obedient, if a little withdrawn, and it's unheard of that he should play truant from his Talmud Torah class. Not yet bar mitzvahed, the kid has already begun to make himself useful around the store, and I look forward to the day he comes into the business as my partner. (I've got a sign made up in anticipation of the event: J. Zipper & Son, Spirits and Fine Wines.) So his conduct is distressing on several counts, not the least of which is how it shows the fanatics' adverse influence on our youth.

"Papa!" exclaims Ziggy, bursting through the door from the street—since when does Ziggy burst? "Papa, Rabbi Shmelke can fly!"

"Shah!" I bark. "Can't you see I'm with a customer?" This is my friend and colleague Harry Nussbaum, proprietor of Memphis Bridge Cigars, whose factory supports better than fifteen employees and is located right here on North Main. Peeling bills from a bankroll as thick as a bible, Nussbaum's in the process of purchasing a case of Passover wine. (From this don't conclude that I'm some exclusively kosher concern; I carry also your vintage clarets and sparkling burgundies, blended whiskeys and sour mash for the yokels, brandies, cordials, brut champagnes—you name it.)

Nussbaum winces, clamping horsey teeth around an unlit cigar. "Shomething ought to be done about thosh people," he mutters, and I heartily concur. As respected men of commerce, we both belong to the executive board of the North Main Street Improvement Committee, which some say is like an Old Country kahal. We chafe at the association, regarding ourselves rather as boosters, watchdogs for the welfare of our district. It's a responsibility we don't take lightly.

When Nussbaum leaves, I turn to Ziggy, his jaw still agape, eyes bugging from his outsize head. Not from my side of the family does he get such a head, bobbling in his turtleneck like a pumpkin in an eggcup. You'd think it was stuffed full of wishes and big ideas, Ziggy's head, though to my knowledge it remains largely vacant.

"You ought to be ashamed of yourself."

"But, Papa, I seen it." Breathless, he twists his academy cap in his hands. "We was on the roof and we peeped through the skylight. First he starts to pray, then all of a sudden his feet don't touch the floor . . ."

"I said, enough!"

Then right away I'm sorry I raised my voice. I should be sorry? But like I say, Ziggy has always been a pliant kid, kind of an amiable mediocrity. Not what you'd call fanciful—where others dream, Ziggy merely sleeps—I'm puzzled he should wait till his twelfth year to carry such tales. I fear he's fallen in with a bad crowd.

Still, it bothers me that I've made him sulk. Between my son and me there have never been secrets—what's to keep secret?—and I don't like how my temper has stung him into furtiveness. But lest he should think I've relented, I'm quick to add, "And never let me hear you played hooky from cheder again."

And that, for the time being, is that.

But at our weekly meeting of the Improvement Committee—to whose board I'm automatically appointed on account of my merchant's credentials—the issue comes up again. It seems that others of our children have conceived a fascination for the Shpinker screwballs, and as a consequence are becoming wayward in their habits. Even our chairman Irving Ostrow of Ostrow's Men's Furnishings, in the tasteful showroom of which we are assembled—even his own son Hershel, known as an exemplary scholar, has lately been delinquent in his studies.

"He hangs around that Auction Street shtibl," says an incredulous Ostrow, referring to the Hasids' sanctuary above Klotwog's Feed Store. "I ask him why and he tells me, like the mountains should tremble"—Ostrow pauses to sip his laxative tea—"'Papa,' he says, 'the Shpinker rebbe can fly.' 'Rebbe' he calls him, like an alter kocker!"

"Godhelpus!" we groan in one voice—Nussbaum, myself, Benny Rosen of Rosen's Delicatessen—having heard this particular rumor once too often. We're all of a single mind in our distaste for such fictions—all save old Kaminsky, the synagogue beadle ("Come-insky" we call him for his greetings at the door to the shul), who keeps the minutes of our councils.

"Maybe the Shmelke, he puts on the children a spell," he suggests out of turn, which is the sort of hokum you'd expect from a beadle.

At length we resolve to nip the thing in the bud. We pass along our apprehensions to the courtly Rabbi Fein, who runs the religious school in the synagogue basement. At our urgency he lets it be known from the pulpit that fraternizing with Hasids, who are after all no better than heretics, can be hazardous to the soul. He hints at physical consequences as well, such as warts and blindness. After that nothing is heard for a while about the goings-on in the little hall above the feed store that serves as the Shpinkers' sanctuary.

What does persist, however, is a certain (what you might call) bohemian-ism that's begun to manifest itself among even the best of our young. Take, for instance, the owlish Hershel Ostrow: in what he no doubt supposes a subtle affectation—though who does he think he's fooling?—he's taken to wearing his father's worn-out homburg; and Mindy Dreyfus, the jeweler's son, has assumed the Prince Albert coat his papa has kept in mothballs since his greenhorn days. A few of the older boys sport incipient beards like the characters who conspire to make bombs at Thompson's Café, where in my opinion they'd be better off. Even my Ziggy, whom we trust to get his own hair cut, he talks Plott the barber into leaving the locks at his temples. He tries to hide them under his cap, which he's begun to wear in the house, though they spiral out like untended runners.

But it's not so much their outward signs of eccentricity as their increasing remoteness that gets under our skin. Even when they're present at meals or their after-school jobs, their minds seem to be elsewhere. This goes as well for Ziggy, never much of a noise to begin with, whose silence these days smacks more of wistful longing than merely having nothing to say.

"Mama," I frown at my wife, Ethel, who's shuffling about the kitchen of our apartment over the liquor store. I'm enjoying her superb golden broth, afloat with eyes of fat that gleam beneath the gas lamp like a peacock's tail; but I nevertheless force a frown. "Mama, give a look on your son."

A good-natured, capable woman, my Ethel, with a figure like a brick mikveh, as they say, she seldom sits down at meals. She prefers to eat on the run, sampling critical spoonfuls as she scoots back and forth between the table and the coal-burning range. At my suggestion, however, she pauses, pretending to have just noticed Ziggy, who's toying absently with his food.

"My son? You mean this one with the confetti over his ears?" She bends to tease his side locks, then straightens, shaking her head. "This one ain't mine. Mine the fairies must of carried him off and left this in his place." She ladles more soup into the bowl he's scarcely touched. "Hey, stranger, eat your knaidel."

Still his mother's child, Ziggy is cajoled from his meditations into a grudging grin, which I fight hard against finding infectious. Surrendering, I make a joke: "Mama, I think the ship you came over on is called the *Ess Ess Mein Kind.*"

Comes the auspicious day of Mr. Crump's visit to North Main Street. This is the political boss's bimonthly progress, when he collects his thank-yous (usually in the form of merchandise) from a grateful Jewish constituency. We have good reason to be grateful, since in exchange for votes and assorted spoils, the Red Snapper, as he's called, has waived the blue laws for our district. He also looks the other way with respect to child labor and the dry law that would have put yours truly out of business. Ordinarily Boss Crump and his entourage, including his handpicked mayor du jour, like to tour the individual shops, receiving the tributes his shvartze valet shleps out to a waiting limousine. But today, tradition notwithstanding, we're drawn out of doors by the mild April weather, where we've put together a more formal welcome.

When the chrome-plated Belgian Minerva pulls to the curb, we're assembled in front of Ridblatt's Bakery on the corner of Jackson Avenue and North Main. Irving Ostrow is offering a brace of suits from his emporium, as solemnly as a fireman presenting a rescued child, while Benny Rosen appears to be wrestling a string of salamis. Harry Nussbaum renders up a bale of cigars, myself a case of schnapps, and Rabbi Fein a ready blessing along with his perennial bread and salt. Puffed and officious in his dual capacity as neighborhood ward heeler and committee chair, Ostrow has also prepared an address: "We citizens of North Main Street pledge to be a feather in the fedora of Mayor Huey, I mean Blunt . . ." (Because who can keep straight Mr. Crump's succession of puppet mayors?)

Behind us, under the bakery awning, Mickey Panitz is ready to strike up his klezmer orchestra; igniting his flash powder, a photographer from the *Commercial Appeal* ducks beneath a black hood. Everyone (with the exception, of course, of the Shpinker zealots, who lack all civic pride) has turned out for the event, lending North Main Street a holiday feel. We bask in Boss Crump's approval, who salutes us with a touch to the rim of his rakish straw skimmer, his smile scattering a galaxy of freckles. This is why what happens next, behind the backs of our visitors, seems doubly shameful, violating as it does such a banner afternoon.

At first we tell ourselves we don't see what we see; we think, maybe a plume of smoke. But looks askance at one another confirm not only that we share the same hallucination but that the hallucination gives every evidence of being real. Even from such a distance it's hard to deny it: around the corner of the next block, something is emerging from the roof of the railroad tenement that houses the Shpinker shtibl. It's a wispy black and gray something that rises out of a propped-open skylight like vapor from an uncorked bottle. Escaping, it climbs into the cloudless sky and hovers over North Main Street, beard and belted caftan aflutter. There's a fur hat resembling the rotary brush of a chimney sweep, a pair of dun-stockinged ankles (to one of which a rope is attached) as spindly as the handles on a scroll. Then it's clear that, risen above the telephone wires and trolley lines, above the water tanks, Rabbi Shmelke floats in a doleful ecstasy.

We begin talking anxiously and at cross-purposes about mutual understanding through public sanitation and so forth. We crank hands left and right, while Mickey Panitz leads his band in a dirgelike rendition of "Dixie." In this way we keep our notables distracted until we can pack them off (photojournalist and all) in their sable limousine. Then, without once looking up again, we repair to Ostrow's Men's Furnishings and convene an extraordinary meeting of the Improvement Committee.

Shooting his sleeves to show flashy cuff links, Ostrow submits a resolution: "I hereby resolve we dispatch to the Shpinkers a delegatz, with the ultimatum they should stop making a nuisance, which it's degrading already to decent citizens, or face a forcible outkicking from the neighborhood. All in agreement say oy."

The only dissenting voice is the one with no vote.

"Your honors know best"—this from Kaminsky, a greenhorn till his dying day—"but ain't it what you call a miracle, this flying rebbe?"

For such irrelevance we decide it also wouldn't hurt to find a new secretary.

En route across the road to the shtibl, in the company of my fellows, I give thanks for small blessings. At least my Ziggy was telling the truth about Shmelke. Though I'm thinking that, with truths like this, it's maybe better he should learn to lie.

We trudge up narrow stairs from the street, pound on a flimsy door, and are admitted by one of Shmelke's unwashed. The dim room lists slightly like the deck of a ship, tilted toward windows that glow from a half-light filtering through the lowered shades. There's a film of dust in the air that lends the graininess of a photogravure to the bearded men seated at the long table, swaying over God only knows what back-numbered lore. By the wall there's an ark stuffed with scrolls, a shelf of moldering books, spice boxes, tarnished candelabra, amulets against the evil eye.

It's all here, I think, all the blind superstition of our ancestors preserved in amber. But how did it manage to follow us over an ocean to such a far-flung outpost as Tennessee? Let the goyim see a room like this, with a ram's horn in place of a clock on the wall, with the shnorrers wrapped in their paraphernalia mumbling hocus-pocus instead of being gainfully employed, and right away the rumors start. The yids are poisoning the water, pishing on communion wafers, murdering Christian children for their blood. Right away somebody's quoting the *Protocols of Zion*. A room like this, give or take one flying rebbe, can upset the delicate balance of the entire American enterprise.

Returned at least in body from the clouds, old Shmelke sits at the head of the table, dispensing his shopworn wisdom. An unlikely source of authority, he appears little more substantial than the lemon shaft pouring over him from the open skylight.

"It is permitted to consult with the guardian spirits of oil and eggs . . . ," he intones, pausing between syllables to suck on a piece of halvah; an "Ahhh" goes up from disciples who lean forward to catch any crumbs. ". . . But sometimes the spirits give false answers." Another sadder but wiser "Ahhh."

When our eyes adjust to the murk, we notice that the ranks of the Shpinkers (who until now have scarcely numbered enough for a minyan) have swelled. They've been joined this afternoon, during Hebrew school hours no less, by a contingent of the sons of North Main Street, my own included. He's standing in his cockeyed academy cap, scrunched between nodding Hasids on the rebbe's left side. To my horror Ziggy, who's shown little enough aptitude for the things of this world, never mind the other, is also nodding to beat the band.

"Home!" I shout, finding myself in four-part harmony with the other committee members. Our outrage since entering having been compounded with interest, we won't be ignored anymore. But while some of the boys do indeed leave their places and make reluctantly for the door, others stand their ground. Among them is Ostrow's brainy son Hershel and my nebbish, that never before disobeyed.

Having turned toward us as one, the disciples look back to their tzaddik, who God forbid should interrupt his discourse on our account. Then Hershel steps forth to confront us, pince-nez identical to Shmelke's perched on his nose. "You see," he explains in hushed tones, though nobody asked him, "figuratively speaking, the rebbe is climbing Jacob's ladder. Each rung corresponds to a letter of tetragrammaton, which in turn corresponds to a level of the soul . . ." And bubkes-bobkes, spouting the gibberish they must've brainwashed him into repeating. I look at Ostrow, who's reaching for his heart pills.

Then who should pipe up but the pipsqueak himself, come around to tug at my sleeve. "Papa"—like he can't decide whether he should plead or insist—"if they don't hold him down by the rope, Rabbi Shmelke can fly away to paradise."

I can hardly believe this is my son. What did I do wrong that he should chase after moth-eaten yiddishe swamis? Did he ever want for anything? Didn't I take him on high holidays to a sensible synagogue, where I showed him how to mouth the prayers nobody remembers the meaning of? Haven't I guaranteed him the life the good Lord intends him for?

Not ordinarily combative, when the occasion calls for it I can speak my mind. To the papery old man whom I hold personally accountable, I ask point-blank, "What have you done to my child?"

Diverted at last from his table talk, Rabbi Shmelke cocks his tallowy head; he seems aware for perhaps the first time of the presence among his faithful of uninvited hangers-on.

"Gay avek!" he croaks at the remaining boys. "Go away." When nobody budges, he lifts a shaggy brow, shrugs his helplessness. Then he resumes in a voice like a violin strung with cobweb, "Allow me to tell you a story . . ."

"A story, a story!" The disciples wag their heads, all of them clearly idiots.

The rebbe commences some foolishness about how the patriarch Isaac's soul went on vacation while his body remained under his father's knife. Along with the others I find myself unable to stop listening, until I feel another tug at my sleeve.

"Papa," Ziggy's whispering, Adam's apple bobbing like a golf ball in a fountain, "they have to let him out the roof or he bumps his head on the ceiling."

"Do I know you?" I say, shaking him off. Then I abruptly turn on my heel and exit, swearing vengeance. I'm down the stairs and already crossing Auction Street, when I realize that my colleagues have joined me in my mortification. I suggest that drastic measures are in order, and as my anger has lent me an unaccustomed cachet, all say aye.

They agree there's not a minute to lose, since every day we become more estranged from our sons. (Or should I say sons and daughters, because you can't exclude old Kaminsky's orphaned granddaughter Ida, a wild girl with an unhealthy passion for books.)

But days pass and Rabbi Fein complains that even with the threat of his ruler, not to mention his assistant Nachum (whom the boys call Knock'em), he can't keep his pupils in Hebrew class. Beyond our command now, our children are turning their backs on opportunity in favor of emulating certifiable cranks. They grow bolder, more and more of them exhibiting a freakish behavior they no longer make any pretense to conceal. For them rebellion is a costume party. They revel in the anomalous touch, some adopting muskrat caps (out of season) to approximate the Hasid's fur shtreimel. Milton Rosen wears a mackintosh that doubles as a caftan, the dumb Herman Wolf uses alphabet blocks for phylacteries. My own Ziggy has taken to picking his shirttails into ritual tassels.

He still turns up periodically for meals, silent affairs at which even Ethel is powerless to humor us. For his own good I lock him in his bedroom after dinner, but he climbs out the window, the little pisher, and scrambles down the fire escape. "Not from my side of the family does he get such a streak of defiance," I tell Ethel, who seems curiously resigned. "I think maybe comes the fairies to take him back again," she says, but am I worried? All right, so I'm worried, but I'm confident that, once the Shpinkers have been summarily dealt with, my son will return to the fold, tail between legs.

Still the problem remains: what precisely should we do? Time passes and the Shpinkers give no indication of developing a civic conscience; neither do they show any discretion when it comes to aiding their blithering rebbe to fly. (If you want to dignify what he does as flying; because in midair he's as bent and deflated as he is on earth, so wilted you have to wonder if he even knows he's left the ground.) In response to their antics, those of us with any self-respect have stopped looking up.

Of course we have our spies, like Old Man Kaminsky, who has nothing better to do than ogle the skies. He tells us that three times a day, morning, noon, and evening, rain or shine, and sometimes nonstop on Shabbos, Shmelke hovers above the chimneys. He marks us from a distance like some wizened dirigible, a sign designating our community as the haven of screwballs and extremists. We're told that instead of studying (a harmless enough endeavor in itself), the shiftless Shpinkers now spend their time testing various grades of rope. From the clothesline purchased at Hekkie's Hardware on Commerce Street, they've graduated to hawser obtained from steamboat chandlers down at the levee. They've taken to braiding lengths of rope, to splicing and paying them out through the skylight, so that Shmelke can float ever higher. Occasionally they might maneuver their rebbe in fishtails and cunning loop-the-loops, causing him to soar and dive; they might send him into electrical storms from which he returns with fluorescent bones. Sometimes, diminished to a mote, the old man disappears in the clouds, only to be reeled back carrying gifts—snuffboxes and kiddush cups made of alloys never seen on this planet before.

Or so says Old Man Kaminsky, whom we dismiss as having also fallen under Shmelke's mind control. We're thankful, in any case, that the Shpinkers now fly their tzaddik high enough that he's ceased to be a serious distraction. (At first the yokels, come to town for the Saturday market, had mistaken him for an advertising ploy, their sons taking potshots with peashooters.) But out of sight isn't necessarily to say that the rebbe is out of mind, though we've gotten used to keeping our noses to the ground. We've begun to forget about him, to forget the problems with our young. What problems? Given the fundamental impossibility of the whole situation, we start to embrace the conviction that his flights are pure fantasy.

Then Ziggy breaks his trancelike silence to drop a bombshell. "I'm studying for bar mitzvah with Rabbi Shmelke," he announces, as Ethel spoons more calf's-foot jelly onto my plate. But while his voice issues the challenge, Ziggy's face, in the shadow of his academy cap, shows he's still testing the water.

Ethel's brisket, tender and savory as it is, sticks in my gorge. I want to tell him the tzaddik's a figment of his imagination and let that be an end to it, but Ziggy's earnestness suggests the tactic won't work.

"What's wrong," I ask, clearing my throat with what emerges as a seismic roar, "ahemmm . . . what's wrong with Rabbi Fein?"

"He ain't as holy."

Directly the heartburn sets in. "And what's holy got to do with it?"

Ziggy looks at me as if my question is hardly deserving of an answer. Condescending to explain, however, he finds it necessary to dismount his high horse, doffing his cap to scratch his bulbous head. "Holy means, you know, like scare . . . I mean sacred."

"Unh-hnh," I say, folding my arms and biting my tongue. Now I'm the soul of patience, which makes him nervous.

"You know, *sacred*," he reasserts, the emphasis for his own sake rather than mine.

"Ahhh," I nod in benign understanding, enjoying how his resolve begins to crack.

"That's right," pursues Ziggy, and tries again to fly in the face of my infernal tolerance, lacking wings. "Like magic."

I'm still nodding, so he repeats himself in case I didn't hear.

"Oh sure, ma-a-agic," I reply, with the good humor of a parent introduced to his child's imaginary friend.

Flustered to the point of fighting back tears, Ziggy nevertheless refuses to surrender, retreating instead behind a wall of hostility.

"You wouldn't know magic if it dumped a load on your head!"

You have to hand it to the kid, the way he persists in his folly; I never would have thought him capable of such high mishegoss. But when the admiration passes, I'm fit to be tied; I'm on my feet, jerking him by the scrawny shoulders, his head whipping back and forth until I think I'm maybe shaking it clear of humbug.

"I'll magic you!" I shout. "Who's your father anyway, that feeble-minded old scarecrow or me? Remember me, Jacob Zipper, that works like a dog so his son can be a person?" Then I see how he's staring daggers; you could puncture your conscience on such daggers, and so I pipe down.

I turn to Ethel, cooling her backside against the hardwood icebox, an oven mitten pressed to her cheek. "So whose side are you on?" I appeal.

She gives me a look. "This is a contest already?"

But tempted as I am to make peace, I feel they've forced my hand; I cuff the boy's ear for good measure and tell my wife, "I don't know him anymore, he's not my son."

Understand, it's a tense time; the news from the Old Country is bad. In Kiev they've got a Jew on trial for blood libel, and over here folks are grumbling about swarms of Hebrews washing onto our shores. Some even blame the wreck of the *Titanic* on the fact that there were Guggenheims onboard. It's a climate created by ignorance, which will surely pass with the coming enlightened age—when our sons will have proved how indispensable we are. But in the meantime we must keep order in our own house.

At the next meeting of the North Main Street Improvement Committee I propose that the time is ripe to act.

Ostrow and the others stir peevishly, their hibernation disturbed. "Act? What act?" It seems they never heard of fanatics in our bosom or the corruption of our youth.

"Wake up!" I exhort them. "We got a problem!"

Slowly, scratching protuberant bellies and unshaven jaws, they begin to snap out of it; they swill sarsaparilla, light cigars, overcoming a collective amnesia to ask me what we should do.

"Am I the chairman?" I protest. "Ostrow's the chairman." But it's clear that my robust agitation has prompted them to look to me for leadership, and I'm damned if I don't feel equal to the test.

"Cut off the head from the body," I'm suddenly inspired to say, "and your monster is kaput."

At sundown the following evening the executive board of the Improvement Committee rounds the corner into Auction Street. There's a softness in the air, the stench of the river temporarily overwhelmed by potted chicken wafting from the windows over the shops. It's a pleasant evening for a stroll, but not for us, who must stay fixed on the critical business at hand. We're all of one mind, I tell myself, though yours truly has been elected to carry the hedge shears—donated for the deed by Hekkie Schatz of Hekkie's Hardware. Ostrow our titular chair, Nussbaum the treasurer, Benny Rosen the whatsit, all have deferred the honor to me, by virtue of what's perceived as my greater indignation.

This time we don't knock but burst into the dusty shtibl. As it turns out our timing is perfect: a knot of disciples—it appears that several are needed to function as anchors—is unraveling the rope beneath the open skylight. Rising into the lemon shaft (now turning primrose), his feet in their felt slippers arched like fins, Rabbi Shmelke chants the Amidah prayer: "Baruch atoh Adonoy, blessed art Thou, our God and God of our Fathers . . ."

The Shpinkers start at our headlong entrance. Then gauging our intentions by the sharp implement I make no attempt to hide, they begin to reel their rebbe back in. My colleagues urge me to do something quick, but I'm frozen to the spot; though Shmelke's descending, I'm still struck with the wonder of watching him rise. "Decease!" cries Ostrow, to no effect whatsoever; then he and the others shove me forward.

Still I dig in my heels. Disoriented, I have the sensation that the room is topsy-turvy; above is below, and vice versa. Standing on the ceiling as the rebbe is hauled up from the depths, we're in danger of coming unglued, of tumbling headfirst through the skylight. I worry for our delinquent sons, who now outnumber the Shpinkers, and in their fantastic getups are almost indistinguishable from the original bunch. Among them, of course, is Ziggy, elflocks curling like bedsprings from under his cap, perched on a chair for the better view.

Then the room rights itself. Holding the handles of the hedge shears, I could say that I'm gripping the wings of a predatory bird, its mind independent of my own. I could say I only hang on for dear life, while it's the shears themselves that swoop forth to bite the rope in two. But the truth is, I do it of my own free will. And when the rope goes slack—think of a serpent when the swami stops playing his pipe—I thrill at the gasps that are exhaled ("Ahhh") all around. After which: quiet, as old Shmelke, still chanting, floats leisurely upward again, into the primrose light that is deepening to plum.

When he's out of sight, my Ziggy is the first to take the initiative—because that's the type of person we Zippers are. The rascal, he bolts for the open window followed by a frantic mob. I too am swept into the general exodus, finding myself somehow impelled over the sill out onto the fire escape. With the others I rush up the clattering stairs behind (incidentally) Ida Kaminsky, who's been hiding there to watch the proceedings. I reach the roof just in time to see my son, never an athletic boy—nor an impulsive or a headstrong or a rebellious one, never to my knowledge any of these—I see him swarm up the slippery pane of the inclined skylight (which slams shut after) and leap for the rope. Whether he means to drag the old man down or hitch a ride, I can't say, but latched on to the dangling cord, he begins, with legs still cycling, to rise along with the crackpot saint.

Then uttering some complicated mystical war cry, Hershel Ostrow, holding on to his homburg, follows Ziggy's lead. With his free hand Hershel grabs my boy's kicking right foot, and I thank God when I see them losing altitude, but this is only a temporary reversal. Because it seems that Rabbi Shmelke, handicaps notwithstanding, has only to warble louder, adjusting the pitch of his prayer to gain height. I console myself that if he continues ascending, the fragile old man will come apart in the sky; the boys will plummet beneath his disembodied leg. Or Ziggy, whose leap I don't believe in the first place, unable to endure the burden of his companion, will let go. I assure myself that none of this is happening.

From beside me the wild Ida Kaminsky has flung herself onto Hershel's ankle, her skirt flaring to show off bloomers—which make a nice ribbon for the tail of a human kite. But even with her the concatenation doesn't end: the shambling Sanford Nussbaum and Mindy Dreyfus, the halfwit Herman Wolf, Rabbi Fein's own pious Abie in his prayer shawl, Milton Rosen in his mackintosh, all take their turn. Eventually every bad seed of North Main Street is fastened to the chain of renegade children trailing in the wake of old Shmelke's ecstasy.

One of the rebbe's zealots, having mounted a chimney pot, makes a leap at the flying parade, but for him they're already out of reach. Then another tries and also fails. Is it because, in wanting to pull their tzaddik back to the earth, his followers are heavy with a ballast of desire? This seems perfectly logical to me, sharing as I do the Hasids' despair.

Which is why I shout "Ziggy, come back! All is forgiven!" and make to jump into the air. In that instant I imagine I grab hold and am carried aloft with the kids. The tin roofs, the trolley lines, the brand-new electric street-lights in their five-globed lamps, swiftly recede, their incandescence humbled by the torched western sky. Across the river the sunset is more radiant than a red flare over a herring barrel, dripping sparks—all the brighter as it's soon to be extinguished by dark clouds swollen with history rolling in from the east. Then just as we're about to sail beyond those clouds, I come back to myself, a stout man and no match for gravity.

Lazar Malkin Enters Heaven

My father-in-law, Lazar Malkin, may he rest in peace, refused to die. This was in keeping with his lifelong stubbornness. Of course there were those who said that he'd passed away already and come back again, as if death were another of his so-called peddling trips, from which he always returned with a sackful of crazy gifts.

There were those in our neighborhood who joked that he'd been dead for years before his end. And there was more than a little truth in this. Hadn't he been declared clinically kaput not once but twice on the operating table? Over the years they'd extracted more of his internal organs than it seemed possible to do without. And what with his wooden leg, his empty left eye socket concealed by a gabardine patch, his missing teeth and sparse white hair, there was hardly enough of old Lazar left in this world to constitute a human being.

"Papa," my wife, Sophie, once asked him, just after the first of his miraculous recoveries, "what was it like to be dead?" She was sometimes untactful, my Sophie, and in this she took after her father—whose child she was by one of his unholy alliances. (Typically obstinate, he had always refused to marry.)

Lazar had looked at her with his good eye, which, despite being set in a face like last week's roast, was usually wet and amused.

"Why ask me?" he wondered, refusing to take the question seriously. "Ask Alabaster the cobbler, who ain't left his shop in fifty years. He makes shoes, you'd think he's building coffins. Ask Petrofsky, whose lunch counter serves nobody but ghosts. Ask Gruber the shammes or Milstein the tinsmith. Ask your husband, who is as good as wearing his sewing machine around his neck . . ."

I protested that he was being unfair, though we both knew that he wasn't. The neighborhood, which was called the Pinch, had been dead since the war. Life and business had moved east, leaving us with our shops falling down around our ears. Myself and the others, we kidded ourselves that North Main Street would come back. Our children would come back again. The ready-made industry, we kept insisting, was just a passing fancy; people would return to quality. So who needed luftmenschen like Lazar to remind us that we were deceived?

"The Pinch ain't the world," he would inform us, before setting off on one of his mysterious peddling expeditions. He would haul himself into the cab of his corroded relic of a truck piled with shmattes and tools got on credit from a local wholesale outfit. Then he would sputter off in some random direction for points unknown.

Weeks later he would return, his pockets as empty as the bed of his truck. But he always brought back souvenirs in his burlap sack, which he prized like the kid in the story who swapped a cow for a handful of beans.

"I want you to have this," he would say to Mr. Alabaster or Gruber or Schloss or me. Then he would give us a harp made out of a crocodile's tail; he would give us a Negro's toe, a root that looked like a little man, a contraption called a go-devil, a singletree, the uses of which he had no idea. "This will make you wise," he told us. "This will make you amorous. This came from Itta Bena and this from Nankipoo"—as if they were places as far away as China, which for all we knew they were.

"Don't thank me," he would say, like he thought we might be speechless with gratitude. Then he would borrow a few bucks and limp away to whatever hole in the wall he was staying in.

Most of my neighbors got rid of Lazar's fetishes and elixirs, complaining that it made them nervous to have them around. I was likewise inclined, but in deference to my wife I kept them. Rather than leave them lying around the apartment, however, I tossed them into the storage shed behind my shop.

No one knew how old Lazar really was, though it was generally agreed that he was far past the age when it was still dignified to be alive. None of us, after all, was a spring chicken anymore. We were worn out from the years of trying to supplement our pensions with the occasional alteration or the sale of a pair of shoelaces. If our time should be near, nobody was complaining. Funerals were anyhow the most festive occasions we had in the Pinch. We would make a day of it, traveling in a long entourage out to the cemetery, then back to North Main for a feast at the home of the bereaved. You might say that death was very popular in our neighborhood. So it aggravated us that Lazar, who preceded us by a whole generation, should persist in hanging around.

He made certain that most of what we knew about him was hearsay. It was his nature to be mysterious. Even Sophie, his daughter by one of his several scandals, knew only the rumors. As to the many versions of his past, she would tell me to take my pick. "I would rather not, if you don't mind," I said. The idea of Lazar Malkin as a figure of romance was a little more than I could handle. But that never stopped Sophie from regaling me by telling stories of her father the way another woman might sing to herself.

He lost his eye as a young man, when he refused to get out of the way of a rampaging Cossack in his village of Podolsk. Walking away from Kamchatka, where he'd been sent for refusing to be drafted into the army of the czar, the frostbite turned to gangrene and he lost his leg. Or was it the other way around? He was dismembered by a Cossack, snowblinded in one eye for good? . . . What did it matter? The only moral I got out of the tales of Lazar's mishegoss was that every time he refused to do what was sensible, there was a little less of him left to refuse with.

It puzzled me that Sophie could continue to have such affection for the old kocker. Hadn't he ruined her mother, among others, at a time when women did not go so willingly to their ruin? Of course, the living proofs of his wickedness were gone now. His old mistresses had long since passed on, and it was assumed there were no offspring other than Sophie. Though sometimes I was haunted by the thought of the surrounding countryside populated by the children of Lazar Malkin.

So what was the attraction? Did the ladies think he was some pirate with his eye patch and clunking artificial leg? That one I still find hard to swallow. Or maybe they thought that with him it didn't count. Because he refused to settle down to any particular life, it was as if he had no legitimate life at all. None worth considering in any case. And I cursed myself for the time I took to think about him, an old fool responsible for making my wife a bastard—though who could think of Sophie in such a light?

"You're a sick man, Lazar," I told him, meaning in more ways than one. "See a doctor."

"I never felt better, I'll dance on your grave," he insisted, asking me incidentally, did I have a little change to spare?

I admit that this did not sit well with me, the idea of his hobbling a jig on my headstone. Lie down already and die, I thought, God forgive me. But from the way he'd been lingering in the neighborhood lately, postponing his journeys, it was apparent to whoever noticed that something was wrong. His unshaven face was the gray of dirty sheets, and his wizened stick of a frame was shrinking visibly. His odor, no longer merely the ripe stench of the unwashed, had about it a musty smell of decay. Despite my imploring, he refused to see a physician, though it wasn't like he hadn't been in the hospital before. (Didn't I have a bundle of his unpaid bills to prove it?) So maybe this time he knew that for what he had there wasn't a cure.

When I didn't see him for a while, I supposed that, regardless of the pain he was in, he had gone off on another of his peddling trips.

"Your father needs a doctor," I informed Sophie over dinner one night.

"He won't go," she said, wagging her chins like, what can you do with such a man? "So I invited him to come stay with us."

She offered me more kreplach, as if my wide-open mouth meant that I must still be hungry. I was thinking of the times he'd sat at our table in the vile, moth-eaten overcoat he wore in all seasons. I was thinking of the dubious mementos he left us with.

"Don't worry," said my good wife. "He won't stay in the apartment . . ."

"Thank God."

". . . But he asked if he could have the shed out back."

"I won't have it!" I shouted, putting my foot down. "I won't have him making a flophouse out of my storehouse."

"Julius," said Sophie in her watch-your-blood-pressure tone of voice, "he's been out there a week already."

I went down to the little brick shed behind the shop. The truth was that I seldom used it—only to dump the odd bolt of material and the broken sewing machines that I was too attached to to throw away. And Lazar's gifts. Though I could see through the window that an oil lamp was burning beneath a halo of mosquitoes, there was no answer to my knock. Entering anyway, I saw cobwebs, mouse droppings, the usual junk—but no Lazar.

Then I was aware of him propped in a chair in a corner, his burlap sack and a few greasy dishes at his feet. It took me so long to notice because I was not used to seeing him sit still. Always he was hopping from his real leg to his phony, being a nuisance, telling us we ought to get out and see more of the world. Now with his leg unhitched and lying across some skeins of mildewed cloth, I could have mistaken him for one of my discarded manikins.

"Lazar," I said, "in hospitals they at least have beds."

"Who sleeps?" he wanted to know, his voice straining up from his hollow chest. This was as much as admitting his frailty. Shocked out of my aggravation, I proceeded to worry.

"You can't live in here," I told him, thinking that no one would confuse this with living. "Pardon my saying so, but it stinks like Gehinnom." I had observed the coffee tin he was using for a slop jar.

"A couple of days," he managed in a pathetic attempt to recover his native chutzpah, "and I'll be back on my feet again. I'll hit the road." When he coughed, there was dust, like when you beat a rug.

I looked over at one of the feet that he hoped to be back on and groaned. It might have been another of his curiosities, taking its place alongside the boar's tusk and the cypress knee.

"Lazar," I implored, astonished at my presumption, "go to heaven already. Your organs and limbs are waiting there for a happy reunion. What do you want to hang around this miserable place anyway?" I made a gesture intended to take in more than the shed, which included the whole of the dilapidated Pinch with its empty shops and abandoned synagogue. Then I understood that for Lazar my gesture had included even more. It took in the high roads to Iuka and Yazoo City, where the shvartzers swapped him moonshine for a yard of calico.

"Heaven," he said in a whisper that was half a shout, turning his head to spit on the floor. "Heaven is wasted on the dead. Anyway, I like it here."

Feeling that my aggravation had returned, I started to leave.

"Julius," he called to me, reaching into the sack at his feet, extracting with his withered fingers I don't know what—some disgusting composition of feathers and bones and hair. "Julius," he wheezed in all sincerity, "I have something for you."

What can you do with such a man?

I went back the following afternoon with Dr. Seligman. Lazar told the doctor don't touch him, and the doctor shrugged like he didn't need to dirty his hands.

"Malkin," he said, "this isn't becoming. You can't borrow time the way you borrow gelt."

Seligman was something of a neighborhood philosopher. Outside the shed he assured me that the old man was past worrying about. "If he thinks he can play hide-and-go-seek with death, then let him. It doesn't hurt anybody but himself." He had such a way of putting things, Seligman.

"But Doc," I said, still not comforted, "it ain't in your backyard that he's playing his farkokte game."

It didn't help, now that the word was out, that my so-called friends and neighbors treated me like I was confining old Lazar against his will. For years they'd wished him out of their hair, and now they behaved as if they actually missed him. Nothing was the same since he failed to turn up at odd hours in their shops, leaving them with some ugly doll made from cornhusks or a rabbit's foot.

"You think I like it," I asked them, "that the old fortz won't get it over with?" Then they looked at me like it wasn't nice to take his name in vain.

Meanwhile Sophie continued to carry her noodle puddings and bowls of chicken broth out to the shed. She was furtive in this activity, as if she were harboring an outlaw, and sometimes I thought she enjoyed the intrigue. More often than not, however, she brought back her plates with the food untouched.

I still looked in on him every couple of days, though it made me nauseous. It spoiled my constitution, the sight of him practically decomposing.

"You're sitting shivah for yourself, that's what," I accused him, holding my nose. When he bothered to communicate, it was only in grunts.

I complained to Sophie: "I was worried a flophouse, but charnel house is more like it."

"Shah!" she said, like it mattered whether the old so-and-so could hear us. "Soon he'll be himself again."

I couldn't believe my ears.

"Petrofsky," I confided at his lunch counter the next day, "my wife's as crazy as Lazar. She thinks he's going to get well."

"So why you got to bury him before his time?"

Petrofsky wasn't the only one to express this sentiment. It was contagious. Alabaster, Ridblatt, Schloss, they were all in the act, all of them suddenly defenders of my undying father-in-law. If I so much as opened my mouth to kvetch about the old man, they told me hush up, they spat against the evil eye. "But only yesterday you said it's unnatural he should live so long," I protested.

"Doc," I told Seligman in the office, where he sat in front of a standing skeleton, "the whole street's gone crazy. They think that maybe a one-legged corpse can dance again."

The doctor looked a little nervous himself, like somebody might be listening. He took off his nickel-rimmed spectacles to speak.

"Maybe they think that if the angel of death can pass over Lazar, he can pass over the whole neighborhood."

"Forgive me, Doctor, but you're crazy too. Since when is everyone so excited to preserve our picturesque community? And anyway, wouldn't your angel look first in an open grave, which after all is what the Pinch has become?" Then I was angry with myself for having stooped to speaking in riddles too.

But in the end I began to succumb to the general contagion. I was afraid for Lazar, I told myself, though—who was I kidding?—like the rest, I was afraid for myself.

"Sophie," I confessed to my wife, who had been treating me like a stranger lately, "I wish that old Lazar was out peddling again." Without him out wandering in the boondocks beyond our neighborhood, returning with his cockamamie gifts, it was like there wasn't a "beyond" anymore. The Pinch, for better or worse, was all there was. This I tried to explain to my Sophie, who squeezed my hand like I was her Julius again.

Each time I looked in on him, it was harder to distinguish the immobile Lazar from the rest of the dust and drek. I described this to Seligman, expecting medical opinion, and got only that it put him in mind of the story of the golem—dormant and moldering in a synagogue attic these six hundred years.

Then there was a new development. There were bits of cloth sticking out of the old man's nostrils and ears, and he refused to open his mouth at all.

"It's to keep his soul from escaping," Sophie told me, mussing my hair as if any ninny could see that. I groaned and rested my head in my hands, trying not to imagine what other orifices he might have plugged up.

After that I didn't visit him anymore. I learned to ignore Sophie, with her kerchief over her face against the smell, going to and fro with the food he refused to eat. I was satisfied it was impossible that he should still be alive, which fact made it easier to forget about him for periods of time.

This was also the tack that my friends and neighbors seemed to be taking. On the subject of Lazar Malkin we had all become deaf and dumb. It was like he was a secret we shared, holding our breath lest someone should find us out.

Meanwhile on North Main Street it was business (or lack of same) as usual.

Of course I wasn't sleeping so well. In the middle of the night I remembered that, among the items and artifacts stored away in my shed, there was my still-breathing father-in-law. This always gave an unpleasant jolt to my system. Then I would get out of bed and make what I called my cocktail—some antacid and a shpritz of soda water. It was summer and the rooms above the shop were an oven, so I would go out to the open back porch for air. I would sip my medicine, looking down at the yard and the shed—where Lazar's lamp had not been kindled for a while.

On one such night, however, I observed that the lamp was burning again. What's more, I detected movement through the little window. Who knew but some miracle had taken place and Lazar was up again? Shivering despite the heat, I grabbed my bathrobe and went down to investigate.

I tiptoed out to the shed, pressed my nose against the filthy windowpane, and told myself that I didn't see what I saw. But while I bit the heel of my hand to keep from crying out loud, he wouldn't go away—the stoop-shouldered man in his middle years, his face sad and creased like the seat of someone's baggy pants. He was wearing a rumpled blue serge suit, its coat a few sizes large to accommodate the hump on his back. Because it fidgeted and twitched, I thought at first that the hump must be alive; then I understood that it was a hidden pair of wings.

So this was he, Malach ha-Mavet, the Angel of Death. I admit to being somewhat disappointed. Such a sight should have been forbidden me, it should have struck me blind and left me gibbering in awe. But all I could feel for the angel's presence was my profoundest sympathy. The poor shnook, he obviously had his work cut out for him. From the way he massaged his temples with the tips of his fingers, his complexion a little bilious (from the smell?), I guessed that he'd been at it for a while. He looked like he'd come a long way expecting more cooperation than this.

"For the last time, Malkin," I could hear him saying, his tone quite similar in its aggravation to the one I'd used with Lazar myself, "are you or aren't you going to give up the ghost?"

In his corner old Lazar was nothing, a heap of dust, his moldy overcoat and eye patch the only indications that he was supposed to resemble a man.

"What are you playing, you ain't at home?" the angel went on. "You're at home. So who do you think you're fooling?"

But no matter how much the angel sighed like he didn't have all night, like the jig was already up, Lazar Malkin kept mum. For this I gave thanks and wondered how, in my moment of weakness, I had been on the side of the angel.

"Awright, awright," the angel was saying, bending his head to squeeze the bridge of his nose. The flame of the lamp leaped with every tired syllable he uttered. "So it ain't vested in me, the authority to take from you what you won't give. So what? I got my orders to bring you back. And if you don't come dead, I take you alive."

There was a stirring in Lazar's corner. Keep still, you fool, I wanted to say. But bony fingers had already emerged from his coatsleeves; they were snatching the plugs of cloth from his ears. The angel leaned forward as if Lazar had spoken, but I could hear nothing—oh, maybe a squeak like a rusty hinge. Then I heard it again.

"Nu?" was what Lazar had said.

The angel began to repeat the part about taking him back, but before he could finish, Lazar interrupted. "Take me where?"

"Where else?" said the angel. "To paradise, of course."

There was a tremor in the corner that produced a commotion of moths.

"Don't make me laugh," the old man replied, actually coughing the distant relation of a chortle. "There ain't no such place."

The angel: "I beg your pardon?"

"You heard me," said Lazar, his voice become amazingly clear.

"Okay," said the angel, trying hard not to seem offended. "We're even. In paradise they'll never believe you're for real."

Where he got the strength then I don't know—unless it was born from the pain that he'd kept to himself all those weeks—but Lazar began to get up. Spiderwebs came apart and bugs abandoned him like he was sprouting out of the ground. Risen to his foot, he cried out,

"There ain't no world but this!"

The flame leaped, the windowpane rattled.

This was apparently the final straw. The angel shook his melancholy head, mourning the loss of his patience. He removed his coat, revealing a sweat-stained shirt and a pitiful pair of wings no larger than a chicken's.

"Understand, this is not my style," he protested, folding his coat, approaching what was left of my father-in-law.

Lazar dropped back into the chair, which collapsed beneath him. When the angel attempted to pull him erect, he struggled. I worried a moment that the old man might crumble to pieces in the angel's embrace. But he was substantial enough to shriek bloody murder, and not too proud to offer bribes: "I got for you a nice feather headdress . . ."

He flopped about and kicked as the angel stuffed him headfirst into his own empty burlap peddler's sack.

Then the world-weary angel manhandled Lazar—whose muffled voice was still trying to bargain from inside his sack—across the cluttered shed. And hefting his armload, the angel of death battered open the back door, then carried his burden, still kicking, over the threshold.

I threw up the window sash and opened my mouth to shout. But I never found my tongue. Because that was when, before the door slammed behind them, I got a glimpse of kingdom come.

It looked exactly like the yard in back of the shop, only—how should I explain it?—sensitive. It was the same brick wall with glass embedded on top, the same ashes and rusty tin cans, but they were tender and ticklish to look at. Intimate like (excuse me) flesh beneath underwear. For the split second that the door stayed open, I felt that I was turned inside out, and what I saw was glowing under my skin in place of my kishkes and heart.

Wiping my eyes, I hurried into the shed and opened the back door. What met me was a wall, some ashes and cans, some unruly weeds and vines, the rear of the derelict coffee factory, the rotten wooden porches of the tenements of our dreary neighborhood. Then I remembered—slapping my forehead, stepping gingerly into the yard—that the shed had never had a back door.

Climbing the stairs to our apartment, I had to laugh out loud.

"Sophie!" I shouted to my wife—who, without waking, told me where to find the bicarbonate of soda. "Sophie," I cried, "set a place at the table for your father. He'll be coming back with God only knows what souvenirs."

Zelik Rifkin and the Tree of Dreams

I. The Lost Tribe

Even by the infernal standards of the Memphis summers, this one was unnaturally hot. So intense was the swelter in the flats above the shops on North Main Street that the wallpaper bubbled and the menorah candles melted into shapes like choirs of ghosts. Great blocks of ice dissolved in their tongs to tiny cubes before the iceman in his saturated apron could carry them upstairs. Ceiling fans turned sluggishly if they turned at all, mired in the heaviness of the humid air. Housewives cooked stuffed kishkes on their windowsills and complained that their own kishkes boiled, their brains stewed in the ovens of their claustrophobic apartments.

All day the population of the Pinch—mostly Jews who liked to call themselves a lost tribe, so far were they scattered from the more kosher habitats of their brethren—kept as much as possible to the shade. Wearing ice bags in place of their yarmulkes they gathered in panting quorums to say prayers invoking rain. In the evenings they sat in folding chairs outside their shops, fanning themselves till all hours with limp newspapers from which the print had run. Later on they brought out picnic baskets and cradles, rolled-up pallets and little spirit lamps. Then they took the short walk over to Market Square Park, where they bedded down alfresco for the night.

A relatively barren parcel of land where an auction block for slaves had once stood, Market Square was tucked behind a row of shops on North Main. It was bordered by an ironworks and the redbrick pile of the Anshei Sphard Synagogue, and the Neighborhood House, where the greenhorns were taught how to box-step and brush their teeth. As a park Market Square had only the barest of parklike attributes. There was a dried-up stone fountain and a ramshackle band pavilion, behind whose trellised skirts local lovebirds conducted trysts. There was an enormous old patriarch oak. It was under the broad boughs of the oak, as if wanting shade from the starry firmament itself, that the citizens of the Pinch made their outdoor dormitory.

II. Friends and Relations

Famous for his cowardice all along the length and breadth of North Main Street, Zelik Rifkin spied on the other boys at their adventures. Often he went out of his way just to frown in disapproval over the foolhardy risks they took. Walking home from the Market Avenue School, for instance, he sometimes made wide detours in order to pass by their haunts. He spooked about the levee, hiding behind rafts of lumber and cotton bales, or peeked around corners, looking up into a slice of sky between alley walls. Then he was likely to see them, the redoubtable Jakie Epstein and his cronies, hurtling in their daredevil competitions from roof to roof.

Taking a dim but fascinated view of their activities, Zelik kibitzed the pranks they played on unsuspecting citizens. From a safe distance he watched them singeing a cop's mustaches with a well-aimed magnifying glass, setting fire to the gazette in a reader's hands. He watched them angling with bamboo poles for the sheitel wigs of the Orthodox wives, or stealing a camera from the pawnshop to take photographs of couples necking under the bandstand, threatening to blackmail them for the evidence.

Sometimes, though it tied his stomach in knots, Zelik was a witness to their shadier exploits. He saw them waltzing the ticket holders in front of the Phoenix Athletic Club for the purpose of deftly picking their pockets, or beating up on trespassing members of the Irish Mackerel Gang in Market Square. Once or twice he was there in the alley behind the Green Owl Café, when racketeers dispatched them into Negro precincts with booklets of policy stubs. He saw them receiving the bottles that Lazar the bootlegger handed them out the Green Owl's back door.

If ever they caught him at his spying, Jakie and the boys might invite Zelik to join in their operations, confident that the invitation alone would scare him away. "Nu, Rifkin," they shouted, "come and help us roll Charlie No Legs for muggles. Come on already, we'll get shikkered blind and jump off the Harahan Bridge."

Flushed from hiding, Zelik would tell them, "Thanks all the same." Then pulling down his golf cap to the bridge of his beaky nose, he'd coax his legs in their baggy knee pants into motion.

He'd duck out of sight, as he did today, and run straight home to his widowed mother.

"It's me, Mama," hailed Zelik upon entering the cramped apartment above Silver's Fruit & Vegetable. He always announced himself as if the remote Mrs. Rifkin, listlessly pumping the treadle of her sewing machine, might take him for somebody else. She might mistake him for one of the dead relations she set such store by, and thus be given a fright. Behind her rose a mound of unstitched jackets and pants like a hill of straw that refused to be spun into gold.

Smiling wanly, more to herself than to her son, Mrs. Rifkin kissed the air next to the cheek that Zelik offered.

"I killed a man this morning" he confided, secure in the knowledge that she never heard him. "I robbed the Planters Bank and rubbed out a teller."

"Just so you're careful," replied his mother, absently feeding fabric to the bobbing needle. "Don't climb too high, you won't sink too low. All I ask is that you be careful. Remember, your father, Mr. Avigdor Rifkin, peace on his soul, was struck down in his prime."

From his vague recollection of his father, a herring-gutted garment peddler with a fruity cough, Zelik doubted that the man had ever had a prime.

Pausing a moment in her labor, Mrs. Rifkin looked up to note the date on a calendar hanging from the faded wallpaper. Produced by a company that had created a device called a rational body brace, the calendar was decorated with illustrations of women in harness. "I see that today is your great-aunt Frieda's yahrzeit," acknowledged Zelik's mother in a tone of dreamy anticipation. "That means we'll have to go to shul after dinner." Sighing wistfully, she tucked a strand of mousy brown hair behind an ear and proceeded with her automatic toil.

For his part, Zelik had no idea who his great-aunt Frieda was. In fact, most of the relations whose birthdays, anniversaries, and memorial yahrzeits (mostly yahrzeits) filled every available date on his mother's calendar, were entirely hearsay to him. He and his mama were the only Rifkins, living or dead, that he knew. But in an otherwise shut-in existence, her trips to the synagogue to light candles and say commemorative prayers were Mrs. Rifkin's sole excursions into the world. They were all she looked forward to, and Zelik, with nothing better to do himself, had acquired the habit of tagging along beside her.

Dumping his schoolbooks in the curtained alcove that served for his bedroom, Zelik excused himself. "Good-bye, Mama, I'm running away to join the circus and ride panthers through hoops of flame." As he started downstairs to his afternoon job in Mr. Silver's market, he could hear his mother faintly uttering her cautionary proverb behind him.

Not gifted with an especially enterprising nature, Zelik was a less than inspired greengrocer's assistant. It was a negligence abetted by the grocer himself, who worried enough for the both of them, making the market the one place where Zelik relaxed.

A troubled man with care lines stamped into his brow as with a brand, Mr. Silver was much too busy looking over his shoulder to keep tabs on a daydreaming stock boy. He was a bachelor, the skittish grocer, said to have fled his native Carpathian village in advance of a rumored pogrom. But despite the considerable distance he'd put between himself and the Old Country, Mr. Silver had yet to feel safe from approaching disaster, and often he confused the local gentiles with the hell-raising Cossacks of his youth. His particular fear was of the Ku Klux Klansmen who staged regular mounted parades up Main Street, with both themselves and their horses enshrouded in sheets and visored cowls.

But for all his apprehensions, Mr. Silver was a generous employer, generous beyond Zelik's worth and occasionally his own means.

"You sure you didn't make a mistake?" Zelik had asked upon receiving his first weekly salary; to which the grocer, sudden prey to a blinking fit in one sad eye, replied, "Maybe you are needing more?" Then he'd thrown in a peck of apricots as a bonus, and enjoined his employee to "Give your mama a health on her head from Leon Silver."

After a while Zelik could take the hint: Mr. Silver's largesse was not so much for the benefit of his assistant as for his assistant's mother. It seemed that the grocer was harboring a secret affection for the seamstress, which he was too timid to express through means more direct than his philanthropy.

At the end of the token few hours he put in at the grocery, Zelik went back upstairs for his Hebrew lesson with Mr. Notowitz. To support herself and her son after the death of her husband, Mrs. Rifkin had taken in piecework from the neighborhood tailors. But even supplemented by contributions from the Anshei Sphard widows' fund, her labors brought only a pittance, and so she had been forced to take in boarders. The current was Aharon Notowitz, a teacher of Hebrew and therefore just a cut above a common shnorrer. Chronically short of the rent, the moth-eaten Mr. Notowitz had offered to compensate his landlady by giving her son "post–bar mitzvah lessons" free of charge. It was a wholly impractical arrangement that would have added to the boarder's liability, were it not for the windfall profits Zelik had come by since going to work at Silver's Fruit & Veg.

He would find the old teacher in his windowless bedroom lit by a dirty skylight, sunk as usual in a hobbled armchair surrounded by heaps of un-shelved books. Formally attired in the gabardine suit he slept in, his beard discolored by ashes and crumbs, eyes like bloodshot fried eggs, Mr. Notowitz seldom got around to actually teaching. Instead he recounted his sorrows. This was fine with Zelik, who'd long since lost the knack of taking religious instruction; it was only as a concession to his mother, who now and then nourished the notion of her son's becoming a rabbi, that he'd agreed to the les-sons in the first place. Moreover, a steady diet of Mrs. Rifkin's memorial days, garnished with the threat of Mr. Silver's transplanted Cossacks, had prepared Zelik to appreciate the old melammed's complaints. By the time he came to hear them, such heartsick lamentations were for Zelik an acquired taste.

Touting himself as a once-celebrated scholar, descended on his mother's side from the archwizard Isaac Luria, Mr. Notowitz had a favorite gripe: he'd lost his faith. "To this farkokte country are following us the demons," he liked to repine, removing a finger from his tufted nostrils to examine the pickings. "But God"—pointing the finger aloft—"He stays behind."

III. Prince of Dreams

That summer, secure within his circle of ritual, apprehension, and regret, Zelik found himself stealing more frequent glimpses outside it. Though he remained true enough to the routine of his days, a restlessness he couldn't account for had seeped into his reluctant bones. He was spending his eve-nings as always in the company of his mother, going along on her commem-orative errands when it was called for. And since school was out, he worked longer hours in the greengrocery; he hung around Mr. Notowitz's rubbish-appointed bedroom. But still he had considerable time on his hands. There were stretches when, lurking aimlessly, Zelik tried to remember what he'd done during previous summers. Then it seemed to him that, every inch his foggy mother's son, he had sleepwalked through the whole of his sixteen years. But if that were the case, he reasoned, to wake up now might be a shock to his system from which he would never recover.

From a furtive vantage Zelik kept watch on the exploits of Jakie Epstein and company. He watched them with his typical nervous censure but found it increasingly difficult to turn away.

Though most of the boys had legitimate jobs of their own to attend to—they hawked newspapers, plucked chickens, sold dry goods in their families' shops—they never seemed to let work get in the way of a good time. With school out they found ample opportunities to run wild. Levy's Candy Store excepted, they tended to avoid North Main Street during off-hours, staying out from under the eyes of parents stationed at the soaped windows of their retail emporiums. Instead they preferred to lurk around the margins of things. They prowled the tenement rooftops and the wagon yards crammed with farmers' tin lizzies, the back alleys with their stables fronting for underworld goings-on. They challenged the rival Goat Hills and Mackerels to baseball in Market Square, games that generally ended in free-for-alls. But mostly they loitered about the cobbles along the levee just below the Pinch.

They sponged dimes from passengers on the paddle-wheeled excursion boats in exchange for the false promise of watching their motorcars. They shot craps in the shadow of cotton bales with roustabouts who told them stories of blown boilers, wrecked packets, crimes of passion, and floods. Defying the treacherous current (to say nothing of the undertow, the parasites, poisonous snakes, and man-eating garfish with which Zelik had heard the water was rife), they held swimming races across the river to Mud Island. On the far shore they drank "gnat's piss" and swapped lies with the fishermen, who lived there in a shantytown made from old Moxie signs.

They swarmed up the arm of a huge, freight-loading gantry crane and dived off. This stunt in itself would have been sufficiently harebrained, but the Pinch Gang liked to gild the lily. From the crane's dizzy pinnacle they executed backward somersaults and cunning jackknives, sometimes (as in the case of Captain Jakie) wearing blindfolds to heighten the danger. Barely clearing the docked barges and houseboats, they shouted obscenities and clutched their testicles before hitting the water. In this way they were sure of getting the attention of the girls, who lolled against bollards and floats pretending not to notice.

When they were done showing off, Jakie and the boys would wander over to where the girls sat sunning themselves. The clown Augie Blot, wearing only wet underpants and goggles, might shake himself like a dog in their vicinity, prompting universal screams. Hyman Myer might invite Sadie Blen to feel his muscles and, if she complied, press her to let him return the favor. A playful tussling would ensue. But sometimes their tussling wasn't so playful, and Zelik, peeping wide-eyed from behind a packing crate or a parked DeSoto, would draw in a horrified breath.

Once he saw the overgrown Lieberman twins, Ike and Izzy, yank Rose Padauer's pinafore over her head. While Ike held the upgathered material in a meaty fist, Izzy whipped off his belt and bound the package tight. "Give a look," cried Ike, the more articulate of the two. "We made a flower."

"Yeah," said Augie Blot with mock sentimentality, "a rose."

The other boys howled, asserting that the change was an improvement, while the girls stomped their feet in angry protest. But shocked as he was, Zelik had to admit that she did indeed look like a flower: a pale yellow one with a pair of kicking, pink-stockinged stems, and frilly white drawers at the blossom's base.

When especially wrought up, Zelik imagined himself, preferably masked, swooping down Douglas Fairbanks–style to rescue the girls from the Pinch Gang's wicked designs. Afterward he was ashamed for indulging such dumb fantasies, involving as they did the childish heroics with which he had no patience. Besides, the truth was that the girls were seldom in any real distress. In fact, they usually gave as good as they got, teasing the boys relentlessly. They cast doubts on the gang's much-vaunted experience of the opposite sex, requesting positive proof of their manhood, reducing them to sheepish blushes, then pushing the advantage: "Whatsa matter, can't you take it?"

One of the girls, Minnie Alabaster by name, was particularly distinguished for her unmercifulness. Her mouth was a neighborhood scandal, causing general embarrassment whenever she opened it. "Your mother seen those warts on your palm?" was her standard greeting to the boys, after which her conversation was likely to degenerate even further. Her remarks were notorious. Regarding the Lieberman brothers, who were forever digging at themselves, she might inquire with alarm, "You guys got carnivals in your pants, or what?" And when Moe Plesofsky had his head shaved due to an infestation of ringworm, she'd thoughtfully observed, "It looks like a putz, only smaller." She always had some off-color joke ("A guy takes a girl for a ride in his car, parks by the river. 'Shtup?' he asks, and she says, 'I usually don't, but you talked me into it.'") or a fanciful aside concerning the foibles of North Main Street:

"So I'm on the streetcar when I hear Mrs. Ridblatt whisper to her husband, 'Shmuel, your business is open.' And he whispers back, 'Is my salesman in or out?'"

Nobody, not even the otherwise unassailable Jakie Epstein, was spared the sting of her tongue. Wary of it, the boys tended not to cross her, seldom daring to make her the object of their gags. Also, though Zelik had seen no hard evidence, it was generally acknowledged that Minnie was Jakie's girl. This was not so much on account of her formidable tongue as her devilish prettiness—her gimlet green eyes and puff of ginger hair cropped after the fashion of Clara Bow, her lips like a twittering scarlet butterfly. The pendulum sway of her hips in the pleated skirts that she wore above her dimpled knees. For such attributes it was assumed that nobody but the gang's intrepid captain should deserve her, though Zelik wondered if anyone had bothered to consult with Minnie herself on this point.

Naturally he was as intimidated by her bold-as-brass manner as he was by the antics of Jakie and the boys. Minnie's forwardness, scalding his ears, was as much a subject of Zelik's eavesdropping disapproval as the Pinch Gang's hazardous stunts. All in all, he concluded, the youth of North Main Street were playing with fire, and you couldn't blame Zelik Rifkin, who played it safe, if they got burned.

But when he was alone, Zelik found that he continued to think about Minnie. He imagined that her brazen exterior concealed untapped tenderness and fidelity. She had a pure and sympathetic heart that only he, with the well-kept secret of his amorous nature (a secret to himself until now), could detect. And at night, under sweat-soaked sheets, he came to realize a not entirely welcome truth: he had conceived an infatuation for Minnie Alabaster. It was a passion out of keeping with any emotion he'd ever experienced—an immoderate, reckless passion, so lofty in its aspiration that it left him, afraid as he was of heights, a prey to chronic nosebleeds; not to mention the gnawing discontent that kept Zelik lingering a little longer in the neighborhood streets.

He became less furtive in his daily espionage, sometimes dawdling in full view of the other kids. This wasn't so much a function of audacity as imprudence, the result of an overwhelming desire to be nearer to Minnie. Thanks to his short stature and the meager frame that enhanced his semi-invisibility, however, Zelik was regarded as harmless if he was regarded at all. Powerless as he was to stay put, he was thus further encouraged to step out from behind the wardrobe in front of Shafetz's Discount or the wooden Indian next to Levy's Candy Store.

At the very worst Zelik's proximity to his peers earned him only the usual spurious invitations, the standard verbal abuse. Twitching his leaky nostrils, Augie Blot might begin the chant, "What's that I'm sniffkin'?" to which the choral response was, "Must be a Rifkin—peeyoo!" Occasionally even Jakie himself, ordinarily above such banter, couldn't resist taking a shot at the figure of fun. "Vey is mir," he might exclaim, popping his gum with a freckled jaw, "it's Zelik the Shiv! Run for your lives!" Then the lot of them would beat it down an alley in stitches.

Sometimes the girls would enter into the ragging, and Minnie Alabaster was often foremost among them. But Zelik had become a glutton for even her most barbed remarks. Once, with her distinctive flair for the dramatic, she'd clutched at a precocious bosom heaving beneath her sailor blouse.

"Come closer," she beckoned the intruder, "Zelik Rifkin, prince of my dreams."

He knew that he ought to feel mortified; she was mocking him shamelessly, but mockery and mortification were second nature to Zelik. What mattered was that she had spoken exclusively to him, and her words—once he'd stripped them of their original context—could be savored in the privacy of his alcove. They could be recalled in such a way as to evoke a sensation that swelled Zelik's shallow breast and surpassed his understanding.

IV. Acrophile

Then came the heat wave that sent the whole of North Main Street to sleep outside in the park. Formerly, during prolonged hot spells, a family might be forced to spend the night on the roof of their building; they would haul up lamps and mattresses until they'd created a kind of poor man's penthouse. But this summer's heat was of a more hellish intensity than the most longtime residents of the Pinch could recall. All day it baked the tenements, so that, even in the slightly less oppressive evening air, the rooftops remained scorching to the touch. The soles of shoes might adhere to the simmering tar paper, arresting movement, leaving you stuck and exposed till the sun rose to bleach your bones. So the families took to the park instead.

Thus far the Rifkins had remained an exception to the late evening exodus, which included even old Mr. Notowitz. Complaining that the foul breath of demons was driving him out of his room, he'd fled the apartment bookless in his filthy suit. (Though not before loosening his necktie and unfastening his collar stud as a statement of how extreme things had become.) Mr. Silver had warned Zelik and anyone else who would listen that the blistering heat was a conspiracy: "It's the Ku Kluxers that they have cooked it up for getting in one spot the Jews. Then by a single swoop they would slaughter them all." But in the end the grocer also succumbed, preferring to be murdered out of doors than suffocated inside.

Zelik supposed that his mother, whose calendar knew no climate, didn't feel the heat so much as others. She appeared no more languid and done in from her drudgery than usual. As for himself, Zelik felt it all right, and what was worse, the terrific heat seemed only to further inflame his passion for Minnie. He yearned for her with a desire that grew like a genie let out of a bottle, too large now to ever stuff back in again. It was a longing beyond his control, that despite himself gave him crazy ideas, and would have kept him awake nights regardless of the weather.

Still, Zelik didn't need his mother with her wholesale distrust of nature to list reasons to stay out of the park. Didn't he already have her litany by heart? There were worms in the grass that crept into your liver through your feet, earwigs that crawled into your brain, mosquitoes indistinguishable in their size and thirst for blood from vampire bats. At night rabid animals stalked the perimeter of the Pinch, with now and again a werewolf among them; and never mind the marauding Klansmen promised by Mr. Silver, when the kids from rival neighborhoods were unfriendly enough.

But on this especially torrid night, as he stood in a window mopping his forehead, watching the neighbors strolling en masse toward Market Square, Zelik achieved a restlessness that challenged his legion of fears. Among the strollers he spied Mr. Alabaster the tinsmith in a knotted headrag, his broad-beamed wife in a fancy leghorn hat, with their pistol of a daughter sashaying behind them, and what once had been clear and present dangers seemed suddenly no more than superstition.

"Mama," Zelik announced at the door of Mrs. Rifkin's bedroom, "I'm off to join the wild Indians and cut the scalps from my enemies."

"Just be careful, tateleh," murmured his mother from her bed. "Chase the wind you nab a devil, stay at home you don't wear out your shoes." Though her voice was much the same waking or sleeping, she nevertheless surprised her son by rolling over to complain about the heat.

In the park the holiday mood of the gathered North Main Street community confirmed Zelik in his feeling that he didn't belong. He felt as if he'd blundered uninvited into the starlit bedroom of strangers, though he was perfectly familiar with everyone there. He saw Bluesteins, Taubenblatts, Rosens, Shapiros, Padauers, Dubrovners, Blens—all of them camped out like pashas on throw-cushioned carpets and folding cots, enjoying the after-hours conviviality. They were exchanging gossip and debating local politics, banqueting on cold chicken and assorted nosherai, decanting samovars to sip glasses of tea through sugar cubes. By lamplight, the perambulators sur-

rounding them like circled wagons, women changed the diapers of bawling infants. They played mah-jongg in upraised sleeping masks while their
husbands—in bathrobes, flicking cigars—fanned themselves with their
poker hands. Here a voice was heard reciting scripture, there another nam-
ing the constellation of Berenice's Hair. A Victrola with a tuba-sized speaker,
blaring a Mischa Elman nocturne, vied with the Original Dixieland Jazz
Band through the crackling static of a wireless radio. Children ran around
in pajamas chasing fireflies, though some already lay curled up on blankets
fast asleep.

Even Mr. Silver, although vigilant in his tasseled nightcap, looked sufficiently comfortable where he sat under cover of a lilac bush, nibbling fruit
from a paper bag. And Mr. Notowitz, wrapped in newspapers like a fish but
recognizable from his gartered ankles and volcanic snores, was the picture
of one who'd slept on stone benches all his life. Meanwhile, having strayed
from their family bivouacs, young people were clustered among the roots at
the foot of the patriarch oak. The boys roughhoused and scratched initials
on the bricks that filled the hollow of the tree trunk like a walled-up door.
The girls turned their backs and conspired in whispers.

As he sidled to within earshot, Zelik could hear Augie Blot proposing
a contest to see which of the Lieberman twins was the dumber. "Okay, Izzy,
first question: are you Izzy or Ike?" Jakie Epstein was leaning against the
tree trunk with folded arms, looking as if the whole proceedings depended
on the grace of his lanky, sandy-haired presence. From her giggling confab
with Sadie Blen and Rose Padauer, Minnie Alabaster turned on a dare to the
silent ringleader: "Hey, Jakie, you still dating that shikse what's-her-name,
Mary Fivefingers?" Some of the neighbors in Zelik's vicinity commented in
exasperation over the mouth on that Alabaster girl.

Then Augie went into his nose-twitching routine. "What's that I'm
smellik?" he called out once or twice before he'd elicited a halfhearted chorus from a couple of the boys: "Must be Zelik." "Rifkin, man of the hour,"
greeted Augie, showing teeth like blasted hoardings. "Jakie, wasn't you just
saying how we needed Rifkin to complete our minyan?"

Jakie frowned his irritation at Augie's putting words in his mouth, especially concerning so uninteresting a subject. But then there was always the
chance that, under Augie's instigation, something interesting might develop.

Zelik knew it was time to back off and dissolve into shadows, but in the
moment that he hesitated (a moth drawn to Minnie's flame) the Liebermans
took hold of his arms. They ushered him forward and planted him directly

in front of Jakie, who took his measure with a dispassionate gaze that made him shrink. He shrank further from his acute awareness that Minnie was looking on with a sardonic grin.

Man of action though he was, Jakie condescended to speech when his office obliged. "You see, Rifkin," he began with a pop of the jaw, "we got this problem. Seems there's this . . . ," leaving the problem for Augie to define.

"This kite," supplied Augie, pointing straight up.

"There's this kite," continued Jakie, "which it is stuck in the top of the tree—ain't that right, Augie? And ain't none of us got the beytsim [Augie, acting as interpreter, clutched himself between the legs] to climb up and fetch it down."

At this Zelik began to struggle against his detainers to no effect. While Augie assured everyone what a lucky break it was that Fearless Rifkin had happened along, the Liebermans hoisted their captive onto the bottommost branch of the oak. When he tried to scramble down, they prevented him, shoving him back onto his swaying perch. Augie Blot struck a match and waved it under his shoe soles until Zelik also had to draw up his dangling feet.

"Now don't he look natural, Jakie," said Augie, stepping back to feign admiration. "A regular Tarzansky, wouldn't you say? He's hugging that branch like I think he must be in love."

"Yeah," concurred Jakie, known sometimes to wax philosophical. "Rifkin wasn't never at home on the earth."

Clinging to his knotty tree limb in a panic, Zelik pleaded, "Have a heart!" He appealed to the neighbors in the grass beyond the serpentine roots, and was told to pipe down, they were trying to sleep. Besides, since he was less than six feet from the ground, those who noticed were more inclined to see humor than danger in his situation.

"Help!" he cried to universal laughter and taunts, one of which resonated in his ears more than the rest.

"Don't worry, Zelik. If you start to fall, you can hang on to your mama's apron strings—which he also uses for tefillin, I got this on good authority."

It was Minnie Alabaster, in whose voice Zelik could take no comfort now. He saw himself, through her eyes, for the pathetic, cowering creature he was, and again in a single night his fears had met their match, overcome this time not by restlessness but shame. And shame, like restlessness, shook you into action. It made you want so badly to distance yourself from the insults hurled from below that, unable to descend, you had no choice but to start climbing.

With a painful deliberateness, his groping all the clumsier for the racing heart that tried to hasten his ascent, Zelik hauled himself aloft. At every stage he paused to catch his breath, embracing boughs hatched with crude hieroglyphics, taking note of a whole new dimension of things to be scared of. There were enormous ants and acorn weevils scurrying along the rope-veined branches like scorpions, warts like eyeballs on spatulate leaves. An unseen owl hooted nearby and Zelik froze, snuffling back tears and wiping his nose, which had begun to bleed. Then a fresh round of abuse spurred him into motion again.

Somewhere during his vertical crawl, far beyond the point where he could see the ground anymore, Zelik realized that the taunts had actually turned to encouragement. Jakie's gang were calling him Shipwreck Zelik after the famous flagpole sitter, saluting him for the way he'd risen to the occasion. That's when, rather than cheered, Zelik was struck by the magnitude of what he'd done, the impossible height he'd attained, and he held fast with all his might to the tree.

Afraid to look down, he squeezed his eyes shut but was afraid of the darkness behind his closed lids. So he opened his eyes and looked up. Just above his head was what appeared to be a cobweb shaped in a spiral like a miniature galaxy. Or could it be in fact the raveled tail of a kite caught in the topmost fork of the oak? His cowardice still screwed to the sticking point, Zelik didn't even dare to reach for it. Instead he clung tighter to the slender bough that nodded with his weight, its bark smooth and unscored by anyone who might have been there before him.

"Attaboy, Zelik!" they shouted; "Rifkin at the roof of the world!" their fickle turnaround galling him even more than their contempt. But though he'd climbed as high as he could manage on the strength of his shame, the wish to get farther from their voices gave him one last boost, and Zelik rose another foot or two into the breezy air.

His head had penetrated the cobweb, which turned out to be nothing more than a patch of fog. It cooled his brain, stilled his heart, and left him with eyes wide open, but what Zelik saw made no earthly sense. He was after all in the top of a tree, a fact miraculous enough in itself. But what he seemed to be looking at, from the level of the pavement no less, was North Main Street—the shops and the firehouse, the tenement flats, the movie theater, the cigar factory, the trolley car lines. It was the same shabby street he lived on, its alleys rank with weeds and wisteria, the cooking odors mingling with the stench of the river and the horse poop of mounted police, though here and there some telling detail suggested a difference.

For one thing there was a moon, a crescent like a silver fish tail, where previously the night had been moonless, and its light was strong as sunlight, if softer, and grainy like a fine yellow mist. The buildings looked mostly the same in their uniform need for repair, though the paint-chipped facades were relieved in some instances by an odd architectural flourish: the lace-worked wrought-iron balcony, entwined in orchids, jutting from the Widow Teitelbaum's window; the giant bare-chested caryatids, which seemed to be breathing, holding up the cornice on either side of Tailor Schloss's door. Projecting from the chimney of a tiny frame house, where a colored family lived beside Blockman's junkyard, was a tall mast complete with yardarms and a billowing, bloodred sail. While the shops were identical to those on the terrestrial street, there were certain items out of keeping with the standard merchandise: the golden ram's horn and the pair of magnificent ivory wings, for instance, among the tarnished brass watches and battered ukuleles in the window of Uncle Sam's Pawn; a manikin decked out in the naughtiest Parisian lingerie and an eye-catching coat of many colors among the racks of irregulars in front of Shapiro's Ready-Made. Through the windows of the Main Street trolley, whose tracks passed not three feet from Zelik's head, he could make out an interior as opulent as a club car on the Twentieth Century Limited.

The neighbors were going about their more or less ordinary business, despite random intrusions of the extraordinary. Mr. Sacharin rolled a herring barrel backward down a ramp from a delivery truck; Mr. Krivetcher arranged his show shelf of only left shoes. Mr. Dreyfus, at a workbench in his shop window, polished a pearl the size of a swami's crystal ball. Max Taubenblatt, in the window of his haberdashery, wearing the hat and tails of a stage magician, prepared to saw his talky wife in half, while next door Lipman the asthmatic cobbler, in lion skins, collapsed the doorposts of his building with a mighty shrug. On a corner Itzhik Bashrig the luftmensch, holding his pail under a faucet, coaxed a pinging shekel from the tap with every flick of his wrist. A woman rode past on Blockman's swayback horse, her naked body concealed by her Godiva hair. The thick blonde tresses were parted in back over a prominent dowager's hump that identified her as Mrs. Blockman herself, the pious junkman's wife.

There was a moment when Zelik wondered if he could have reached heaven. But the monkeyshines of his neighbors were not altogether of the type he associated with a kosher idea of heaven. Besides, so far as he knew, none of these people were dead yet. Having made this assumption, however, Zelik figured he ought to confirm it, and immediately thrust his head back under the quiet whirlpool of fog. He looked down through the web of branches at the sleeping neighborhood spread out around the base of the tree. Then it occurred to him: what sleepers did was dream. And dreams, one might suppose, rose like heat until they found their common level. There they might settle at a height where some dauntless climber, provided he had the means of ascent, could reach them. He could enter the community of dreams and witness the high jinks to his heart's delight.

But as he looked down Zelik lost the sense of rapture he'd had only moments ago, and with it he very nearly lost his balance. Reminded that he was still, God forbid, umpteen feet above the earth (where dawn was already breaking), Zelik's fear of heights reasserted itself with a nauseating rush. Desperate, he clung to the oak for dear life.

Once the nebbish had climbed out of sight and shown no signs of coming down, the Pinch Gang began to lose interest. Augie Blot started torturing a bullfrog, pretending to read the future in its entrails, which were ultimately used to terrorize the girls. Eventually, grown bored and sleepy, they'd all wandered off to join their families. In the morning, reassembled at the foot of the oak, yawning and disheveled from a night under the stars, the remnants of last night's party remembered Zelik. Because the leaves were too thick to determine if he was still dangling somewhere above, Augie Blot was for calling the fire department, while Jakie dispatched his nimbler lieutenants to investigate.

When they saw him being lowered through the branches from which he'd been pried, they marvelled that he'd stuck it out overnight. Moe Plesofsky and some of the others proposed that Rifkin be made an honorary gang member on the spot. Such fanatical endurance surely entitled him to waive the trials by fire, water, and theft that constituted a traditional initiation. But on closer inspection, when he'd been dropped to the ground in a limp but still quivering heap, they thought better of their benevolent impulses. All of a sudden it was clear that, regardless of what may have compelled him up the tree in the first place, it was fear that had kept Zelik aloft.

"Jellyfish Rifkin," jeered Augie, stepping over to lift one of Zelik's scrawny arms, "the winner and still champeen coward of North Main Street." Several others joined in the derision, but ramrod Jakie Epstein advised them to button their lips. "He ain't worth the wasted breath," Jakie added quickly, lest they mistake him for a defender of the underdog.

Some of the neighbors, pulling up suspender straps and massaging sore spines as they passed on the way to their homes, did a double take at the sight of the pitiful Rifkin kid. They gazed at him as if, though familiar, he was a stranger whose face they'd seen somewhere before. Among the passersby were the Alabasters, with their tousle-headed daughter in tow. Getting a load of Zelik, she gave him a flirtatious wink, then screwed up her face like she didn't know what had gotten into her.

For his part, Zelik—cap caked in bird droppings, shirt and plus fours hung with twigs—wondered if he was still in a dream.

V. SHEDDING SKIN

Trudging home in the already hothouse sunshine, Zelik found his mother, who'd yet to miss him, dragging around the kitchen in her tatty dressing gown. She was setting the breakfast table with typical burnt offerings.

"Today's the anniversary," she announced with an enervated reverence, "of your great-grandma, the Bubbe Bobke's passing, who died of what they died of in those days. So after supper you'll come with me to shul?"

"Mama," confessed Zelik, presenting the bedraggled spectacle of himself as evidence, "I spent the night in a tree."

"As long as you were careful, my yingele. If you climb a ladder, count every rung. You know, your father, Mr. Rifkin . . ."

Not that Zelik needed any reminding about the perils that awaited him abroad. Hadn't last night's adventure been lesson enough, leaving him more than ever a bundle of nerves? Should someone say boo, he'd have clung to his mama's bristly ankles and pulled her gown over his head. So jangled was he this morning that he could scarcely recollect how, for a while in the crown of an oak tree, he'd been brave.

But as the day progressed and Zelik went through his perfunctory paces in Mr. Silver's market—grinding coffee, weighing cantaloupes, shucking corn to the weary rhythm of she-loves-me, she-loves-me-not—he began to recall with more clarity what he'd seen from the top of the tree. Or rather, the memory overtook his brain despite his best efforts to resist it. The exhilaration of the previous night returned, dispelling his nervousness, infecting his tepid bloodstream till his insides ran with rapids and cascades. In the end, Zelik's vision of a cockeyed North Main Street eclipsed even his hopeless mooning over Minnie, and he longed to see that ethereal place again more than he longed to see her.

Later that afternoon in Mr. Notowitz's bedroom, as his teacher belched whitefish and remembered past glories, Zelik thought he knew precisely what the old man was talking about. There was the part for instance where, wiping his face with the fringe of his flyblown beard, the teacher brooded,

"Once the Tree of Life I have climbed and plucked the sacred citron—I, Aharon Notowitz, that knew personally what are calling the wise men a holy influx. This by the heart and yea even in the pants I am knowing, when I would wear the garment of light that it was custom-tailored—"

"I know just what you mean," put in Zelik from the edge of his chair.

"You?" said the teacher, his blood-rimmed yellow eyes coming to rest on his student for possibly the first time in their acquaintance. "Pishteppel, what do you know?"

The concept being brand-new to him, Zelik had to grope for the words. "It's like . . . being awake in your dreams."

"Dreams shmeams," grumbled the old man, though Zelik thought his sourness lacked its customary conviction. "Kholem iz nit gelebt, dreamed ain't lived."

Zelik looked forward eagerly to accompanying his mother to the synagogue that evening, if only for the time it would kill. Absorbed as he was in his anticipation, however, he couldn't help noticing that, despite the ever-oppressive heat, Mrs. Rifkin looked a touch livelier than usual. The indications consisted in nothing more than a slightly diminished slouch to her walk, a clean frock, a hint of rouge, a head-hugging flapper chapeau. But they were enough to make her son question whether the exuberance he could hardly suppress was somehow contagious.

Because sundown came so late during the summer months, the service on this Shabbos evening didn't begin till after nine o'clock. It was ordinarily a lengthy affair, during which, in a ritual unique to North Main Street, prominent citizens were called up to read from the Torah. Leaving their seats by the eastern wall, these men, often dressed as if for the links, would whisper in the sexton's ear before ascending the bima; then the sexton would relate in a booming voice their competitive contributions to the synagogue building fund. But tonight the service was cut short on account of the general asphyxiation. After Cantor Abrams had lifted his megaphone for a show-stopping Adon Olom, Rabbi Fein rose puffing in his bowler to make an announcement: the ladies of Hadassah would be on hand with provisions for those who elected to stay the night in Market Square.

To Zelik's astonishment his mama, who as a rule never ventured farther from home than the shul, heaved a sigh and submitted fatalistically: "Who knows, maybe it'll do us good. Coming, kepeleh?"

In the park Mrs. Rifkin set about her mechanical housekeeping as if she were accustomed to sleeping out of doors. Choosing a spot on the edge of the crowd—somewhat duplicating the apartment's floorplan in its vicinity to Mr. Notowitz on his bench—she spread the horse blanket dispensed by the Hadassah. She kicked off her shoes, removed her costume jewelry, and took a yahrzeit candle from her purse. Zelik wondered why he should have expected that the candle would already be lit.

Nearby under the lilac Mr. Silver sat, nibbling dried fruit. Upon seeing the Rifkins he rose and shuffled over, removing his sleeping cap. Zelik waited for him to warn them of impending disaster, but instead he only offered some of his prunes. "Very good on my ulcer, they told me, and for the voiding of the bowel," he assured them, risking an experimental smile at Mrs. Rifkin. It was as close to a declaration of affection as Zelik had ever known him to make. Something, it seemed, was in the air.

Zelik stuck close to his mother, who, after muttering prayers and laying her head beside the flickering candle, surprised him again by the ease with which she fell asleep. Once asleep, however, she was her old self again, moaning in the way that distinguished her troubled slumber. From where he sat in parched grass that still retained the heat of the day, Zelik could just make out the other kids under the tree. He strained for a glimpse of Minnie but felt no special disappointment when he couldn't see her. Instead he was content to lean back against the pillow of his wadded sack coat, listening to the A&P Gypsies drowning in a surf of static, the laughter of his neighbors growing spotty before subsiding into yawns.

The hour was late and he too ought to be dog-weary, having had not one wink of sleep the night before, but tired was the last thing that Zelik felt. Warily he got to his feet, beginning to creep about the margins of his neighbors' encampments, picking his way toward the base of the oak. He looked here and there amid the lumber mill of snoring to make certain that no one was watching, then jumped up to grab hold of an overhanging limb.

"I don't do this," Zelik reminded himself as he clambered for a foothold.

"Zelik Rifkin doesn't climb trees." So who was it clutching that knot shaped like an old man's grimace, who fending off the flapping of an angry bird whose nest he'd nudged with his head? This is not to say that the dread of almost everything, by which Zelik identified himself, wasn't perfectly alive and well in his system. But tonight anxiety didn't rattle his nerves so much as strum them, tuning them to musical vibrations as he climbed into the cooler air.

In the giddy branches at the top of the tree, without hesitating, Zelik stuck his head through the spiral ceiling of fog. Again he was presented with the street of dreams. Citizens passing by on foot or in automobiles waved cordial salutations to Zelik's disembodied head. Blind Eli Rosen sounded an *aooga* horn as he rounded the corner in a block-long, articulated touring car; Miss Bialy of the Neighborhood House fluttered her hankie from the window of a solid glass four-in-hand. Filling his lungs with the fumes and aromas that were a tonic to him now, Zelik exchanged his grip on the oak for a hold of the pavement. He pulled himself up, scrambling from what turned out to be a manhole, its cover lying to one side like a huge plug nickel.

He stood in the middle of the street, poised to investigate, when he was struck by a mildly disturbing thought: what if, just as this morning he'd nearly forgotten last night, in wandering away from the manhole he forgot where he'd come from? To refresh himself with regard to his bearings, Zelik dropped to his knees and poked his head back into the hole. What he saw under the fog was a skinny kid in golf cap and baggy knee pants, hugging the wavering branches of a tree.

"This is me," Zelik surmised, curiously inspecting the flesh and bones out of which he seemed to have climbed. It troubled him a bit that his abandoned self should have reverted to so terror-stricken an attitude. Feeling, nonetheless, quite corporeal from his loftier vantage, fully clothed and ready for a little fun, Zelik withdrew his head from the fog as if he'd kept it under water too long. Then, with another breath, he took another look: still there. Again he raised his head, gave a shrug, then got to his feet and set off to explore.

He began with the Idle Hour Cinema, where, as a regular feature of the Amateur Night venue, the little Elster girl was winding up a tap dance in blackface and bubble eyes. Following her the manager, Mr. Forbitz, announced, "For your special delectation . . . ," drawing a curtain to reveal Tamkin the cobbler's apprentice immersed in an outsize fishbowl, a knife in his teeth, wrestling a large man-eating reptile with a thrashing tail. At the Phoenix Athletic Club they were dragging Eddie Kid Katz, the local palooka, out of the ring, after which the cadaverous Galitzianer rebbe entered in satin trunks. Coached from a corner by a party resembling the champ Benny Leonard himself, he delivered a sucker punch to the apparently glass jaw of a giant wearing biblical sandals and a ribbon-braided beard. From a dolphin's-head spigot on the marble fountain in his candy store, Mr. Levy filled a glass with sparkling liquid, levitating as he sipped it several inches above the sawdusted floor. In his butcher shop Old Man Dubrovner, tiptoeing into the meat locker, parted hanging slabs of beef to behold what looked like the Queen of Sheba, suspended in a block of ice.

Zelik took in everything with the peculiar wisdom with which he felt himself newly endowed. He understood, for instance, that although most of these prodigies were authored by individuals, there were some involving two or more dreamers at once. This could of course be explained by the fact that the neighborhood slept together, and their dreams were therefore likely to mingle and converge. It was a condition that sometimes made it hard to determine where one person's dream left off and another's began.

Such was the case in the mikveh where the Rubenesque Mrs. Kipper, her lower anatomy that of a glittering goldfish, was performing a solitary water ballet, while Mr. Shafetz of Shafetz's Discount looked on indulgently in his fez, blowing words of love in the smoke from a nargileh pipe. It was the case with the Pinch Gang, who were everywhere, performing stunts compared with which their daylight exploits were sissy stuff. They danced without nets on crisscrossed clotheslines strung high across the alleys. At the river they commandeered the sumptuous barge of the Cotton Carnival royalty, dallying with the maids of honor after forcing their irate escorts to walk the plank.

Returning their greetings, Zelik heartily applauded their reckless abandon. He felt that, while only a spectator, he somehow as good as participated in their mischief. In fact, it occurred to him that being wide awake gave one a sort of edge over the dreamers. You had the power, should you want to use it, to interfere with or even alter the course of their dreams.

But why would you want to do that when everyone already appeared to be having such a good time? Or rather, almost everyone—because, across the street at Silver's Fruit & Veg, the harried proprietor cringed behind his cash register with his apron over his head. A posse of mounted Ku Klux Klansmen, wearing cowls that bore the insignia of the Black Hundred and brandishing Cossack sabers, had ridden roughshod into the grocery. They were dangling a thick noose from a light fixture, threatening to stretch the grocer's Jew neck.

"We gon' do you like they done that'ere Leo Franko down Atlanta-ways."

Nor was everything hunky-dory in the apartment over the market. Mrs. Rifkin was as usual at her sewing, but back in his stifling bedroom Mr. Notowitz was beleaguered by giggling demons. Shaggy little creatures with beaks and crumpled horns, with goat shanks and barbed tails that struck sparks from whatever they touched, were tearing pages from his sacred texts and tossing them gleefully into the air. Bleating depravity, they tugged at his soup-stained beard and knotted the wisps of his hair while the old man asked the Lord why he'd been singled out for such a distinction. And when he looked again, Zelik saw how his mother, idle behind her antiquated Singer, was staring in dumbstruck confusion at the calendar on the wall. She was studying the glaringly empty square of a single vacant day wherein there was nothing at all to commemorate.

An old hand at nightmare himself, Zelik certainly knew them when he saw them, and so backed away from the situations of his mother and friends. It wasn't that he was frightened; nothing here seemed to frighten him, which was the point. All of a sudden Zelik missed his native jumpiness, the nerves that set off alarms throughout his body. Light-footed, he missed the lumpish body in which he'd never felt much at home. Maybe, he thought, it was time to go and check on himself in the tree.

Making one last scenic loop on the way, he passed by the Anshei Sphard shul, through whose portals he saw dreams that had not so much merged as collided. Inside, Minnie Alabaster was being manhandled, dragged kicking and screaming down the aisle by the Lieberman twins. In a gown of white chiffon and a veil sent flying from her tossing ginger hair, she shouted oaths that caused even Jakie's goons to turn crimson about the jug ears. On the altar stood Captain Jakie himself, looking a little chafed in his top hat and cutaway, with his best man, Augie Blot, beside him in snazzy pinstripes, a pistol trained on the frowning Rabbi Fein.

In the door of the synagogue Zelik had reached the conclusion that, given such complicated circumstances, you could hardly apportion blame, when Minnie twisted in her struggle to cry out to him, "Shmuck, you got lead for bones or what!" At that moment, having wrestled her up the stairs to the canopy, the Liebermans hoisted her wedding dress and bound it tightly over her head. They held her pinned in place but still kicking as the rabbi began dolefully to read the marriage vows.

Satisfied that all was not only big fun in this quarter, that one person's dream might be another's nightmare, Zelik turned and retreated to his manhole. He dropped back into his vacated skin, which welcomed him like a warm bath of worry and fear.

VI. In Which Zelik Has an Agenda

With the ounce of residual chutzpah still left to him, Zelik managed a slow descent on his own steam, reaching the ground just in time for sunrise. Where yesterday his muscles had smarted exquisitely, unaccustomed as they were to strenuous exercise, today he hurt in his very bones, not to mention his head and his heart. All that afternoon in Mr. Silver's market he groaned aloud with every least effort, until the grocer was moved to say, "You don't look so good already. Have a sit." No martyr to his condition, Zelik wanted to tell his employer, unusually spruce of late in a rakish straw boater, what he knew no one would believe. In fact, but for the souvenir of his general aches and pains, Zelik was no longer so sure what he believed himself.

"Maybe I overdid it in this heat," he agreed with Mr. Silver, and sat down.

Later on he swapped complaints tit for tat with Mr. Notowitz, griping about the unpleasant consequences of slipping in and out of one's own skin, but fell into a self-conscious silence when he had the impression that the old man was listening for a change. He was irked by his mother's unbecoming friskiness that evening, her air of expectancy. Why should she be in such an all-fired hurry to get to Market Square, where all she did, after a brief chat with Mr. Silver, was lie down and sink abruptly into fitful sleep?

As it turned out, Mrs. Rifkin wasn't the only one bent on retiring early. All around the neighbors stretched ostentatiously, excusing themselves from bridge circles and checkers, plumping pillows as if they couldn't wait to commence the business of dreaming. Not a bad idea, thought Zelik, who'd had no rest for two nights running, but he was still too keyed up and racked with pain to relax. Unable to get comfortable, he rose, feeling that despite wide-open eyes he was walking in his sleep, limping resistlessly toward the oak. He was in no shape to even consider climbing, which thank you but he'd had quite enough of in any case. Though didn't the conventional wisdom have it that more of what brought on the affliction was sometimes the best remedy . . . ?

At the top of the tree, hoisting himself with an excruciating effort into the dreamscape of North Main, Zelik was buoyant and light-headed once again. What's more, he found himself in possession of a program. Making straight for the greengrocery, where Mr. Silver's recurrent nightmare was still in progress, he leapt adroitly astride the haunch of one of the horses, un-seating its hooded rider with a shove while retaining his sword. He spurred the spirited Arabian into the market, laying about with his blade and snatch-ing up the terrified grocer, whom he folded over the horse's flying mane. The Klansmen reared and spat curses in the name of the Exalted Kleagle before beating a frustrated retreat. Leaving Mr. Silver seated now upon the charger, proudly erect as if posing for an equestrian portrait, Zelik dismounted and picked up a Klansman's fallen hood. He took a grease pencil from the check-out counter, scrawled a Star of David above the peepholes, and pulled the linen cowl over his head—a wizard's hat.

He shot upstairs past his wilted mama, saying, "Don't go away!" then burst into the room where Mr. Notowitz was suffering from demons. "It is I, your hallowed ancestor Isaac Luria," he announced, "scourge of goblins and fiends." He took up a book at random from the gutted pile on the floor. "And this is the Book of Raziel that the angels gave to Adam, which he lost like a klutz when he got kicked out of the Garden. It's the book that answers the question how to look on the Almighty without you should go crazy or blind." He licked a finger, fanned the pages, gave a satisfied nod, and ad-dressed the assembled evil spirits by name:

"Igrat, Pirpik, Qatzefoni, Asherlutz, Hormin son of Lilith,
Mahalath
  ahalath
    halath
      alath
        lath
          ath
            th
              h, enough already! Shoyn genug!"

Whining that they'd been dealt with unfairly, calling Zelik a spoilsport and worse, the demons began to vanish, from their hooves and chicken feet to their spiky, cyclopean heads. To the tune of his old teacher's blubbering grati-tude, Zelik made his exit and doffed the hood. He marched past his mother, who was mired in fabric, and stepped up to her calendar, writing boldly with his marker in the single vacant square (whose date was incidentally the pres-ent day): RACHEL RIFKIN'S COMING OUT. Then, gently, he raised her from the sewing machine and led her out of the cramped apartment down into the enchanted street. There Mr. Silver, saying "Hi ho, Leon Silver!" invited her to take a ride on his milk-white steed.

After that Zelik might have rested. On earth he would have rested, tuckered out from the sheer exertion of having imagined such events. But here one thing led to another, the momentum building, carrying him forward as on the crest of a wave that crashed at the threshold of the Anshei Sphard shul. Entering, Zelik plucked the cantor's megaphone from its wall sconce, thinking it might come in handy. He stole into the women's gallery to better survey the scene on the altar, still in full swing, the hostage rabbi still pronouncing nuptials over a battling bride. Zelik tapped his temple until a strategy revealed itself. He untied from the railing a rope attached to the Everlasting Light, which in turn hung suspended from a rafter over the wedding canopy, directly above the head of the gun-toting Augie Blot. Then he let go, allowing the lamp, like a small red meteor, to drop through the canopy and flatten Augie's yarmulke. As Augie crumpled, Zelik broadcasted through the booming megaphone, "It's the voice of the Lord here. Now cut the hanky-panky."

Exchanging fearful glances, the knuckleheaded Liebermans unhanded their captive and bolted, tumbling over each other in their efforts to be first down the aisle and out the doors. Meanwhile Jakie Epstein, ferocious when provoked, had taken up the fallen Augie's pistol, pointing it left and right. "What's that I'm sniffkin'!" he called out, proving it wasn't so easy to pull the wool over his eyes even in dreams.

Welcoming the challenge, Zelik mounted the railing, the rope that held the counterweight of the lamp still in his hands. He swung down from the gallery in a sweeping pendulum arc, neatly kicking the gun out of Jakie's grasp and catching it on the upswing in midair. Then he dropped to the altar and aimed the gun at Jakie, who raised his arms in defeat, muttering as he retired that they would see who had the final laugh. Nevertheless, Zelik thought he'd detected a trace of the ringleader's smile, as if Jakie were pleased at long last to have a worthy adversary. Tossing aside the pistol, Zelik unfastened the knot that bound Minnie's dress over her head and stepped back to watch the lace and chiffon fall like petals unfolding. As they faced each other—Minnie drinking in an adoring Zelik with quizzical jade green eyes—the rabbi read the conclusion of the ceremony and advised the groom to stomp the glass.

Lifting Minnie in his arms, thrilled to his toes by what a featherweight she proved to be, Zelik carried her down the aisle past pews now filled with neighbors shouting, "Mazel tov!" With his thoughts turned toward their honeymoon, he carried his bride out of the synagogue to a manhole in the middle of North Main Street. But when he'd stepped into the tree and settled back into his skin, he found that he was empty-handed except for the swaying branches he clung to for dear life.

The next day was agony all over again. Having never been drunk, Zelik thought this was what it must feel like to be hungover, so muddied in his brain were his memories of nocturnal derring-do. "Reckless shmeckless," he scoffed at himself Mr. Notowitz–style. Nervous and full of self-pity, he was valiant only in dreams.

Building a pyramid of apples in front of the market during the hottest part of the afternoon, Zelik pictured himself a slave in Egypt. Mr. Silver he tried to cast in the role of pharaoh, which wasn't so easy given the grocer's recent high spirits. How could you account for such a change in the timid little man? Where he should have been bemoaning evil prospects for the future, here he was making plans.

"So, Zelik, I think maybe I'm purchasing to raise them in the yard some chickens. I would make a competition by Makowsky and Dubrovner that they could use a kick in the toches. Don't you agree?" Then he inquired as to what time the Rifkins might be walking to the park tonight.

Zelik had no opinions to speak of concerning Mr. Silver's business, but for all his nagging discomfort, he wasn't unflattered that his opinion should have been sought. He even went so far as to make a pretense of weighing the matter thoughtfully.

Later, stepping into the hotbox of Mr. Notowitz's bedroom for his abortive Hebrew lesson, Zelik found the teacher poring feverishly over his texts. Stripped for once to his threadbare shirtsleeves, he was squeezing a boil on his neck with one hand, jotting notes and drawing diagrams in the broad margins with the other. When Zelik hemmed, the old man looked up and greeted him with unprecedented warmth.

"Ah, my prize pupil, make a guess what I do. Go ahead, make already a guess." Zelik opened his mouth to say that he hadn't a clue. "I, in my capacity that I call myself the Pseudo-Abulafia, am hereby attempting the splitting of the Ineffable Name. So what you get when you do strictly by the formula from *The Kumquat Orchard* of Rabbi Velvl . . ."—here he made a few more mad scribbles—". . . is you get for your trouble a fair likeness of the Cosmic Adam in his magic hat!"

"Come again," was all that Zelik could think to say.

But the old man's enthusiasm remained irrepressible. "So nu, what are you waiting?" he urged. "Give a look."

Zelik looked and saw a doodle resembling one of the multiglobed streetlamps along North Main, lit upon by a flock of crows. This he reported dutifully to Mr. Notowitz, who exhorted him to look again. "Don't tell to me you can't see him. Of course you can see him," the teacher assured his student, his optimism generating acid in Zelik's stomach. "Is possible, anything!"

Having deserted her sewing machine early that evening, Mrs. Rifkin was not to be found in the kitchen either. Zelik located her in her bedroom, primping in front of a mirror. She was mildly distressed at having nearly forgotten her cousin (three times removed) Zygmund's yahrzeit, who had died of something someplace far away.

"But what's the fuss, eh, tateleh? After all, the old fortz was cold before I got born. Now tell the truth, which do you prefer?"—holding up two kinds of earrings—"these ones or these with the thingamajigs that look like . . ." She laughed throatily, then blushed over what she thought they looked like.

Zelik was further bewildered at the attention paid him by his neighbors in Market Square. Before tonight, the most he could have expected from the citizens of North Main Street was their indifference, but now they hailed him with an amiable familiarity. They pinched his knobby shoulder and patted his back, gave him good-humored cuffs on the ear. Some paused to pass a little time in his company, asking his views on the affairs of the day: from the bull market to the films of Vilma Banky, the prospects for Prohibition repeal, the Monkey Trial, the duration of the heat wave, the fashionable positive thinking method of Dr. Émile Coué. When Zelik protested that he wasn't really up on current events, they pooh-poohed his modesty. And Minnie Alabaster blew him a kiss.

Her parents had stopped by the Rifkin bivouac to get Zelik's thoughts on a touring company currently playing the Orpheum Theatre. This was when their daughter, posed beside them with one arm akimbo, touched her fingers to her full, pursed lips and blew in Zelik's direction. Stupefied, he slapped his cheek, having actually felt the sting of her kiss, though it might have been only a coincidental mosquito bite.

What was happening, Zelik wondered, that everyone should be giving him such a red carpet treatment, after years of either ignoring him or making fun? Why this sudden about-face? They were a fickle bunch, his neighbors—that was all he could figure, and Minnie he deemed the most fickle of the lot. Another thing Zelik couldn't understand was how he could feel so crippled

with exhaustion and still not be ready to sleep. He blamed the capricious-
ness of North Main Street for playing on his nerves. This was not to say he
would have wanted them to fall back on their former disposition; it was just
that this being regarded as a person, for whatever reasons, was new to him.
It would take a little getting used to. In the meantime the wisest course
might be to stick to the shadows, keeping a safe distance from unpredictable neighbors, going where—once the park was quiet and he could rouse
his aching bones—Zelik felt himself to be in control.

VII. Mensch

Though the summer never relented, the population of the Pinch seemed less
oppressed by it than before. Something of the festive mood they displayed
in the park at night was now extended to their daylight behavior. Rather
than languish in helpless misery, they invented ways to beat the heat. They
became less rigorous in observing their shop hours, taking siestas and making frequent trips to the public baths. Mrs. Bluestein designed a tunic made
from twin enema bags filled with ice, which she threatened to have patented
when it was copied by the tailor Schloss. Another trend was set by Mr.
Shapiro, who strung a hammock between his shop awning and show rack,
then hired neighborhood children to fan him with broad-brimmed fedoras.
Everyone wore looser, skimpier garments, even pajamas and dressing gowns
by day, lending North Main Street the aspect of a Baghdad seraglio. And
one and all went out of their way to pay their respects to Zelik Rifkin.

   With never a mention of any event that might have led to their change of
heart, the shopkeepers sought him out. They asked his advice about embar-
rassingly personal matters, about the finer points of religious law as if he'd
been a rabbi; they showed him a deference they might have accorded a local
hero. Nor did they flinch at the improvised answers that Zelik had begun to
find the temerity to hand them. Their wives dropped by to worry over him,
agreeing with clucking tongues that the boy was too thin, plying him with
pastries and noodle puddings that he should keep up his strength—though
they never said what for. Sometimes they teased him that what he needed
was a nice girl.

   Grown accustomed to their attentions, Zelik had stopped wasting time
in wondering whether he deserved them. What went on during business
hours was of little concern to him, his days being only anxious preludes to
his nocturnal escapades. After all, in the small hours, between foiling various

nightmares, outmaneuvering Jakie Epstein along the way, he was with Minnie. A doting spouse, she'd set up housekeeping on a tiny painted ark drawn by swans in the Gayoso Bayou, and had begun to hint mysteriously that they might one day need an extra room. Reluctantly leaving her ardent embraces, Zelik set off on his self-appointed rounds of interfering in dreams. When there were no horrors to vanquish, he contented himself with making matches, such as the one between the bookish spinster Miss Weintraub and the handsome young novelist F. Scott Fitzgerald, his first marriage annulled after his wife discovered his Jewish descent. All were in attendance at the reception atop the fleabag Cochran Hotel, where a lavish roof garden had miraculously appeared. There was a cake the size of a carnival float, Kid Ory's Creole Jazz Band playing Old World klezmer standards, and Zelik himself in the role of wedding jester, using risqué material gleaned from his pretty bride in another life.

So, if the neighbors wanted to treat him like a celebrity, it was their affair. Zelik saw no reason why he ought to discourage them. Moreover, since his body had adjusted to its nightly dislocations and he was no longer bent double with pain, he was better prepared to receive their solicitous gestures with a certain grace.

Around the market these days Mr. Silver, his perspiration glistening hair oil, hummed freilach airs as he weighed the produce, striking cash register keys to end a refrain. He spoke now in a jovial singsong to his customers, attempting jokes that he generally mangled, tossing the bonus of an extra string bean into their sacks. With his popular employee he liked to intimate how he had in mind a certain someone for a partnership, just as soon as that someone finished school.

"Incidentally," he would always inquire after his exchanges with Zelik, brushing off the freshly starched apron that Mrs. Rifkin had monogrammed, "what time do you and your mama walk tonight in Market Square?"

A little earlier every evening Mr. Silver and Mrs. Rifkin—he in his spats with a hamper of laxative fruit, she all done up in her veiled cloche and high-vamped shoes—strolled to the park, shmoozing animatedly on the way. Zelik would trail behind them as discreetly as possible, given the attention he drew wherever he went. Sometimes Mr. Notowitz also joined their party, his informally open collar allowing the free sway of his wattled throat. Taking his student's arm, he might assure him he had the makings of an authentic tzaddik, and once paid Zelik the highest compliment: "I am seeing in you the young Aharon Notowitz." If the student reminded his teacher that he'd never before shown any special aptitude for learning, the old man insisted that such modesty was itself a sign of wisdom. Then Zelik would have to gloat a bit despite himself, grinning complacently at the back of his mother's head. For the newly bobbed curls that peeked from under her hat, her coquettishness bespeaking a second girlhood, he felt in part responsible, though he couldn't say exactly how.

In another development Jakie Epstein had begun to send around delegations inviting Zelik to attend various functions of the gang. While making change or uncrating bananas (careless lately of tarantulas lurking among them), Zelik might feel a tug at his sleeve, then look up to find Augie Blot in his aviator goggles.

"Jakie wants to know if you'd like to be a umpire," he might say, spitting tobacco juice through a gap in his teeth to show it was all the same to him; or, "Jakie wants to know if you'd like to watch us beat the kreplach out of the Mackerel Gang."

At first Zelik tested the water gingerly, thinking he smelled something fishy. Since when had they ever requested his company except to make him the butt of a joke? But now, putting his suspicions to rest, they seemed genuinely pleased to see him, asking his advice about everything from placing numbers bets to the speculated girth of Mrs. Kipper's bosom. Encouraged, Zelik began hanging around with the boys more often. He was tickled to have been accepted without having to spend the night on Beale Street or set fire to a schoolmistress or desecrate the Torah scrolls. But what was most appealing about his chumminess with the Pinch Gang was the opportunities it afforded Zelik to be close to Minnie.

Meanwhile she was making unashamedly aggressive overtures toward him. She'd begun by targeting him as the particular audience for her dubious humor ("So, Zelik, Doc Seligman walks into the deli and asks Mrs. Rosen if she's got hemorrhoids. 'Sorry, darling,' she says, 'only what's on the menu.'"), then graduated to a more personal approach. "They say you been hiding your light under a bushel basket at Silver's," she might tease him, pouting provocatively. "Mind if I take a peek under your bushel?" Eventually even less circumspect, she would steal up behind him to whisper pet endearments: "Zisss-keit, Sweet Patootie, my naughty Uncle Zelik, when are you coming to babysit your ickle Minnie?"

Always in his presence she managed to be fiddling with a stocking or dropping a scented handkerchief. Inhaling a lipstick-stained cigarette, she blew smoke rings that settled like halos over Zelik's head. And if the other boys, Jakie included, ever thought it unfair that the nebbish should command so much of Minnie's attention, they never let on.

Amazingly, Zelik wasn't afraid of her anymore. After a while he could weather her flirtations without his heart beginning to hum like a beehive whose vibrations he could feel in his pants. Cozy under his mantle of local maven, he forgot all those weeks of desperate yearning, and received her advances with a courtliness due the tender bride he knew her to be in her dreams.

He even found the nerve to return her flattery, if not quite in kind. "Minnie, you're a doll," he'd attempted on a note of confidence that fizzled when the words wouldn't come. "You're a . . . doll." But when the object of his tribute, instead of mocking him, winked as though the sally had struck home, Zelik was heartened. He could do no wrong. Moved to bolder experimentation, he cribbed lines from the Song of Songs, domesticating them to the immediate surroundings.

"Thine eyes are as sunbeams in wine bottles," he extolled, reading from an unscrolled scrap of paper with halting formality. "Thy hair like when you lift the lid on a stove, thy teeth like freshly scrubbed stones in the potter's field. Thy neck is the obelisk in Confederate Park, thine tsitskehs a pair of puppies. The smell of thy garments is the smell of Ridblatt's Bakery. Behold, my neshomaleh, leaping on the cobbles, skipping on the shells of snapping turtles . . ."

Minnie rewarded him by squirming kittenishly, the words seeming to have touched her in intimate places. "Stop!" she pleaded, pulling her beret over her ears, after which she purred, "Sweetie, I'm yours!" Guilty of having kindled blushes in so many others, Minnie turned crimson herself, then grew sober: it was a grave responsibility to be thus adored. She dropped her forward manner and her trademark salty language, swapping them for an uncharacteristic hauteur. Having absorbed by association some of the fawning respect universally heaped on her "fella" (as Zelik was lately acknowledged to be), Minnie Alabaster began to put on airs.

It seemed to Zelik that he now had just about everything one could want in this world, and assumed it had all come about by the grace of his activities in another. But since his neighbors had never once referred to having seen him in their dreams, you might have argued otherwise. You could believe, for example, that they'd simply come around to appreciating virtues in the kid that he himself had not recognized before.

At first their homage had served only to violate his privacy; it distracted him from the driven anticipation of his nightly ascent up the oak. Nothing on earth was as beguiling or even, paradoxically, as real as what waited for him at the top of the tree. Then the quality of life in the Pinch had changed: the neighbors ceased to utter discouraging words except about the weather. And, wonder of wonders, Minnie had given him her affection. Suddenly the daylight North Main Street was making a bid to compete with its nocturnal counterpart. In fact, they were neck and neck, and Zelik, drawn irresistibly to each, was never so content as to spend his days in one and his nights in the other.

Honored in the greengrocery, he still went through his stock boy's motions, though he was often interrupted by neighbors dropping by to bend his ear. Mr. Silver, if he worried about anything beyond the knot in his new cravat, worried that his assistant might become fatigued. With a paternal interest in Zelik's welfare, not to say a newfound sympathy for matters of the heart, he would advise his employee to take off early and go visit his girl.

A creature of habit, Zelik never failed to look in on Mr. Notowitz, whom he frequently found in the throes of mystical transport, naked but for his holey underwear. "Here by the gate of paradise is Notowitz!" the old man might proclaim, the sparse hair horizontal at his temples. "Behold that it is as an elevator up the trunk of the Tree of Life—I'm talking my room. You are maybe wanting to ride?" Zelik, who never rode when he could climb, would tell the teacher, "I'll take a rain check," then excuse himself and hurry off to preside over the doings of the Pinch Gang.

With Minnie on his arm he was practically holding court, a solemn and discerning presence at their assorted pranks and brawls. They even made sure he had a grandstand view of their more disreputable enterprises—the bootlegging, the petty thefts. For himself Zelik was happy to turn a blind eye to such proceedings, but sometimes, lest they offend her sensibilities, he thought it better to lead Minnie away. He took her for walks to show her off along streets where he had previously wandered in stealth all alone; and in the evenings, touching fingertips to each other's lips, the sweethearts exchanged a fond good night. The moment seemed all the more delicate against the backdrop of the noisy park, its racket increased by the conspicuous billing and cooing of Mrs. Rifkin and the grocer. Afterward, when everyone else was bedded down and sleeping, Zelik would climb the tree and meddle in their dreams.

It was an embarrassment of riches, the bounty that he now enjoyed, though it had displaced somewhat the sweet suspense of waiting each day for night to fall. Lately, while his body still longed in every fiber to make the climb, Zelik, his mind becalmed, wondered what was the hurry. Owing to his popularity, the neighbors had relocated their encampments until the Rifkins replaced the oak as centerpiece of the gathered community. This made it chancier to go creeping among them. Moreover, should anyone catch him climbing, what with their great concern for his welfare, they would insist he come down at once before hurting himself. And sometimes it occurred to Zelik that, for their sake, maybe he ought to be a bit more careful.

Also, when he thought of it, his meteoric rise to respectability rivaled anything he'd encountered in dreams. Dreams could scarcely improve on the bliss that was Zelik's daily fare. In coming to share his neighbors' estimation of him, he felt almost as if North Main Street, in both its terrestrial and celestial manifestations, belonged to him; as if all that went on in that neighborhood above the sleeping park were contained in a dream of Zelik's own. Or was it a hallucination, since who wouldn't start to see things if they'd missed as much sleep as he?

Then came a night when the thought of his marathon wakefulness made him yawn. All around him his neighbors were already deep in slumber, and exposed as he was, Zelik figured it must be catching. Maybe a short nap would refresh him for the climb. Yawning luxuriously, he stretched out on the davenport that Shafetz's Discount had donated for his comfort. (His mother had been provided a chaise longue.) With his fingers locked behind his head, eyes closed to the shooting stars, he began to doze, falling into a dream about Minnie. In it he was dissatisfied with their hand-holding dalliance and had begun, despite her giggling protests, to fumble under her clothes. He was jolted awake to a throbbing sense of something unfinished, but presently succumbed to drowsiness again.

VIII. A Change in the Weather

In the days following the abandonment of his nightly climb, Zelik looked forward to sleeping as much as he'd previously looked forward to scaling the oak. He slept long and deep, and in the mornings had to be roused by his mother with persistent shaking. Throughout the rest of the day he took every occasion to catnap, catching his winks where he might, convinced that his record insomnia had finally caught up with him. Meanwhile his neighbors continued to greet him affably enough, though they sometimes caught themselves in midsentence, pausing in irritation as if suddenly aware of having transgressed some personal code. Frequently stuporous, however, Zelik was the last to notice that their attitude toward him had grown chillier and more remote.

Even his closest acquaintances got into the act. There was the afternoon, for instance, when, sacked out for a snooze on a cooler at the rear of the market, Zelik was rudely awakened by the grocer. "Stop with the loafing already," snapped Mr. Silver, his cheeks sagging from the weight of the bags under his eyes. "Troubles I got enough of without I should have a goldbrick on the job."

Hitting a snag in his mystical investigations—the critical twelfth combination of the letters of the Tetragrammaton having failed to induce the visionary state—Mr. Notowitz, who'd reverted to his moss-grown suit, blamed his difficulties on his student's untimely entrance.

"Where you been, you never heard of knocking?" he demanded, rapping his forehead with a bony fist until he'd raised a lump. "Come in, Mr. Rifkin, that he walks in the way of the Torah repairing its breaches. Better he should walk in the way of his mama repairing britches." With this he violently blew his nose in the crook of his sleeve.

Dowdy again in a washed-out housefrock, her face lackluster in the absence of shadow and rouge, Mrs. Rifkin asked her son if he'd mind correcting the tilt of her neglected calendar. And while he was at it, he should tear off the July page, since August was already half over, though where the time had gone she didn't know.

There was also discontent in the ranks of the Pinch Gang, who'd begun to express impatience with the way Zelik remained always the spectator. It started one late afternoon on the levee, when Ike, the semiarticulate twin, asked Zelik, "How come you don't never do nothing but sit and look?" Seated on a bollard with Minnie beside him, her elbow resting on his shoulder, Zelik rolled his eyes in a groggy smirk. He expected others to do the same rather than dignify such a stupid question. But Jakie himself, drying off after a dip in the river, his stringy muscles atwitch in his soaking skivvies, seconded Lieberman's query. This left it to the irreverent Augie Blot to set them straight.

"'Cause he's a rare bird, ain't you heard? A yellow-bellied Zelik." He went on to call him names intended to dissolve any lingering illusion that the emperor was wearing clothes.

Zelik puffed himself up, speechless at Augie's show of insubordination. Truly, it was a harsher judgment than the others seemed prepared to accept, and with a pop of the jaw Jakie offered the accused a chance to allay their suspicions.

"Whyn't you dive off the crane if you ain't afraid?"

Swallowing hard, Zelik maintained his composure. "What for should I want to get all wet?"

When Augie suggested he already was, Minnie cut him short, forgetting herself in a curse that dismissed Jakie's mouthpiece for a pink-eyed, limp-petseled bed wetter. Then swelling the bodice of her sailor blouse, she was haughty again. "Go ahead, sweetie, give the monkeys a thrill." She patted her mouth in a yawn, bored at the prospect of yet another example of her boyfriend's fearlessness.

Aggravated, wanting a nap, Zelik turned to remind his companion that he didn't have to prove himself, when he saw in the set of her features that he must. Petulantly, he slid from the bollard and kicked off his shoes. He removed his cap and shirt, handing them to Minnie, who received them as if this were part of an established routine. Aware of how his pallor contrasted with the suntanned bodies of the gang, he was also conscious of the fact that Jakie Epstein didn't have a corner on knotty biceps, Zelik's clandestine tree-climbing activities having whipped him into pretty fair shape.

He strolled up to the greasy traveling platform from which a tall crane leaned out over the river, and sprang onto the ladder. In seconds he was scrambling up the girders of the crane itself, using the large bolts encrusted with pigeon drek for toeholds, climbing with an easy agility. Then it was bracing to demonstrate before an audience what had become for Zelik an almost involuntary exercise; although, as he mounted higher, he discovered he was a little out of practice. He was slightly winded as he neared the top, not to say dizzy from the contraption's tilt and sway, and the sun, glinting off the tin roofs of houseboats and the river, stung his eyes whenever Zelik dared to look down. Here he awoke to the realization that, for all his dream heroics, he had yet to disprove the famous Rifkin chickenheartedness by day. It was a truth that stopped him cold, left him clinging to the girders for dear life, listening to insults hurled from the cobbles and feeling his nose begin to bleed.

After that Minnie became increasingly difficult to live with, though she continued to stick by Zelik with a stubbornness that challenged anyone to so much as look askance. But where her beau had turned back before her eyes into a milquetoast, Minnie had begun to act the floozy again. She'd revived her teasing manner that called into question the virility of the other boys, sometimes suckering them into flirtations that she abruptly thwarted. Once more she was telling stories that cast their families in compromising roles: "So Nathan Shapiro meets his papa coming out of a bordel on Beale Street, and his papa says, 'Don't be angry, sonny. Would you want I should wake your mama at such an hour for a dollar?'" And always she looked over her shoulder for Zelik's reaction.

Then the first time he'd presumed to suggest that this kind of behavior wasn't becoming, Minnie turned on him. She yanked him behind the Market Square bandstand and offered him another chance to prove his mettle. "What do you say, my big strong ape-mensch," she breathlessly invited, watering Zelik's eyes with her cheap perfume, "won't you give your angel food girlie a little fun?"

"I don't know what's got into you, Minnie." Zelik tried to stand firm in his disapproval, though neither of them was fooled. Both understood that he was simply afraid to touch her, at least in her fleshly daylight incarnation.

"Okay, kiddo," sniffed Minnie, twisting her neck to admire the bare shoulder that her boat-necked blouse revealed, "if you can't show me a good time, there's others who can." Pausing to light a cigarette, she flicked the match at Zelik before traipsing off.

Brooding but undaunted, Zelik resolved to fix things the next time he saw her, if not here on earth then elsewhere. He determined to make good again in dreams what he'd botched in waking life. How had he let the situation get so out of hand in the first place? It was true of course that, during his drowsy absence, the street at the top of the oak had all but faded into unreality; but now this only increased Zelik's urgency to reconfirm what had to have been more than just the fruits of an overwrought imagination.

At dusk on the same day that Minnie had called his bluff, however, there was a distinctly literal chill in the air. There was a breeze that the neighbors were welcoming as the harbinger of an early autumn, their reward for having survived such a scorching summer.

"Thank God that tonight in our own beds we will sleep," sighed Mr. Silver, who had recently begun talking about Klan raids in the park again.

"What are you saying!" cried his young assistant, on hand to fly into a panic. "This summer ain't over by a long shot. You'll see, the temperature'll soar. Don't be taken in by a little breeze."

The grocer was perplexed that anyone should seem to want the heat to endure. "Meshuggeh," he grumbled, turning away, washing his hands of an employee who, beyond feckless, was crazy to boot.

Zelik wandered up North Main Street, listening to the shopkeepers trading expressions of relief over the change in the weather. Taking every opportunity to contradict them, he insisted they shouldn't relax: "Don't you know we're in for more of the same!" But the neighbors only shook their heads, no longer influenced by what the screwball Rifkin kid might believe.

That night Zelik went to the empty park all alone. Not only had the wind picked up, with a blustery edge that gave him gooseflesh, but a fierce storm was threatening. Huge, billowing thunderheads obscured the moon, their interiors lit like intermittent X-rays. Then the sky cracked open and a gully-washer ensued. Running home in the torrential downpour, fording gutters flash flooded to his knees, Zelik was drenched to the marrow. Even changed into his nightshirt and nestled under the covers, he couldn't stop trembling.

At first unable to sleep, he fell at length into an agitated insensibility, dreaming that the oak was struck by lightning at its crown, riven limbs tumbling to earth in sizzling flames. He woke up sopping all over again, the sheets clammy from his sweat. For an instant Zelik thought his prayers had been answered: the heat had returned with an intensity that made a furnace of the apartment. But how could this be, when the rain was still drumming away in the alley outside? It was a mystery that goaded Zelik into abandoning his bed for the cluttered living room. His mother and Mr. Notowitz, a sheet draped like a prayer shawl over his shoulders, were already at the windows, looking onto a stormy North Main Street aglow beneath a hyacinth orange sky.

The word went from building to building that the great wooden barn of the Phoenix Athletic Club had been struck by lightning. "It went up just like matchsticks," everyone said. Although the boxing arena stood a block away on Front Street, the heat from its conflagration was so furious that the windows of the Rifkin apartment were too hot to touch. Over the clanging engines from five alarms, they could hear the nickering screams of horses in a stable near the arena that had also caught fire. They could hear the sound of shattering glass as windows were bursting all over the Pinch.

IX. Jacob's Ladder

For a day or so it was hard to tell whether the overcast sky was due to dark clouds or the smoke from the smoldering arena. But soon the cooler air blew away the smoke, the sun reappeared, and the season turned.

By now Zelik's status in the community had degenerated from merely discredited to outcast. Nostalgic for his former condition of near-invisibility, he lurked in backstreets, avoiding as best he could the scornful glances of his neighbors, the taunts of Jakie's gang. From the way everyone behaved, you'd have thought he was personally responsible for whatever disappointment they'd experienced in life.

To make matters worse, Zelik's friend and employer, reeling from a recent attack of gentile phobia (he claimed it was the Klan that torched the boxing arena, infested as it was with a certain ghetto element), informed his so-called assistant that he would have to lay him off. "It ain't so hotsy-totsy, the produce business," explained Mr. Silver.

Zelik put up a token resistance. "So what happened to 'With a certain cute boychik, soon I am making a partnership'?"

"That was couple weeks ago already," said the grocer, pausing a moment to plaintively recall the past. "To tell the truth, what it is that ain't good for business is you."

Neither was it good for business, thought Zelik, that Mr. Silver shook in his bluchers every time some yokel walked in from the wagon yard. And what about his recent quarrel with Mrs. Rifkin? (It had begun trivially enough with the seamstress accusing her suitor of having falsely advertised inferior merchandise, but ended in the mutual dissolution of their romance.) Let Silver deny that had anything to do with the sudden dismissal of his faithful employee. But Zelik wasn't really inclined to argue. The job had entailed more public exposure than he had the heart to suffer, and, besides, who needed the grocer's penny-ante charity?

Meanwhile Mr. Notowitz's experiments in practical Kabbalah had entirely broken down, and the old teacher had withdrawn into a sullen and demon-ridden silence. If he emerged for meals, he ate little; he complained that feasting all summer on the fruit of the Tree of Life had given him terminal gas. As for Mrs. Rifkin, with the courtship of Leon Silver blotted from her memory, she'd resumed her fanatical devotion to the calendar of events in other people's lives.

As the following months ushered in the bitter winter of Zelik Rifkin's discontent, no one else in the Pinch appeared to be doing much better. Everyone griped that business had fallen off. They blamed their lack of prosperity—which was a new line, as if they'd just waked up to the fact that they were poor—on the treachery of their Irish and Italian competitors; though the butcher Makowsky was heard to say of the butcher Dubrovner, who promptly returned the compliment, that he was not above certain underhanded practices of his own. Most agreed with Mr. Silver that the mayor of Memphis, a self-styled potentate nicknamed the Red Snapper, was perfectly capable of reinstituting the blood libel. A pogrom might be imminent.

But of all the available scapegoats on which the neighborhood pinned their woes, Zelik remained a sentimental favorite, the Pinch's own resident Jonah. The latest complaint to become popular along North Main Street was chronic insomnia, which had infected enough to be declared an epidemic. Despite unusually cold weather otherwise suited for a deep winter's hibernation, the neighbors grew ever more irritable from loss of sleep. For this they were also disposed to blame the Rifkin kid, though direct expressions of annoyance had to be reserved for the rare occasions when he was sighted. Thus, having once been revered for no apparent reason, Zelik was now just as unreasonably despised.

The worst was of course that Minnie wanted nothing to do with him. In the face of her active disdain, however, Zelik's pining for his ginger-haired precious had if anything intensified. But this was not the wistfully chivalrous brand of longing that had satisfied him in the days when he was secure in her adoration. Now Zelik wanted to encircle her slender waist and squeeze for all he was worth. He wanted to nibble her succulent earlobe, bury his nose in the warmth of her boobies, bite the delectable flesh above her rolled stocking while murmuring forbidden words. He cursed and berated himself for the opportunities he'd let slip by, for neglecting to act on the nerve that he'd deceived himself into thinking he had.

Leaning out of doorways in his earflaps and ulster, parting racks of pants gone stiff from the chilly air, Zelik spied on Minnie. He watched her gossiping as she left Levy's Candy Store with Rose Padauer and Sadie Blen, heard her twitting the boys with her racy remarks, the choicest of which she'd begun to save for Jakie Epstein. Holding his breath so its steam wouldn't give him away, he saw Minnie urge Jakie to drop back from the others, tugging him into an alley where they could bundle and pet.

The unending cold snap did nothing to take the edge off his terrible wanting, and eventually a day arrived when desire got the better of fear. Having waited for the lovebirds to part company in a gravel drive behind the cigar factory, Zelik pitched forward through a sprinkling of snowflakes to block Minnie's path.

"M-n-n-n." His chattering teeth prevented him from getting beyond a blue-lipped approximation of her name.

Hugging herself in her mackinaw against the raw January wind, Minnie wondered aloud, "What did I ever see in you? Gevalt!" She slapped her brow with a mittened palm. "I must of had a hole in my head."

In the instant before she started away, Zelik saw in her emerald eyes that she scarcely even considered him worth pitying. Frantically hoping that a second look might erase the first, he lunged for her arm and spun her around.

"Nobody!" she hissed. "You got wet lokshen noodles where your backbone ought to be."

He was sobbing when he embraced her, the sobs mounting to a caterwaul as they tussled, as he tried to thrust his fingers between the buttons of her coat. It was a clumsy assault, too blind and confused to be effective, and Minnie handily repulsed him with a knee to his groin. He slumped against a bill-plastered wall and slid to the gravel, Minnie already showing him her heels, though she turned back briefly to deliver a kick for good measure to his shin. While the hot tears cooled to an icy glaze on his cheeks, Zelik surrendered to the contemplation of his basest act of cowardice so far.

Warmer weather brought little relief, though with a heady bouquet of growing things in the air, the open hostility of his neighbors toward Zelik seemed to have subsided. His disgrace, lacking any sound basis in circumstance, was apparently forgotten along with the dreadful winter, and the street resumed its original indifference with regard to the Rifkin kid. Not that it mattered. By now Zelik had more than enough disgust for himself to compensate for what his neighbors no longer took the trouble to feel.

He had for some time discontinued his spying operations, leaving home only to attend the Market Avenue School, in whose dusty corridors and classrooms he'd perfected his nonentity. Otherwise, except on those evenings when he accompanied her to the synagogue for prayers and yitzkor services, Zelik remained his mother's shut-in companion. He left his days to be defined, like hers, by the calendar of banner events—a new calendar published by a company that made wrought-iron anvils. Avoiding their cranky boarder, Zelik occupied himself with daydreams in which nobody ever turned out a hero, though sometimes, if only to break the monotony, he might be moved to inquire about the relatives they mourned. Maybe one of them had an interesting life. But in the end he dropped the questions, having confirmed that his toilworn mother hardly knew any more about them than he.

School let out and spring turned imperceptibly to summer, a mild summer like an apology for the previous year's inferno. But the balmy days were too good to last, and somewhere around mid-July the heat was once again cranked up full force. The shopkeepers lolled in their sweaty undershirts, their faces hidden beneath wet rags. On their heads they wore newspapers folded into admiral's hats, smeared headlines declaring no end in sight for the dog days. The k'nackers claimed they were dredging boiled mussels from the river, that Kaplan the real-estate agent had cornered the market in shade, while the pious tended to view the heat wave as a finsternish, another plague visited for their sins on North Main Street by an angry God. Eentsy Lazarov had been spotted in the arms of her shaigetz in the balcony of the Orpheum Theatre, Morris Hanover seen departing a hog-nosed café on Beale Street eating treyf. Though if it occurred to anyone to blame the unbearable weather on Zelik Rifkin, they were never heard to say.

Like every other apartment in the Pinch, the one above Silver's Fruit & Veg was practically beyond habitation. Its occupants were unable to draw a breath without feeling as if someone else had drawn it before them; there seemed not enough of that torpid air to go around. This, Zelik told himself, was what he deserved, though the heaviness of this particular afternoon left him wondering if there might be a limit even for him. Raising himself from his prostration atop a pile of clothes in need of mending, he panted hopefully, "Did anybody die today?"

With barely the strength to pump the treadle on her hobbling machine, Mrs. Rifkin glanced at the calendar. "Your great-uncle Gershon," she sighed.

Of Uncle Gershon Zelik knew only that he'd perished of death long ago in some unpronounceable village in Europe, and that his memorial meant he and his mother, please God, would leave the apartment tonight. It never entered his head anymore that he might go out alone.

Because it was Shabbos, the whole of North Main Street was in the synagogue, flapping their prayerbooks like an aviary to try and stir a breeze. There were several instances of fainting, not to be confused with swoons in the gallery during the cantor's megaphone vocals. Dehydrated babies wailed and daveners gibbered in no identifiable tongue. Finally Rabbi Fein, so farshvitst you'd have thought his bowler was an upturned bucket, hauled himself onto the pulpit to deliver his benedictory sermon. Wrapped in his wringing tallis like a bath towel, he reeled as he recited what purported to be a midrash on the subject of Jacob's Ladder.

". . . You had at the bottom of the ladder the angels, that they looked like old men in their caftans, their wings scrawny as a chicken's. But the closer they are getting, these angels, to the top of the ladder, the more antsy-pantsy and fuller of pep they become. Then it's off with the clothes, they're throwing them willy-nilly, and hallelujah! youthful figures they got now, with lovely wings that make a nice cool breeze."

The rabbi cleared his throat and recovered his composure. "The lesson from this text we are learning," he began with authority; then his eyes started to shift and he muttered hastily that the congregation were free to draw their own conclusions. He raised his voice to announce that the ladies of the synagogue auxiliary would be on hand with provisions for those who elected to stay the night in Market Square.

X. The Ceiling of Fate

Too depleted from the ordeal of the service to protest, Mrs. Rifkin allowed her son to lead her across the street into the park. There they joined the others milling about like survivors of a shipwreck, receiving from the ladies blankets for making pallets and collapsible cups of iced tea. On the far edge of the circle of neighbors, Zelik spread the blanket and saw that his wilting mother was settled comfortably for the night. Sitting beside her, he patted his chest through his shirt in an effort to quiet the frightened fluttering within.

Everyone was there: Mr. Silver beneath the lilac with his galluses hanging, swilling stomach bitters to chase down his prunes; Mr. Notowitz disguised as refuse on his bench. Some members of the Pinch Gang could be seen shadowboxing under the tree, a knot of girls (Zelik wondered idly if Minnie was among them) conspiring nearby. Now and then neighbors passed seeking extra hands for card games, looking to stake claims on unoccupied pieces of ground, but not one gave the Rifkin kid so much as a "How do ya do." They ignored Zelik so completely he might have doubted his very existence, which, under the circumstances, he found somehow reassuring.

In the moonless sky, however, there were occasional flashes of lightning, promising rain and threatening to reduce the oak to a burning bush. Zelik could feel this particular worry beginning to spawn nameless others until he was permeated with a general dread. Over and over, as the neighbors extinguished their lanterns and allowed their Victrolas to wind down, he had to remind himself that this was only heat lightning, which was nothing but the echo of a storm too far away to matter.

To his mother he whispered, in order not to wake her, "Good night, Mama, I'm off to climb a tree to the Land of Nod," then started at her mumbled words of caution. He got to his feet and made his way among his neighbors, casting rueful glances at their recumbent forms, as if they'd fallen in battle instead of merely fallen asleep.

He stepped onto a humpbacked root and jumped, clambering painfully aloft. Due to a long inertia his muscles were unused to climbing, never mind the state of his nerves, and Zelik groaned his torment at every stage of the ascent. Too scared to look down, he nevertheless managed to lose his footing from time to time, and had to hug the tree until his breath returned. Somewhere during the climb his groans turned to whimpers, though after a certain height Zelik's suffering began to sound in his own ears as if it belonged to someone else.

When he'd surfaced from under the fog, he filled his lungs with sparkling courage, his eyes with crazy dreams. Slipping neatly out of his body, Zelik stood astride the manhole to watch the shenanigans of North Main. The Widow Teitelbaum was on her balcony, serenaded by a singing cowboy bearing a marked resemblance to Cantor Abrams in Stetson and chaps. Sacharin the herringmonger tossed promotional handbills from on board a flying fish, and Lazar the red-whiskered bootlegger, unscrewing a fire plug, deluged the gutters with an amber flood of beer. But anxious as he was to commence his rounds, Zelik restrained himself; there was a piece of business he had first to attend to.

Dropping back into the tree, he hung by his knees and surveyed the park below. From this topsy-turvy vantage Zelik felt almost as if he were at the bottom of the oak again, looking up into a dark canopy hung with dreamers. He judged that all was as it should be with them, just as it was with his own outmoded self, fearfully clutching the branches under the ceiling of fog. Reaching down, Zelik took hold of those tenacious fingers and endeavored to pry them loose. His old golf-capped, knee-pantsed, skin-and-bones double struggled to retain its balance. To make sure that it didn't, Zelik gave it a little shove. As he swung back up onto the airborne pavement, he heard the thrashing beneath him, the desolate shriek, which he muffled by sliding the iron manhole cover in place. Then nothing remained but to stroll off into the thick of things.

The Lord and Morton Gruber

Morton Gruber, czar of a string of lucrative coin-operated laundries, gave his wife a perfunctory peck and got out of bed. With a brain still thickly encrusted with dreams—a recurring one in particular in which he was force-fed leaden slugs—he padded downstairs to the kitchen. Crossing freshly waxed tiles to an island with a copper roof, he lit a gas burner on the stainless-steel range. As he was reaching for the kettle, the flame shot up and a voice called out his name.

"MORTON GRUBER."

The kettle slipped out of his hand and clattered noisily over the tiles. From the upstairs bedroom came the voice of his wife shouting, "Morty, what have you done?"

"Nothing," replied Morton. "Go back to sleep." But he was talking not so much to his wife as to the unruly flame.

Again the flame spouted up in a fierce red column, piercing the copper hood and scorching the ceiling.

"MORTON GRUBER, THIS IS THE LORD."

Morton folded his vulnerable belly into the monogrammed silk of his bathrobe and backed toward a window, glancing out over manicured lawns as if for help.

"It's God, Morty," repeated the flame, modulating itself to a milder blue blaze, "and you're going to be my prophet."

Groaning aloud, Morton rolled his eyes in an appeal to heaven: "Who needs this?" He caught sight of the blackened spot on the ceiling. "This we don't need, no way. Thanks but no thanks." For a man whose livelihood depended on the precision of manufactured appliances, this kind of thing was unacceptable. It was more than the law allowed.

As the flame was burning evenly now, Morton took courage. "It never happened," he assured himself, studiously avoiding the ceiling with his puffy eyes. "I wasn't awake yet, that's all." He wagged his broad face this way and that, pounded his temple with the heel of his hand, dislodging clusters of dreams like old snow. "Now I'm awake, all right, okay. I don't hear nothing."

The flame danced and Morton flung himself back up against the window, cracking a pane.

"DON'T FIGHT IT, GRUBER."

Careless of his blood pressure, Morton felt his hackles rising—that such an unnatural occurrence should take place in his home. My home, he reflected, with its gracefully appointed fixtures, its scrubbed and polished surfaces, its mortgage paid off a decade ago. Then squaring off with the range, he mocked in defiance, "'Don't fight it, Gruber.'" This he repeated until it came to him: "You sound like me."

"I am you, in a sense," from the burner, spitting sparks as if a throat were being cleared, "but let's not get into that. The thing is, I want you to . . ."

But at that point Morton had clapped his hands over his ears and fled the room.

Back upstairs he hid his head beneath a pillow, his well-padded rump in the air. "Lolly," he spoke into pastel satin sheets, "what would you say if I told you that I just heard the voice of the Lord?"

Still drowsing, Morton's wife lifted her sleeping visor and uttered a soft interrogative grunt. Morton emerged from under the pillow, his sparse hair in bedeviled tufts, and restated his question with an unmuffled tongue.

Lolly opened her eyes far enough to admit the sight of her agitated husband, then shut them again. "See a doctor," was her automatic reply, and completing the reflex, "you're overworked."

She and Morton both knew of course that this was not the case. In the past few years, since their wayward son, Jason, had finally begun to take an interest in the business, Morton had found himself in a state of semi-retirement. He still went to the office, shuffled papers, and made supervisory noises. But most of his time was spent on the phone to his former partner, who countered his chronic boasting with endless reminiscences.

Catnapping again, Lolly surfaced enough to inquire, "So what did He say?"

"Who?" wondered Morton, still hugging his pillow, already wishing he'd kept his mouth shut.

"You know, the Lord."

Morton gave his wife an incredulous frown. What did she mean by dignifying what he was trying his best to discredit in his mind? He was ready to bite off her head when he heard it again, the voice like his own, rattling the long-settled foundation.

"GRUBERRR."

Morton's jowls flapped as his head swiveled left and right, searching among the haremlike furnishings for a sign.

"What do you think, I need props?" the voice resounded. "I don't need props. Listen, putz, YOU'RE IT."

"I'm it?" echoed Morton in a whisper. He looked to Lolly to maybe tell him otherwise; but, with her eyes still closed, she gave no indication of having heard a thing.

Then an irresistible impulse to protest swelled within him: who was lord of this particular manor anyway? But on second thought, he'd better, for Lolly's sake, spare her a potential scene. Curbing his temper, and with a humility that went against his nature, Morton asked the draperied walls, "Why me?"

"There was a lottery in heaven and you won," came the voice, sardonically. "What's the difference? I'm the Lord and you're my prophet. Now get off your tush and spread the word."

Morton's jaw sagged into receding chins, his eyes shifting warily. "Um," he tendered, still humble, "begging Your pardon, but what is the word?"

Said the voice: "What else, shmendrick? DOOM."

Finding it suddenly difficult to breathe, Morton tugged at the lapels of his pajamas, bursting buttons and baring his hairy chest. He was on his knees in the middle of the canopied bed, his clenched fists raised in supplication.

"Get off my back, why dontcha!" he railed. "Can't You see I'm a happy man?"

At this Lolly sat up and, remarking her husband's condition, let out a piercing scream. She wrapped her arms about his sweating torso as if to drag him back down to earth.

"Oh, Morty!" she moaned, tears filling the parched cracks in her cold cream. "Morty"—trying to rock him against her breast—"you're having a breakdown."

"That's it," cried Morton, clutching at a final straw. "I'm nuts!" But who would believe it of such a solid citizen as he?

"I'm crazy," Morton confessed to the elegant doctor seated behind his barge-sized desk, a wreath of degrees on the wall above his head.

The doctor nodded un-hmm, collapsing the cathedral roof of his fingers. He cast down his impassive eyes and made a note on the pad in his lap, then lifted his eyes back over the rims of his glasses. It was an expression that said to Morton, What else is new?

"I hear voices," Morton hastened to add, but was forced to qualify, "Well, actually, *a* voice."

The doctor nodded again with a hint of vigor, arched a brow. Encouraged, Morton practically grinned as he delivered the goods.

"The voice says it's the Lord."

When the doctor nodded with apparent satisfaction and made another note, Morton relaxed. He locked his hands behind his head, leaned back in his chair, and prepared himself to hear the verdict. But the doctor's pen was still poised above his pad, implying that Morton should go on. His quizzical look seemed to say through sealed lips, This is not an audition.

Morton awarded himself high marks in interpreting the doctor's body language, but was it for this that he'd come? Quiz him about his potty training, the ancient history of his love life, anything. At these prices, was it too much to ask that the shrink should occasionally open his mouth?

In the continuing silence Morton determined to prove that two could play at this game—though not for long. Never a patient man—for him a clock was as good as a taxi meter—it was Morton who eventually broke the deadlock. Testily he got to his feet.

"The talk I don't need, I get free of charge," he snapped. "But when I pay, what do I get but . . ." Here he pantomimed the doctor's note taking. "I might as well be talking to myself."

Jotting down another note, the doctor spoke, easily abandoning whatever principle had kept him mum. "So, Mr. Gruber, what else does this voice of yours say?"

Morton was disappointed on a couple of counts: first, that the doctor did not have an exotic foreign accent; and second, that his question, where originality was concerned, was not much improvement over Lolly's. Rather than answer, he chose to stand and glower.

The doctor stroked his beard like a pet, considering, then directed Morton's attention to a leather-upholstered chaise longue.

"Would you perhaps like to lie down?"

Morton knitted his brow, suspicious of appeasement. Then he relented, thinking he had maybe been a bit too temperamental. Moreover, it was true that he always thought better on his back.

"Why not?" He shrugged. "God forbid I shouldn't get my money's worth."

Lying on the couch, Morton twined his fingers over the mound of his stomach and felt talkative.

"It comes to me from out of the blue, the voice, and tells me I'm it—a prophet, y'know. Me, Morton Gruber." He chuckled at the absurdity of it. "The only profit I understand is the kind that puts bread on the table, if you take my meaning." Then he wheezed in outright amusement over his joke.

Having removed himself to a chair at the head of the chaise, the doctor crossed his legs and flipped a page of the erstwhile notepad in his lap. "And how long," he matter-of-factly inquired, "has this delusion of yours persisted?"

"What delusion?" replied Morton, suddenly on his guard again. "My voice is real." Then he allowed himself to gloat over the way he'd outfoxed the doc.

To admit that he believed in the voice, this was smart; it would get him labeled certifiably farmisht. Then the doctor would have no recourse but to prescribe a nice sanatorium in the country. There Morton would sit in the sun, pampered and spoon-fed by young nurses. He would play dominoes with contented lunatics between naps. In a couple of weeks, refreshed from his holiday, he'd come home a new man. And that, he presumed, would be that.

Still, there was something unkosher here; he needed to think. But behind him the doctor, who naturally couldn't keep quiet when you wanted him to, was speaking even as he scribbled.

"Mr. Gruber, would you consider yourself a religious man?"

"Eh?" said Morton, taken unaware. "I ain't no fanatic, if that's what you mean." He and his family were members of the Reform synagogue, nu? Like everyone else, he was hedging his bets against the afterlife. So what was this headshrinker getting at, anyway?

"Then would you say that this delusion—" continued the doctor, when Morton interrupted.

"There's that word again." He sat up and growled. "Didn't I tell you already? It ain't a delusion!"

Now he thought he understood what was bothering him. It was the doctor's insinuating tone he resented; but more than that, it was the nasty way he had of taking Morton's voice in vain. Again Morton was on his feet.

"My voice is real," he reiterated, not without a touch of pride. "And there's nothing wrong with me that a little letting off steam wouldn't cure."

As he stomped out of the office, he thanked the doctor very much and told him what he could do with his bill.

Stepping out of the elevator into the columned foyer of the doctor's building, Morton was staggered off balance by the public address.

"THE LORD PAGING MORTON GRUBER" reverberated about the marble walls.

He froze to the spot, jostled by passersby whose faces showed no particular signs of alarm. Nevertheless, feeling conspicuous, Morton looked around for someplace to hide. He ducked into a phone booth, folded the door shut, and gazed out as if from inside a block of ice. The phone rang and, though he knew better, he lifted the receiver slowly to his ear.

"Gruber," said the hearty voice that rightfully belonged to himself, "God here."

"Gimme a break, willya?" cried Morton, then shuddered to the marrow as he remembered Whom he was supposed to be talking to.

Taking advantage of his subsequent speechlessness, the voice was carrying on: "Now, sonny boy, leave us not mince words—" when Morton, struck by a technicality (or a doubt, if you will), found the sudden nerve to break in.

"I thought You said You didn't need props."

"Who needs?" replied the voice. "But it makes a nice effect, don't you think?" Then back to business. "Anyhow, I'm talking DOOM here, Gruber. Not just your nickel-and-dime decline-and-fall stuff, but apocalypse, kiddo— a big bang-up finish like the big bang I started with . . ."

Morton experimentally replaced the receiver, while the voice continued loud and clear. There was a moment when he was certain that ulcers were spawning in his intestines; his pulse was outrunning the capacity of his tired blood to keep up. So this was what it was like to talk to God, he reflected. It was enough to make you nostalgic for a little heartburn.

". . . Now what I want," pursued the Lord, "is that you should get off the pot, then sit down and write Me a book . . ."

Slow down a minute, Morton had it in mind to say. A book? What did a book have to do with wandering around collaring strangers, with kvetching and making a general nuisance in the marketplace? Wasn't that, after all, what prophets did? Kvetching, Morton thought he might know something about. But a book?

". . . A sort of scripture, y'know; like a new testament . . ." the Lord was proposing, as Morton picked up the receiver again. It was a pointless gesture, but it made him feel slightly more comfortable.

"Excuse me."

". . . It's the age-old story with a newfangled twist . . ."

"Beg pardon," Morton found himself respectfully submitting, albeit he was no expert in such things, "but ain't you got a new testament already?"

The Lord sounded frankly peeved. "Two thousand years old is new?"

"It still sells, don't it?" Morton interjected with reverence.

"So do rabbits' feet, but whodoyaknow that's lucky anymore?"

Morton wasn't sure that he saw the connection; he wondered if it was possible for God to blaspheme.

"The point is, Gruber, that the thing has got to be written," insisted the Lord. It was the tone that Morton so often used, usually to no avail, when arguing with his wife and son.

The shoe on the other foot for a change, he let slip a single obstinate syllable: "Why?" And heartened, as one good word called for another, "Why a book if we're all doomed anyway?"

Pleased with himself, Morton rested his case. He thought he already knew the answer: this doom business was all a joke, right—just to frighten everybody back into line? But with the lengthening silence on the other end, Morton's momentary confidence dwindled. It occurred to him that his question might have stumped the Lord, and while not a praying man, he prayed that it hadn't.

Finally came the considered reply, confirming the worst: "To tell you the God's honest truth, I don't know." And a weary afterthought: "Something to do with the triumph of the spirit and all that."

Such an admission of something less than omniscience made Morton sick at heart. It pulled the rug out, though he couldn't say why; made him swallow hard and wipe his bullet-sweating brow.

Lord, he rehearsed subvocally until he could find his tongue. "Lord," he hoarsely appealed.

"Yeah, Morty." At least they were back on a first-name basis.

"Lord, you're scaring the pants offa me."

Then he hung up the phone and beat it out of the booth.

Safe in his office Morton collected his fugitive wits and wondered what made him think he was safe. Had these paneled walls been soundproofed against the meddlesome voice of You-Know-Who? Still, he couldn't help feeling that here he was in his own domain; that at least among his ledgers and due bills, his antique adding machine, the company calendars decades out of date, he was, relatively speaking, the boss.

The offices of the Suds-O-Mat Self-Service Laundries were situated in a meticulously landscaped suburban plaza a mile or so from Morton's own neighborhood. It was where, at the pushy behest of his progressive son, Jason, Morton had finally agreed to move the seat of their operations. It was an exodus he'd postponed for years, clinging to his former premises on the rundown North Main Street where Morton had grown up. To his son's accusation that sentiment alone had kept him in that seedy building, Morton replied that it was only for the sake of cheap rent. There was not, he contended, a sentimental bone in his body.

"So why," Jason had needled him with the zeal of a recent convert to free enterprise, "why did you bring your old office with you, right down to the original dust?"

It was the kind of disrespectful remark that kept Morton constantly put out with his only son. Where did he get off questioning (as Morton saw it) his father's authority, especially now when that authority was little more than token? Wasn't it enough that Jason was lately regarded as the driving force behind the business, while Morton was reduced to a well-pensioned figurehead?

Without Morton's foresight there would have been no business. If he hadn't had such faith in the future over a quarter of a century ago, they might still be back in steam cleaning with his ex-partner Louie Gold; though Gold wasn't complaining. Blithely, if at a constant loss, he operated the laundry that he and Morton had begun in their youth. Despite Morton's hooting derision he hung on to it with a curator's loyalty to the past. He lived above it with his wife, while around him the neighborhood collapsed into vacant lots and arid weeds.

He even had the nerve to patronize Morton, his success notwithstanding, as if Morton were a prodigal who would eventually return to the fold.

"I'm making money hand over toches," Morton would boast during the phone calls that were a daily ritual since he'd emigrated from North Main. "Only yesterday my real estate investments . . ." But Louie would interrupt in the wistful tone that suggested Morton's priorities were not straight.

"Guess who dropped in" or "passed away" or "Remember the time we cut cheder with Anastasia Tomashefsky?" he might say, as if memories, not money, were the standard currency.

"Wake up, Louie!" Morton was frequently compelled to shout, real life being such a far cry from the past. But not today. Today he didn't feel like shouting. Having had it on good authority that there was no future, it seemed to Morton more urgent than ever to tap his repository of memories.

"Louie," he greeted cheerlessly, the telephone having become for him a loathsome instrument.

"Morty," hailed Louie, "how's the weather out there in paradise?"

"Louie," Morton tried again edgewise, but his old friend was already off and running.

"Hey, Morty, you'll never guess who dropped by. Remember Hyman Nieman, old Numb Nuts Nieman? The time he was swimming in the river? He swam nearly across and said, 'I can't make it,' then turned around and swam back again."

Impatient as he was to get a word in, Morton savored the recollection. A sweet mental laxative, it set loose an image of himself as a boy on the levee, hopping from bare foot to foot on the hot cobblestones. The image purged, Morton was instantly restored to a worried late middle age.

"Louie, will you stop?" he pleaded. "I got tsores."

There was a courteous silence momentarily overruled by curiosity. "What's the matter, Morty?"

But Morton's clenched jaw refused to release what he held on the tip of his tongue. Maybe he was being a little too hasty. Here he'd been designated the Lord's confidant, and what did he do but broadcast it all over town. Already Lolly knew (which meant that her canasta club knew, and so on); then there was Dr. Whatsit, and now he was spilling the beans to Louie. But wasn't that what a prophet did?

A voice that was not the voice seemed to prompt him: save it for the book. Only what did Morton know from books? The last one he'd read was *Forever Amber* in 1948, and then he'd skipped all but the raciest parts. He was very perplexed.

"Morty, speak to me. It's Louie, your pal."

"Louie," said Morton with uncustomary sincerity, "we've always leveled with each other, right?"

"Right."

"You don't still hold a grudge 'cause I left you for the coin-ops?"

"Water under the bridge."

"Louie."

"What, Morty?"

But divine revelation no longer seemed to be the most pressing subject at hand. "Louie, do you think I'm a happy man?"

"Happy," Louie considered. "What's happy? You live in a palace, drive a car as long as my debit column. Ain't that happy?"

"Louie, you didn't answer my question."

A ponderous sigh at the other end. "You ain't *un*happy, though I wouldn't exactly call you happy. Comfortable, that's what you are."

Morton had to smirk over Louie's attempt at diplomacy. "Not today I ain't," he confessed.

"So what are you today, Morty?"

"I'm scared."

"Morty, Morty," warbled Louie, "come down to the laundry. We'll walk around the old neighborhood. Y'know, sometimes I think I can still smell Mrs. Ridblatt baking challah—"

Thinking he could smell it too, Morton violently blew his nose.

"Louie, will you shut up with the ghosts already? What is it with you and ghosts? Maybe you're one of them, Louie. You're a ghost too."

In the lull of Louie's sulking, Morton attempted an apology, but his ex-partner shouted him down.

"If what you are is living, then I'd rather be a ghost. I can't help you, Gruber. Go and see a rabbi." After which a clunk and a dial tone.

"So?" asked Lolly for the third or fourth time, following Morton around the house as he searched for his cigars. "So?" she repeated, as he settled with an *oy* into a reclining armchair. Then Jason, whom she'd alerted to his father's freakish condition, burst in in time to lend his two cents' worth.

Toying with the remote control, which in turn flashed random lives across the television screen, Morton prolonged his family's suspense.

"So?" he mocked them under his breath. "So what?"

"So what did the doctor say?"

Advancing the serial images before they could capture his interest, Morton heaved the hybrid of a shrug and a sigh. "I'm beyond doctors, Lolly," he asserted with a suggestion of vanity. "For what I got, who knows? Maybe it's time to call in the rabbi."

Lolly slapped her forehead and made her "Can you believe this" face at the ceiling. Out of the corner of his eye Morton registered her expression: boy, did she have the wrong supreme being.

"It's all right, Mama," said Jason, taking charge. A veteran no-account who had lately contracted ambition, he was resplendent with self-esteem, his gold chain glinting at his open throat. "Papa," he said, inclining his coiffured head to signify that the moment of reckoning had arrived, "don't you think it's time you threw in the towel?"

Morton turned in his chair, about to breathe fire. But rather than play any further into his family's hands, he checked himself. He raised the volume and continued to switch the channels, his attention arrested for a split second by the image of Charlton Heston on Sinai.

Still he was sensitive to the sound of his wife and son in commiseration, muttering an exchange that might have been a Kaddish. Swiveling toward them in annoyance, Morton barked, "I'll get some advice from the rabbi tomorrow. He'll fix me up, you'll see." Then he waved his hand, indicating that the subject was formally closed.

Jason, who would have to have the last word, mumbled in phony deference, "He has spoken."

Born out of his conversation with Louie, visiting the rabbi was a whim that had ripened into a conviction. At first Morton hadn't known he was serious himself. In this resolve he hesitated long enough to mourn the man he'd been only days before. For him, for the old Morton Gruber, such superstitious bunkum would have been beneath contempt.

Nor did the atmosphere of the opulent new synagogue, diamond-in-the-roughly situated among the pines, help to dispel Morton's doubts. The rabbi's office, give or take a few Jewish artifacts—the spice box, the shofar mounted on a plaque like a leaping bass—was practically interchangeable with the shrink's. The rabbi himself was youthful and nattily dressed, his hands folded patiently atop his barge-sized desk, the bouquet of his aftershave suffusing the room.

Completely unruffled by his congregant's pronouncements, he spoke to Morton the way an adult speaks man-to-man to a child. Breezily he dismissed Morton's experience as unfashionable.

"Sometimes," he averred, removing his tinted glasses, "we personify the conscience and call it the word of God. I've done this myself. But you know, Morton"—who for some reason resented the intimate use of his given name—"word-of-mouth prophecy is a thing of the past. It belongs to the infancy of our faith. Today the Lord uses far subtler means of communicating His will . . ."

But Morton had already given up listening. He half suspected that the rabbi was in cahoots with his son to hasten his obsolescence. Why couldn't he get it through anyone's head that what was happening to him was the one and only real thing? His spine curved like a question mark under the terrible onus of his familiarity with the absolute.

Upon hearing the phrase "aural hallucination" released like a ring of smoke from the rabbi's mouth, Morton got up to take his leave. He thanked the rabbi politely (for nothing) and showed himself to the door.

On his way out, however, he followed an impulse to duck into the lavish sanctuary. He saw the carpeted altar backed by a sumptuous tapestry depicting the usual miracles, and upon the altar an old man in a baggy black suit. Morton recognized him as the doddering Rabbi Fishbein, the former spiritual leader of Temple Emanuel. But that was before the synagogue had moved from its original location downtown just off North Main Street. A kind of rabbi emeritus now, he was something of an embarrassment to the congregation, having delegated to himself in senility the tasks of a beadle. Puttering about in his stockinged feet, he dusted the standing candelabra, arranged the flowers.

As uncomfortable with the rabbi's Old Country habits as anyone else, Morton found himself today unaccountably drawn to the moth-eaten old man. With his ashen complexion fraying into his unkempt whiskers, his yarmulke like a listing cupola, he looked perfectly benign, even holy; though what did Morton know from holy? Nevertheless Morton, a shnorrer, not a chooser, thought it was maybe worth a try. Maybe this scarecrow Fishbein knew just the right mumbo jumbo to get Morton out of his predicament.

Adopting the humility that was becoming second nature to him lately, Morton shambled to the foot of the altar and cleared his throat.

"Rabbi," he submitted, "God won't leave me alone."

The old man paused, dabbing his forehead thoughtfully with the dustcloth. Without the least alteration of his generally bemused features, he looked down at Morton. It was a look that might at any moment break into a radiant piety, and Morton, bending his psoriatic scalp, would be there to receive its curative benefits.

But when the old rabbi spoke, his eyes flared like gas flames, and his whiskers stood out from the gale of his words. His voice was the voice that was borrowed from Morton, His wonders to perform.

"So, Morty, consider yourself a lucky boy."

Unprepared for this meanest of the Lord's parlor tricks, Morton practically retched, swatting the air as he backed away. He puffed on unsteady legs up the aisle, hounded by the voice that shook the scrolls in their ark and guttered the Everlasting Light.

"What did you think, you could shake Me in My own house? Dybbuks you cast out, Gruber—THE LORD YOU INVITE IN!"

In a last-ditch effort to take up the thread of his ordinary life, Morton went that afternoon to inspect the latest Suds-O-Mat installation. Swallowing what was left of his pride, he'd prevailed upon Jason (who tried to beg off) to take him along. While Jason was outside talking with a contractor, Morton poked about a rainbow array of washers, testing a surface here, feeding a quarter there. He was trying to take some satisfaction in this farthest outpost of his little empire.

But nothing helped. His business, to tell the truth, had meant little enough to him these past few years. Now, in the face of recent developments, it meant even less. This preoccupation with his disembodied voice had monopolized all the available significance. It filled him with an awful apprehension that left no room for less demanding concerns—for his native aggravation, say, or his gastric distress. But how, he asked himself, could this have come to pass? How could his brain have become so completely occupied by the fear of God—unless the space had been vacant in the first place?

He was standing in front of one of the huge tumble dryers, contemplating his distorted reflection in the porthole glass. Is that how I look to a fish? he wondered, peering closer. Then the porthole came suddenly unlatched, opening in his face, and the voice of the Lord chastised him once again. Stumbling backward, Morton listened fatalistically and nursed his bloody nose.

"Enough hide-and-go-seek, eh, Morty?" A torrid breath was expelled from the dryer. "It begins to get boring."

Hangdog, Morton sniffled a token "What do you want from me?"

"A book, boychik, only a book. Something . . . in a popular vein."

Morton was chuckling dolefully to himself. "What's so funny?"

"Me write a book?" He shook his head. "I ain't written more than my name on a check since grammar school."

"So what? You're divinely inspired now."

Morton had to laugh over that one. So this was inspiration? Being badgered and bullied and frightened half out of your skull? Okay, all right, he would consider himself inspired. And taking the Lord at His word, Morton thereupon conceived a gem of a rejoinder.

"Look," he suggested, "why don't You just forget about this book business and spare the world." Then, drawing on some remote recollection of how things were done in the Bible, he added, "You made a believer out of a hard case like me. Ain't that enough?"

"You trying to bargain with Me, Gruber?" boomed the empty dryer drum, the door swinging emphatically on its hinges, spanking air.

"It ain't done?"

After a long moment the Lord responded, sounding profoundly fatigued. "Well . . . to be honest, the whole thing is out of my hands."

Suspicious, Morton felt compelled to ask what he thought he was probably better off not knowing. "What do You mean? Ain't You the Lord God Almighty?" Then he waited, embarrassed and uncomfortable in his role as inquisitor.

Came the voice, the big wind reduced to a balmy breeze: "The Lord, yes. Almighty not no more." Another pause, Morton folding his arms. "Y'see, I gave away all my secrets already. So now you guys are in charge."

Morton was confused. "Wait a minute. Lemme get this straight. You mean we, the humans, we're the ones running the show?"

"I cannot tell a lie."

"Then . . ." began Morton, nodding to welcome a little light. If men ran the world, then what was the problem? Sure, they'd made some mistakes—who wouldn't? But it was never too late to put things back in order. Give a little here, take a little there, and everything's shipshape again. And if He could be believed, there would be no more meddling on the part of Providence.

Morton took a deep breath, the tears of gratitude welling up, when the Lord, having apparently read his mind, threw down an inexorable wet blanket.

"Forget it, mortal. Your days are numbered."

"So You're telling me . . . what are you telling me?" stammered Morton, the clouds reappearing, mushrooming over his temporarily rosy horizon.

"Must I paint you a picture?" asked the Lord. "Anyway," He continued dreamily, "who could resist? I'd do the same if I still had the power."

Morton had heard all he wanted to hear. Irate, he was impressed by the reserves of his own audacity. His wrath restored his self-esteem.

"If You're so Goddamned impotent," he shouted, accompanied by the percussion of his heart, "then what the hell am I listening to You for?"

"Because"—Morton felt himself pitched head foremost into the humid dryer—"I'm still the Lord!" The porthole slammed shut, the drum began to spin, and saith the Lord, "I AIN'T DEAD YET, YOU SHMUCK."

Braced inside the dryer, Morton ogled the topsy-turvy launderette through the circular window. It was the way the world would look being flushed down a toilet. And cramped, nauseous, stifled as he was, Morton still hoped that he wouldn't be evicted from this vantage too soon.

Distracted now beyond reason, Morton decided to run away to some heathen country where they never heard of the Lord. But the thought of His voice speaking from shrunken heads or out of the mouths of tigers gave him pause. Instead he clung to what was familiar, driving alone about the city streets after the networks had signed off. At 3:00 a.m. he turned up on Louie Gold's doorstep, looking like he'd been deposited there by a storm.

"Boy howdy, you gimme a scare!" exclaimed Louie, adjusting his cock-eyed spectacles, fastening his bathrobe. "What do you mean coming round here at this unholy hour?"

"Louie," greeted Morton, trying his best not to plead, "how about we take a stroll around the old neighborhood?"

As they shambled along North Main Street, Louie remarked to Morton more than once, "Don't say I never did you no favors." But in the end he forgot his annoyance, warming as always to his role as curator of their mutual past. Every gutted storefront and weed-choked lot recalled some checkered incident from their youth.

"Hey, Morty," he might say, pointing toward a tilting tenement, "remember the night we smoked muggles on Plesofsky's roof ? Remember the time we rode the dumbwaiter at the Cochran Hotel? And Saturday evenings, Morty, Saturday evening. Hot rye bread, dancing pickaninnies, and tootsies . . ."

Rather than fight them, Morton tonight embraced Louie's remembrances; he silently thanked him for keeping them fresh all the years. And as they crossed the street at Auction and started back down the other side, Morton detected a few awakening memories of his own. There was Lolly, for instance, as she was when he'd met her—a plump, playful girl waving an ostrich feather at a synagogue dance. He asked her if she was there all alone and she told him yeah—smiling slyly, nodding toward a bow-tied nebbish—except for her date.

Then the whole street was busy with figments: Mr. Zimmerman hawking "irregular" trousers, Mrs. Ridblatt accusing the butcher of highway robbery, Yudl the melammed wading through traffic with his nose in a book.

Though he couldn't explain it, they had all become suddenly sacred to Morton. It exhilarated him past understanding, this return by popular demand of Morton's own personal history.

It struck him that he ought to write a memoir, though what did Morton know from memoirs? And anyway, where was the sense in it, when he had it from an indisputable source that there might be no one around to read such a thing? Still, Morton's newfound notion would not let him go.

"Y'know, Louie," he opined, savoring a little the sound of his own voice, "in the beginning was the Word. So why not the same thing in the end?"

Then he had packed his bags and declared that he was going away for a while. A trip, he assured all concerned, would do him good.

"Away?" wailed Lolly, appealing to Jason and an imaginary jury. "Away where? Where away?" her powdered jaw still working in search of other combinations of the phrase.

"Papa, sit down. We'll talk," asserted Jason, clutching the back of Morton's armchair the way a matador holds a cape. Then, having made no immediate impression on his father, he took a couple of calculated steps forward, as if stepping into somebody else's shoes. "It's no use," he judged, offering his mother condolences. "He won't listen to reason, so what can you do?"

At the door Morton turned to take in the sad spectacle of his abandoned family. Even as he looked at them he missed them in his bones. Then he plodded down the porch steps cherishing his mental snapshot: his wife with her hysterical devotion, her cheeks irrigated by freshets of purple mascara; his son with his luxuriant chest hair like smoke above the volcano on his Hawaiian shirt, suppressing his unspoken affection with a "Good riddance."

"The family Gruber minus its head," he lamented aloud, labeling the snapshot. "My family finally at a loss for words." For himself the words came so easily of late; words like *passionate*, *vulnerable*, and *clairvoyant* came tripping from his tongue, leaving an aftertaste of spices. And while he already desperately missed his place in the bosom of his family, Morton took some consolation in his newly acquired facility with language.

At midnight he boarded a train for God knows where. He could not have said whether he was fleeing his fate or running headlong to meet it. For the moment being in motion was enough; it was the be-all and end-all as far as Morton was concerned. Outside his window the darkness was interfered with periodically by lights signaling pockets of humanity. Like luminous gallstones the lights had their coefficient warmth in the depths of Morton's gut.

A riot of sensations performed themselves in his breast, while Morton identified them, like long-lost children, in the order that they appeared. "Sorrow and pity," he whispered, "chutzpah, rapture, a fine wooziness." Conspicuously absent among them, he noted, was fear.

It was as if his yearning for the past, with which he'd lately become infected, had spread to include the here and now. Whatever caught his eye he immediately longed for; all his appetites were active. He wanted, for instance, that sandwich leaking green olives that an old man across the aisle was nibbling out of tinfoil. That flashbulb of an amethyst that the gentleman with the briefcase was sporting on his pinky. That young girl in the beret with her downcast eyes and her dimpled knees, like a pair of small faces, peeking out from under a tartan skirt. Everything he looked at had its place among his desires.

Morton wanted the words to express his current attachments, and bingo, there they were.

"That lopsided grin of a moon," he pronounced as he gazed out the window, "like Lolly's dentures in the pocket of her black negligee." It gave him gooseflesh, the way he'd contracted the gift of gab. He'd come into his own exclusive voice, an all-purpose eloquence, suitable for pulpit, stump, after dinner, or you name it.

Eventually he arrived at a station in a town on the edge of the continent. He took a taxi out beyond the swampland to a beach, then waddled with his baggage over sand strewn with the skeletons of creatures and foundered craft. He looked out across the dark water, embossed with threads of silver, toward lands more traditionally associated with prophets. On the horizon there was heat lightning as if some glorious battle were in progress. There was a familiar, not-so-resonant voice, which Morton knew better than to confuse with the flashing sky.

"Morty," came the voice, sounding out of breath, as if it had struggled to catch him up. "Help me!"

"So," said Morton, folding his arms, relishing the upper hand, "You don't speak in capitals no more."

"I'm nowhere, Morty, banished from the farkokte world I created. Like something on a shelf in a hockshop, I'm waiting to be redeemed. Redeem me, why don't you! For God's sake, make me a book, give me a home!"

Morton shrugged a bit impishly, having perceived what he took to be a truth. "I guess some things ain't already written, eh, Lord?"

"Wise guy," snapped back the Lord, an impishness of his own in reserve. "You're free to guess." There was a suggestion of thunder and a couple of waves tossing phosphorescent caps.

Morton waved his hands in counterfeit fright; he whistled a spooky impersonation of the wind. "Hoo hoo," he laughed, "give a listen to Mr. Mysterious here." Then, lifting his eyes, Morton winked at where he figured a gallery of eavesdropping angels ought to be.

Returning by the next train, Morton moved, for a man of his age and weight, with considerable stealth. He took a few prized items from the offices of Suds-O-Mat and made his way back to the old neighborhood. Dodging ghosts, he ducked down an alley, slipped behind a flap of corrugated tin, and was greeted by a timeless mildew.

In his old second-story office he rehung an out-of-date calendar, cleared the bottles left by derelicts from the relic of a rolltop desk. He arranged the photographs of Lolly and Jason, blew a mantle of dust from a yellowed ledger, and composed himself to take dictation from the Lord.

At first Morton wasn't entirely comfortable with the collaboration. God, feeling himself again, was too full of propaganda and threats. Too much "Babylon shall become heaps, a dwelling place for vermin"—that old hobbyhorse. But after a while Morton learned to temper the more sanctimonious, tub-thumping stuff with here and there an amusing anecdote of his own. As a consequence, there was soon a preponderance of narrative drawn from Morton's own very rich past. There was a danger of his eclipsing the Lord's message beyond recognition. But Morton was too intoxicated by the ease of his writing to worry. He was convinced that, if not completely faithful to the letter, he was at least being true to the spirit of the Word of God.

Under the pressure of the promised end of history, he wrote with a balanced grace. He wrote as if his book were an ark upon which he and his God and his family—and as large a circle of others as there was time enough to include—would weather oblivion. Sometimes, however, it bothered him that posterity would never read these pages. Then he thought he would tear them out of the ledger, stuff them in bottles, and fling them into the universe. Sometimes he despaired of finishing before the end.

But the ordered accumulation of words was usually satisfaction enough.

And his single-minded diligence in transcribing them, Morton came to believe, was even stronger than death. If not here, then he might complete his task in heaven. There, watched over by cherubs with feather dusters, engraved upon tablets of gilded stone, the book would take its place in celestial archives. It would bear this inscription under the title, in what he prayed would not be considered false modesty:

BY THE LORD GOD ALMIGHTY AS TOLD TO MORTON GRUBER.

Shimmele Fly-by-Night

Everyone ran away from my father. My mama ran away from him into the scrawny arms of Mr. Blen the hatter, who was so frightened of my father that he fled the Pinch with my mama at his coattails. My sister, Fagie, ran away from him to the sanctuary of the Green Owl Café, managed by her fiancé, the bootlegger Nutty Iskowitz. The neighborhood kids ran away from him, afraid of his fiery beard, its edges ragged from the tufts he pulled out of it in his wrath. They were scared of his voice and his bloodstained apron, his colossal hands, the shredded left thumb on which he tested the sharpness of his knives, his furious eyes in the shadow of the black homburg he never took off.

The kids along North Main Street ran away from him to their mothers, who told them, "Read your lessons, eat your whitefish, don't wet the bed, or Red Dubrovner will get you."

They ran away from me too, though you couldn't exactly call it running. They turned their backs and whispered whenever they saw me, like I might be my father's spy. This I was used to since I was little. Then—running from behind my sister's skirts as we crossed through the Market Square Park—I used to chase after them. But eventually I got the idea that they weren't playing games with me, that for them the son of my father was something to beware of. So I got used to being lonely, and sometimes I thought it wasn't the butcher but me that they feared. Then I was able to enjoy their silent treatment a little. What bothered me was when they broke their silence and dared each other to make cracks about my family. What bothered me was when some wise guy got the nerve up to ask, "Hey, Shimmie, why don't you run away?"

It was Papa's theory that our neighborhood was haunted. He believed that the gamblers and fancy women, the river rats and drunken Indians who used to live there, were now dybbuks. They were taking possession of the Jewish shopkeepers and their children one by one.

"It's the truth, cholilleh!" he would declare in his borscht-thick accent, kissing his mezuzah and spitting against the evil eye. And if someone who didn't know about his rotten disposition should say otherwise, suggesting that the Pinch wasn't so bad—if they said that it wasn't Russia, after all—my father would insist it was worse.

"Some golden land!" he would groan, slapping his barrel chest. Then he would count on his fingers the ways that we were persecuted: by the infernal heat and the crooked politicians, the high water at Pesach, the diseases that followed the floods, the yokels in their white sheets that they bought whole-sale at Zimmerman's Emporium.

It was the peculiar quality of my father's voice that it could grumble and bark and whine all at once. And coming as it did out of his flame-red beard, it was as good as if delivered from a burning bush. He was at his best when he was laying into his own kind.

"This North Main Street, I'm telling you, it's a regular circus parade . . . and bingo bango bongo"—hopping from one foot to the other, pounding the cash register keys—"here comes the Jews! They are shaving off their beards and peddling corsets on Shabbos, they are stuffing themselves with chazzerai. They are running away to join the vaudeville. They are forgetting their mama-loshen, which ends up where? In the mouths of the shvartzers is where. The shvartzers have stolen our tongue!"

It was true that the local colored porters and maids seemed to have an especially good ear for Yiddish. There was even a street musician who sang "Oif'n Pripechik" to his own accompaniment on washboard and jug.

"Pretty soon they pick up all the Jewishness that the Jews are throwing away. Then nu? What will the Jews have left? Cold cuts and dry goods is what."

But as bad as the Pinch was, the South outside its boundaries (accord-ing to my father) was even worse. The river was awash with dead men and snakes. Beyond our neighborhood the poor people married their own moth-ers and had two-headed children. For sport they wrestled pigs and cut the private parts off Negroes, which they framed and hung up in the barber-shops. The South beyond the Pinch was Gehinnom, it was Sitra Achra, the other side; and it was seeping into Jewish homes the way the creepers poked through the tenement walls.

I had no reason not to believe my father. When had I ever been far-ther from home than the Market Square school? After class I went for my

Hebrew lesson to Mr. Notowitz, the melammed, in his rooms across from Blockman's junkyard. An ancient mildewed gentleman with breath like a toilet, he would prod me with his walking stick through my alef-bais; this until, convinced of my ineptitude, he sat down at the table and fell asleep. From Mr. Notowitz I went straight home to work in the shop. On Saturdays my father took me with him to shul, on Sundays to the Auction Street stockyard. During the rare unsupervised moments when I was out of his sight, I didn't know what to do with myself. Then, like my miserable mama, I tended to sit in an upstairs window and look out onto the tummel of North Main Street.

If he hadn't been the only ordained ritual slaughterer in the Pinch, my father with his temper would have chased away what business he had. But as it was, the women had to come to Dubrovner's for their kosher meats. They came to him by the dozens on Shabbos eve, carrying live chickens from the market by their trussed-up feet. As they approached the shop, the cackling would swell to an unholy pitch, reminding my father of one of his pet complaints.

"Gevalt, the noise!" he would cry, clapping his hands over his ears. He was forever at odds with the pandemonium of the streets: with the bell from the Chickasaw Ironworks, the calliopes from the excursion boats on the river, the shouts of the newsboys, the songs of the cantor at the Anshei Sphard shul—though none of them gave his own bellowing any serious competition.

In any event, when the ladies had gathered in the shop with their chickens, my father would roll his sleeves above his ham-sized forearms. He would take up his blade and, muttering a benediction that sounded more like a curse, shut the birds up for good and all. Then he would call me: "Shimmele Goylem, pipsqueak, shlemiel!"

It was my job to hang up the chickens in the stinking rear of the shop. I hung them upside down on a row of hooks so they could finish twitching and leaking blood onto the sawdusted floor. The women would look on with a kind of reverence, as if the chickens had been justly punished for daring to squawk in the face of Red Dubrovner.

Then they took their seats in a half-circle of folding chairs near the open back door. In faded kerchiefs and dowdy dresses ringed in sweat under the arms, they sat with their knees apart, waiting for me to drop a dead bird into their laps. After that they proceeded to flick the feathers, tossing them by the fistful into the air. In this way, in the sweltering rear of Dubrovner's, the wives of North Main Street became the engineers of a blizzard.

Feathers would swirl and spiral around the dangling lightbulb, flurrying down from the ceiling and settling in drifts over the filthy floor. Then we were no longer in the back of the butcher shop, but in the snowy woods of Byelorussia. Or so I imagined. I imagined it not because I'd ever been in any such woods, but because my papa, resting after one of his outbursts, would sometimes recall them.

"You had the mud and the drek but what's new?" He would shrug, brushing chicken guts and toenails from his apron. "Then comes the snow—kadosh kadosh . . ." Here he closed his eyes, his fingers wriggling an imitation of falling snowflakes. "Kadosh kadosh and everything's kosher again."

It was the same snow, I once heard him suppose, that had covered the bodies of his family, murdered by Cossacks in a village pogrom. The pogrom had occurred after my father, fleeing military conscription and chasing rumors of freedom, had already run away to America. This he'd let out before he knew what he was saying. Then angry with himself for his moment of weakness, he clenched a fist to shout, "Here it only pishes dirty rain!"

That's how it was with the storms of feathers. They lulled my father into thoughtfulness just long enough to make him mad all over again. Then he would come from behind his butcher's block, swatting blowflies away from his beard, and accuse the women of everything under the sun. He blamed them for bad weather, bank panics, arson, for binding their husbands to their steam presses and lasts by the cords of their own phylacteries. And sometimes he accused them of cutting the cords. He accused them of putting ideas in my mama's head.

"Yentes!" he bawled at the wives, who had the good sense to keep their heads bent over their laps. "Where is your gossip? Y-t-t y-t-t, why don't you! Shmoose!" Then he would sway in front of them, pressing his palms together and fluttering his eyelids, a housewife expressing concern. "Poor maidele, how she suffers; on a dog I wouldn't wish it . . ."

He always turned around to make sure that none of his antics were lost on Mama. Usually she was standing behind the marble counter preparing to dress the chickens. Thin as a candle, she was often caught gazing wistfully at a naked bird, like maybe she recognized it from better days.

"What do you think, that's your cousin Chaim on his deathbed?" my father would growl, making me think of the Lord goading Abraham to butcher his son. "It's a chicken, cut out his kishkes!" And later on, when he caught her hesitating, he began to say, "What do you think, that's your precious Mr. Blen?"

How Papa hit on the notion of a romance between my mama and the little hatter, I'll never know. Mr. Blen, with his nervous stammer and banjo eyes, his yarmulke riding his wavy hair like a buoy, was the least likely candidate for anyone's suitor, never mind the wife of the terrible Dubrovner. But it was like my father to expect miracles at his own expense.

"I know what you tell my Rosie," he hounded the women, always in my mama's hearing. "You tell her, run away from your momzer husband. You tell her to go to the shmendrick Blen, that he's pining away in his shop for you. You tell her"—raising his voice in a rasping falsetto—"'He needs you, which is more than we can say for the crazy butcher, not to mention your floozy of a daughter and your nebbish son . . .'"

On her own, I don't think it would have occurred to my long-suffering mama that there was anywhere else to go. So maybe, without any faculties of resistance, she finally gave in to the power of my father's suggestion. Maybe his constant kvetching browbeat her into a glimpse of another life. Because one day, between the meat scales and the butcher paper, I saw her blush. Then the first blush must have awakened others, spreading like a rash, until the whole length and breadth of my mousy mama became inflamed.

That's how it started, the itch of her late-blooming passion. It kept her from sleep and drove her to highlight her tired eyes. She marcelled her stringy hair and swapped her drab gaberdine for a taffeta shirtwaist with lavender trim. It probably wasn't as complete a shedding of her old worn-out skin as she must have hoped for: not quite a butterfly, she was more of a caterpillar with wings. Still, it was enough to give her the nerve to throw her couple of dresses, along with her mother's candlesticks, into a carpetbag one day and walk out of the apartment above the butcher shop forever.

As I was never much of a match for my ferocious father, it seemed to me that my mama and the hatter had been paired in heaven. Where neither of them had made much of an impression when they were around, now that they were gone they were legendary. Though everyone naturally fell silent when they saw my father coming, the story was in the air. Who didn't know how Mama, with baggage in hand, had entered Blen's Custom Millinery in the early morning? Who but my papa hadn't heard the women in the gallery at the synagogue, or the old kockers on their bench in front of Petrofsky's fruitstand, repeating my mama's words: "Wolfie, mein basherter, my destined one. God help us, I belong to you."

After that it's unclear whether Mr. Blen was fleeing Mama (who pursued him) or whether they were burning their bridges together. In any case, they were last seen boarding a streetcar amid a spray of sparks.

To be honest, neither my sister nor I missed our mama very much. What was there to miss in her daylong sighs, her taking to bed with a headache, her staring dumbly at dead chickens, dumbly out the window at North Main? Papa, of course, made up for our lack of concern. He howled his shame and rifled the pages of his grease-stained *Shulchan Arukh*, looking to brand himself the male equivalent of aguneh, abandoned wife.

"Am I the only one who doesn't run away from this farkokte place?" he cried, though only Mama was gone. But that was his favorite refrain. In his tantrums he always talked like he was completely alone, betrayed by one and all. Still, I could tell that some of the heart had gone out of his hysterics. It wasn't the same complaining about Mama's leaving him, now that her desertion was fact.

Nevertheless he went through the paces he was famous for. He caterwauled and butted the doorposts with his head until he'd ruined the crown of his homburg. He bloodied his own nose, blackened his eyes, carrying on in the way that kept alive the tall tales of Red Dubrovner's mishegoss. But to me the whole thing lacked conviction. I'd seen worse when he had no reason at all to be mad.

At one point during his demonstration he tore off his lapels; he went down to the meat locker and brought up a case of his home-brewed kiddush wine. With every bottle he swilled, his roaring diminished a little, until finally he had drunk himself into silence. Then the sounds of North Main Street—the shmeikeling shopkeepers, the delivery wagons, the bells—had their turn. They took up the roaring where my father left off. And that's when I got the willies: not from the butcher's ranting, which was the familiar music of my days, but from the thunderous noise the world made when he stopped. I was scared when all I could hear was the world and my father's small voice—when he'd pulled his tallis from under his apron to cover his head—saying a Kaddish for Mama.

In the shop downstairs, however, it was business as usual. Papa continued haranguing the women, who continued flicking their chickens with heads bowed. But upstairs was another story. Abandoned by Mama, the apartment over the shop was worse off than before.

Nobody would have accused my poor footsore mama of being a housekeeper, but at least she had swept up the wreckage in the wake of my father's wrath. Now that she was gone, the place was a shameful dump. Glass dropped out of a crack in the skylight and the kitchen table listed from a broken leg. The pan under the icebox had overflowed, warping the floorboards. As I watched my father sniffing around in the debris, I saw it coming.

"Faigele!" he bawled. "Where is my shikse daughter?"

That was when he must have realized that my sister Fagie was seldom at home. Afterward, whenever she stopped by for a bite to eat or to wind her Victrola in the bedroom we shared, Papa would start in on her.

"Vildeh moid!" he wailed, with or without his audience of women. "She got to run, you know, she got to skidoo. They are missing her already in the speakeasies of Babylon . . ." Then he would lift alternate feet in a grotesque black bottom, slapping the soles of his shoes.

But Fagie could take the hint without all Papa's displays. Nobody needed to put ideas in her head. Hadn't she been gallivanting, chasing boys and making scandal, for a couple of years?

She was a pip, my sister—a flashy dresser, always with bracelets and beads, high-heeled pumps and seamed stockings rolled below the knee. Her short pleated skirts swished as she walked, the necklines plunging toward the bosom she didn't have. Her carroty spit curls dangled like burlesque side locks, and her cheeks—feverish anyway—were heavily rouged.

"I can't do anything with her," our mama used to grieve before she went away—which was no news, as what was there that Mama could do anything with? Meanwhile Papa might call her nafkeleh on principle; he might, finding part of a barbecue sandwich she'd brought home from the Pig n Whistle, bellow until his blood vessels burst. But mostly, too busy with his general ravings, he took small notice of my sister's shenanigans until after Mama was gone.

Then all it took was his declaring that she would depart soon for the

Unterworld, that already she smelled of sulfur and deep-fried sin, to send Fagie straight into the arms of Nutty Iskowitz.

He was the local bootlegger, owner of the notorious Green Owl Café and of the largest piece of the broken-down middleweight boxer Eddie Kid Katz. Nutty wore padded suits and two-tone shoes, and pomaded his hair until it looked like record grooves. On any day you could see him driving his Studebaker down Main Street, unaware that half the neighborhood kids were hanging on to the fenders and running boards. For all the shadiness of his reputation, nobody seemed to take him very seriously, least of all Fagie.

"The Czar of Market Square, he calls himself," she would sigh to me with a *ha*. "He's a czar all right: he fortzes Mrs. Rosen's meatballs and it's a pogrom." She would joke about his pitted weasel features, his jaw always snapping gum. "A face he ain't got, only a pair of profiles."

But she liked him all the same. I could tell by the way that she squirmed when she spoke of him, toying with the gaudy jewelry he bought her. She bragged about his connections with ward heelers and the celebrities of Beale Street, whose gambling houses he claimed to supply with his bathtub gin. She described for me with affection the rooms above the café where Nutty held court, the green felt craps tables overhung with blue muggle smoke.

It made me nervous to hear about her life, all of it so foreign to the butcher shop. But I was glad, on the other hand, that Fagie had finally found herself a sweetheart. The others had always run away from her on account of her meshuggener father, and because, frankly, Fagie was no prize. Only it seemed like what was discouraging to everyone else was what attracted Nutty, which was maybe how he got his name.

"He thinks it makes him some kind of a macher to be seen with Red Dubrovner's daughter," Fagie told me once while buffing her nails. "It's his idea of living dangerously." And later she mentioned offhandedly that he had asked her to stand under the canopy with him.

"So I says to him, 'What do you think, it's going to rain?'" Then she left off plucking an eyebrow to squeeze my hand. "Oh, Shimmie," she said, "it looks like I found my ticket out of this bughouse."

I thought of pointing out that, as big noises went, Nutty was second only to our father in the Pinch, but it didn't seem like my place to say so.

Papa, for all his prophesying the worst, was the last to know that my sister and Nutty had become an item. This was owing partially to me. While secrets tend to make me nauseous, I had helped to keep my father in the dark. I covered for Fagie in her absences, straightening up the apartment and cooking the briskets, everything short of which my father considered treyf. So—except for Papa's appetite, which had fallen off lately—everything was going along as usual. Then Fagie had to spoil it all by waltzing into the shop with her boyfriend on her arm.

They strolled in—Fagie swinging her beads, Nutty under a fedora, a thumb in his lapel—looking like this must be how the other half lives. Behind them loomed an individual whose chest and biceps strained the seams of his pinstripe suit. I guessed that this was Eddie Kid Katz, Nutty's partial property and bodyguard, in whose puffy eyes there shone not a speck of light. With his lantern jaw working its chewing gum in time to his boss's, he took up his post by the open front doors, while Fagie and Nutty browsed the meat cases, casually approaching the butcher.

He stood in his sleeveless undershirt behind his chopping block. The sweat poured off him, beads of it glistening in the hair on his shoulders like raindrops on a bird's nest. Busy trimming the flanks of salted beef that I was shlepping in from the locker, he didn't even bother to look up.

"Papa," said Fagie, tightening her grip on Nutty's arm, "I want you to meet my fiancé."

Still he didn't look up, though his slicing became more vigorous, and I could tell that he was biting his tongue. But though she knew better, Fagie continued to needle him: "Papa, maybe you didn't hear . . ."

I don't know what she was up to, asking for trouble that way. It was like they were sightseeing and she'd brought Nutty to show him the most celebrated temper in the Pinch. So it must have disappointed them when Papa, who looked like he was going to explode, only fizzled.

"Lilith," he hissed, calling on the Lord to witness what a brazen thing was his daughter, that she should soak in a mikveh for ninety years. And that was it. He went back to his trimming and chopping.

Nutty looked over his shoulder at Eddie Kid Katz as if to say, "So this is the big wind?" I wanted to shout over the counter that he hadn't seen anything yet, just wait until Papa got hot . . .

Meanwhile Nutty was making motions as if he were taking control. Giving Fagie back her arm, he shoved her politely to one side. Then squaring his shoulders, checking his shirt cuffs, he planted himself directly in front of the butcher.

"Now, Papa," he began, patronizing and familiar, rocking back and forth on his heels, "we come here in good faith, didn't we, to ask for your blessing? So please, spare us the 'Vey is mir,' just say 'Mazel tov' and we're on our way." Evidently pleased with his speech, he glanced over his shoulder again.

He turned back around in time to see the vein at my father's temple pulse like blue lightning. Impaling a loin roast with his cleaver, Papa started to tremble, taking hold of the underside of his chopping block to steady himself. But the huge wooden block, despite its weight, wasn't anchor enough for his rage. As his temper rose, so did the chopping block, coming away from the floor with all four legs.

From the way the bootlegger's jaw dropped, the gum rolling out of his mouth, you'd have thought that Papa was lifting the block by magic, and not just by dint of his awful strength. Mr. Iskowitz, I imagined myself saying, meet Red Dubrovner.

With the tendons like roots in his neck, his teeth clenched about the tip of his tongue, Papa bent his knees to hoist the chopping block over his head. Except for Eddie Kid Katz, who went on noisily chewing his gum, nobody breathed. We were spellbound watching the way that the block was suspended above my papa—like Moses about to smash the tablets of the law. In a minute, I knew, he would let loose his tongue and spit out whole plagues of abuse. He would froth into his beard.

But Nutty Iskowitz, snapping out of his stupor, wasn't hanging around for that. Taking cautious steps backward, he grabbed my sister (whose eyes were still glued to the block) and dragged her behind him out the front doors. Not so impressed, the stone-faced palooka turned and strutted slowly after them.

No sooner had they gone than my father dropped his chopping block. He let it fall on top of his head, rattling his teeth, which bit off the tip of his tongue. It plopped like a little strawberry onto his apron bib. Then Papa folded under the weight of the block, his thick body crumpling like the crown of his homburg. The building shuddered and the floorboards splintered beneath him.

Later that evening he sat motionless in the kitchen upstairs. On the crippled table in front of him were his open *Shulchan Arukh* and three empty bottles of his kiddush wine. In his mouth was a piece of melting ice; an ice pack was perched atop his bald and swollen head, fastened there by his blue-striped tallis. Standing beside him in the coppery light, I saw a mouse crawl unnoticed over his shoulder. The Saturday night hullabaloo started up outside the window, nearly drowning out the voice of my father lisping a Kaddish for his daughter, Fagie.

In the weeks that followed he never took his eyes off me. He must have thought, now that Mama and Fagie were gone, I too would soon be running away. The worst of it was that he watched me without ever speaking his mind. True, he still let off steam from time to time in the shop, parading his anger in front of the women on Shabbos eve. But he would trip now over his hobbled tongue before he got very far, then fall silent. And upstairs in the apartment, which I was still taking pains to keep straight, he seldom spoke a word.

What's more, he was losing weight. Brooding at the kitchen table like he was sitting shivah, he refused to eat his bloody briskets—though he might occasionally pick at the tripes he brought home from the slaughterhouse. His shoulders had begun to droop and his beard was getting sparse and lusterless. Bags like bruises appeared beneath his eyes.

Meanwhile business, such as it was, had fallen off. The wives, no longer so shy about gossiping in his presence, still brought their chickens, of course. But in Mama's absence they then carried the carcasses across to Makowsky, my father's nonreverend competitor, who dressed them out for a dime. Cradling the dead birds with lolling necks, they would file a little smugly past Red Dubrovner, as if there was maybe a better show over the road.

I wanted to tell him, Don't worry on my account, I'm not going anywhere; but I didn't even like to mention the possibility. I didn't like to think about leaving my father's sight. What was there, anyway, outside our neighborhood? Swamps and vicious three-legged dogs and yokels who hitched Jewish boys up to their plows—as my papa had always assured us. And now that he wasn't shouting about it, I was more fearful than ever, now that the sounds in the distance were coming so clear: the whistles of the packet boats, the singing of the roustabouts on the levee.

But one afternoon I didn't wait, as I usually did, for my Hebrew teacher, Mr. Notowitz, to wake up and dismiss me. Instead, leaving him asleep at the table, I picked my way through his fish bones and stacks of books and slipped quietly out of his apartment.

Following my feet I found myself headed up Main Street toward the Green Owl Café. I was drawn there by my fondness for Fagie. Though she'd never hung around much, now that I knew she wasn't coming back I missed her. I missed her dirty mouth and the reek of her cheap perfume. Hadn't she always been more of a mama to me than Mama? What harm would it do, I wondered, if I paid her a visit? I would drop by briefly on the way home from cheder—it was that simple. So why did my heart hammer my chest like it wanted out?

Then I was standing on the curb at Poplar Avenue—which I'd never in my life been across—looking for any excuse to turn around. But the avenue didn't appear to be different from any other street; it was no Red Sea. The other side was still Main Street, still shops and offices, and there was the Green Owl less than a block away. So I hitched up my shorts and crossed over.

The curtained door of the dingy café was the only one on the street that was closed against the muggy sunlight. I was shuffling in front of it, having second thoughts, when the door suddenly opened and a customer came out. I expected raucous noise to tumble down on top of me, saw myself bolting away. But as I heard nothing, only the knocking of what I guessed were billiard balls, I took a deep breath and sidled in.

The men sat at tables under harsh lights, in the sluggish air stirred by ceiling fans. They were drinking from porcelain mugs which they took under the tables to refill, spitting dolefully into dented cuspidors. From my father's ravings I'd imagined that they would be brawling and sinning openly. So I was relieved, if a little disappointed, by their silence. All things considered, the Anshei Sphard shul, with its reeling and chattering daveners, was more like I'd expected the café to be.

Then I realized that the quiet was due in part to the fact that everyone was looking at me. Accustomed to being practically invisible, I was close to backing out the door when the man behind the counter, wiping a spoon in his apron, asked me, "What can we do for you, small change?"

I swallowed and told him I was looking for Fagie Dubrovner.

"Sorry, sweetpea," he replied, turning his head aside to wink. "She's already spoken for."

Everyone chuckled over the way I was blushing. "But I'm her brother," I explained.

"Ohhh," nodded the man behind the counter. "In that case . . ." and he jerked his thumb toward the stairs in back of the pool table.

Upstairs it was even harder to breathe than down. The smoke hung so thick I had to wave it aside like cobwebs in order to see. Then everything was pretty much as Fagie had described, only faded. The draperies were threadbare, the windowpanes painted an ugly red. The men in vests and gartered shirtsleeves, standing over the dice table, looked grim, like they were peering into somebody's open casket.

Fagie saw me before I saw her.

"Shimmie!" she hailed from a table in the back. At the table, which was littered with amber bottles, a group of men sat playing cards. Nutty Iskowitz was among them in striped suspenders, a cigar stuck in his mouth, and behind him in his too-tight suit stood Eddie Kid Katz. With his arms folded, the boxer made me think of a genie popped out of one of the cuspidors downstairs.

"Look, everybody," said Fagie, risen from Nutty's side, her tassels swishing as she crossed the room to hug me. "It's my long-lost baby brother." But nobody even bothered to turn around.

"Hello, brother-in-law," Nutty Iskowitz called out to me, leaning back in his chair to study his hand of cards. "I'll buy you a pair of long pants for the wedding."

"You're coming, ain't you, kiddo?" asked Fagie, breathing toilet water and whiskey in my face. "Every gonif in town will be there."

Somehow it hadn't entered my mind that Fagie would be having a wedding. On the Other Side, where Papa claimed she had gone, who had weddings? Now that I knew hers was coming, I was excited for Fagie's sake. But I was sorry for myself, knowing that the butcher would never let me attend.

"That's right," said Nutty, laying down his cards, locking his fingers behind his head in an attitude more suited to blowing his horn. "Nothing's too good for my angel drawers . . ."

Fagie beamed through her makeup as she told me how they were renting the banquet hall of the Cochran Hotel. She practically crooned the words "catered affair," waving her handkerchief lah-de-dah over the elegance of it all. But all I could think of, as she carried on, was that it was past the time when I should have been home from Mr. Notowitz's.

Meanwhile Nutty was still putting on the dog.

"Shapiro's got his whole sweatshop working on her gown," he was saying. "The train's so long we can use it for a chupeh. And wait till she gets a load of the ring." Here he crossed his legs on top of the table and shut his eyes. "We'll bring down a wonder rabbi from Chicago, and Eddie here can jump out of the cake, and to close the show, we'll set a flock of chickens free . . ."

At this Fagie's face suddenly clouded. "No chickens!" she snapped, turning hotly toward Nutty. "I want real birds—pigeons and doves."

"Awright, awright," protested Nutty, "whatever my little knish . . ." Then his eyes went wide as he righted his chair, hopping abruptly to his feet. "Nail down the furniture, boys," he exclaimed, showing the empty palm of one hand, tugging at Eddie's coat sleeve with the other. "It's him again!"

At the head of the stairs stood my father in his homburg and apron. Stoop-shouldered and pale, he was resting his chin against his sinking chest, so that his beard resembled a shirtfront. He was moving his lips, trying, I suppose, to tell me that he'd come to take me home. But no sounds emerged from his mouth.

The whole room, distracted from gambling, was braced for some kind of eruption. Then Fagie, having sized up our papa's condition, took the liberty of putting words on his tongue.

"I come," she said, making her voice sound Russian and gruff, "to give a blessing on my daughter's marriage." After which the gamblers relaxed into horse laughter and guffaws. Encouraged by their response and Papa's continued speechlessness, Fagie went on.

"I will slaughter a bull in her honor, with my bare hands, kayne horeh."

Everyone was howling over her impersonation. Stepping from behind Eddie, Nutty sauntered over to put an arm around her shoulder. "What a gal!" He grinned, while he put his other arm around me.

I wished I could enter into the spirit of it all, but when I tried to laugh with them, my papa's downcast presence reminded me of my place. His lips were no longer moving and he appeared to be shrinking, the general hilarity affecting him like salt on a snail. So I broke away and hurried to his side.

As I began to lead him out, Fagie shook her head and gave me a look like, So long, it's been nice to know you.

When we were back across the avenue, my father's hangdog silence was even more of a spectacle. Everyone noticed how he trudged in front of their shops, his eyes fixed on his feet. Seated in a folding chair outside his dry goods store, Mr. Bluestein was the first to say it.

"Whaddayaknow, Dubrovner's lost his temper."

That was his joke, and he liked it so much that he shouted it to his wife in her upstairs window, resting her bosom in a flower box. She passed it on to Mrs. Ridblatt in a neighboring window, who called down to Mr. Sacharin rolling a herring barrel into his market. He shared the information with a couple of firemen outside the Number 4 station, who dispatched their idiot mascot, Arthur, to Mrs. Rosen's next door. In a little while the newsboys would get wind of it. Pretty soon the whole street, when they got over the shock, would maybe turn out to give the butcher back some of his own.

It was up to me to do something.

"Papa," I said, clearing my throat to speak a little louder. "Papa, I don't think the Green Owl is so bad."

Don't ask me how but it worked. I heard a rumbling in his belly as his chest began to swell. His beard bristled and the blue vein flashed at his temple.

"Then go back!" he cried, miraculously overcoming the handicap of his lisp. "Go to the goyim, why don't you! Gey in drerd arayn! Run away!" I was trotting to keep up with him now, staying out of the way of his flailing arms, of his fingers squeezing air.

"Or maybe you want to wait for the dark. You burn your skullcap and black your face with ashes, you hide in a shvartzer's wagon and roll away. Or sail away, that's good. You wait for the floods, you put a washtub in the bayou—you're a regular Hucklebee Dubrovner. You hop on the ice truck, you hop on the freight train that is crossing over the bridge. You tie your tallis to a stick—Shimmele Luftmensch; you sprinkle salt on the Pinch, you don't turn around . . ."

He was himself again, sounding off to spite the whole neighborhood. Mothers grabbed their children and merchants pulled down the shades inside their shops, while Papa continued his rampage, suggesting so many colorful ways of departing that you might have thought he'd considered them for himself.

But by the time we got back to the shop, he was spent. Gloomy again and short of breath, he slogged up the stairs to our stuffy apartment. In the kitchen he slumped into a chair and laid his head across the sticky tabletop. Seeing him like that, dead silent in the failing light, I thought I knew what he was feeling: that he was all alone in a deserted house.

"Papa, get up!" I pleaded, trying to shake him by his hairy shoulders. "Tell me I'm a no-good, I'm running away! Say, 'Shimmele Shnorrer, you take up with gypsies . . .'"

Unable to move him, I was shaking myself over what might come next. In a little while, I thought, he would lift his head slowly. He would pick himself up, go down to the meat locker, and return with his ritual wine. He would drink two or three bottles, cover his head, and say the Kaddish for me.

But since he was behaving anyway like I'd already left him, I left him, creeping stealthily out of the room. I went down to the locker in the rear of the shop and pulled open the thick wooden door. I hauled out a case of wine from under the hanging flanks of beef, dragging it through sawdust to the screen door in back, then down some clattering steps into the yard. Then I returned to the locker for the remaining case.

With chattering teeth I uncorked a bottle of wine. I poured it into an empty birdbath, which stood choked by rotten vines in the center of the yard. I did the same with another and another, asking my father's forgiveness for every bottle that I poured. Soon the wine was slopping over the bowl, spilling onto the broken stones, sending up steam toward the setting sun.

Down to the last bottle, I suddenly realized how thirsty my labor had made me. It was Friday evening, so I said the blessing before I drank. The first sip, which set off a pleasant tingling inside me, called for a deeper swallow. Refreshed but a little dizzy, I went over to the low brick wall that surrounded the yard, squatting there with my back against the bricks as I continued to drink. It was then that the birds began to come.

They were pigeons—some blue and gray, some mottled albino. Swooping down into the birdbath, they fluttered and splashed and preened, battling for space in the crowded bowl. Edged out, they glided to the ground and wobbled about. Some keeled over as if they were stalled; some came to rest within inches of my feet. Watching them, I worried that the wine had gone bad; they were poisoned and so was I. Then a hiccup brought home to me my own condition, and I understood the birds were drunk.

This got me tickled. The more they stumbled and capsized, making trilling sounds that might have been snores, the more amused I became. In the end I had to laugh out loud, clapping a hand over my mouth. I tried to get hold of myself. After all, my father might appear at any moment—and what would he find? Me sitting in the mud made from his own spilled wine, a flock of shikkered pigeons at my feet.

And in the midst of it, remembering my sister's request for pigeons, pigeons and doves to set loose at her wedding, I had an idea.

Wiping tears from my eyes, I fumbled back into the shop, snatched a spool of shaggy twine from a counter, and returned to the yard. I unraveled a length and bit if off, then stooped to tie the end around the leg of a snoozing pigeon. The bird only twitched a little and moaned, and I was encouraged to try another. By the time I had run out of twine, there were strings attached to nearly all the birds in the yard.

I dried my sweaty hands on my shorts and, taking up all the loose ends, went back to the wall and sat down. Now I had only to wait for the birds to sober up and begin to stir. And when they rose into the air, I would carry them like a bunch of balloons to my sister, Fagie.

I took one last swallow of wine and tied my fistful of string through a belt loop. Then I closed my eyes to imagine how they would greet me: "Hurray for Shimmele Badchen, the wedding jester!"

I was waked by a tugging that jerked me forward and up. Before my eyes were open I knew that it was my father, I could feel the wind from his wrath in my hair.

But when I looked, I saw it wasn't Papa but the birds who were carrying me aloft. Already I was as high as our kitchen window, through which I glimpsed a dark and empty room. I was dangling by the seat of my pants, swinging just above my father as he came out onto the steps behind his shop.

He might have reached up then and grabbed me, and pulled me back into his arms. He might at least have called my name.

"Shout, Papa!" I cried, still hoping he would scare the birds into letting me down. "Say, 'Cruel boychik, you give me a this, you break my that!'"

But he only stood there looking helpless and small, the feathers falling into his upturned face.

So maybe he took the grubby pigeons for angels, I don't know. By then I was over the rooftops, the neighborhood diminishing to a huddle of tenements below me. And what with all the commotion of the birds, their pitching and diving and beating their wings above my head, what with the breezes flapping in my baggy shorts, I had enough trouble just trying to stay horizontal. I had my hands full with pawing the evening air—which was smoldering red in the west, beyond the river, over Arkansas. I had my own problems now with learning to dip and soar, never mind worrying about the butcher.

Moishe the Just

It was the summer we spent on the roof, spying on our neighbors across the street. There was Ivan Salky, Harold Panitz, the late Nathan Siripkin, and me. We would kneel on the sticky tar paper, our chins propped on top of a low parapet encrusted with bird droppings. In this way we watched the clumsy progress of the courtship of Billy Rubin and the shoemaker's daughter. We saw, like a puppet play in silhouette, Old Man Crow beating his wife behind drawn shades. Through their open windows we saw the noisy family Pinkus gesticulating over their hysterical evening meal. We saw Eddie Kid Katz sparring with shadows and the amply endowed Widow Taubenblatt in her bath, but even with her we got bored.

"What if Billy Rubin went for her tush? What if Kid Katz got decked by his own shadow?" Nathan would needle us in a constant catechism. It was his never-ending campaign to infect us with his cockeyed fantasies.

But we had already begun to grow out of them. Didn't we know better than anyone that our neighborhood held no particular secrets? What people did in the privacy of their apartments at night was not so different from their antics in the street by day. Old Man Crow abused his wife outside their haberdashery; the Pinkuses, behind their lunch counter, were hysterical. The Widow Taubenblatt, although not naked, struck distinctly suggestive poses at her cash register. So when, at the close of day, they entered their rooms and the windows above North Main Street shed light on their private lives, there were no surprises. And even Nathan Siripkin's more modest speculations couldn't lead us to expect them.

"What if Moishe Purim was a *lamed vovnik*?" asked Nathan one sweltering evening toward the end of June. By then the novelty of our espionage had nearly worn off. Ivan and Harold and I were hardly paying attention to the predictable performances of our neighbors. Instead we worried about the future; we sniffed the breeze that blew in off the river. Like a whiff of what was coming, it smelled fishy.

But Nathan still had the gift of recalling us from our distraction and suckering us into his own. Despite ourselves we were curious—as Nathan must have calculated—to find out exactly what a lamed vovnik was.

"You know," said Nathan offhandedly, as if we only needed reminding, "like a saint. There's always thirty-six of them living secretly in different places. They're the excuse God gives himself not to blow us the hell out of the universe."

We were a little slow to take his meaning. Cheder boys all, we were nevertheless reluctant learners, content with no more than a nodding acquaintance with our exotic heritage. What interested us in those lean years was free enterprise. At the risk of a rap from the ruler of Rabbi Fishbein, we stole glances out the dirty windows of the Talmud Torah class. We worried that other kids were staking claim to the corners we sold papers on; they were peddling our bottles to the bootleggers down on Beale Street.

Among us only Nathan Siripkin still had time for the old superstitions, which he was not above exploiting for his own ends. That night, for instance, by way of recalling our errant attention, he went so far as to propose that the lowly Moishe was one of God's elect.

"Name me one person in the Pinch that's holier," he challenged, his eye-glasses glinting moonlight, head nodding like an overripe melon on the scrawny stalk of his neck. And we had to admit that if destitution and monotonous ritual observance were the measure, Moishe was certainly holy.

Of all the neighbors we spied on, his activities were the most forgettable. Each dusk, with a homecoming kiss to the doorpost, he climbed six flights of stairs to his junk-cluttered room. He switched on an unshaded bulb and, shedding the bulk of his person, unpeeled himself of two or three overcoats. Anointing his hands at a grimy sink, he sat down to his packing crate and praised the Lord for a mostly imaginary repast of kosher leavings. Then, with his party cap of a yarmulke perched precariously atop his mottled head, he swayed for hours over an open scripture. Repeatedly he buried the hatchet of his face in its crumb-strewn pages, so that it looked as if he were bobbing for wisdom. Though Nathan had often made cruder suggestions as to what he might be about.

But now he was taking another tack.

For years Nathan Siripkin had appointed himself the task of keeping us amused. It was his compulsion. Spunky for such a nebbish, he could ferret out whatever squalor and romance our neighborhood had to offer. He'd introduced us, always with his air of a proprietor, to the disreputable goings-on upstairs at the Green Owl Café. He'd led us into the sewers (catacombs, he called them) beneath North Main Street, which were given over to a refuge for forgotten men. And whenever it looked like the neighborhood might be depleted of spectacle, Nathan replenished it from his own fanciful reserves.

At his instigation we'd been trespassers, truants, and now Peeping Toms. But lately, waking up to the fact that there was life outside the Pinch, we had begun to develop an immunity to his big ideas.

To salvage what was left of his influence, Nathan made an effort to outdo himself. He provided us with the cross-sectioned lives of our neighbors, taking it personally when our interest flagged. Given the extremes he went to to hold our attention, you'd have thought their lives depended on our watching to give them significance. But none of Nathan's embroideries was making much of an impression anymore.

Then he presented the theory that Moishe Purim was one of those for whose sake God neglected to destroy the world, and suddenly we were all ears.

Not exactly a luftmensch—like so many that wandered North Main Street in those days—old Moishe had barely visible means of support. His own dilapidated beast of burden, he pulled a rattling wooden cart with rubber tires around the Pinch. In it he collected scrap metal, which he sold to Blockman's junkyard; he took in cast-off garments, kitchen utensils, broken clocks and gramophones, which he hocked for peanuts over at Kaplan's loans. With his perpetually bemused expression, his rheumy eyes rolled up under his heavy lids, he was oblivious to traffic and streetcars and barking dogs. He never solicited, though our parents, when they heard his jingling approach, took him the unwanted bits of their past. These he dutifully hauled away.

"It's like," Nathan once commented (he was big on pestilence and disasters), "the way people in the plague used to bring out their dead." But that was before he was committed to the idea that old Moishe was a saint.

I don't know why we were so susceptible. After all, we were practical kids whose first allegiance was to the power of the almighty buck. Maybe it was the times, which, besides being tough, were also a little scary. The news from abroad—our parents never tired of telling us—was bleak. Relations were beginning to get lost. And if momzers like Father Coughlin were any indication, what was happening there might happen here. So maybe we were primed for giving our cagey suspicions a rest. In any case, at Nathan Siripkin's invitation, we began to follow Moishe around the Pinch.

At first we told ourselves that we were only humoring Nathan—but then we were taken in by the old contagion. School was out and we were working in our families' shops; we were hawking papers, delivering piecework, selling policy. But we stole time to meet in the afternoons. It was then that Nathan attempted to bear out in broad daylight what he'd concluded during our evenings on the roof.

"Have a look," he charged us, waving in the direction of the old man like he was shaking him out of his unbuttoned sleeve. "He's got one foot in this world and one foot in the other."

"Looks to me like he's got both feet in the gutter," said Ivan Salky. That was the cue to elbow each other and hoot at Nathan's expense—which we did. But, playing it safe, we kept our hilarity to a minimum.

"So why don't we ask him if he's a lamed whatsit already?" Harold Panitz, whose flair for the obvious could always be counted on, wanted to know.

Nathan did his famous slow burn. He spent a moment in suffering our boorishness bravely, then took the opportunity to reveal to us the paradoxical nature of the just man.

"Because, putz, if a lamed vovnik suspects that he's holy, he ain't holy anymore. It's a secret . . ."

"Between us and the Lord," I threw in irreverently, trying to one-up Nathan's presumptions. Because I was smart (I read books), Nathan sometimes treated me like I was his protégé. This of course made me stick even closer to the others. Now he gave me one of his meaningful glances, as if we both understood what a mouthful I'd said.

He was such a pisher, Nathan Siripkin, with his outsized head of copper curls boiling out of his overheated brain. Behind his back we took great pleasure in mocking him: we supposed that he was from Mars, that his swollen brain would one day burst through the walls of his skull. Then all hell would break loose; a carnival of demented creatures would run amok through the streets of the Pinch. But for all of our mutinous jokes, we remained more or less his grudging disciples. We were intrigued that, in the face of so much pressing reality, Nathan continued to treat his fabrications with such high seriousness.

Despite all the commotion of North Main Street, he put a finger to his lips whenever we were shadowing Moishe. This was doubly irrelevant since Moishe was so obviously indifferent to his surroundings. Streetcars would clang, hook-and-ladders peel out of the Number 4 station, and the old man would appear in their dust, serenely trudging. Elevators bearing piano crates and porters would rise up out of the pavement as Moishe passed over. Children might stampede, pigeons pelt the rim of his hat, paint buckets graze his shoulders as they toppled off scaffolds. And demons, as Nathan assured us, might pull his beard and tug at the wisps of his hair. But nothing could distract the junk collector from his self-appointed rounds.

"That's what they're like," Nathan had whispered, beckoning us into a doorway for the confidence. "They walk around in a trance all day while God looks out for them."

We had to admit that the old kocker turned out to be more interesting than we'd bargained for. For the hour or so that we tailed him in the afternoons, we were fascinated. We were under the impression, unspoken of course, that so long as we were riding the junk collector's coattails, we were also preserved from harm. What with the world going to hell in a handbag, it was nice to think that our neighborhood was still, so to speak, safe for democracy. Nothing threatened us anymore: not Rabbi Fishbein's ruler or the bullying Mackerel Gang, not the butcher's rotten temper or the promise of high water or the voices from the radio prophesying war. Whatever perils lurked along the length of North Main Street parted like the Red Sea for Moishe, and for us as we crept stealthily behind him.

Naturally Nathan assumed full credit for the sense of well-being that Moishe had lulled us into.

"You have to understand," he explained in his most aggravating tone of condescension, "he's in direct communication with the Lord. Break that connection and he's just like you and me."

Then we chafed a little at the implication that we were like Nathan. It made us prickly and uncomfortable. Ivan Salky, lowering the bill of his cap, was the first among us to utter a word of dissent.

"All right," he said, swallowing hard to get it out, "so the old geek don't know how to get out of the rain. He's too feeble-minded to understand he's a bum. So nu?"

And as Ivan remained unstruck by lightning, the spell was lifted. Harold Panitz and I were encouraged to second and third our discontent. So Moishe ignored traffic signals, walked on freshly poured cement, lived on crumbs and Hebrew characters. He was a strange one, there was no denying it; but a saint? Show us some solid evidence.

There was a satisfaction we always took in turning on Nathan, even if it meant we were the victims of our own rebellion. Sure, we'd gotten a kick out of following Moishe, and yes, there was something about him that made us feel at peace with the world. But we were ready to forfeit it all in an instant for the sake of putting Nathan on the spot.

"Okay, okay," he protested, "I get your drift." Making his martyr's face, he pressed the palms of his hands to his temples as if to still the metronome of his head, which continued its nodding. Apparently for his own benefit he recited an axiom—this by way of gathering his wits.

"You don't judge a holy man by what he does so much as by what he don't do. Now what don't he do?" There was a pause during which we looked at one another while Nathan's brain went into labor. Eventually, releasing his temples, he gave birth to this assumption:

"He don't get led into temptation, that's what!"

Then it became a question of what temptation to place before Moishe, by virtue of his resistance to which he would prove he was holy.

Impatient as he was with our insubordination, Nathan Siripkin could never pass up a chance to be devious. Quickly forgetting to feel persecuted, he got down to business. He summarily ruled out the lesser vices, deeming it unlikely that, say, a barbecued spare rib dangled in front of Moishe's nose would offer him any genuine allure. By the same token, it was hard to imagine him being drawn into a craps game or a policy scam. How could he be seduced by what he probably couldn't even identify? And as for placing some item of value in his path, the lifting of which would make him a thief, what would he notice that wasn't dropped directly into his cart? No, what was called for was a kind of temptation that even Moishe could not ignore.

Had we offered any assistance, Nathan would have received it as interfering with the intricate workings of his mind. Which was fine with us. It wasn't so much that we lacked imagination, though why should we tax our own when we could rely upon his? And anyway, we didn't like to lose an opportunity of watching him warm to inspiration—the way he would wad up his face, yank his corkscrewing hair like he was trying to unstopper ideas. In a while his features would resolve themselves into an insipid grin; a forefinger would shoot up eureka-wise. Then he would reveal some half-baked prescription, just as now he announced what might have been a watchword:

"Anastasia!"

Ivan Salky, Harold Panitz, and I exchanged glances to the effect that we were not in the slightest surprised.

Anastasia Tomashefsky, with her greasy hair and her thick body as shapeless as a laundry bag, was most of what we knew about the charms of the opposite sex. Where the Widow Taubenblatt was our tantalizing but unattainable ideal, Anastasia could be had for the price of a potato knish. True, we had not had much of her, but the odd glimpse of raw pink nipple, the casually exposed dirty underwear, had been enough to frighten us out of wanting more. Although she was a discovery of Nathan's, even he became squeamish when it came to taking advantage of what she offered. Though we fortified ourselves with boasts of our wicked intentions, we blenched at the critical moments, remembering rumors of the disfiguring diseases that might ensue.

But on Moishe's account we took heart. We were disinterested parties engaging her services for the sake of a bold experiment. It cost us three danishes, a pound of chopped liver, and considerable time lost in persuasion.

"You want me to what? In front of who?" Anastasia kept asking, not so much shocked as bewildered by what we proposed. We snickered into our sleeves as Nathan, juggling invisible grapefruits, mimed a demonstration of what we had in mind. In the end Anastasia, who was nothing if not a good sport, joined in the general hilarity.

"The old fart'll have a heart attack!" she squealed in unwholesome abandon—giving some of us cause for second thoughts. But we knew that Nathan had already been goaded beyond the point of no return.

After dinner we convened as usual on the roof. Through a collapsible spyglass that Nathan had managed to get out of hock for the occasion, we took turns in sighting old Moishe bent over his book. He was one floor above us and a street width away, but seeing him like that—tobacco-colored in the weathered telescope lens—was like putting an eye to his keyhole. But where on the one hand he seemed so close, on the other he seemed even farther away, in a remoter place and time. It was a sensation that kept us interested for a while, then began to tire us out. But just when we'd practically given up believing that the appointment would be kept, Moishe got up to answer the door.

Who knows what we expected to happen? For all our predictions about his jumping into her arms and worse, I don't think we really imagined that Moishe would ever succumb to temptation. But what we weren't prepared for was the offhand regard with which he greeted Anastasia at the door.

She stood there in her hoisted brassiere, her blouse held professionally open, like a gonif might open his coat to display his wares. Though we couldn't see Moishe's expression, it couldn't have been so different from the blinking complacency he wore when he turned around. Then he crept away from her as if she might have been walking in her sleep and he was taking pains not to wake her up. (While for her part Anastasia stole a peek at her drooping boobies, like she had to make sure that they were still there.) From his cot the old man removed a mouse-gray blanket and padded back to the doorway. He draped the blanket over Anastasia's nakedness the way you put a shade over a lamp that's too bright. Then, ever so gently, he closed the door in her face.

It was the proper way for a saint to behave; of that we were all agreed. Like Nathan had said: you know them by what they don't do. But who couldn't help feeling disappointed that nothing unspeakable had taken place? Already we were grousing, what a wet blanket was Moishe, what a shnook—when Nathan, in a theatrically maritime stance, spectacles on his forehead, spyglass to his eye, told us, "Shah! Pipe down." We turned back toward his window in time to see the old man blowing dust from a plum-colored bottle of wine.

Uncorking the bottle between his bony knees, he raised it hastily, plugging his lips like he was stanching a wound. We held our breath watching him drink but had to breathe again before he stopped; and Nathan assured us that the bottle was nearly empty when he put it down. Then, as the spirits began to move him, he commenced what, for want of another word, must be called a dance. He danced with his knees bent stiffly, his fleshless arms stretching out of his ragged sleeves. His fingers snapped, whiskers furled, while his head lolled from side to side, as if he were being electrocuted in slow motion.

"He's nuts!" blurted Harold Panitz, but this time we echoed Nathan in saying shut up. Then we astonished ourselves a little, since what was there to be quiet for? Unless we were listening for the same music that Moishe must have thought he heard.

In a window beneath him Billy Rubin was tentatively putting an arm around his sweetheart, who promptly removed it, and in another window the Pinkuses were slinging food. Behind a butter-yellow shade Old Man Crow was lifting a vase to brain his wife. Kid Katz was cranking out deep knee bends, and the widow, in her unfastened dressing gown, was gazing into a mirror. They were doing what they always did, though it all took place tonight—or so you might have concluded—by the grace of Moishe's doddering dance. He could have been their puppeteer.

We remained transfixed until the old goat's unending contortions began eventually to wear us down. Enough was enough, we complained; such monkeyshines were unnatural in a man of his age. And one by one we left the roof, all but Nathan, who kept his spyglass trained exclusively on Moishe.

The next night, in the absence of any further drama (Moishe fell typically asleep over his book), we were full of contentiousness again. So he hadn't tried to shtup Anastasia, we said—so what? With a body like hers, it didn't take a saint to resist. And anyway, what had his lunatic dance been all about? Was it right that a just man—one of the thirty-six pillars of the civilized world, as Nathan was fond of saying—should get drunk and hop about all alone in his room?

Unprepared for our attack, Nathan Siripkin fell uncharacteristically into sulking, which antagonized us all the more. At one point, his spectacles fogging, head nodding woodpeckerishly, he seemed actually to be in pain.

"You guys got no faith!" he accused, prompting us to look at one another in consternation. What was this foreign currency that we were suddenly supposed to possess? Where could you spend it around here? It was unlike Nathan to stoop to such tactics by way of shirking the burden of proof.

After a while, however, he began to come around. "All right, okay"—he dismissed the problem with a wave—"so we'll tempt him again. We'll swipe some muggles from Nutty Iskowitz or we'll . . ." We could see he was clutching at straws.

Then it was Ivan Salky who brought Nathan up short.

"Enough temptation," he stated flatly, leading with his lantern jaw. "What we want is a miracle." He turned to Harold Panitz and me for confirmation, and we uniformly wagged our heads. Though we hadn't known it until that moment when Ivan became our spokesman, nothing short of a miracle would ever convince us of Moishe's sanctity.

Nathan eyed us in acute exasperation. "Schmucks."

"If he's really what you say, he can do a miracle," said I, feeling my oats, ignoring the glance I got from Nathan of utter betrayal.

"Of course he can do a miracle," sighed Nathan, as if it went without saying. "Only he just don't know that he can."

"Oh, neat, oh, very convenient." We mugged and rolled our eyes. We were back to the business of knowing the holy man by what he didn't do.

Then pop-eyed Harold Panitz tugged at Nathan's sleeve and asked an inspired question.

"Can he die?"

Ivan Salky and I lit up at the astuteness of this; we slapped Harold's back in hearty congratulation. Death was surely the thing by which, if it turned out he wasn't prey to it in the ordinary sense, Moishe could be proved a saint.

Cornered, Nathan had to confess it was so: a lamed vovnik never passed on until God himself decided it was time. "Then He takes them up to paradise alive." But this was a phenomenon you might have to wait an eternity to see, and we didn't have that kind of patience. We were confident that Nathan, calling upon his wily devices, could settle the matter more instantly.

"Prove it now!" we insisted, as proud of our ultimatum as we were frightened at having delivered it. Because we saw how Nathan Siripkin, stilling his head in the vise of his forefinger and thumb, had already begun to consider. Already he was plotting how to place the poor junk collector's life in jeopardy.

It was a little chilling, the way Nathan put himself through his paces. Traditionally, by the time he'd converted us to his current obsession, he was carried away by something new. We might just be getting the hang of finding the loose change beneath the bleachers at the Phoenix boxing arena when Nathan would talk us into, say, volunteering for the hypnotist at the Idle Hour talent night. In his fickleness he was always one step ahead of us.

So you'd have thought that we'd been contrary enough over Moishe for Nathan to take the hint. As a variety of entertainment—who should know better than him?—the old man had had his day. But this one Nathan refused to give up gracefully; he hung on to his fixed idea about the junk collector as if it were a matter of life and death.

At night on the roof, lounging against the dusty skylight, we listened to him presenting designs for what he'd begun to call his "saint trap." But this wasn't the old Nathan Siripkin, full of infectious mischief and crackpot illusions. Something about him had changed. Not only did he seem to have bought his own spiel, but he'd become fanatically single-minded in his scheming. In fact he might have been as determined to disprove the junkman's authenticity as to prove it.

At first he invoked what he knew to be the classical fates of saints—goyishe saints, that is, since the Jewish ones were immortal. There was stoning, of course, immolation, crucifixion, and so on, though none of these were up-to-date enough for his purposes. Still he continued to lean toward the apocalyptic. He was sold for a while on the notion that the earth might be made to open up beneath Moishe. Bridges could collapse, freight elevators might plummet down bottomless shafts. And as the town was situated on a famous fault line, giant fissures might be caused to erupt along the surface of North Main Street.

When we reasoned that the technical know-how for such assassinations was beyond our modest means, Nathan shifted without ceremony to an alternate vision.

"How about we drop a live wire in his bathtub?" he submitted. His bones would be illumined through his ashen skin, and he would dance again at his own transfiguration.

Rather than do him the courtesy of egging him on, we pressed him to consider more conservative measures. It was how we attempted to call his bluff. Since when, we wondered, did Moishe ever take a bath? And who knew (in response to Nathan's next proposal that we poison the old man's wine) when he might be moved to drink again?

At one point Harold Panitz, aiming for the heart of the matter, said, "Why don't we just hit the old buzzard over the head?" But Nathan only laughed him to scorn. It was just the kind of guileless suggestion you might expect from the unsophisticated Harold.

Then Nathan thought a little longer. He was stalling, of course, and he knew that we knew. Having failed to back us off with his loftier ideas, he was forced to come down to earth. He went through all the motions, bludgeoning his brow with the heel of his hand, and after a time his forefinger shot up like a perennial sprout.

"I got it!" he announced, davening from the neck up only. "We'll drop some big weight on his head."

Climbing up the fire escape outside Moishe's building, we were supposed to pass for a party of honest workmen. Though if called upon to do so, even Nathan would have been hard pressed to account for all our paraphernalia. There were the ropes, for instance, and the beltful of tools in which Nathan was festooned, so that he clanked like Marley's ghost. Then came the armload of boards against which Harold Panitz appeared to be fighting a losing battle. Not to mention the anvil that Ivan Salky and I—stopping every few steps to gasp for breath and look over our shoulders—reluctantly lugged.

To spur us on, Nathan kept comparing us to an expedition up a mountain, but that only made the ascent seem more punishing.

He'd campaigned for a millstone, which was supposed to signify the weight of the world's woe, or something of that order. But for the sake of expediency (and in lieu of a vault, his second choice), he'd conceded to the more available anvil, which we stole from Harold's father's tinsmithy. It was a scored and misshapen hunk of iron, about which Nathan wasn't happy until he'd dignified it with a mythological status: "It's like the one they pulled the sword out of in King Arthur." Though he sounded a little less than convinced.

From his girdle of tools Nathan had drawn forth a crowbar with a mighty flourish. It proved unnecessary, however, as Moishe's window, the corner one overlooking Auction Street, was already open. Then it seemed natural enough that we should be standing inside his room. Hadn't it been for us like some kind of stage? So now we were a crew come to rearrange the props between acts. But after a few moments the atmosphere began to oppress us. We lowered our heads in the presence of his makeshift table, his fractured cot, the orphaned steam irons and mixers, the broken clocks with their arms in a semaphore of all hours. There was the fetor of fish and stale pee, odors dense as ghosts that were trying to crowd us out of the room.

"Right," chirped Nathan, rubbing his hands, still refusing to take the hint, "let's get to work." But he was no less lumpish than the rest of us. For all his big ideas, he hadn't a clue about how to proceed with rigging his booby trap. It was up to Ivan Salky, the handyman's son, to take the initiative.

Standing on a crate precariously balanced in the lap of a listing chair, he hammered a pair of pulleys into the ceiling. Cracks spread out in the plaster like fossilized lightning. Then Ivan threaded ropes through the pulleys, making a kind of cat's cradle. He took the plank, into which I'd been busily boring a hole, and secured it among the ropes like the seat of a swing. He knotted some twine, passed it through the plank and over his network of ropes, then looped it around the dangling light cord. Climbing down, he began to test his contraption, switching the light off and on— which caused the swing to dip in a mechanical approximation of Nathan's perpetual nod.

It only remained to mount the anvil in place. This we accomplished, after a couple of abortive efforts, through the offices of a tottering human totem pole. With the anvil in its cradle, the totem pole collapsed, and we picked ourselves up to admire our handiwork. Sinister device that it was, it hung in the center of that seedy room as conspicuously as a chandelier. No one but the heedless Moishe could have failed to see it immediately upon walking in.

Then Nathan Siripkin pronounced his verdict: "Rube Goldberg meets Edgar Allan Poe." Apparently he was satisfied.

We'd been expecting him at any moment to relent. Having played along with him until now, we were ready for him to admit the joke had gone far enough. But Nathan continued to make a good show of it. Diabolical architect of Moishe's execution, he still professed a faith in miracles. And if he saw any contradiction, it wasn't obvious; not unless you considered his grinding teeth, his feverish hopping about, as evidence.

He was orchestrating exactly how the saint trap ought to be sprung.

"He'll pull the cord like this," said Nathan, teasing us with a tug at thin air, "and the anvil will fall. But it'll never touch a hair on his head." And for a second you could almost see it: the anvil suspended and radiant, balanced on the pinnacle of the junkman's paper yarmulke.

Then Harold Panitz, whose skepticism was sometimes in question, asked, "So what if God decides it's his time?"

Nathan shrugged it off with the cavalier assurance that trumpets would blow, angels descend. He grinned skittishly in the face of our lack of conviction, taking us to task. "Don't bother me with technicalities. Besides, in times as screwy as these, do you think that God can spare a single lamed vovnik?"

It was the only occasion in anyone's recollection that Nathan Siripkin had stooped to acknowledge the times.

That night, around dusk, by prior arrangement, Ivan and Harold and I met on the roof before Nathan arrived. In the west the setting sun, like a broken yolk, was running an angry red all over the sky, spilling into the river. Somewhere in the east, beyond the ocean, a storm—as our parents liked to remind us—was brewing. And there we were on a roof above our crummy neighborhood, feeling particularly exposed to the elements, like we might be marooned. Ivan Salky pulled the bill of his cap down nearly to the bridge of his nose, and Harold Panitz kept looking like, Who knows, maybe Nathan could be right.

But we were wise to Nathan Siripkin; we understood how this had turned into a contest of wills. This whole elaborate plot was for our benefit; it was intended to scare us into subscribing to his latest, crowning mishegoss. No doubt Nathan assumed that any moment now we would lose our nerve, but we were one step ahead of him. We were resolved that come what may we would let him play his hand through to the bitter end.

Then the skylight slid open and Nathan emerged with his hands in his pockets, his head barely nodding, whistling a tune. Gone was his jumping-bean agitation of the afternoon. Not that we were fooled for a minute by his confidence—which was maybe the point. Maybe he wanted us to think he didn't require our endorsement to believe that something was true.

Our hearts sank as he cautioned us not to do precisely what we'd sworn, despite him, not to do: "Nobody but nobody tries to warn him, see?"

Having put it to us so bluntly, he felt obliged to reiterate: if we tipped off Moishe to the danger, everything would have to come out. He would learn what the trap was for; he would know who he was, and as a consequence he wouldn't be who he was anymore. It was the same old screwball logic that he had hooked us with in the first place. Only tonight it seemed like another kind of trap, one in which Nathan himself was already caught. And he was crazy if he expected us to join him.

Still, we waited in our typical genuflection on the bubbling tar paper, passing the spyglass back and forth. We chewed jawbreakers, mopped sweat from our foreheads, and avoided each other's eyes.

Then ("Moishe ahoy") we spotted him pushing his cart along North Main Street, weaving a path between the five-globed streetlamps and the sparks from the trolley cars. He left his cart in an alley beside his building, then entered the vestibule, where he would climb the six flights of stairs up to his room. He would climb the stairs at a weary trudge, pausing perhaps on every landing, cautioning his heart to stop rattling the cage of his brittle ribs. Minutes would elapse before he reached the top. There was plenty of time, if we shook a leg, to divert him from what was in store.

Then the time had run out and we looked to Nathan as if he might for God's sake turn back the clock. But Nathan wasn't there.

He must have dived headlong through the skylight, ridden banisters down to the street, then shot up the fire escape on the other side. He must have bolted through the window just in time to intercept the junkman's fate. In any case, when the light came on in Moishe's room, I saw through the spyglass, which I'd wrestled out of Harold's hands, the old man stumbling backward. I saw Nathan, who must have shoved him, crumpling under the fallen anvil, dropping out of the golden frame of the lens.

Lowering the glass, I saw how everything had spilled out through the crack in Nathan Siripkin's size nine head: the old man with outstretched arms and upturned face, dancing his grief; the klutzy kid stealing a kiss and getting a slap from a skinny girl; a couple of families giving each other hell; a palooka delivering a Sunday punch to phantoms; a lonely woman in her bath.

At the inquest we held on to a hope against all odds, that old Moishe was deaf and dumb. But when it all came out, how we'd tried to prove that the junk collector was one of the holy thirty-six, he opened his mouth. Gesturing shame with a pair of crooked forefingers, he spoke in an accent thick as sour cream.

"Bed, bed boychikls. Somebody better potch dere tushies."

When he saw that no one but him was laughing, he suddenly appeared perplexed. His amused expression sagged like a sack whose bottom drops out in the rain. It was an expression that we were certain had echoes; it was repeated maybe thirty-five times, until every other lamed vovnik wherever he might be had lost his innocence too.

That was something that Nathan had neglected to tell us, a piece of the legend we figured out for ourselves. When you exposed one just man, you as good as exposed the lot. We understood this better after the storm finally broke in Europe. At the same time the swollen river overflowed the Pinch. North Main Street was under water, and the high ground was awash with homeless families and bedraggled animals. For those of us who were able to read the signs, we knew that it was the beginning of the end of the world.

Aaron Makes a Match

"Aunt Esther, have you ever been penetrated by a man?" asked her nephew, Aaron Bronsky, who was concerned.

"What is this, a proposition?" replied his maiden aunt, nodding her head in a palsy. "Listen, don't worry about me, worry about you. Your childhood is a mockery; your mind is a public convenience. Go climb a tree, tear your pants, get dirty. Here's another book." And with the help of her nephew, she rose from her love seat and went to the tall shelves that surrounded the room.

It had been for years Aunt Esther's habit to make Aaron the gift of a book upon each of his visits. As a consequence her library had become severely depleted. The books had originally belonged to her father's father, who had somehow managed to lug them across an ocean from Bratislava. Family tradition had it that he was mad, as the task would imply and the sepia photograph above the fireplace confirmed. His hair and whiskers were an ice storm out of which peered his terrible eyes. In the days before his spectacles, Aaron had spent hours in front of mirrors, trying to duplicate the look on his great-grandfather's face.

The books consisted mostly of arcane volumes in decaying leather, with titles such as *The Testament of Solomon* or *The Secrets of Abramelin the Mage as Delivered by Abraham the Jew unto His Son Lamech, A.D. 1458.* Interspersed among these were a few dubious pamphlets with naughty illustrations.

"Take," said Aunt Esther, removing from a shelf one of the heavier tomes. "Read." As Aaron thanked her and made for the door with his prize, she followed him with more injunctions: "Ruin your health, go blind. Haven't you heard of recess? Haven't you heard of life?" All of which made Aaron feel that he was stealing a golden goose.

Then he had stepped into the evening and shut the ponderous front door.

Looking back through its rippled diamond panes, he could see the little woman, like a harlequin in a block of ice, still standing on the other side.

Back home Aaron entered his bedroom, which had come to house the bulk of Aunt Esther's library. The books were stacked about the floor in dense and tottering heaps. To negotiate a path from the door to the bed required the skill of a Theseus. Aaron himself had been known to get lost for days.

"Milton, your son has buried himself alive," his mother would complain to the newspaper behind which her husband was hidden.

Counting his books, fingering their bindings, blowing the dust from their pages, Aaron was sometimes even moved to read them. This earned him the neighborhood nickname of Aaron the Scholar, whose eyeglasses were rumored to be made from the bottoms of pop bottles, whose feces were full of undigested words.

Thus happily outcast, Aaron kept to himself. The clutter of his bedroom could not have accommodated loneliness. One thing, however, disturbed him in his otherwise comfortable solitude: that, as his own store of books was increased, his aunt's was diminished. He imagined his own house and hers at either end of a seesaw. With every book he carried home, his house was brought closer to earth, while his aunt's—with its congeries of vacant rooms—rose higher into the air. The imbalance haunted him.

Then there was the recent confidence, imparted to him with relish by W. Cecil Blankenship, the neighborhood's evil genius.

"Unless your aunt Esther gets penetrated by the male of the species," pronounced Cecil, "she will dry up inside and out." Then, with variations on his theme: "Her navel will fall off and her bodily orifices will . . ." But Aaron was already walking away. Although he had only an abstract grasp of what Cecil's prophecy implied, he worried that it might be even now in effect; that his aunt's wizened figure and her prunelike complexion were not necessarily due to her age.

These thoughts preoccupied him, as he sat on the floor and opened the latest addition to his library. Out of its leaves fell a yellowed pamphlet bearing the title *The Doge at His Dalliance* in formal calligraphy. Aaron inspected its contents. Through a progress of antique daguerreotypes, a man and a woman, exotically undressed, were involved in a series of impossible postures. Their activities were framed by a minimum of poignant commentary. Putting aside all other considerations, Aaron gave the pamphlet his undivided attention.

When, well after midnight, he felt that he had the bulk of its details by heart, he stopped to clean his glasses. Replacing them, he caught sight of the weathered volume from which the pamphlet had fallen. Itself profusely illustrated, it was a dictionary of angels.

Though it hurt his pride to do so, Aaron went to consult Cecil Blankenship. He was usually to be found in the loft, properly known as the Asylum of St. Mary of Bethlehem, above his family's two-car garage. This was where Cecil conducted his unspeakable experiments and entertained his friends.

The asylum was reached by passing between a Studebaker and a Dodge sedan, then climbing a rope ladder to knock at a trapdoor.

"Password," came a voice from above.

"Cecil, can I see you for a minute?" asked Aaron, impatient of protocol.

"Well, as I live and breathe," declared Cecil, "to what do I owe the pleasure . . . ?" And so on. Cecil frequently patterned his speech after the villains of melodrama. Then resuming his official tone, "Say, 'The horror, the horror.'"

Aaron complied and found himself promptly hauled into the presence of the archfiend of Alabama Street. Cecil was alone in his chambers, tastefully appointed (as he liked to say) with the furniture of bad dreams. Homemade manacles containing a human skeleton hung from the rafters; on the creaking floor were a whip, a crown of thorns, a reinforced birdcage labeled The Iron Mask of Torquemada. On a table in the corner, amid tubes and scorched beakers, lay a rodent without a head. The austerity was a little mitigated by, here and there, a filthy magazine.

"Have you come to be solemnly mortified?" intoned Cecil with his sidewise grin, his strawberry cowlick like a wave at sunset.

Because he was anxious not to know what Cecil was talking about, Aaron, by way of an answer, produced his pamphlet. Opening it to its choicest sequence of photographs, he asked, "Cecil, is this penetration?"

After careful scrutiny, Cecil placed his hand over his heart. Lifting his pink eyes toward paradise, he became pious. "I'm dying," he said.

Aaron took this response to be an affirmative. Seeing no reason to prolong his visit, he thanked Cecil for his expertise and turned to go. A hand at his belt held him forcibly restrained.

"Give me that," said Cecil, suggesting an alternative, "or I'll kill you."

Aaron shrugged and endeavored to open the trapdoor. Said Cecil on second thought, "Give me, and I'll make you an honorary Inmate."

Aaron thanked but no-thanked him and persisted in trying to make his escape.

"Gimme and I'll give you . . ." —Cecil looked round the loft, spotted a murky aquarium—". . . some rare and colorful tropical fish."

So that evening Aaron introduced his books to a large glass jar full of tiny incandescent fish. Through the night he watched them, like expiring matches, drift to the bottom of the jar; later on, setting out for another world, they would rise as far as the surface and float. Nothing in his books could tell him what Cecil had also neglected to: that the fish could only survive in water of a controlled equatorial temperature.

This was not the first time that Cecil had had the last laugh. Once, ransacking his own laboratory, he'd left a trail of broken glass and dead animals leading to Aaron's door. Reprisals included the desecration of Aaron's bicycle, as performed by the Inmates at Cecil's behest. After that there were notes in Aaron's mailbox to the effect that his aunt Esther, a figure of fun, could be spied upon in her bath. The evidence consisted of graphic descriptions of the remoter parts of Aunt Esther's anatomy. The notes were signed: "Yours in regurgitation, the Inmates of the Asylum of St. Mary of Bethlehem."

Then there was the occasion of the grammar school science fair. Cecil had submitted a stillborn infant—acquired from godknowswhere—immersed in a beaker of formaldehyde. Wires were attached to it so that, when a button was pushed, it jiggled about. Despite his insistence that the child was in fact a homunculus in a *vas hermeticum*, Cecil took none of the prizes.

Perhaps it was his disappointment on this count that prompted Cecil to scapegoat Aaron. Science had never been Aaron's strong point. That year he had taken advantage of his mother's last operation to place her pair of gallstones in the fair. Floating in a small glass container, they were accompanied by a modest cardboard sign that stated simply what they were. Cecil, for it could have been none other, replaced the sign with an enormous placard:

SACRED RELIC of the TESTICLES of
JESUS CHRIST OUR LORD

announced the placard in rainbow pastels.

The prank, beyond the embarrassment it caused his family, secured Aaron's ostracism at school. Not that Aaron was especially aware of it. The opinion of his peers concerned him no more than the oaks outside his bedroom window. The oaks lined a street in a city on a river where steamboats had once disembarked: all of which was a matter of indifference to Aaron. What concerned him were his books and, lately, the question of his aunt's virginity.

"Aunt Esther, why don't you marry?" asked Aaron upon his next visit.

"Because," replied his aunt, wistfully lifting the cover of an album on the table beside her love seat. With her crooked fingers, she fanned the pages, flashing the glossy autographed images of Valentino, Navarro, Bushman.

"Because all the best men are taken." The phrase, in this context, had a strange connotation. Then, recovering her senses, "What are you talking marriage? I got one foot already in the Bosom of Abraham."

It was true, observed Aaron, that Aunt Esther had seen better days. Her mottled scalp was visible beneath the sparseness of her iron-gray hair; the pouches beneath her eyes were marsupial in depth, and blue veins embroidered her shins. Her chest was concave. She was a comprehensive catalogue of the symptoms of desiccation for want of a man.

"Why don't I marry?" continued the aunt, ruffling under her nephew's regard. "Why don't you be a prizefighter, go to sea, you nebbish, you milksop, you bookworm . . ."

Meanwhile Aaron was discreetly making his exit. Aunt Esther had been raised to her feet by the strength of her own why-don't-yous, some of which included violence and the pursuit of sin. It occurred to Aaron, as he reached the door, that it was through no accident that the provocative pamphlet had fallen into his hands. Perhaps his aunt, to alleviate her boredom, meant to arouse his manhood prematurely through the medium of stimulating pictures. These reflections saw him through the front door and into the night, oblivious to Aunt Esther's "Wait, here's a book!"

It was the first time he'd left her house empty handed. She needed, he reasoned, to be left in possession of what little remained of her library. This might console her until her nephew could implement the resolution he formulated on his walk home.

It was a resolution reinforced by an item of which W. Cecil Blankenship had once apprised him.

"Her membrane will have ossified beyond penetration by ordinary men," he'd pronounced from a shadow, as Aaron walked by.

He entered his bedroom as if there weren't a moment to lose. Without hesitation he took up the dictionary of angels and, having small patience with lesser lights, turned instantly to the chapter on archangels. Then, suddenly cautious of overmuch haste, he browsed.

The prints of the more prestigious seraphim were very imposing. There was Michael in residence in Seventh Heaven, Israfel with a scissors hold on Jacob. Uriel was confounding Ezra with riddles, and Gabriel, seated on His left hand, was gossiping with God. Raphael, with ritual gravity, was showing Tobit the proper way to clean fish. Aaron was taken with their august countenances, both at home and interfering with humankind. But one in particular had captured his discriminating eye.

Azrael, with his mane of black curls and his magnificent wings, was taking his ease in the shade of the Tree of Life. In a drawing by Doré, he was seated next to Solomon entertaining a rajah. He was depicted elsewhere with the handful of dust that completed the assembly of Adam. He was obviously one of the worldlier and more resourceful of angels. Also there was something in the penetrating glint of his eye that convinced Aaron he need look no further. Without bothering to read his pedigree, he decided aloud, "Azrael, you are it."

Then toppling a precarious stack of books, Aaron unearthed an incunabulum in a limp leather binding. The inscription on the title page professed that the following had been translated from parchments found in Jerusalem catacombs. The parchments had contained the keys to the conjuration of spirits, both celestial and infernal. Aaron shuddered to think how such a book might be used in the hands of a W. Cecil Blankenship, then shuddered to think how he intended to use it himself. He examined its pages for fingerprints of necromancers who might have preceded him, and wondered about their purposes.

"Maybe I should start with something less ambitious," he considered, thinking fondly upon the relative security of white rabbits and sleight of hand. But, summoning his courage, he called upon the blood of his great-grandfather to stand him in good stead.

No doubt Cecil Blankenship would have proceeded with scientific integrity. He would have made his scroll from the vellum of a lamb that he'd butchered himself, drawn his forty-four pentacles with a quill shaped from the third feather of a gander's left wing. He would have forged his own sword and tempered it in blood drawn from his little sister, then donned a silk robe embroidered in the consecrated letters of Tetragrammaton. Or so Aaron imagined, himself a great believer in the elimination of red tape.

For an approximation of sorcerer's garb, he made do with a bathrobe, a prayer shawl, and a paper party hat. He substituted an antenna for the speci-fied wand of virgin hazel. Clearing a space on the floor, he drew with a piece of chalk a magic circle, or rather oblong, and stepped within. Ignoring the preliminary ten-thousand-word incantation, he commenced straightaway to chant the unutterable names, guaranteed to attract the attention of the denizens of kingdom come.

Outside his room he could hear his mother, who was given to listening at his door, complaining, "Milton, your son is doing funny business," to her husband the newspaper.

Having repeated the entire register of unutterables to no avail, Aaron took up an alternative tack.

"Azrael, come now or else . . ." he warned, reciting the list of disfigura-tions to which reluctant spirits are subject. Although he began zealously enough with leprosy and gangrene, by the time he arrived at hemorrhoids his exhilaration was spent. He was weary of nothing happening, losing faith. From an angel's eye he saw himself: a skinny kid in a dark room on a small planet sunk in a whirlpool of stars. What, after all, had he done to deserve the indulgence of immortals?

"Maybe I should have sacrificed something," he wondered, picturing Cecil Blankenship disemboweling his younger sister. Then, intercepting a tear with his finger, Aaron sat down, a little surprised to find himself so soon defeated.

"Azrael," he muttered, in broken tones, abandoning all pretense to cere-mony, "my aunt Esther needs love."

"So what does she look like, your aunt?" came a voice from nowhere in particular, which brought Aaron to his feet. Stepping out of the chalk circle, he fell over books and switched on the overhead light, then promptly switched it off. In that moment in the dark he prayed that the mistake, which he'd only just glimpsed, might be rectified, then turned the switch again, illuminating the answer to his prayers.

There in the circle, in place of himself, unaccompanied by thunder or other effects, stood a seedy old man in a threadbare black suit a couple of sizes too large. In his horny right hand he was holding an account book, in his left a rubber-tipped walking stick of standard orthopedic supply.

"I know what you're thinking already," he croaked, "but the wings I leave up there," raising his tired rust-red eyes. "On earth you take what you can get."

"You couldn't get better than that?" asked Aaron, unable to mask his disappointment.

"I'm inconspicuous," the old man protested, "and anyway what are you, the Baal Shem of Oz?" Self-consciously Aaron took off the party hat and shawl. "Now about your aunt," goaded the old man, "you were saying . . . ?"

But Aaron, having found not one hint of sublimity in the shabby phenomenon before him, was brooding. Particularly saddened by the sight of the old man's hairless pate, he was wondering if its speckled irritation could be due to the heat of a halo. Finally he asked point-blank, "Are you the archangel Azrael?"

"Yeah, that's me. Now what about . . . ?"

"Then prove it; do me a miracle."

"It's not miracle enough I'm here?" the alleged Azrael wanted to know. But Aaron's obstinate expression said not.

"So what do you want I should do? A nice card trick maybe?" And laying aside his cane, he actually produced from the pocket of his coat a deck of dog-eared tarot, at which Aaron frowned. "All right, okay," sighed the self-avowed angel, in a voice which implied that Aaron had asked for it. He restored the cards to his pocket, then withdrew what Aaron expected to be a feather duster, a scarf without end, but was in fact a small pencil.

"Your father's name in full, surname first," he inquired, opening his ledger officially.

"Bronsky, Milton G.," Aaron volunteered, forfeiting his father for the sake of curiosity.

The angel thumbed through pages, licked the lead, and made a mark. Directly a screaming was heard from the other side of the bedroom door.

"Your papa is now exhibiting the symptoms of heart failure," stated Azrael. "Falling over his newspaper, he tears convulsively at his breast." The whoops and cries for help from his mother seeming to confirm as much, Aaron was satisfied. Gloating, the angel erased his mark and blew; the screaming ceased.

"Your papa resumes his reading of the funnies," reported Azrael, "which, incidentally, are one page away from the obits."

"My aunt Esther needs a husband," submitted Aaron.

"Ah," said the angel, interested, looking almost spry, "a coincidence. It so happens I'm in the market for a bride." Then with a wanton inflection: "Between you and me, eternity can be a very lonesome place."

Aaron could not help appearing doubtful.

"Don't worry, Mr. Wise Guy," said the angel, developing a rash, "I'm completely functional. You can start to call me Uncle, if you wish." And seeing that Aaron still had scruples, he continued with a ludicrous yellow-toothed grin, "You just introduce us, and let my charm do the rest."

"But . . .," Aaron tried again.

"But me no buts; and to set your mind at ease, I give you another miracle." So saying, he disappeared. A plume of dust, as when one shuts a casket, ensued.

"Aunt Esther, I brought you a suitor," said Aaron, and anticipating her disapproval: "it's the best I could do."

She stood at the threshold of her pile of a house, peering past the porch light at the angel, who was bowing. The top of his head, caught in the light, served as a proxy for a crimson moon on an otherwise pitch-black night.

Then he stepped into view with his walking stick and various accessories adopted for the occasion. There was, for instance, in his moth-eaten lapel a partially decomposed boutonniere. The scent he was wearing was a heady mixture of camphor and carbolic acid. Business deferring to pleasure, he had tucked his account book away.

"Aunt Esther," announced Aaron with uncertainty, "this is Uncle Azrael from the other side—" "Of the family," he had been about to say. But the angel cut him short, creaking forward to take the maiden aunt's hand in his own.

"I'm bewitched," he said, lifting her hand to his mouth, kissing the swollen joints. The sound complementing the gesture was that of a plaster being pulled from a sore. Aunt Esther removed her hand and examined it curiously, as if to verify it was still the original. She seemed reassured.

"Aaron," continued the angel, ogling the spinster, "you were too modest." Aaron's head felt incongruous upon his shoulders. "She ain't just a lady of culture and taste, she's a regular shaineh maidl."

Aaron was prepared for the worst. All the way over he'd imagined their reception: Aunt Esther's shock over Azrael's squalid appearance, her bristling at his impertinence. How she would slam the door, then open a window to call names: alter kocker, philanderer, toad; nor would her nephew be spared her indignation: anemic pismire who would sell his own flesh and blood.

But here she was, tittering slightly, her crow's-feet radiant as fishtails about her smiling eyes. With unprecedented impulsiveness, she had taken Uncle Azrael's arm, saying, "Aaron, where have you been keeping this delightful old heartbreaker?"

And Aaron, to his utter amazement, saw his aunt wink at his make-believe uncle, who smugly returned the confidence in kind. Then, leading him through the hallway into the library, Aunt Esther deposited the angel in her love seat and herself beside him. Aaron sheepishly followed.

Beginning to feel like an unwanted chaperone, he took a chair opposite the heavenly host and hostess. Aunt Esther, with spasms and feverish cheeks, was cajoling Uncle Azrael, "So tell me about yourself."

"So twist my arm," said the angel, sniggering consumptively.

"You're a card, you are," persisted the aunt, placing her hand on his knee.

"That's right, I'm the thirteenth trump."

Attending these proceedings, Aaron was resentful of the ease with which Azrael had entered his aunt's good graces. Although he had always credited Aunt Esther with formidable resistance, it was difficult now to tell who was courting who.

"You're a wicked one," scolded Aunt Esther, close to a stroke. She was all aglow, eyes moist, the folds beneath her chin like curtains of northern lights. Her imaginary bosom heaved dangerously. Transported, she had squeezed Uncle Azrael's knee, causing the leg to kick involuntarily. As a result, a cherished glass decanter, standing on the coffee table in front of them, was smashed.

"Which reminds me," said Aunt Esther in the subsequent silence, "can I offer you some wine?" Then, unable to contain herself, she started to laugh. No proof against such contagion, Uncle Azrael joined in the cackling, interrupting the hilarity only to gingerly spit phlegm into a handkerchief.

Aaron was, frankly, a little disgusted. As matchmaker, he felt called upon to maintain the proprieties.

"Ahem," he said, his authority counting for nothing. The couple had become conspiratorial in their mirth.

"Uncle Azrael," offered Aaron, "is from out of town, you know." And louder, "I believe that he's traveled extensively." Then, taxing his conversational skills, "Is it true that you've been as far as New Orleans?"

The angel put a finger on his lips and cupped a tufted ear. "Did you hear something? I thought I heard something," he confessed to the aunt, who shook her head no. This was the signal for more incontinent laughter.

"Uncle Azrael is also an amateur magician," cited Aaron, who had yet to take the hint.

"There it is again," said the angel, cocking his head in the attitude of one who receives communications from beyond. "It sounds like . . . yeah, that's it; it's Aaron's mama calling him to come home." And Aunt Esther merrily threw in for good measure, "Aaron, why don't you take a book with you on your way out." Then, joining hands in a collision of fingers, they congratulated each other upon their mischief.

Trying to control his pouting lower lip, Aaron took his leave. As for Aunt Esther's books, she could keep them; he might even bring the ones she had given him back. And with this thought, he felt suddenly free, saw himself with only a kerchief on a stick, setting off for Cathay, say, or New Orleans.

But before he left, he thought he might take a souvenir. So, as his lingering presence was already forgotten, he removed from the mantelpiece the photograph of his great-grandfather and walked out the door. He carried it home to his bedroom and placed it on top of his tallest stack of books. There by flashlight he meditated upon the face, wishing that he were himself the fierce old scholar, seated in a study house in Bratislava, a volume of Mishnah open before him, *The Doge at His Dalliance* hidden inside the text.

Sometime during the small hours, Aaron, fallen asleep in his clothes, was waked by a visitation. Before him stood the down-at-heels seraph, more disheveled than usual. His shirtfront was furled and his funereal suit had been pulled off one of his shoulders. His hoary head was wreathed in lipstick traces, like erysipelas or roses.

"Your aunt and I, we don't believe in long engagements," he asserted, leaning jauntily against his cane, adding that the date had been set for a week from Sunday.

"Say mazel tov," he prompted, but before Aaron could respond, he vanished with nominal effects.

The family were of course scandalized over the announcement of Aunt Esther's banns. Although prepared to humor her more harmless eccentricities, they now felt obliged to protect her from herself. A December bride was one thing, but Aunt Esther was practically into her thirteenth month. And who was this luftmensch, this Azrael? What were his credentials and where did he hail from and why did he look like *The Golem Takes a Bride*? Where was his shadow? But after they'd met him, one by one they came under his spell. No one any longer seemed conscious of his nastiness or his pungent scarecrow's attire. They could only repeat how fortunate was Esther to have found such a doting and urbane companion for her declining years.

"But what can a man like Uncle Azrael see in a meshuggeneh like Esther?" Aaron heard his mother wonder. Already the family were calling him Uncle.

But to Aaron's mind, the angel was the unworthier party. The shame was that his aunt had so readily succumbed to the designs of a creature disreputably fallen from grace. Then, remembering how he had engineered the fall, Aaron was forced to acknowledge the shame as his own. In the days that followed her wedding announcement, Aunt Esther kept company almost exclusively with Uncle Azrael; therefore Aaron, left to his own devices, had plenty of time to indulge in regret.

Sometimes he thought he might sabotage the ceremony. When the rabbi asked if there was any reason why this man and woman should not be joined together, Aaron would step forward.

"Uncle Azrael's not a man," he would shout, "he's . . ." and the relatives would all concur; for didn't they think him an angel already?

"Where does it say that mortals are forbidden to marry with seraphim?" he could hear the more irate among them protesting.

So Aaron contemplated abduction. He would steal his aunt Esther and smuggle her, possibly wrapped in a carpet, into countries where even angels feared to tread. They would spend their days swatting scorpions, eating grubs, and Aaron would bask once again in his aunt's abuse: you pipsqueak, you nothing. Then, recalled from his daydreams, Aaron recollected that his aunt was already happy. It was his own dejection that was making him wish he might have left well enough alone.

Usually impatient with pathos, he asked himself, "What have I set loose on the world?"

Came the Sunday of the wedding, and Aaron was putting on his suit. It was his navy blue bar mitzvah suit, pockets full of mothballs, which his mother had laid out for him that morning. In it he remembered that he was supposed to have come of age. This thought made him as skittish as if he were the bridegroom, then led him to imagine that the wedding was his own.

"Aaron," his mother was calling from beyond the bedroom door, "come on already, we're late."

"I'm not going through with it," said Aaron to himself, practicing second thoughts, picturing a synagogue full of outraged relations.

"Huh?" said his mother, who thought she heard something. "Come on. Don't forget you gotta give the bride away."

At this Aaron tried on the resolution that practice had made perfect.

"I'm not going through with it." And blaming his books for finally crowding him out of his room, he opened his window and stepped into a tree, then leaped out of earshot as his mother paged him again.

In lieu of faraway places, Aaron was in search of the childhood his aunt had accused him of losing. Without an authentic chum to give him asylum, he made his way toward the Blankenship garage.

"The horror!" cried Aaron, rapping upon the trapdoor until it opened.

Straightaway he was hoisted by a couple of Cecil's lieutenants into the groaning loft. Flanked by half a dozen kids in surgical masks, in rain slickers doubling as laboratory coats, Cecil sat cross-legged in similar attire, saying, "To what do we owe this unexpected . . ." et cetera.

"I ran away from Aunt Esther's wedding," admitted Aaron, thus explaining his suit; though he wondered why, given the circumstances, he should feel self-conscious.

"Your visit is very opportune," said Cecil, his mask puffing in and out of his mouth as he spoke, muffling his voice. He explained that this afternoon he had gathered his colleagues to witness a mysterious biological phenomenon.

His colleagues fidgeted and poked one another impatiently, ill becoming the solemnity of the occasion. The truth was that they were Cecil's faithful disciples only as long as he kept them entertained. And as they had lately grown bored with the customary atrocities upon animals, their host (or Warden, as he preferred to be called) was forced to greater lengths to amuse them. Already, embezzling the St. Mary of Bethlehem treasury, Cecil had managed to engage the services of Desdemona Malone. For half an hour she had ticklishly submitted to the anatomical researches of the Inmates; after which, weeping disconsolately, she asked for a priest. Today Cecil promised something altogether different.

"So if someone would provide Aaron with a mask . . . ," he suggested, as preliminary to their getting under way. A comical kid took from among the instruments of torture the bottomless birdcage which served for the Iron Mask of Torquemada. This he placed over Aaron's head, who sat down from the weight of it. Unwieldy as it was, he thought better of trying to remove it, at least until the comical kid had taken his foot from its crown.

When the laughter subsided, Cecil went on, "Today we have with us Mr. Genghis Padauer, come all the way from Leath Street in the interest of science." Not to mention the five dollars out of Cecil's mother's sinking fund.

A gangling, flatheaded older boy in mufti sat to one side, gravely scratching his acned chin.

"Under our strict clinical supervision," said Cecil, "Genghis has agreed to show us sperm."

At a signal from Cecil, Genghis took a checkered handkerchief from the pocket of his dungarees, spreading it over his lap. He might have been about to eat his lunch. Then, searching for something, he slipped his right hand underneath the kerchief. Directly the handkerchief, coming to life, stood up and jerked about. Genghis appeared fascinated by the activity in his own lap, as if waiting for an imp he had captured to be still. The floorboards accelerated their bouncing, and Genghis, rolling his eyes toward the rafters, grunted once. Then, tugging at a furtive zipper, he held forth for inspection the kerchief containing the residue of his passion.

The Inmates climbed over each other for the privilege of being the first to see. While a couple pretended that they were going to be sick, the rest were unusually reverent. Crawling forward, Cecil dipped a finger into the nacreous substance, proving its ropy consistency.

"Gentlemen," he declared, removing his mask as if to punctuate a successful operation, "I give you the elixir of life."

From inside his birdcage, Aaron was impressed. Although he essentially hated and feared Cecil Blankenship, he couldn't help feeling at that moment a glimmer of brotherhood.

"And now," said Cecil, while he had their attention, "for our next experiment, let us turn to Aaron the Scholar. Take down his pants!"

The Inmates, in their inflammable mood, needed little encouragement. Howling diabolically, they pinned his arms and pulled his blue serge trousers to his ankles. Thus overwhelmed by boys in masks, Aaron was robbed of his composure.

"For your express delectation," Cecil shouted over the din, coruscating in his plastic rain slicker, "we present to you this album of photographs, entitled *Aunt Esther's Honeymoon*" —holding open before Aaron's eyes the pamphlet called *The Doge at His Dalliance*.

Gazing disinterestedly at the pictures through the bars of his cage, Aaron was elsewhere. He was standing beside the chupeh, proudly consigning his aunt to her marriage. He was applauding as Uncle Azrael crushed the glass. Then, despite his distance, he was recalled to the immediate proceedings by the awareness of his risen member.

Sitting up, Aaron took stock of the details of his humiliation: his bitterness, his certainty that he would never forgive, the sudden high-pitched ratcheting sound that superseded the fiendish laughter, Cecil Blankenship's ecstatic broken-toothed grin; which was the last thing that Aaron saw before the lights went out and he found himself temporarily in midair.

The beams that supported the loft had snapped, the floorboards given way. The collapse of the Asylum of St. Mary of Bethlehem, from an excess of pandemonium, was as complete as that of the House of Usher. The boys dropped through darkness onto the roofs of the Blankenship family vehicles, from which they tumbled off into adolescence; all except Aaron, who merely fell out of his cage.

Pulling up his trousers, Aaron ran several blocks without a backward glance. Crossing Poplar Avenue, he did not stop until he reached the doors of a ponderous copper-domed building, its stained glass windows garish with the setting sun. Stepping in out of the afterglow, he passed through a vestibule and entered the sanctuary, vacant of its congregation. Prompted, however, by distant music in a nonliturgical mode, he left the shul and ascended a flight of stairs. In the assembly hall, beneath a succession of lambent chandeliers, the wedding reception was already winding down.

Kitchen porters were removing plates of chicken bones, marzipan crumbs, and gold fillings, decanting wine. A few elderly guests were still seated at the long banquet tables; some dozing, some resurrecting old quarrels and complaining of pain. Meanwhile an orchestra, looking as if it had emerged from the face of a clock, was playing a waltz. Pregnant cousins and their apprehensive husbands, uncles and infant nieces, the bachelor rabbi and his sister, were shuffling about the polished floor. In their midst, executing a kind of geriatric apache, the newlyweds amorously doddered.

Looking a bit like a superannuated ringmaster in his tails, Uncle Azrael lurched with his bride through a series of hyperbolical postures. Aunt Esther for her part, breathless in white satin, clung to the groom for dear life. The other dancers, a little frightened, tried with varying success to make way for them.

Standing unnoticed at the edge of the dance floor, catching his breath, Aaron seemed to have, at least momentarily, outrun his shame and indignation. Not many Uncle Azraels, he whimsically considered, could dance on the head of a pin. And watching the married couple turn like a broken dreidl, he exulted.

"Tonight my aunt will get laid," he sighed, dropping a tear into his spectacles. A corollary to this thought occurred to him: if matrimony could make of his dilapidated aunt a woman, perhaps it could make of an angel a man. Hence the old spellbinder's preposterous animation: he was celebrating his return to mortality.

"Mazel tov," whispered Aaron, imagining a cozy future. He saw himself and his aunt and uncle, seated before shelves to which he intended restoring their borrowed books. His aunt would be knitting an endless scarf for his uncle, who would sit reminiscing about the life to come; while Aaron luxuriated in their contentment, safe from his enemies, growing wise.

Just then, stepping forward in his waistcoat, the violinist had become a fiddler, striking up a lively tune from a recent Broadway show. Aaron saw Uncle Azrael's wrinkles rearrange themselves like paper catching fire. He was smiling at Aunt Esther, as if this were their song, taking her agued hand. Aunt Esther in turn took the hand of a cousin, who took the hand of a husband, and so on, until the entire unseated wedding party were concatenated. Then, led by Uncle Azrael, lifting his spindle shanks unnaturally high, they hokey-pokeyed.

They moved around the floor in a serpentine romp, eventually passing Aaron, whom his uncle incited the relations to encircle. Without interrupting the dance, Uncle Azrael greeted him, tweaking his cheek in transit.

"Wouldya look at what the cat drug in!" he exclaimed. "We thought you'd been stolen by gypsies."

Next came his aunt, who was finding it difficult to simultaneously hop and speak.

"Aaron, you fragment," she managed to scold him, "you made me give myself away." And her lips, particularly bloodless that evening, shaped a coquettish kiss.

Aaron blushed, while the rest of the dancers filed past, beckoning him to join the chain. Thanking them, protesting his weak linkdom, he modestly declined. Nevertheless, orbited by so many faces, he was feeling slightly indispensable.

The dancers wove a circle round him thrice, then moved away, following their leader, whose kicking legs revealed his gartered socks. Aaron might have applauded had they not left him richer by a goblet of wine in either of his hands. Thirsty, he drained the first glass to the health of the newlyweds: long life. Then, to assuage his worries that their health might be impaired through behavior unbefitting their years (be they three score and ten or, in the case of the groom, ten thousand), he drank the second. Through the upturned crystal, emptied of wine, he viewed the galloping procession; trailing out of an exit behind Azrael and Esther, they appeared to be dissolving into the bottom of Aaron's glass.

The fiddler stopped playing and Aaron's heart sank. Turning to place the goblets on a table, he happened to see Uncle Azrael's metal cane among the bread crusts and ashes. Obviously the sprightly bridegroom had no real use for it.

"But on the other hand," reasoned Aaron, looking for a loophole, "there might be a sentimental attachment." The cane did, after all, convey a sense of authority, not to mention its many practical uses. Surely his new uncle would be grateful for its return.

"Bless you, boychik," Uncle Azrael would say, "and so long as you are here, why don't you accompany your aunt and myself on our honeymoon?"

Speculating on the places where retired angels might go (the constellation of the Great Bear, maybe, or New Orleans), Aaron picked up the cane and fled the hall. On his way out he caught sight of his mother, seated on a bench, informing an open edition of the *Hebrew Watchman*, "Milton, your son's run amok."

Aaron bolted down the steps and shoved through the wedding guests, who stood on the sidewalk throwing rice at a departing black taxicab.

"Wait for me!" he called, sprinting after it, swallowing exhaust for the length of a block. As the taxi accelerated, undaunted, Aaron vaulted fences and streaked down alleys. Never before so fleet, he felt lighter by at least an entire roomful of books.

After running for some minutes, he reached his aunt's house, in front of which a shadowy driver was loading trunks into the back of a taxi. Hurtling up the steps, Aaron made straight for the library, whence issued the screams.

On the carpet in front of the love seat, Aunt Esther in her bridal gown lay shrieking. Desperately she held on to the ankle of another, an upright Aunt Esther, distinguished from the prostrate by her sensible, if wintry, traveling attire; and by her transparency. The standing Aunt Esther, while attempting to retain her balance, shook the foot to which her corporeal counterpart was fastened. She might have been trying to kick off an ill-fitting shoe.

Meanwhile Uncle Azrael, restored to his somber worm-perforated suit, was holding his open ledger in one hand while tugging at the ankle of the fallen Aunt Esther with his other.

"This is highly irregular," he groaned in exasperation.

With a grace becoming her newly acquired matrimonial status, the upright Aunt Esther welcomed her nephew. The room swam through her pellucid countenance, as she beseeched the boy above the noise of her double, "Aaron, you doormat, be a sweetheart and make her let me go."

Despite his trembling, Aaron managed to hang on to his wits. Anxious to be of service, wanting to redeem his absence from the wedding, he quickly weighed his allegiances. Hadn't his sympathies always lain more with the spirit of Aunt Esther rather than with the flesh? Reasoning thus, Aaron dropped the cane and knelt on the emerald carpet. He grasped the hands of the dying woman and prized her crooked fingers, one by one, from about the scrawny ankle of her soul. There followed a medley of all the rigors that the former old maid had been heir to over the years. Then, with the surcease of her rattling, Aunt Esther said, "Gott in Himmel," and gave up the ghost.

"Good riddance," sighed Uncle Azrael, sneezing, wiping his nose with a sleeve, offering his arm. "Come, my neshomaleh, my queen, let us fly."

And so the ageless couple departed the house, exchanging its vestigial library for an evening in April. Left behind, Aaron considered closing the mouth and the terrified eyes of the corpse, lighting candles, sitting vigil beside its putrefaction for the remainder of his days.

"I will be the friendless custodian of this solitary house," he told himself, just to hear how it sounded. Satisfied that it sounded absurd, he shouted, "Wait, I'm coming with you!" then staggered after the angel and his mate out the door, bearing the cane.

Azrael was committing the soul of Esther to the backseat of the taxicab. He turned around at Aaron's approach, discarding the ledger in favor of the cane. This he tore out of Aaron's hand and lifted above his head. It was a gesture of such furious and mighty dimensions (rending the seams of his suit) that his bare-boned frame could scarcely contain it. To assume it, he had first to rise in stature, to fling back his head, had nearly to spread his wings. Aaron, protecting his face, fell backward onto the grass. Through the lattice of his fingers, he observed how a crescent moon sat athwart the tip of the upraised cane like a scythe. Then the angel had ducked into the taxi and roared, "Take us home!" to the driver, who screeched away.

Aaron sat on the curb and felt sorry for himself. He would have liked to be left with a little something more in exchange for the sacrifice of his aunt. A garter, perhaps, or a bridal bouquet. But all he had to console himself with was the gift of the ledger, quarto-sized and with a pencil stuck in its spiral spine. Inspecting its columns of debits and credits, he frowned, as if an account book were all that remained of his childhood.

"Thank you for nothing!" he inveighed against heaven, and as it seemed so far away, "kiss my you-know-what." Which, lifting his flank, he indicated, so that there might be no mistake.

Then, by the light of the streetlamp and with the help of the wind, he thumbed idly through the pages of the ledger, looking for familiar names. Among those he recognized, there was of course his own and that of one Blankenship, Wolfgang Cecil; beside which, removing the pencil, he made a mark.

Legend of the Lost

His odyssey began on the day Mendy Dreyfus's girlfriend, Blossom Wurzberg, dared him to take the plunge. This was on a Sunday afternoon in spring when the couple, at Blossom's suggestion, had visited the county fair, an annual anachronism that took place at an ordinarily desolate tract in the heart of the city. The event had all the classic attractions—vertiginous rides thronged with vomiting children, corn dog and fried dough concessions, livestock corrals featuring hogs as big as Volkswagens. In one corner of the general pandemonium a giant portable crane had been erected, surrounded by onlookers with upturned heads. From the crane there dangled a gondola like a roofless cage, and from the gondola—once it was raised halfway to heaven—leaped fools, their legs attached to a long elastic cord. After hurtling several hundred feet toward the earth, the leapers, when the cord was stretched to its limit, were snapped in the nick of time back into the air, where they bounced around yo-yo fashion. Then they ceased bouncing and hung limply inverted until they were lowered to the ground, like (thought Mendy with grudging admiration) spent Houdinis.

He of course understood that Blossom had not intended him to take her dare seriously; it was simply in the nature of a dig. She knew well enough that he was afraid of heights, of depths, the dark. What wasn't Mendy Dreyfus scared of? But his timidity had always been a sore point for a young man whose imagination often ran to heroic scenarios, in which the reluctant assistant in his father's failing fabric shop performed feats of derring-do. And today, after a lovemaking session in her apartment during which Blossom had as usual mocked his poor performance, Mendy was feeling especially sensitive to her salting his wounds.

"Go ahead, why don't you?" she teased him, her asymmetrical anatomy ill-served by the gypsy apparel she wore. "Don't let me stop you, I know you're dying to do it."

Which prompted Mendy to ask himself, shielding his eyes to watch another reckless idiot fling himself from the platform dangling high in the firmament: What would she think of me if I actually did it? What would I think of myself? Then the buzzing of this impossible notion in his bulb-shaped cranium began to overwhelm even the chant of the spectators ("Bun-gee! Bun-gee!") and the rock standards blaring from speakers on telephone poles. His stomach churned and his head grew light as he heard himself declare in his heart that he'd had enough for one day of Blossom's needling.

"All right," he assented, borrowing a phrase he'd once heard uttered by an Indian brave in a movie (Mendy was something of a movie buff), "today is a good day to die." Because it had occurred to him that if he simply resigned himself to a premature end, proving his nonexistent courage didn't seem so forbidding. He wasn't so much taking a foolish risk as committing suicide. So be it.

Leaving Blossom rooted in disbelief, Mendy sidled through the crowd, stepped between barriers, and presented himself to a sun-bronzed, bare-chested attendant as a candidate for lunacy. After paying an exorbitant sum without blinking, he signed a waiver and was strapped into a complicated harness binding his torso and loins. He was escorted into the wire mesh cage by the attendant, then hauled without ceremony to a height from which he believed he could discern the curvature of the earth. The crowd below, encircling the area in the center of which an air mattress (the size of a post-age stamp) had been placed, seethed like insects—like the humanity Orson Welles expressed contempt for from the top of the Vienna Ferris wheel in *The Third Man*. But Mendy's contempt was generally reserved for himself. Standing frozen at the opened gate of the gondola with his temples repeating the hammer blows of his heart, he knew there was no question of his going through with it: among his catalogue of fears, the fear of death still figured prominently. Nor would it be the first time he'd made some rash gesture only to abort it at the eleventh second, but given the multitude ogling him from below, this time his cowardice promised even greater mortification than Mendy was accustomed to.

"Bun-gee!" chanted the crowd, like the natives in a jungle film before toss-ing their victim into the beast's carnivorous maw. Through chattering teeth Mendy submitted to his chaperone, "I changed my mind."

Replied the attendant, his square-jawed features fixed in an implacable mask, "You paid your money, you take your chances." Then the mask cracked slightly to admit the ghost of a grin: "Don't embarrass us."

Mendy wasn't sure he'd heard him right; the wind at that altitude was whistling in his ears: it muted the noise of the crowd, muted even the rattling of the cage due to his seismic trembling. "I don't think you understand," he tried again, close to tears. "I've decided not to jump."

The attendant considered a weighty moment, then having reached a conclusion said, "That's what you think," and shoved Mendy from the platform.

Popular belief has it that, when plummeting toward oblivion, your whole life will flash before your eyes. But Mendy's life, largely a series of petty humiliations, had not been particularly memorable. What did flash, however (give or take the theft of his tricycle, his baptism in a boys' room toilet by high school thugs), were reruns of his favorite movies—*The Scarlet Pimpernel* in which Leslie Howard is transformed from fop to fearless avenger during the Reign of Terror, *The Mask of Zorro* in which Tyrone Power is similarly transformed to aid the oppressed of a fabled California. There was even a moment when he wondered (with a wistfulness that did little to mitigate his terror) if, when the cord snapped taut, he might revisit more films on the rebound. Then the bungee cord snapped but did not stay taut, its moorings, compromised by so many previous jumps, having unraveled at the moment of impact—so that after a jolt during which his clenched teeth kept his stomach from being ejected out his mouth, the cord trailed behind Mendy like a broken umbilical as the earth rocketed forth to slap him into extinction.

It was at this juncture that Mendy's soul, a pallid swatch of a thing responsible for his lifelong faintheartedness, chose to bail. Such an abandonment was in distinct violation of cosmic law; but given the current state of the fallen world (in which the old authority was much eroded), Mendy's soul concluded that the law might be judged obsolete and could be waived. So rather than stick around for the inevitable, Mendy's soul decided to spare itself a bitter end by escaping through a nether orifice with an inaudible sigh. As it turned out, however, the postage-stamp air mattress was larger than it had appeared from space; it was, as Mendy pitched toward it, now the size of an ottoman, now a haymow. Tumbling toches over teakettle, he landed on his backside with a resounding smack dead-center of the mattress, which deflated beneath him like a risen loaf punched by a fist. Cradled in the rippling nylon, Mendy felt himself lowered to the ground as on the roof of a collapsing parachute.

Burnished attendants, duplicates of the one who'd pushed him out of the gondola, rushed to Mendy's side. This was not so much to offer assistance as to expedite his removal from a scene that could only discourage confidence in their enterprise. But the crowd, having seen what they'd seen, gaped in silence at the gaunt young man with his rusty shock of hair, as he stood up (albeit unsteadily) and, liberated from his bungee corset, walked from the site of his fall without a scratch. Having elbowed her way toward him, Blossom was suddenly at Mendy's side, all jangling bracelets and flapping scarves, demonstrating a concern that might once have touched her thin-skinned boyfriend. But since he'd disengaged himself from the air mattress and discovered his feet again, Mendy cast a cold eye on the circle of astonishment that hedged him in. Unaccustomed as he was to being the center of attention, he found it even less interesting than being bullied or ignored.

He was accosted by a local disk jockey with a silver ponytail thrusting a microphone in the survivor's face. The man had been interviewing the bungee jumpers, asking them—between playing tracks of oldies—their impressions of what he called their near-death experience. And since Mendy had come nearest of anyone, the DJ was moved to dart from his trailer and detain him before he got away.

"I'm standing here at the leaper colony with a guy who's just fallen out of the sky and lived to tell the tale. I kid you not, this one flew too near the sun, ladies and germs, and dropped to earth like a sandbag into an air bag, and yours truly, the old windbag, was witness to a full-tilt miracle. So tell us if you will, Mister . . . I didn't catch the name? We're all aflutter to know, what was it like?"

With a flatness uninformed by his typically apologetic tone, Mendy replied, "I dunno, awesome I guess."

His lack of conviction stunned the interviewer into a momentary speechlessness, though he rallied to say, "Sorry, I didn't catch the name . . . ?" Too late, however, as Mendy, content to be hustled away by a proprietary Blossom through a gauntlet of backslapping onlookers, had already left the scene.

Back at Blossom's carriage house in the city's garden district (she was a divorce lawyer and made a tidy living), Mendy stood somewhat woodenly in the center of her rattan-furnished bedroom, while she tugged with an uncharacteristic urgency at his shirt and fly. Heatedly she removed her own flounced skirt and blouse and vintage underwear to reveal a figure whose pronounced collarbones and pannier-like hips Mendy had frankly never found very appealing. Was his frequent impotence due to the fact that he had not actually desired his girlfriend? He was confused, but no more in-

terested in answering the question than in satisfying Blossom's pushy pruri-
ence, which the incident at the fair seemed to have piqued.

"Oh, Mendy, are you all right?" she panted, shoving him backward onto
the bed, though he'd had enough of being shoved for one day. "Maybe we
should have waited for a doctor; I think they called an ambulance, but you
don't seem to have any broken bones." Naked herself, she inspected his parts,
stroking them as she nuzzled and rubbed against him. "I know I should let
you rest," she cooed. "You've been through so much today, but I just don't
seem able to keep my hands off you. You were so bold!"

And you're so ridiculous, thought Mendy, with your orange dye job like
an orangutan's mane—an observation he was suddenly aware of having uttered aloud.

Blossom froze in mid-embrace, and Mendy watched as a tear issued
from her mascaraed eye, leaving a dark snail's trail down her concave cheek.
What had come over him? Was he trying to pay her back for all the insults
she'd hurled at him over the years of their tired relationship? If so, then
vengeance was not especially sweet; neither was it sour. It was tasteless.
While on the other hand, his cruelty seemed to serve as a further spur to
Blossom's passion, for she'd begun to grind her hips more vigorously against
him. Curious as to where it was leading, Mendy persisted in his experiment.

"What's more, you got a throat like an ostrich that swallowed a rock, or
is that lump some kind of rudimentary Adam's apple?"

She registered the barb with a moan of pain (or was it a spasm of pleasure?), while Mendy searched his mind for some explanation for his aber-
rant behavior. His ordinary frame of reference, the movies, seemed currently
unavailable to him, and without that perspective Mendy concluded that his
mistreatment of Blossom was entirely original. It vaguely pleased him, his
newfound originality. Meanwhile the floodgates had opened, black stream-
ers extending Blossom's fake lashes to spidery lengths. But the more she
wept, the more she wriggled her body in a desperate effort to arouse her
boyfriend's in turn. "Look at how we fit together," she insisted, squirming as
if to create more friction, kneading his member the way an arthritic squeezes
a ball of putty. "I never noticed before what a good fit we are." In the end her
ardent entreaties did in fact elicit a response from Mendy, who observed
with mild amusement that his organ was engorged. Then, because he was
able, he impaled the woman upon it; he turned her over and took her from
behind with a savage lack of tenderness. When he was done, he rolled onto
his back, while she crawled forward to drape herself like flotsam across his

chest and thank him profusely. Still weeping, she purred her devotion to Mendy, who told her it was over.

"You're funny." Forcing a giggle through her tears to show what a good sport she was: she got the joke. But Mendy was already up and getting dressed.

"Didn't you tell me you were only marking time till Humphrey Bogart arrives?" he said. "Well, he's arrived, sweetheart, and now he's leaving."

This dramatic change in her nebbish boyfriend provoked ever more extreme protestations of fidelity from Blossom, but Mendy was no longer listening. It really was over, though he had to confess he had taken some satisfaction in the sensation of being mean to her.

The following morning in the shop Mendy was unrolling a length of fabric that Mrs. Altfeder, a frequent customer, wanted to examine for the purpose of making drapes. His father was perched on a stool behind the register reading his paper. He was flanked by upright bolts of cloth like—his son had often thought—a sage amidst painted papyrus scrolls; and in fact Mr. Dreyfus Sr. had been something of a scholar during his youth in his native Galicia. He was reading aloud, as was his habit, from an article about a daredevil who'd fallen to earth unharmed after the malfunction of some cockamamie fairgrounds contraption.

"Says here, 'he is believed to be an area man, but his identity remains unknown as he abruptly fled the scene.' How do you like that?" Mr. Dreyfus squinted over the top of the paper. "Nu, Mendel," he asked, "vos iz *bun-gee?*"

But Mendy was too preoccupied to respond.

A frail man with a sad comb-over and a rheumatic heart, Mendel Sr. sat observing his son, a serviceable if feckless employee. Still Mr. Dreyfus gave thanks for small blessings. While he might have been more outgoing, Mendy was courteous enough; he was competent at measuring and cutting, displaying the goods to their best advantage in the grainy sunlight that suffused the shop's oriental clutter. Of course Mr. Dreyfus would have liked his son to have a bit more ambition. But he understood that the shop was Mendy's safe harbor, the place in which the boy (he was twenty-eight) was free to imagine becoming the pride of the Bengal Lancers or the scourge of the Spanish Main. It was clear to the father that his son's heart was never really in his duties.

Meanwhile Mrs. Altfeder, a complaisant woman with a pompadoured wig, was humbly protesting that today's material seemed inferior to the remnants she'd purchased a few months before.

"Take it or leave it," said Mendy. Having raised his paper, Mr. Dreyfus lowered it again, unable to believe his ears. "Or would you prefer cloth of gold, that when I unroll it, for a bonus, Eddie Fisher tumbles out? Or why not a nice shot silk that you can swaddle your big behind in and dance for your husband that hasn't had a woody in twenty years?"

Mrs. Altfeder, the tears standing in her froggy eyes, looked from Mendy to his father, who could only return her stunned expression as his newspaper slipped to the floor. Then both of them looked to Mendy, who seemed as surprised by his utterance as they. While he offered no apologies, felt no remorse, he wondered what had gotten into him; or rather, what had gone out of him? Because he'd felt, since yesterday, that he'd been relieved of an enormous weight, which, once removed, allowed long-suppressed sentiments to surface. This unburdening gave him a peculiar tingle that helped fill the vacuum of sensation he'd experienced (give or take his ravishing of Blossom) since falling from the sky the day before.

When his father slid from his stool and waddled forward to insist that he apologize to Mrs. Altfeder at once, Mendy told him to stay out of it. He was practically a detached audience to his own anger, which he hadn't known he possessed; he wasn't even sure the anger was real, but expressing it allowed him to feel something, which was better than the nearly nothing he'd felt since Sunday.

"What's more, you can stay out of my life from now on," he said, "and on second thought I'll do you a favor and stay out of yours. I've been a hostage to this place long enough." At that he flung his apron ("Who needs an apron in a shmatteh shop?") in his father's flushed face and stiff-armed a tailor's dummy from its base as he slammed out the door.

He showed up that evening for dinner, however, tail between legs. This was because, while his soul had decamped, Mendy still had a heart after all. And that heart still thrummed from the phantom vibrations of his departed neshomah like fiddle strings teased by the wind. Moreover, it was Shabbos eve and, in the absence of his own (which had first taken refuge in a june bug before finding more permanent residence in the faux alligator handbag of a lady on her way to Altoona), Mendy had been endowed like all Jews with a neshomah yetirah, a second soul. Or so his father, full of choice bits of superstition, had always maintained. But the second soul, if it indeed existed, was clearly as ill-accommodated by Mendy's person as his original had been; and after a brief spasm of sympathy for his father, who had assumed a disconsolate posture, his weak chin resting on his pigeon breast, Mendy felt his shame and compassion sputter out. The airlessness of the Dreyfus household had stilled the fiddle strings.

Never especially observant himself, Mendy had always enjoyed spending the Sabbath with his family. He liked the timelessness of the ritual and the warmth of their modest house in a neighborhood that had been, before its subdivision in the 1920s, an old forest. He'd never seriously imagined leaving it, though tonight his home seemed to have no significance for him at all, and Mendy could scarcely remember a time when it had.

Said his mother, shuffling into the dining room on thick ankles, her swollen toes poking like jujubes out of terry cloth mules, "Your papa says you was at work today a regular Mr. Jekyll and Hyde." Placing the twin loaves of braided challah and bottle of sweet kiddush wine before her unresponsive husband. "Vi gaitz, boychikl?"

Put in mind by her remark of the film adaptations of Stevenson's classic tale, Mendy tried to remember in which version Fredric March or Spencer Tracy had made the transition from man to monster without makeup. Unable to recall, he let it go. The heat in his chest evoked by his mother's concern—like a feeble flame under a hot air balloon—never reached his brain. Though conscious of the comfort he'd taken over the years from his family's hearth, Mendy could only shrug his indifference to the hurt he was causing them tonight.

"Is it Blossom?" asked his mother, breaking wind with a sound like shuffling cards as she lowered herself into a chair. She'd always worried that the flighty girl would one day wound her only son. "Did she upset you?"

"That's over," pronounced Mendy without a twinge of regret. "She's history." The word had a disturbing resonance in that dimly lit room.

Interpreting her son's cool response as a cover for deep injury, Mrs. Dreyfus wiped her face in her apron and turned to her sullen husband. "The boy is just upset that his girlfriend gives him the air," she offered, a potato-shaped woman whose Old Country accent remained as thick as sour cream.

Mr. Dreyfus looked up hopefully from his brooding. "Okay, Mendy, I forgive you."

Mendy considered. "I don't remember that I asked you to forgive me."

"Oy," said Mr. Dreyfus, his chin collapsing again like a trapdoor in a gallows, while his wife assured him that the boy would come around. "Mendele," she said to him, reaching across the table to lay a meaty hand on his arm, "something's wrong you can't talk to us, then maybe the rabbi?"

Sniffed Mendy, "Don't make me laugh." Then, removing her hand from his arm as if plucking a spider, he excused himself from the table and, soon after, left the house for good. Some months later his father had a heart attack and passed away, and while his mother lingered on in loneliness, to say nothing of penury, she never saw her son on earth again.

"Don't make me laugh," said Rabbi Rappaport, actually tilting back his head to let go a guffaw. He recovered himself momentarily, wiped a tear from his eye, then surrendered again to a whinnying laughter. He was an imposing man, the rabbi, with a salt-and-pepper beard, his plump cheeks imbued with a healthy tan, presumably from the many excursions he led to the Holy Land. He wore a colorful pillbox kipah perched jauntily atop a head like a Toby mug. But despite his good-humored aspect, it was hard not to view his reaction as other than mockery.

Seated in a straight-back chair before the rabbi's desk, strewn with kitschy klezmer figurines, Mendy Dreyfus was reminded of a character whose name he couldn't recall from a movie he didn't remember. The persistence of real life had lately eclipsed his recollection of films.

"What do you mean, lost your soul?" said the rabbi, catching his breath. "I got news for you, Mr.—Mendel was it?—you're a modern man. Angst and neurasthenia you got, shpilkes you got maybe in spades, but souls went out with voodoo and kayne horeh. Your *soul*"—he shook his head over the wacky proposition—"that's a good one. You want soul, go ask Wilson Pickett. I'm only a poor clergyman, gimme a break."

Unimpressed by the rabbi's jollying tone, or the mezuzah nestled like an ingot in the boiling chest hair revealed by his open collar, Mendy said flatly, "It was only a figure of speech."

Several days had passed since he'd left his parents' house and failed to return to the fabric shop, during which time Mendy had wandered the city like a golem. (That is, like the clay monster a medieval rabbi had once brought to life by stuffing a parchment bearing the name of God in its mouth. It was a legend Mendy's father had been fond of recalling.) He'd taken a room in a Depression-era motor court called Wigwam Village, known as a popular site for assignations and suicides. It was situated on a forgotten side street near the decaying heart of the city's downtown business district. Its individual units, cleaned once a decade, were constructed in the shape of ferrocement Indian tepees, though they likewise resembled an assembly of Klansmen's hoods. Following the habits of his prelapsarian self, Mendy had spent his

days at the movies, watching epics about peasant revolts and men who abandoned civilization to live with savages. These were the types of sagas he'd
always relied upon to stimulate a weak constitution, but now they failed to
move him in any significant way. That's when he conceived the idea that his
impassivity was due to the loss of his soul. It was a purely abstract notion, no
more than a metaphor really, though his first thought after conceiving it was,
good riddance. Then he wondered where such rancor came from. Feeling
restless (restlessness being one of the few familiar emotions left in his repertoire), he decided to follow his mother's suggestion and get a rabbi's take on
the subject. Not that he'd ever sought advice from that quarter before.

He drove his old warhorse Buick out east to the new synagogue. This
was the jewel box in its suburban setting at the end of a dogwood parade
that had replaced the crumbling brick edifice of Mendy's youth—a Gothic
shul presided over by an aged rabbi with toxic halitosis who was already in
mothballs at the time of Mendy's bar mitzvah. Still marginally Orthodox,
the new synagogue with its progressive spiritual leader had cleansed away
much of the mildew of tradition.

Having visited the place only once or twice with his parents on High
Holidays, Mendy was a little taken aback by the trim receptionist in the
stained-glass vestibule, who asked him to please state his business. He was
making small progress in his effort to explain why he was there, when Rabbi
Rappaport himself came striding briskly by the receptionist's desk. He nodded perfunctorily and passed on, as Mendy scurried after him and the receptionist rolled her eyes to indicate that this one was meshuggeh. Cornered by
the intruder, the casually attired rabbi rocked impatiently on his heels, while
Mendy assured him he wanted only a moment of his time.

The rabbi let escape an audible sigh. "Come into my office," he said, looking both ways as if he didn't want to be seen in such dubious company.
He led Mendy into a paneled chamber, where he lowered himself into a
recliner behind his laden desk. "So what can I do for you?" he asked, glancing at his watch.

Seated with his back to a museum case full of porcelain Hasidim and
troll dolls waving Israeli flags, Mendy said that he felt like he'd lost his soul.

That's when the rabbi's fixed expression expanded into a grin and he
laughed out loud, while his visitor protested that he hadn't intended the
remark to be taken literally. Watery-eyed, Rabbi Rappaport invited Mendy
to lighten up, suggesting that the former shop assistant had lost his sense
of humor as well. Mendy thoughtfully absorbed the insight, even acknowl-

edged its veracity, then noted amid the objects on the rabbi's desk an Old Testament scripture bound in Moroccan leather. Rising abruptly to his feet, he opened the Bible and thumbed its vellum pages until he found a cherished psalm of his father's: "How sweet are Thy words to my palate! Yea, sweeter than honey to my mouth!" Following an impulse that originated somewhere deep in his bowels, Mendy tore out the page with the psalm. Never in the least athletic, he vaulted over the desk, scattering the souvenirs on top in the process, and on the other side stuffed the wadded page between the rabbi's gaping lips. Then he exited the office with the man of God still sputtering behind him. Leaving the building, Mendy felt a further surge of energy and wished he'd taken the trouble to find the man's phylacteries, which he might for good measure have strangled him with.

That night, while Mendy sat idly watching pornography on the cable TV (there was only pornography on the cable TV) in a motel room appointed in hanging fly strips, the faux alligator handbag in which his soul had sought sanctuary was snatched by a thief. The thief, who'd wrenched the bag from the fingers of its proprietress outside a dollar store in Altoona, hopped in his car and headed east. As he drove he emptied onto the seat beside him the contents of the bag, which he tossed out the window. The bag landed squarely on a fresh cowpat in a blue-green pasture at dusk. There Mendy's soul might have resided in contentment for all eternity, had not Mr. Dreyfus Sr., in the days before his own death, said the Kaddish for his delinquent son. Thus was Mendy's timid soul released despite itself to wander again, realizing in its homelessness a nostalgia for the familiarity of its original host.

Meanwhile there was a drumming at the door of Mendy's motel unit, which he got listlessly to his feet to answer. No sooner had he opened the door than a woman in a pink velour mini, a bloody mouse swelling under her right eye, lunged shrieking into the circular room. At her spiked heels was a knob-headed fellow, gold rings through his nostril and ears, who grabbed her by the magenta hair, which came off in his hand. Further enraged at the sight of her cropped head, revealing her callow age, the man lurched after her, hurling his weight against the door of the bathroom where she'd taken shelter. The hinges burst and the door caved in to disclose the girl hunkered in fright beneath the sink, from where the man dragged her by the kicking ankles.

Observing her situation, Mendy appreciated that the girl was in distress, though it was no particular concern of his. Then the intruder, veins outstanding beneath his tattooed skin, paused in the process of hauling his prey toward the door to explain (as a courtesy?) to the room's occupant, "Sometime the bitches do get hysterical." When he added with a chuckle, "You ain't seen nothing, am I right, my man?," Mendy, who could not tell a lie, begged to contradict him. This prompted the man to relinquish the girl and take a poke at the occupant. Clipped in the temple, Mendy was launched briefly among asteroids before returning to a consciousness of intense pain. But rather than render him passive as in bygone days, the pain served as a spur, and Mendy rose from the bed where he'd fallen to spring onto the back of his attacker. Because he was busy once again with throttling the girl, the man was unprepared to find himself mounted by a demon pummeling his head and tearing the gold ring from his nostril. Snorting blood that hung in a mist over the disordered room, the man bucked his assailant from his back and howled murderous oaths as he staggered, cupping his nose, out the door.

From the place where he lay, bloody himself but indifferent to his bruises, Mendy regarded the girl still curled in a fetal position. He crawled over to better inspect her, inhaling her venereal odor enhanced by fear, which excited him. Unfolding her knees from her chin, he pushed the stretch skirt to her waist, yanked off her patent leather boots, and peeled the skin of her torn pantyhose; then he shucked his pants and spread her unresisting thighs to invade her with a barbarous ferocity, after which he rolled off her and was instantly miles away. The girl sat up without bothering to correct her disarranged attire, though she restored the wig to her head. "I guess you thought you had that coming," she said, gingerly touching the carbuncle of her eye, "but next time you might ask." Though he failed to respond, she anyway told him that her name was Choyce and wondered, with an automatic wink of her good eye, if he was peddling anyone else's pussy.

She had, as it happened, other sisters of the stroll who had also been turned out by Suede, the hotheaded pimp whom Mendy had bested, and in the wake of Suede's initial defeat they began, furtively at first, to visit his vanquisher. Soon Mendy became aware that he stood to come into an inheritance. The prospect was confirmed by Choyce, practical minded beyond her years: she made it clear the girls were prepared to acknowledge themselves as Mendy's property provided he was willing to take care of them. In this way Mendy made the acquaintance of Mimosa, Licorice, and Lamé, a rainbow assortment of hookers whose wares he was invited to sample with the same merciless abandon with which he'd taken possession of Choyce. Satisfied by his ungentle behavior that he was made of more durable stuff

than his appearance implied, they shifted their loyalties from their former flesh broker. Suede had after all proved himself ineffectual and had in
any case made himself scarce since his humiliation at the hands of Mendy
Dreyfus.

Though Mendy neither encouraged nor frustrated their attentions, the
hookers, who seemed to have no fixed abodes, began by degrees to move
their base of operations from doorways and the backseats of parked cars to
the petrified tepees of the antiquated motor court. They also proceeded to
advise Mendy with regard to defending both himself and them. Mimo, a
Mexican girl who'd been traded to Suede along with a shipment of amphet-
amines in exchange for a cache of small arms, tutored him in the use of a
.38-caliber handgun. With it Mendy distracted himself by firing at rats in
the vacant lot behind the motel. (It was an area of the city in which gunfire
was not uncommon.) Lamé, a near albino allergic to sunlight who wore her
nocturnal teddy throughout the day, took a special interest in tending to
Mendy's sartorial needs. She tricked out his nondescript wardrobe with velvet jogging suits, a maxi coat with leopard skin collar and cuffs, and boots
with stacked heels; while Licorice, indigo-skinned with implants like water
balloons, crowned him with a plush fedora like a capsized chanterelle.

Mendy took some satisfaction in the ostentation of his outward appearance, which included the gun he carried in a holster under his arm. But the
holster was on a bureau out of reach the night Suede returned to redeem
his pride and livelihood. He stormed into the room with his own weapon
drawn and his infected beak in a sling to find Mendy in a heated dalliance
with Mimo and Choyce.

"You got merchandise belongs to me," he declared, as Mendy rose from
the bed manning an erection the size of a knockwurst. With his penis seeming to challenge the pimp's menacing revolver, Mendy delivered his reply:
"Consider yourself dispossessed," then ejaculated on the disgraced pimp's
bell-bottom pants leg.

After a moment's confusion, the pimp responded by firing a bullet straight
through Mendy's leaden eye. The bullet's trajectory jarred loose a medley
of memories that seemed to belong to someone else, sweet memories of
hearth and home and black-and-white movies that served ultimately to fuel
Mendy's outrage. Bouncing off the wall against which the concussion had
hurled him, he lunged at the shooter despite his dreadful wound. Flailing
wildly, he toppled his nemesis (who dropped the gun), which inspired the
girls to join in kicking the fallen pimp, perforating his cheeks with their

stiletto heels. During the course of their collective brutalization of Suede, the trauma of Mendy's injury caught up with him and he collapsed to the floor. While he recovered in the hospital after the bullet had been successfully dislodged from his frontal lobe (his eye, a smashed jelly baby, was scraped from its socket), Mendy's violated brain spat sparks into his otherwise vapid imagination. That's when he came to understand that he either had several lives or was simply incapable of dying. He registered the information with a twitch of interest that tickled the roundhouse stitches wreathing his shaved head. With a similar quiver he received the news, delivered in whispers by the girls who visited his bedside, that they had trussed the pimp with their knotted stockings and tossed him in the trunk of Mendy's Buick (soon to be replaced by a Lincoln Town Car). They drove him out onto a sandbar in the river, where they buried him up to the neck, then steered the car over his head, which crunched like an egg. Afterward they dug him up and threw his body in the river, where it was dragged down by the weight of the gold chains that, out of respect, they'd refrained from removing.

They punctuated their story with a little ceremony in which they conferred on Mendy the distinction of being their sole procurer. They made it official with a badge of office in the form of an ornamental eye patch embroidered by Lamé, who had certain domestic skills. Strapping on the patch, they christened him with the street alias of Captain Blood. While the name had no more meaning for Mendy than for the whores, who'd merely liked the sound of it, hearing it spoken swelled his heart. Apparently he still had a heart.

Since he'd been admitted to the hospital with a gunshot wound, there was naturally a police investigation, but in the absence of a perpetrator there was little follow-up. The police were at any rate disinclined to put much energy into investigating infamies committed by underworld types on other underworld types. Their neglect was also encouraged by the baksheesh and sexual favors rendered to the cops by the girls, compliments of Captain Blood. Still, the newspapers got wind of the incident and the miraculous survival of a man who'd been shot in the head. But before the journalists could broadcast the marvel of his recovery, Captain Blood had quit the hospital against medical advice and returned to the fastness of Wigwam Village. All that appeared in the papers was a sketchy article about an area man who had survived a bullet in the brain.

From that time the girls belonged well and truly to Captain Blood, and the authority he wielded over them was yet another sensation that helped fill the vacuum within. Though he regarded himself as impervious to the fate of his predecessor, the captain still subscribed to the custom, endorsed by the girls themselves, of keeping them in line through fear. They were all damaged goods, the whores in Captain Blood's stable, and while their vocation required that they make a show of high spirits, it was largely due to the drugs they ingested that they refrained from lacerating themselves. Captain Blood, who had entertained morbid thoughts of his own in his former life, discovered that the anodynes the girls used—the heroin, crystal meth, and cocaine (the drug of Choyce)—were as effective as sex in supplanting the emptiness at his core. The drugs also abetted the firing neurons that trailed periodic comets across the path the bullet had traced through his brain, obviating consciousness. So Captain Blood joined his string of girls in their indulgences and in chemically induced fevers used them severely, exhausting himself in a debauchery chased with alcohol. It was a debilitating regimen that, while it took its toll on those around him, seemed in fact to nourish Captain Blood, whose stringy muscles were the toughened complement to his piratical eye patch. All his appetites were voracious, including his taste for the soul food the whores had delivered from a local beanery.

As addicted to physical abuse as they were to drugs, the girls professed a blind devotion to their captain inspired by his perceived heartlessness. He returned their affection with generally brutish treatment, which was after all what they expected, but occasionally, between bouts of dissipation, he might guide their hands to his thumping breast. "See," he would declare, "I got a heart," though with no soul to serve as gofer between that organ and his head, the possibility of sympathizing with others was moot.

Soon the girls were turning all their tricks in the motor court, whose manager, a toothless old man with a gut like a herniated inner tube, gave them the run of the place. In exchange he received a reasonable tribute and was allowed certain slavering liberties with the ladies. Thus was Wigwam Village effectively transformed into a brothel. The hookers freely turned over the take from the "parties" with their johns to their new sugar pimp, who had no business acumen whatsoever, though the acquisition of capital proved to be yet another intoxicant. Meanwhile Choyce, along with the daily rotation of her cotton candy wigs, handled the finances; she kept meticulous accounts and doled out allowances to the girls while reserving the lion's share for Captain Blood. She alerted him to the considerable portion of their assets absorbed by the purchase of illicit drugs, and having extracted a quizzical *Nu?* from the captain, respectfully proposed that they diversify:

they could consolidate the sale of sex with substance trafficking. That way they might have at hand the pharmaceuticals they required while benefiting from the profits of a cottage industry on their doorstep.

Inquiries were made of a dealer known as Mud Boy, a name derived from his carnal proclivities, whose healthy respect for Captain Blood had helped spread the pimp's reputation abroad. Mud Boy was prevailed on to consult with his manufacturer, who was in turn persuaded of the advantage of transferring his laboratory facilities to one (then two) of the motel units, which the Blood Consortium—as the enterprising whores had dubbed their merger—would furnish free of charge. The manufacturer would of course be liable to the consortium for a percentage of his income, but this tax would also guarantee his protection by the captain. As a fringe benefit, should his revenues fall short, the manufacturer—a tonsured technocrat with a sweet tooth—could make up the difference in trade from the girls. In this way Captain Blood found himself the czar of a burgeoning criminal empire.

On any given evening Wigwam Village was a regular circus of sin, a showcase for most of the vices known to man. In one unit, for instance, you might find Lamé, having dispensed with a client's depravities, injecting herself in some remote part of her anatomy as yet unmarked by tracks; while next door Licorice, in a leather livery wielding her "Licorice whip," flogged an off-duty cop strappadoed from a rafter by his heels. In yet another unit, the manufacturer, wearing a respirator mask, could be found directing his crew in "cooking" over-the-counter cold remedies. They crushed the capsules marinating in a denatured alcohol that stunk like cat piss, and mixed solvents and phosphorus corrosives in a hell's kitchen of plastic helixes, bubbling Pyrex containers, and Rubbermaid vats. The johns and junkies came and went, many of them indistinguishable from the local thugs the girls had conscripted to aid in the defense of the village—which was now a place the daylight world (police included) steered clear of, while at night every strain of degenerate came looking for fun.

Artillery was also in abundance, much of it obtained through a straw purchaser the manufacturer had employed in his preconsortium days. This so-called liar and buyer oversaw a steady influx of premium death-dealing devices: Beretta semiautomatics, Thompson submachine guns, Lewis assault rifles, Kalashnikovs, and Beano hand grenades, whose serial numbers the crew blotted out with battery acid. Those weapons undeployed by the Village defense community were marked up for resale at black market prices and exhibited in yet another of the motel units.

As a crossroads of hustlers, gangsters, and corporate swells in sedans with tinted windows ("equipped with driver's-side douche bags," as the sharp-tongued Licorice was wont to say), Wigwam Village in the heat of summer was a powder keg. Presiding over his nightmare kingdom, Captain Blood sometimes lay distracted in the seraglio into which Lamé had transformed his conical room; then his minions were dispatched to quell disorder in his stead. But more often the captain preferred doing his own dirty work. If greedy competitors attempted a trespass into any of the consortium's operations, Captain Blood, if he wasn't indisposed, never hesitated to meet them with force, making certain to place himself directly in harm's way. His reputation for fearlessness, and for the insanity his fearlessness implied, was on occasion its own caveat, prompting the more judicious to think twice; though there were always ambitious punks eager to challenge the primacy of Captain Blood.

There were skirmishes from which the captain emerged with fresh wounds that disfigured him further. Wounds that themselves seemed sentient, like the phantom retina through which, when he raised his patch, the Captain thought he could see all the way to the dead end of history. In various encounters Captain Blood had lost the motor coordination of his left hand, curled into a claw since being pinned to a doorpost by a jailhouse shank; he lost an earlobe chewed away in a brawl. In one fabled face-off, he received a bullet through the chest that, in his towering rage, he scarcely noticed, though like his previous head wound, this one required hospitalization; and again, while the doctors debated the possibility of his survival (and compromised cops sat vigil outside his door), Captain Blood resurfaced in his compound in a matter of days.

The city, much of whose vice and contraband Captain Blood and his hirelings now controlled, bore no resemblance to the city of his birth. That one he scarcely remembered, though it lay unchanged in its pleasant situation but a few miles away. His own enclave was a tawdry inferno with him as its ringmaster, orchestrating activities that resulted in an exponential increase in regional despair. This was somehow gratifying to the captain, as was his loutish treatment of the girls (or at least those who still survived—because Mimo had died from septicemia resulting from a botched abortion and Lamé from an overdose of scag cut with Red Devil lye), as well as his battles with would-be rivals who violated his domain. Occasionally, when he passed a mirror, Captain Blood, if he saw anyone at all, saw therein a one-eyed stranger with auburn hair and ropy muscles furnished by the quantities of "ice" he consumed; though violence and the adrenaline it triggered had become as essential as methedrine and in fact made the drugs largely superfluous. Violence trumped all other stimuli.

Choyce, who was often the target of his primal furies, believed that she and the captain had a special relationship. She admired him for his lack of illusions. Unlike Suede and the parade of chicken hawks that had preceded him, her new pimp was no hypocrite; he expressed no sentimental remorse after his punishing abuses, which seemed anyway more experimental than personal. Once, however, the girl, having secreted in her battered psyche some vestigial scrap of innocence, found the gumption to ask the captain, "Do Jews believe in God?" Then she shuddered from a pleasing chill when he replied, "Don't make me laugh."

In the meantime, unlike its former host, Captain Blood's disembodied soul was attracted to old haunts. In fact, having retraced the route of its wayward transit, it scoured the city for the whereabouts of its prior vessel, unwittingly brushing the cheek of the quondam Mendy Dreyfus, unrecognizable in his soulless incarnation; while Captain Blood himself was barely aware of a passing breeze. And so his fugitive soul continued its wandering. Better to remain elusive than captive again in a container other than the one to which it had initially belonged, that one being evidently extinct. Eventually, though, Mendy's soul floated into my own zone of influence, attracted by the trap I had unconsciously constructed for it.

Every empire contains within it the seeds of its own destruction, and Captain Blood's was no different. The end came when someone lit a cigarette, flicked a switch, dropped a gallon of ether, or sneezed—these were the theories, since no eyewitnesses survived to report the event. Whatever the case, experts agreed that some infernal match had been made between combustible vapors and volatile organic compounds brokered by chemical flames. The two meth labs combined with the weapons magazine in a fireball that engulfed the Village and blasted a fleet of cement tepees into the stratosphere—or so went the apocryphal version told for a generation to explain the origin of the weed-choked crater where Wigwam Village once stood. Nearly everyone—whores, pervs, and outlaws alike—was atomized in flagrante, their cinders buried beneath a debris that shrouded the entire metropolitan area in a day of perpetual night. The newspaper editorials had a field day extolling the timely biblical solution that had rid the city of its festering nest of iniquity.

Buried in the rubble himself and nearly incinerated, Captain Blood had dragged himself out of the ashes, turning to stone a group of rubberneckers loitering at the edge of the site. He was hospitalized once again (by now the doctors and staff scarcely blinked) and released—having distributed among them what he'd retained of the consortium hush fund—with third-degree burns over much of his body. A criminal legend, he was a horror to behold, his head bereft of all but a few tufts of hair, his ears cauterized to gnocchi, crocodile skin howling in a torment that thrilled him and drove him to wander farther afield.

In the bleached-stone streets of the Holy Land, to which he'd been drawn by his wounds, priests crossed themselves, mullahs chanted the azala prayer, and black-fedoraed haredi uttered a hasty "Kayn ayn horeh!" ("No evil eye!") at the sight of him. Occasionally he was mistaken for a leper by those who had no idea what lepers looked like but thought that the captain—designated a corporal in a militia of right-wing ideologues unofficially attached to the Israel Defense Forces—looked like one. He enjoyed the shock he caused to pedestrians but sometimes cowled himself in a tallis or checked kaffiyeh to pass as neither one thing nor the other. The regular army had naturally refused admission to a creature as maimed as he, but there were brigades of irregulars just this side of vigilantes who appreciated his zeal for violence; and then there was the eye patch that drew comparisons to a former general of renown. His rank was an arbitrary appointment, since, as a human weapon— "human" being a relative term in his case—Baal ha-Mavet, the Master of Death as he was now known, was an exception. He was not especially shadowy in his movements, nor was he fleet of foot; he possessed no expertise with military hardware (though he'd acquired a certain skill in the use of his treyf sticker) and couldn't even speak the language of his compatriots, much less the enemy. But he inspired dread wherever he was deployed.

He'd been enticed to this part of the world by the opportunities it afforded to inflict pain, pain having become a constant companion that prompted the Baal ha-Mavet to visit more of the same upon others. At home in places where angels feared to tread, he burrowed through the tunnels of weapons smugglers like a physic through tortured intestines. He entered refugee camps with walls graffitied in blood and perimeters of gutted refrigerators and automobiles. He hacked his way through the strung laundry of Hamas or Fatah, invading their mudbrick hovels to assassinate assassins; swarmed over asbestos roofs bristling with antennae, over domed roofs from which smoke curled like plumes from trepanned skulls. He ransacked caves where the stored explosives of the resistance shared berths with the bones of the patriarchs. When he closed his eye he still saw the bulldozed dwellings and uprooted kitchen gardens, the watchtowers, stacked sandbags, and mounted machine guns; he sniffed sulfur and the musk of burning rubber, heard percussion grenades and the screams of prisoners, the voices of muezzins over speakers from neon minarets crying, "Itbach al-Yahud! Slaughter the Jews!" He saw vehicles foundering in quicksand, fugitives trapped in funnels of light from helicopter gunships, the walking dead stumbling toward a horizon lit by phosphorus bombs.

There was of course another Holy Land, in which people made love and money amid flowering bougainvillea and tamarind; they opened mechanized shutters onto vistas of the Mediterranean flecked with bellying sails. But that Eretz Israel was only a rumor to which the Baal ha-Mavet had never really subscribed. That one existed somewhere in the precincts of recorded time, whereas the Death dwelled in a timeless element on a bald hilltop besieged by enemies. He lived among a people who, when they weren't playing havoc with their neighbors, tended their goats and irrigated their orange groves with water redirected from their neighbors' wells. They quoted scripture ("He who shows mercy to the cruel is destined to be cruel to the merciful") and imagined themselves the contemporaries of Judah Maccabee, Bar Kochba, and Joseph Trumpeldor. They watched over their flocks and their feral children at play beside an open sewer in the shade of dusty terebinths—as did the Death, who hunkered alongside them in their trailers, squatted in their noisome privies, frightened their clodhopping women wearing turbans and dirt-length skirts. For them he felt not a twinge of desire, desire having dissolved into an altogether tepid sensation, though the hatred that was rife in the settlement could still give him a charge. Former sappers, paratroopers, and Shin Bet inquisitors, the settlers identified themselves first as farmers. They plowed the fields with automatic rifles strapped over their shoulders and tefillin fastened to their foreheads like truncated horns. They had purged themselves of the neuroses of the Diaspora ("If one comes to slay you, slay him first; do not be overly righteous"), their world concurrent with Jericho, Masada, and Tel Hai.

Each time a piguah, an action, was instigated on their side of the border (itself a capricious demarcation), the settlers exacted a tenfold retribution on the other side. And sometimes, impatient, they provoked actions themselves that called for immediate retaliation. They murdered the Canaanites in reprisals inciting reactions that prompted more reprisals, which they ex-

ulted in, these muscular Hebrew warriors, who had restored the pious valor
of their ancestors; who were at once a useful adjunct and a chronic embarrassment to the regular army.

They were a brotherhood of heroes, who, while they admired the Baal
ha-Mavet in their fashion, never quite admitted him into their fraternity. His
fortitude was of another order. A secret weapon whose secret was open, he
had acquired a reputation that induced fear among men—the martyrs and
freedom fighters in their ski masks and fatigues—who prided themselves
on having none. Renowned as were his deeds, however, you couldn't have called
him a living legend, since no one regarded him as certifiably mortal; the Baal
ha-Mavet's fame was not that of a person, nor was he judged by human
standards. No one assumed that his flayed skin concealed an ordinary man,
since, beyond his excessive bloodlust, he gave no indication of human frailty;
he evidenced no frailties at all. Naturally, in a climate where myth held dominion over history, a figure such as the Death enjoyed a mythic stature:
he was a species that some wonder rabbi had molded from desert clay, ani-
mated with spells, and dispatched to aid them in their holy endeavors.

A miscellany of miracles was attributed to him: there were tunnel cave-
ins from which he disinterred himself with a regularity his comrades grew
accustomed to; there was the suicide detonation at a checkpoint near Jabalia,
where he was retrieved from among the jackstraw carcasses and zipped into
a rubber body bag. In a makeshift morgue under corrugated zinc, he extri-
cated himself from the bag with his treyf sticker in an act of self-resurrection
during which he experienced a cramp in the arch of his foot. (It was a spasm
that attempted, albeit abortively, to communicate to his brain the memory of
Robert Donat in *The Count of Monte Cristo*—in particular the scene where
Donat as Edmond Dantès frees himself from his shroud after being tossed
into the bay from the parapet of the Château d'If.)

But the truth was that there was still a man of sorts behind ha-Mavet's
unsightly visage, and for that one the shedding of blood had ceased to be
an entirely satisfying activity. While his own wounds cried out continually
for the blood of others, his mind was often detached from the suffering he
caused; and sometimes when he lifted his eye patch like a gunport and his
empty socket was flooded with visions, he wanted something he could not
name. Of course that longing was never as strong as his urge to skewer his
victims, but resisting its tug, the Death felt increasingly tired.

The fear he evoked in others had begun to bore him, the round of reprisals and counterattacks become monotonous. This is not to say he wasn't

still rankled when someone failed to grant him the deference that was his due—which was the case on a summer afternoon in the Mea Shearim quarter of Jerusalem. It was unusual for ha-Mavet to visit the city, attuned as was his temperament to lunar landscapes and given his hostility to the habitations of rational men. But in the Old World atmosphere of Mea Shearim (the seculars quipped it was the Jurassic Park of Judaism) time was at least as inconsequential as in the settlements, and the inhabitants just as moonstruck. He was on his way to meet with a group of fanatics conspiring to blow up the Haram al-Sharif, the Temple Mount, in the hope of triggering Armageddon. ("On Mount Moriah, which is desolate, there the foxes walk . . . ," they lamented in anticipation of the aftermath.) The Baal ha-Mavet had no special political stake in the matter but simply resonated to the idea of a conflagration with universal consequences, and the fanatics meant to exploit his attitude to their own ends.

The walls were posted in placards admonishing immodest dress and deriding opposing sects, the streets swept with sand from the simoom winds. While the majority of black hats made spitting gestures as the stranger passed, one old graybeard, apparently frozen by the manifest sight of him, refused to get out of his path. What's more, the squat rabbinical gentleman in his beaver shtreimel, his beard furled like a baby's bib, seemed transfixed by the Baal ha-Mavet's naked eye. Recognizing in the old man a throwback to Galut, the long exile that had reduced the Jews to craven usurers and kowtowers to authority, the Death felt an exhilarating contempt. He cursed what he perceived as the fear that nailed the old man in place and lifted a hand to slap him out of his way. But catching sight of his own grisly reflection in the rabbi's moist eye, he too was paralyzed and unable to deliver the blow.

Said the old man in a perfectly unruffled Yiddish that ha-Mavet was surprised to find he understood: "You poor shmo, you lost your neshomah." It was his parents' mother tongue; the Master of Death, it seemed, had had parents.

"Are you my father?" he was suddenly compelled to ask.

"God forbid."

"Then get out of my way." He made to step around the old man, who, nimble for his years, scooted sideways to block his progress.

"I'm talking your soul," said the rabbi, whose manner on second thought was less fearful than concerned. "I can see you ain't got one."

"So," said the Baal ha-Mavet, "this is news?" But in fact it was.

Then the old man took the occasion to invite the stranger into his home, it was Shabbos, and actually grasped him by the misshapen hand to lead him over the nearby threshold; while the Death, though perplexed, allowed himself to be led. He couldn't recall the last time he'd entered a proper house. This one, despite its chapfallen facade, was rather spacious inside, its parlor sunk below street level and surrounded by sagging shelves of tarnished menorahs and rams' horns like helical deaf-aids; there were spice boxes, hamsas, talismans, and siddurim—all of which, the rabbi assured his guest, with a wave, were for sale. When he had doffed his shtreimel, revealing a skullcap hedged about by linty curls, the old rabbi bade his guest to sit facing him in an adjacent armchair. He called to his wife to prepare some tea, which the blockish woman served Russian-style with lump sugar, trundling into the parlor on fallen arches, her thick wig center-parted like an exposed brain. Placing the tray on a low table between them, she stole a glance at the Baal ha-Mavet then fled the room with her apron over her face. The rabbi excused his wife's discourteous behavior with a harumph, while his guest wondered how it was he was still held captive by the old man's sallow eye.

"What am I doing here?" he growled, at odds with the mercantile clutter of his surroundings.

"Enough already with the shreklikheit," said the rabbi dismissively, pulling wire spectacles over either ear. He dipped a macaroon into his tea and took a bite, ignoring the crumbs that fell into his beard, then became pedagogical. "We know that from nefesh, ruach, and neshomah, it consists, your three-part soul, and when departs the neshomah, which it's the essential piece, your nefesh and ruach, they shrivel up like, excuse me"—grabbing himself significantly through his caftan—"an old man's beytsim." Leaning forward to better examine his guest, the rabbi crossed and uncrossed his eyes. "I am a student of the science that by a person's forehead I can read the invisible inscription that denotes his character. You"—adjusting his squint—"you got wrote on your forehead the letters mem and tav, which means death, but that I can fix in a jiffy." He leaned over further, smelling faintly of gas, and traced with the bitten nail of his index finger a sign on his guest's mottled brow. Ha-Mavet, who'd lost also the memory of having been touched by another, experienced a prickling in his skin that he deeply resented. "Now you got aleph, mem, and tav, that instead of 'death' spells 'truth', which it should make you feel better."

He went on to explain that it was clear ha-Mavet had had an old and enervated soul, one that had suffered much through too many gilgulim, or incarnations. "So it didn't have anymore the heart to stick with you through thick and thin." The problem was, when the neshomah, the divine element, abandons a man, its place is taken up by an impure spirit from the left-hand side, which occupies the abode of the soul. "But, yingele, I can assure you, wherever it is, your neshomah, it misses you." It might be confined to a hat or an insect or even, nishtu gedacht, a gentile, or it might be simply adrift, but you could be sure that, whatever its state, it was homesick for its former host.

Feeling confined by the wings of his armchair, the Baal ha-Mavet blurted his impatience with the old man's foolishness: "Why should I care about the chickenshit thing?"

"Because you can't again feel what it is to be human without it."

"What's the big deal about human?"

The rabbi shrugged an exaggerated shrug, his round shoulders as if lifted by the arching of his caterpillar brows. "So long as you're alive, you might as well be a person, no? Besides"—he relaxed again, locking fingers over his spreading paunch—"HaShem don't want Jews to be warriors. Worriers He prefers them to be."

Beyond aggravation, the Death was on the verge of making for the door, when there came a colossal boom that rocked the planet beneath them and shook the Judaica clattering from its shelves. Through a grated window he could make out the volcanic roiling of mile-high smoke, a golden dome launched like an unstoppered cork into the beryl blue sky. He felt a pang of sorrow that he hadn't been the one to punch in the code on the cellular phone (its numbers corresponding to an appropriate chapter and verse from Ezekiel), thus detonating the chain of dynamite sticks snaking their way through the catacombs under the Temple Mount. Then the sorrow spread like a black infusion throughout his system, engendering there an exquisite new ache that superseded all his old wounds (which had lately gone numb), until he was stricken with the pain of missing his displaced soul.

The rabbi remarked somewhat in afterthought that the explosion was reminiscent of shevirat ha-kelim, the big bang that had succeeded the cosmic tantrum. This was when HaShem, disappointed in His creation, had retreated in a huff into his sanctum and slammed the door behind him— which caused the bang that scattered the sparks of righteousness over the earth. "For every Jew it is his task to gather up from where they hide the sparks and restore them to their source."

At that the Baal ha-Mavet declared that he'd had enough and, rising abruptly, bolted out of the rabbi's house. The old imposter called after him that it was customary to leave the tzaddik some gratuity. With the Temple

Mount in flames, sirens and gunshots heard throughout Jerusalem, riots erupting all over the Palestinian territories, settlements attacked and their inhabitants slain, Mendy Dreyfus no longer felt like looking for something else to destroy. Instead, he sought a reunion with what, unbeknownst to him till now, he'd been hungering after these several years.

But where does one search for a runaway soul? You might visit holy places in the hope that souls clustered there; but when Mendy made his way through anarchic streets to the Western Wall, arguably the holiest site in the Holy Land, he found that its stones had already tumbled to rubble, and that all the souls nesting in its caper-clogged crannies (alongside letters to God) had fled. In fact, souls were everywhere in flight, and if you'd had Mendy's second sight via his empty socket, you might have glimpsed them—at least those that weren't still trapped in TV chassis or the breasts of the bereaved; you might have seen, had it not been veiled in ash, a flock of souls flitting across the face of the moon. Where they were headed, who knew, but Mendy figured that, if it was heaven, the joke was on them, because no one could expect any longer to get there from here.

In any case, after the thunderclap at the Haram al-Sharif, mortars and rockets, some armed with chemical warheads, had been launched from a hundred hidden sites into Israeli cities. A fully mobilized IDF had responded with furious air and ground assaults on every Palestinian town and refugee camp. The Third Intifada was broadcast live on CNN, clips of fleeing women and children being wasted by Israeli battalions shown repeatedly on Al Jazeera, accompanied by outraged commentary from every corner of the Arab world. All over the Middle East and Muslim South Asia, leaves were cancelled and armies placed on high alert; in Damascus a long-dormant al-Qaeda sleeper cell was activated. Western governments, and a few Gulf states, urged calm and condemned the violence on both sides. The Security Council met in emergency session but couldn't agree on a resolution: Russia, particularly surly, called Israel a "terrorist state." The Syrian al-Qaeda cell, meanwhile, had secretly assembled a dirty bomb, mounted it on a short-range missile of Pakistani design and Iranian manufacture, and launched it successfully into Tel Aviv. The result was predictably catastrophic. Mossad quickly determined the launch point and provenance of the missile, and the prime minister authorized retaliatory strikes against Syria, Iran, and Pakistan. Multiple-warhead nuclear missiles were launched from the Negev toward Damascus, Tehran, and Islamabad. Russian air defense, on the qui vive since the Cold War, instantly detected the launches, whose trajectories could not at this stage be distinguished from those of an attack on Russia herself; so Moscow initiated a launch cycle of its own missile defenses. American early warning systems registered Russia's launch preparations, the U.S. military went to DEFCON 1, and so on—while true believers everywhere, their eyes seared by thermal pulses that rent the ozone curtain to tatters, their teeth blasted by the cold that followed hard upon the total eclipse of light, waited in vain to be raptured aloft.

Mendy thought he should maybe return to where he'd started from, but that place had become this place, time and history having surrendered to an eternity modeled on an ancient blueprint of Judgment Day. The whole planet, scorched beyond a hope of photosynthesis, turned creakily beneath a blanket of perpetually sifting black snow. Every survivor was a prophet, gibbering amid toppled doorposts smeared against the Destroyer's visitation with hyssop dipped in blood; they crouched among toxic gases emitted from smoldering polymers and unburied bodies, citing Exodus: "A fine dust will settle over the land and it shall become on man and beast a burning rash erupting in boils; a darkness will be upon the land, a darkness one can feel . . ." Evolution was reversed, once-mortal creatures no longer walking upright but dragging themselves across the dunes eating filth. As hairless and blistered as the storied Baal ha-Mavet himself, they murdered whatever might provide them a tainted nourishment that their afflicted bodies could not by any means digest. They fought over every vestige of the world that was: an ultraviolet fish, a soda bottle as elastic as a cartoon grin, a plastic water gun fused to a turtle's shell; they killed for a clock without hands or a goggle-eyed girl. Though he moved indistinguishably among them, Mendy shared no part of their pain, their suffering having derived from loss while his came from renewed memories.

Now that the slaughter that had been his special element was pandemic, Mendy steered clear of the open graves of what once had been cities, from which limping corpses emerged. He girded his loins with the hides of moldering beasts, ate radioactive locusts, tubers that glowed in the dark, and sucked pea-green milk from the udders of cankered cows. His injured anatomy was further racked by symptoms of typhus, by thyroid nodules and lesions like bloated leeches; his deflated stomach was pasted like wet cellophane to his twisted spine. He was assaulted by the bone chill of the global winter and the relentless solar flux that followed the settling of the planetary dust storm. But while he was proportionately more dead than alive, a lone figure huddling in culverts, Mendy Dreyfus was still unable to give up the ghost. He still hoped to put himself in the way of something sacred. In this manner the years passed, the decades, a century or more. Here and there a grapevine challenged death's supremacy; a lizard flickered, a polecat yowled, greenflies swarmed; a cypress sprouted a single leaf and a tribe of what passed for humanity clung to a barren wadi around a contaminated well. When they weren't busy butchering each other, they might manage to eke a puckered carob or a bleeding turnip out of the parched soil; they might tend a herd of livestock consisting of six-legged mutants, a camel with a trio of humps. To such settlements Mendy gave a wide berth, though he was known to take the liberty on occasion of raiding their wattles to cull a creature or two from their flocks.

He was shepherding one such animal (identifiable as some breed of teratological goat) in the Judean desert near the wilderness of Ein Gedi, when the thing slipped its tether and bounded off into the sandstone hills. It was skittering, the goat-thing, along the pink cliffs that rimmed the Dead Sea, when it suddenly disappeared. Having scrambled up to the ledge where it vanished, Mendy discovered the hearth-sized opening of a cave from which emanated a cool draft. Dropping to all fours, he could hear the animal chomping on something just inside. He wriggled through the pinched entrance to find the creature, encircled in light from a chimney hole, standing atop a heap of rubbish from a bygone era. There were charred tins, Teflon containers, a ruined tie-dyed dashiki, and a small hill of mildewed paperbacks stashed there long ago by some immemorial hermit saint. Indifferent to his presence, the goat-thing stood munching a book with one of its mouths, nibbling as contentedly as if it were feeding on provender. Crawling forward, Mendy examined the weather-swollen condition of the other texts, some of whose faded titles he could still make out in the velvety light: *Stalking the Wild Asparagus, The Teachings of Don Juan, The Whole Earth Catalog, The I Ching.* At his approach the goat-thing dropped the book and, bleating like a fractured shofar, beat it further back into the darkness of the cavern. Tempted to follow, Mendy was stalled by a maverick impulse, and instead picked up the book the goat-thing had abandoned. It had been eons since he'd read a book, but after only a few sentences he found this one oddly intriguing. Clutching it in his mangled hand as he crawled back out of the cave, Mendy squatted on a rock he carelessly shared with a sunning serpent and continued reading.

The ravaged book, entitled *The Legend of the Lost*, was about a guy who goes bungee jumping (whatever that is) and loses his soul. All right, so it wasn't such an original story, but neither was Mendy's an original soul. Anyway, as it turns out, every story, regardless of how slight, is destined to be the repository of a lost soul, and in contriving this one, I had inadvertently captured Mendy's. I'd pressed it there between the pages of the narrative like the petals of an old boutonniere that blossomed again in Mendy's lights and lungs as he read the tale. In this way he reabsorbed his own prodigal neshomah in the reading: the words became flesh even as his sere flesh began to wither, the years catching up with and overtaking him, so that he and his restored soul, which cleaved to him now for dear life, started to decompose along with the book itself, its pages returning to a flaky pulp as he read them.

But despite his own disintegrating frame Mendy Dreyfus was tickled; he laughed aloud at the stirring sensation of his own rapid wasting away, which brought to mind an old movie—what was it? oh yeah: *Lost Horizon*—in which the heroine, played by Jane Wyatt, ages a hundred years on the spot, crumbling to powder upon leaving the rarefied atmosphere of Shangri-La. The hero, Ronald Colman, however, escapes intact to recommence his solitary wandering. His fate was not unlike that of my own soul, whose sloughed corpus had been defunct since the nuclear winter. Then pleased to have had at least one devoted reader, my restless soul was released from hovering about the mouth of the cave, and distancing itself from the windblown remains of Mendy's story, began to prowl the earth in search of a home of its own.

II

THE LOWER EAST SIDE, NEW YORK

The Sin of Elijah

Somewhere during the couple of millennia that I'd been commuting between heaven and earth, I, Elijah the Tishbite—former prophet of the Northern Kingdom of Israel, translated to Paradise in a chariot of flame while yet alive—became a voyeur. Call me weak, but after you've attended no end of circumcisions, performed untold numbers of virtuous deeds and righteous meddlings in a multitude of disguises, your piety can begin to wear a little thin. Besides, good works had ceased to generate the kind of respect they'd once commanded in the world, a situation that took its toll on one's self-esteem; so that even I, old as I was, had become susceptible from time to time to the yetser hora, the evil impulse.

That's how I came to spy on the Fefers, Feyvush and Gitl, in their love nest on the Lower East Side of New York. You might say that observing the passions of mortals, often with stern disapproval, had always been a hobby of mine; but of late it was their more intimate pursuits that took my fancy. Still, I had standards. As a whiff of sanctity always clung to my person from my sojourns in the Upper Eden, I lost interest where the dalliance of mortals was undiluted by some measure of earnest affection. And the young Fefer couple, they adored each other with a love that surpassed their own understanding. Indeed, so fervent was the heat of their voluptuous intercourse that they sometimes feared it might consume them and they would perish of sheer ecstasy.

I happened upon them one miserable midsummer evening when I was making my rounds of the East Side ghetto, which in those years was much in need of my benevolent visitations. I did a lot of good, believe me, spreading banquets on the tables of desolate families in their coal cellars, exposing the villains posing as suitors to young girls fresh off the boat. I even engaged in spirited disputes with the apikorsin, the unbelievers, in an effort to vindicate God's justice to man—a thankless task, to say the least, in that swarming, heretical, typhus-infested neighborhood. So was it any wonder that with the volume of dirty work that fell to my hands, I should occasionally seek some momentary diversion?

You might call it a waste that one with my gift for camouflage, who could have gained clandestine admittance backstage at the Ziegfeld Follies when Anna Held climbed out of her milk bath, or slipped unnoticed into the green room at the People's Theatre where Tomashefsky romped au naturel with his zaftig harem, that I should return time and again to the tenement flat of Feyvush and Gitl Fefer. But then you never saw the Fefers at their amorous business.

To be sure, they weren't what you'd call prepossessing. Feyvush, a cobbler by profession, was stoop-shouldered and hollow-breasted, nose like a parrot's beak, hair a wreath of swiftly evaporating black foam. His bride was a green-eyed, pear-shaped little hausfrau, freckles stippling her cheeks as if dripped from the brush that daubed her rust-red pompadour. Had you seen them in the streets—Feyvush with nostrils flaring from the stench, his arm hooked through Gitl's, from whose free hand dangled the carcass of an unflicked chicken—you would have deemed them in no way remarkable. But at night when they turned down the gas lamp in their stuffy bedroom, its window giving onto the fire escape (where I stooped to watch), they were the Irene and Vernon Castle of the clammy sheets.

At first they might betray a charming awkwardness. Feyvush would fumble with the buttons of Gitl's shirtwaist, tugging a little frantically at corset laces, hooks, and eyes. He might haul without ceremony the shapeless muslin shift over her head, shove the itchy cotton drawers below her knees. Just as impatiently Gitl would yank down the straps of her spouse's suspenders, pluck the studs from his shirt, the rivets from his fly; she would thrust chubby fingers between the seams of his union suit with the same impulsiveness that she plunged her hand in a barrel to snatch a herring. Then they would tumble onto the sagging iron bed, its rusty springs complaining like a startled henhouse. At the initial shock of flesh pressing flesh, they would clip, squeeze, and fondle whatever was most convenient, as if each sought a desperate assurance that the other was real. But once they'd determined as much, they slowed the pace; they lulled their frenzy to a rhythmic investigation of secret contours, like a getting acquainted of the blind.

They postponed the moment of their union for as long as they could stand to. While Feyvush sucked her nipples till they stood up like gumdrops, Gitl gaily pulled out clumps of her husband's hair; while he traced with his nose the line of ginger fur below her navel the way a flame follows a fuse, she held his hips like a rampant divining rod over her womb. When their loins were finally locked together, it jarred them so that they froze for an instant, each seeming to ask the other in tender astonishment, "What did we do?" Then the bed would gallop from wardrobe to washstand and the neighbors pound on their ceilings with brooms, until Feyvush and Gitl spent themselves, I swear it, in a shower of sparks. It was an eruption that in others might have catapulted their spirits clear out of their bodies—but not the Fefers, who clung tenaciously to each other rather than suffer even a momentary separation from their better half.

Afterward, as they lay in a tangle, hiding their faces in mutual embarrassment over such a bounty of delight, I would slope off. My prurient interests satisfied, I was released from impure thoughts; I was free, a stickiness in the pants notwithstanding, to carry on with cleansing lepers and catering the weddings of the honest poor. So as you see, my spying on the Fefers was a tonic, a clear case of the ends justifying the means.

How was it I contrived to stumble upon such a talented pair in the first place? Suffice it that, when you've been around for nearly three thousand years, you develop antennae. It's a sensitivity that, in my case, was partial compensation for the loss of my oracular faculty, an exchange of roles from clairvoyant to voyeur. While I might not be able to predict the future with certainty anymore, I could intuit where and when someone was getting a heartfelt shtupping.

But like I say, I didn't let my fascination with the Fefers interfere with the performance of good works; the tally of my mitzvot was as great as ever. Greater perhaps, since my broader interests kept me closer than usual to earth, sometimes neglecting the tasks that involved a return to Kingdom Come. (Sometimes I put off escorting souls back to the afterlife, a job I'd never relished, involving as it did what amounted to cleaning up after the Angel of Death.) Whenever the opportunity arose, my preoccupation with Feyvush and Gitl might move me to play the detective. While traveling in their native Galicia, for instance, I would stop by the study house, the only light on an otherwise deserted street in the abandoned village of Krok. This was the Fefers' home village, a place existing just this side of memory, reduced by pogrom and expulsions to broken chimneys, a haunted bathhouse, scattered pages of the synagogue register among the dead leaves. The only survivors being a dropsical rabbi and his skeleton crew of disciples, it was to them I appealed for specifics.

"Who could forget?" replied the old rabbi, stroking a snuff-yellow beard, the wen on his brow like a sightless third eye. "After their wedding he comes to me, this Feyvush: 'Rabbi,' he says guiltily, 'is not such unspeakable pleasure a sin?' I tell him: 'In the view of Yohanan ben Dabai, a man may do what he will with his wife; within the zone of the marriage bed all is permitted.' He thanks me and runs off before I can give him the opinion of Rabbi Eliezer, who suggests that, while having intercourse, one should think on arcane points of law . . ."

I liked to imagine their wedding night. Hadn't I witnessed enough of them in my time—burlesque affairs wherein the child bride and groom, martyrs to arranged marriages, had never set eyes on each other before? They were usually frightened to near paralysis, their only preparation a lecture from some doting melammed, or a long-suffering mother's manual of medieval advice. "What's God been doing since He created the world?" goes the old query. Answer: "He's been busy making matches." But the demoralized condition of the children to whose nuptials I was assigned smacked more of the intervention of pushy families than the hand of God.

No wonder I was so often called on to give a timid bridegroom a nudge. Employing my protean powers—now regrettably obsolete, though I still regard myself a master of stealth—I might take the form of a bat or the shimmying flame of a hurricane lamp to scare the couple into each other's arms. (Why I never lost patience and stood in for the fainthearted husband myself, I can't say.) Certainly there's no reason to suppose that Dvora Malkeh's Feyvush, the cobbler's apprentice, was any braver when it came to bedding his own stranger bride—his Gitl, who at fifteen was two years his junior, the only daughter of Chaim Rupture the porter, her dowry a hobbled goat and a dented tin kiddush cup. It was not what you'd have called a brilliant match.

Still, I liked to picture the moment when they're alone for the first time in their bridal chamber, which was probably some shelf above a stove encircled by horse blankets. In the dark Feyvush has summoned the courage to strip to his talis koton, its ritual fringes dangling a flimsy curtain over his knocking knees. Gitl has peeled in one anxious motion to her starchless shift and slid gingerly beneath the thistledown, where she's joined after a small eternity by the tremulous groom. They lie there without speaking, without touching, having forgotten (respectively) the rabbi's sage instruction and the diagrams in *The Saffron Sacrament*. They only know that the warm (albeit shuddering) flesh beside them has a magnetism as strong as gravity, so that each feels they've been falling their whole lives into the other's embrace. And afterward there's nothing on earth—neither goat's teat nor cobbler's last, pickle jar, poppy seed, Cossack's knout, or holy scroll—that doesn't echo their common devotion.

Or so I imagined. I also guessed that their tiny hamlet must have begun to seem too cramped to contain such an abundance of mutual affection. It needed a shtetl, say, the size of Tarnopol, or a teeming city as large as Lodz, to accommodate them; or better: for a love that defied possibility, a land where the impossible (as was popularly bruited) was the order of the day. America was hardly an original idea—I never said the Fefers were original, only unique—but emboldened by the way that wedded bliss had transformed their ramshackle birthplace, they must have been curious to see how love traveled.

You might have thought the long ocean passage, at the end of which waited only a dingy dumbbell tenement on Orchard Street, would have cooled their ardor. Were their New World circumstances any friendlier to romance than the Old? Feyvush worked twelve-hour days in a bootmaking loft above the butcher's shambles in Gouverneur Slip; while Gitl haggled with fishmongers and supplemented her husband's mean wages stitching artificial flowers for ladies' hats. The streets swarmed with hucksters, ganefs, and handkerchief girls who solicited in the shadows of buildings draped in black bunting. Every day the funeral trains of cholera victims plied the market crush, displacing vendors crying spoiled meat above the locust hum of the sewing machines. The summers brought a heat that made ovens of the tenements, sending the occupants to their roofs where they inhaled a cloud of blue flies; and in winter the ice hung in tusks from the common faucets, the truck horses froze upright in their tracks beside the curb. But if the ills of the ghetto were any impediment to their ongoing conjugal fervor, you couldn't have proved it by the Feyvush and Gitl I knew.

They were after all no strangers to squalor, and the corruptions of the East Side had a vitality not incompatible with the Fefers' own sweet delirium. Certainly there was a stench, but there was also an exhilaration: there were passions on display in the music halls and the Yiddish theaters, where Jacob Adler or Bertha Kalish could be counted on nightly to tear their emotions to shreds. You had the dancing academies where the greenhorns groped one another in a macabre approximation of the turkey trot, the Canal Street cafés where the poets and revolutionaries fought pitched battles with arsenals of words. You had the shrill and insomniac streets. Content as they were to keep to themselves, the Fefers were not above rubbernecking. They

liked to browse the Tenth Ward's gallery of passions, comparing them—
with some measure of pride—unfavorably to their own.

Sometimes I thought the Fefers nurtured their desire for each other as
if it were an altogether separate entity, a member of the family if you will.
Of course the mystery remained that such heroic lovemaking as theirs had
yet to produce any offspring, which was certainly not for want of trying.
Indeed, they'd never lost sight of the sacramental aspect of their intimacy, or
the taboos against sharing a bed for purposes other than procreation. They
had regularly consulted with local midwives, and purchased an assortment
of bendls, simples, and fertility charms to no avail. (Gitl had even gone so
far as to flush her system with mandrake enemas against a possible evil eye.)
But once, as I knelt outside their window during a smallpox-ridden summer
(when caskets the size of bread pans were carried from the tenements night
and day), I heard Feyvush suggest, "Maybe no babies is for such a plenty of
pleasure the price we got to pay?"

You didn't have to be a prophet to see it coming. What could you expect
when a pair of mortals routinely achieved orgasms like Krakatoa, their loins
shooting sparks like the uncorking of a bottle of pyrotechnical champagne?
Something had to give, and with hindsight I can see that it had to happen
on Shabbos, when married folk are enjoined to go at their copulation as
if ridden by demons. Their fervent cleaving to one another (dveikuss, the
Kabbalists call it) is supposed to hasten the advent of Messiah, or some such
poppycock. Anyway, the Fefers had gathered momentum over the years,
enduring climaxes of such convulsive magnitude that their frames could
scarcely contain the exaltation. And since they clung to each other with a
ferocity that refused to release spirit from flesh, it was only a matter of time
until their transports carried them bodily aloft.

I was in Paradise when it happened, doing clerical work. Certain book-
keeping tasks were entrusted to me, such as totting up the debits and credits
of incoming souls—tedious work that I alternated with the more restful occupation of weaving garlands of prayers; but even this had become somewhat
monotonous, a mindless therapy befitting the sanatorium-like atmosphere
of Kingdom Come. For such employment I chose a quiet stone bench (what
bench wasn't quiet?) along a garden path near the bandstand. (Paradise back
then resembled those sepia views of Baden-Baden or Saratoga Springs in
their heyday; though of late the place, fallen into neglect, has more in com-

mon with the seedier precincts of Miami Beach.) At dusk I closed the ledger
and tossed the garlands into the boughs of the Tree of Life, already so festooned with ribbons of prayer that the dead, in their wistfulness, compared
it to a live oak hung with Spanish moss. Myself, I thought of a peddler of
suspenders on the Lower East Side.

I was making my way along a petal-strewn walk toward the gates in my
honorary angel getup—quilted smoking jacket, tasseled fez, a pair of rigid,
lint-white wings. Constructed of chicken wire and papier-mâché, they were
just for show, the wings, about as useful as an ostrich's. I confess this was a
source of some resentment, since why shouldn't I merit the genuine article?
As for the outfit, having selected it myself I couldn't complain; certainly it
was smart, though the truth was I preferred my terrestrial shmattes. But in
my empyrean role as Sandolphon the Psychopomp, whose responsibilities
included the orientation of lost souls, I was expected to keep up appearances.

So I'm headed toward the park gates when I notice this hubbub around a
turreted gazebo. Maybe I should qualify "hubbub," since the dead, taking the
air in their light golfing costumes and garden-party gowns, were seldom moved
to curiosity. Nevertheless, a number had paused in their twilight stroll to inspect some new development under the pavilion on the lawn. Approaching, I
charged the spectators to make way. Then I ascended the short flight of steps
to see an uninvited iron bed supplanting the tasteful wicker furniture; and on
that rumpled, bow-footed bed lay the Fefers, man and wife, in flagrante de-
licto. Feyvush, with his pants still down around his hairy ankles, and Gitl, her
shift rucked to the neck, were holding on to each other for dear life.

As you may know, it wasn't without precedent for unlicensed mortals
to enter the Garden alive. Through the ages you'd had a smattering of over-
zealous mystics who'd arrived by dint of pious contemplation, only to expire
outright from the exertion. But to my knowledge Feyvush and Gitl were the
first to have made the trip via the agency of ecstatic intercourse. They had,
in effect, shtupped their way to heaven.

I moved forward to cover their nakedness with the quilt, though there
was really no need for modesty in the Upper Eden, where unlike in the fallen
one innocence still obtained.

"I bet you're wondering where it is that you are," was all I could think
to say.

They nodded in saucer-eyed unison. When I told them Paradise, their
eyes flicked left and right like synchronized wipers on a pair of stalled
locomobiles. Then just as I'd begun to introduce myself ("the mock-angel

Sandolphon here, although you might know me better as . . ."), an imperious voice cut me off.

"I'll take care of this—that is of course if *you* don't mind . . ."

It was the archangel Metatron, né Enoch ben Seth, celestial magistrate, commissary, archivist, and scribe. Sometimes called Prince of the Face (his was a chiseled death mask with one severely arched brow), he stood with his hands clasped before him, a thin gray eminence rocking on his heels. He was dressed like an undertaker in a sable homburg and frock coat, its seams neatly split at the shoulders to make room for an impressive set of ivory wings. Unlike my own pantomime pair, Enoch's worked. While much too dignified to actually use them, he was not above preening them in my presence, flaunting the wings as an emblem of a higher status that he seldom let me forget. He had it in for me because I served as a reminder that he too had once been a human being. Like me he'd been translated in the prime of life in an apotheosis of flames to Kingdom Come. Never mind that his assumption had included the further awards of functional feathers and an investiture as full seraph: he still couldn't forgive me for recalling his humble origins, the humanity he'd never entirely outgrown.

"Welcome to the Upper Eden," the archangel greeted the bedridden couple, "the bottommost borough of Olam ha-Ba, the World to Come." And on a cautionary note, "You realize of course that your arrival here is somewhat, how shall we say, premature?"

With the quilt hoisted to their chins, the Fefers nodded in concert—as what else should they do?

"However," continued Enoch, whose flashier handle I'd never gotten used to, which insubordination he duly noted, "accidents will happen, eh? And we must make the best of an irregular state of affairs. So"—he gave a dispassionate sniff, brushing stardust or dandruff from an otherwise immaculate sleeve—"if you'll be so good as to follow me, I'll show you to your quarters." He turned abruptly and for a moment we were nose to nose (my potato to Enoch's flutey yam), until I was forced to step aside.

Feyvush and Gitl exchanged bewildered glances, then shrugged. Clutching the quilt about their shoulders, they climbed out of bed—Feyvush stumbling over his trousers as Gitl stifled a nervous laugh—and scrambled to catch up with the peremptory angel. They trailed him down the steps of the gazebo under the boughs of the Tree of Life, in which the firefly lanterns had just become visible in the gloaming. Behind them the little knot of immortals drifted off in their interminable promenade.

"What's the hurry?" I wanted to call out to the Fefers; I wanted a chance to give them the benefit of my experience to help them get their bearings. Wasn't that the least I could do for the pair who'd provided me with such a spicy pastime over the years? Outranked, however, I had no alternative but to tag along unobtrusively.

Enoch led them down the hedge-bordered broadwalk between wrought-iron gates, their arch bearing the designation GANEYDN in gilded Hebrew characters. They crossed a cobbled avenue, ascended some steps onto a veranda where thousands of cypress rockers ticked like a chorus of pendulums. (Understand that Paradise never went in for the showier effects: none of your sardonyx portals and myriads of ministering angels wrapped in clouds of glory, no rivers of balsam, honey, and wine. There, in deference to the sensibilities of the deceased, earthly standards abide; the splendor remains human scale, though odd details from the loftier regions sometimes trickle down.)

Through mahogany doors thrown open to the balmy air, they entered the lobby of the grand hotel that serves as dormitory for the dead. Arrested by their admiration for the acres of carpets and carved furniture, the formal portraits of archons in their cedar of Lebanon frames, the chandeliers, Feyvush and Gitl lagged behind. They craned their necks to watch phoenixes smoldering like smudge pots gliding beneath the arcaded ceiling, while Enoch herded them into the elevator's brass cage. Banking on the honeymoon suite, I took the stairs and, preternaturally spry for my years, slipped in after them as Enoch was showing the couple their rooms. Here again the Fefers were stunned by sumptuous appointments: the marble-topped whatnot, the divan stuffed with angel's hair, the Brussels lace draperies framing balustraded windows open to a view of the park. From its bandstand you could hear the silvery yodel of a famous dead cantor chanting the evening prayers.

Inconspicuous behind the open door, my head wreathed in a Tiffany lamp shade, I watched the liveried cherubs parade into the bedroom, dumping their burdens of fresh apparel on the canopied bed.

"I trust you'll find these accommodations satisfactory," Enoch was saying in all insincerity, "and that your stay here will be a pleasant one." Rubbing the hands he was doubtless eager to wash of this business, he began to mince backward toward the door.

Under the quilt that mantled the Fefers, Feyvush started as from a poke in the ribs. He looked askance at his wife, who gave him a nod of encouragement, then ventured a timid, "Um, if it please your honor"—another nudge—"for how long do we supposed to stay here?"

Replied Enoch, "Why, forever of course."

Another dig with her elbow failed to move her tongue-tied husband, and Gitl spoke up herself. "You mean we ain't got to die?"

"God forbid," exhaled Enoch a touch sarcastically, his patience with their naïveté at an end: it was a scandal how the living lacked even the minimal sophistication of the dead. "Now, if there are no further questions ...?" Already backed into the corridor, he reminded them that room service was only a bellpull away, and was gone.

Closing the door (behind which my camouflaged presence made no impression at all), Feyvush turned to Gitl and asked, "Should we have gave him a tip?"

Gitl practically choked in her attempt to suppress a titter whose contagion spread to Feyvush. With a toothy grin making fish-shaped crescents of his goggle eyes, he proceeded to pinch her all over, and together they dissolved in a fit of hysterics that buckled their knees. They rolled about on the emerald carpet, then picked themselves up in breathless dishevelment, abandoning their quilt to make a beeline for the bedroom.

Oh boy, I thought, God forgive me; now they'll have it off in heaven and their aphrodisiac whoops will drive the neutered seraphim to acts of depravity. But instead of flinging themselves headlong onto the satin counterpane, they paused to inspect their laid-out wardrobe—or "trousseau" as Gitl insisted on calling it.

Donning a wing-collar shirt with boiled bosom, creased flannel trousers, and a yachting blazer with a yellow Shield of David crest, Feyvush struck rakish poses for his bride. Gitl wriggled into a silk corset cover, over which she pulled an Empire tea gown, over which an ungirded floral kimono. At the smoky-mirrored dressing table she daubed her round face with scented powders; she made raccoon's eyes of her own with an excess of shadow, scattered a shpritz of sparkles over the bonfire of her hair. Between her blown breasts she hung a sapphire the size of a gasolier.

While she carried on playing dress-up, Feyvush tugged experimentally on the bellpull, which was answered by an almost instantaneous knock at the door. Feyvush opened it to admit a tea trolley wheeled by a silent creature (pillbox hat and rudimentary wings) who'd no sooner appeared than bowed himself out. Relaxing the hand that held the waived gratuity, Feyvush fell to contemplating the pitcher and covered dish on the trolley. Pleased with her primping, Gitl rose to take the initiative. The truth was, the young Mrs. Fefer was no great shakes in the kitchen, the couple having always done their "cooking" (as Talmud puts it) in bed. Nevertheless, with a marked efficiency, she lifted the silver lid from the dish, faltering at the sight of the medicinal blue bottle underneath. Undiscouraged, however, she tipped a bit of liver brown powder from the bottle onto the plate, then mixed in a few drops of water from the crystal pitcher. There was a foaming after which the powder assumed the consistency of clotted tapioca. Gitl dipped in a finger, gave it a tentative lick, smacked her lips, and sighed. Then she dipped the finger again, placing it this time on her husband's extended tongue. Feyvush too closed his eyes and sighed, which was the signal for them both to tuck in with silver spoons. Cheeks bulging, they exulted over the succulent feast of milchik and fleishik flavors that only manna can evoke.

Having placated their bellies, you might have expected them to turn to the satisfaction of other appetites. But instead of going back to the bedroom, they went to the open windows and again looked out over the Garden. Listening to the still-warbling cantor (to be followed in that evening's program by a concert of Victor Herbert standards—though not before at least half a century'd passed on earth), they were so enraptured they forgot to embrace. Up here where perfection was the sine qua non, their felicity was complete, and they required no language or gesture to improve on what was already ideal.

Heartsick, I replaced the lamp shade and slunk out. I know it was unbecoming my rank and position to be disappointed on account of mere mortals; after all, if the Fefers had finally arrived at the logical destination of their transports, then good on them! What affair was it of mine? But now that it was time I mounted another expedition to the fallen world—babies, paupers, and skeptics were proliferating like mad—I found I lacked the necessary incentive. This is not to say I was content to stay on in Paradise, where I was quite frankly bored, but neither did a world without the Fefers have much appeal.

It didn't help that I ran into them everywhere, tipping my fez somewhat coolly whenever we crossed paths—which was often, since Feyvush and Gitl, holding hands out of habit, never tired of exploring the afterlife. At first I tried to ignore them, but idle myself, I fell into an old habit of my own. I tailed them as they joined the ranks of the perpetual strollers meandering among the topiary hedges, loitering along the gravel walks and bridle paths. I supposed that for a tourist the Garden did have its attractions: you've got your quaint scale reproductions of the industries of the upper heavens, such as a mill for grinding manna, a quarry of souls. There's a zoo that houses some of the beasts that run wild in the more ethereal realms: a three-legged "man of the mountain," a sullen behemoth with barnacled hide, a petting zoo containing a salamander hatched from a myrtle flame. But having re-adjusted my metabolism to conform to the hours of earth, I wondered when the Fefers would wake up. When would they notice, say, that the fragrant purple dusk advanced at only a glacial pace toward dawn; that the dead, however well dressed and courteous, were rather, well, stiff and cold?

In the end, though, my vigilance paid off. After what you would call about a week (though the Shabbos eve candles still burned in the celestial yeshivas), I was fortunate enough to be on hand when the couple sounded their first note of discontent. Hidden in plain sight in their suite (in the pendulum cabinet of a grandfather clock), I overheard Feyvush broach a troubling subject with his wife. Having sampled some of the outdoor prayer minyans that clustered about the velvet lawns, he complained, "It ain't true, Gitteleh, the stories that they tell about the world." Because in their discourses on the supernatural aspects of history, the dead, due to a faulty collective memory, tended to overlook the essential part of being alive: that it was natural.

Seated at her dressing table, languidly unscrolling the bobbin of her pompadour, letting it fall like carrot shavings over her forehead, Gitl ventured a complaint of her own. He should know that in the palatial bath-house she attended—it was no longer unusual for the couple to spend time apart—the ladies snubbed her.

"For them to be flesh and blood is a sin."

She was wearing a glove-silk chemise that might have formerly inspired her husband to feats of erotic derring-do. Stepping closer, Feyvush tried to reassure her, "I think they're jealous."

Gitl gave a careless shrug.

At her shoulder Feyvush continued cautiously, "Gitl, remember how"—pausing to gather courage—"remember how on the Day of Atonement we played 'blowing the shofar'?"

Gitl stopped fussing with her hair, nodded reflexively.

"Do you remember how on Purim I would part like the pages of Megillah ..."—here an intake of air in the lungs of both parties—"... your legs?"

Again an almost mechanical nod.

"Gitl," submitted Feyvush just above a whisper, "do you miss it that I don't touch you that way no more?"

She put down the tortoiseshell hairbrush, cocked her head thoughtfully, then released an arpeggio of racking sobs. "Like the breath of life I miss it!"

she wailed, as Feyvush, his own frustrations confirmed, fell to his knees and echoed her lament.

"Gitteleh," he bawled, burying his face in her lap, "ain't nobody fency yentzing in Kingdom Come!" Then lifting his head to blow his nose on a brocaded shirtsleeve, drying his eyes with same, he hesitantly offered, "Maybe we could try to go home . . ."

"Hallelujah!"

This was me bursting forth from the clock to congratulate them on a bold resolution. "Now you're talking!" I assured them. "Of course it won't be easy; into the Garden you got without a dispensation but without a dispensation they won't never let you leave . . ." Then I observed how the Fefers, not yet sufficiently jaded from their stay in heaven, were taken aback. Having leapt to their feet, they'd begun to slide away from me along the paneled walls, which was understandable: for despite my natty attire, my features had become somewhat crepe-hung over the ages, my rheumy eyes tending toward the hyacinth red.

Recalling the introduction I never completed upon their arrival, I started over. "Allow me to present myself: the prophet Elijah, at your service. You would recognize me better in the rags I wear in the world." And as they still appeared dubious, Gitl smearing her already runny mascara as if in an effort to wipe me from her eye, I entreated them to relax: "You can trust me." I explained that I wanted to help them get back to where they belonged.

This at least had the effect of halting their retreat, which in turn called my bluff.

"You should understand," I began to equivocate, "there ain't much I can do personally. Sure, I'm licensed to usher souls from downstairs to up, but regarding vicey-versey I got no jurisdiction, my hands are tied. And from here to there you don't measure the distance in miles but years, so don't even think about starting the journey on your own . . ."

At that point Gitl, making chins (their ambrosial diet had endowed her with several extra), planted an elbow in Feyvush's ribs. He coughed once before speaking. "If it please your honor"—his listless tone not half so respectful as he'd been with Enoch—"what is it exactly you meaning to do?"

I felt a foolish grin spreading like eczema across my face. "What I have in mind . . . ," I announced on a note of confidence that instantly fell flat, because I didn't really have a clue. Rallying nonetheless, I voiced my determination to intercede with the archangel Metatron on the couple's behalf.

But who was I kidding? That stickler for the letter of the Law, he wouldn't have done me a favor if his immortality depended on it. Still, a promise was a promise, so I sought out his high-and-mightiness in his apartments in the dignitaries' wing of the hotel. (My own were among the cottages of the superannuated cherubim.)

Addressing him by his given name, I'm straightaway off on the wrong foot.

"Sorry . . . I mean Metatron, Prince of the Face (such a face!), Lesser Lord of the Seventy Names, and so forth," I said, attempting to smooth his ruffled pride. It seemed that Enoch had never gotten over the treatment attending his translation to heaven, when the hosts mockingly claimed they could smell one of woman born from parasangs away. "Anyhow"—putting my foot in it deeper—"they had a nice holiday, the Fefers, but they would like already to go back where they came."

Seated behind the captain's desk in his office sipping a demitasse with uplifted pinky, his back to a wall of framed citations and awards, the archangel assumed an expression of puzzled innocence. Did I have to spell it out?

"You know, like home."

"Home?" inquired Enoch as if butter wouldn't melt on his unctuous tongue. "Why, this is their home for all eternity."

Apparently I wasn't going to be invited to sit down. "But they ain't happy here," I persisted.

"Not happy in Paradise?" Plunking down his cup and saucer as if the concept was unheard of.

"It's possible," I allowed a bit too emphatically. Enoch clucked his tongue, which provoked me to state the obvious. "Lookit, they ain't dead yet."

"A mere technicality," pooh-poohed the archangel. "Besides, for those who've dwelt in Abraham's Bosom, the earth should no longer hold any real attraction."

Although I was more or less living proof to the contrary, rather than risk antagonizing him again, I kept mum on that subject. Instead: "Have a heart," I appealed to him. "You were alive when you came here . . ." Which didn't sound the way I meant it to. "Didn't you ever want to go back?"

"Back?" Enoch was incredulous. "Back to what, making shoes?"

That he'd lowered his guard enough to mention his mortal profession made me think I saw an angle. "Feyvush is a cobbler," I humbly submitted.

"Then he's well out of it." The seraph stressed the point by raising his arched brow even higher, creating ripples that spoiled the symmetry of his widow's peak. "Besides, when I stitched leather, it was as if I fastened the world above to the world below."

"But don't you see," I pleaded, the tassel of my fez dancing like a spider before my eyes till I slapped it away, "that's what it was like when Feyvush would yentz with his bride . . ." This was definitely not the tack to have taken.

"Like I said, he's better off," snapped Enoch, rising abruptly from his swivel chair to spread his magnificent wings. "And since when is any of this *your* business?"

The conversation closed, I turned to go, muttering something about how I guessed I was just a sentimental fool.

"Elijah . . . ," the angel called my name after a fashion guaranteed to inspire maximum guilt.

"Sandolphon," I corrected him under my breath.

". . . I think it's time you tended to your terrestrial errands."

"Funny," I replied in an insipid singsong, "I was thinking the same thing."

You'll say I should have left well enough alone, and maybe you're right. After all, without my meddling the Fefers would still be in heaven and I pursuing my charitable rounds on earth—instead of sentenced for my delinquency to stand here at this crossroads directing traffic, pointing the pious toward the gates, the wicked in the other direction, not unlike (to my everlasting shame) that Nazi doctor on the railroad platform during the last apocalypse. But who'd have thought that, with my commendable record of good works, I wasn't entitled to a single trespass?

When I offered the Fefers my plan, Gitl elbowed Feyvush, then interrupted his diffident "If it please your honor—" to challenge me herself: "What for do you want to help us?"

"Because"—since my audience with the archangel I'd developed a ready answer—"I can't stand to see nobody downhearted in Paradise. This is my curse, that such rachmones, such compassion I got, I can't stand it to see nobody downhearted anywhere." Which was true enough. It was an attitude that kept me constantly at odds with the angelic orders, with Enoch and Raziel and Death (between whom and myself there was a history of feuding) and the rest of that cold-blooded crew. It was my age-old humanitarian impulse that compelled me to come to the aid of the Fefers, right? and not just a selfish desire to see them at their shtupping again.

Departing the hotel, we moved through whatever pockets of darkness the unending dusk provided—hard to find in a park whose every corner was illuminated by menorahs and fairy lights. Dressed for traveling (Feyvush in an ulster and fore-and-aft cap, Gitl in automobile cape and sensible shoes), they were irked with me, my charges, for making them leave behind a pair of overstuffed Gladstone bags. Their aggravation signified an ambivalence that, in my haste to get started, I chose to ignore, and looking back I confess I might have been a little pushy. Anyway, in order not to call attention to ourselves (small danger among the indifferent immortals), I pretended I was conducting yet another couple of greenhorns on a sightseeing tour of the Garden.

"Here you got your rose trellis made out of what's left of Jacob's Ladder, and over there, that scrawny thing propped on a crutch, that's the Etz ha-Daat, the Tree of Knowledge . . ."

When I was sure no one was looking, I hauled the Fefers behind me into the shadows beneath the bloated roots of the Tree of Life. From a hanger in their midst I removed my universal luftmensch outfit—watch cap, galoshes, and patched overcoat—which I quick-changed into after discarding my Sandolphon duds. Then I led the fugitives into a narrow cavern that snaked its way under the Tree trunk, fetching up at the rust-cankered door of a dumbwaiter.

I'd discovered it some time ago while looking for an easier passage to earth. My ordination as honorary angel, while retarding the aging process, had not, as you know, halted it entirely; so I was in need of a less strenuous means of descent than was afforded by the branches of the Tree of Life. An antique device left over from the days when the Lord still frequented the Garden to send the odd miracle below, the dumbwaiter was just the thing. It was a sturdy enough contraption that, notwithstanding the sponginess of its wooden cabinet and the agonizing groan of its cables, had endured the test of time.

The problem was that the dumbwaiter's compactness was not intended to accommodate three people. A meager, collapsible old man, I'd always found it sufficiently roomy; but while the Fefers were not large, Gitl had never been exactly svelte, and both of them had put on weight during their "honeymoon." Nevertheless, making a virtue of necessity, they folded themselves into a tandem pair of Ss and allowed me to stuff them into the tight compartment. This must have been awkward for them at first, since they hadn't held each other in a while, but as I wedged myself into the box behind them and started to lower us down the long shaft, Feyvush and Gitl began to generate a sultry heat.

They ceased their griping about cramped quarters and began to make purring noises of a type that brought tears to my eyes. I felt an excitement beyond that which accrued from our gathering speed, as the tug of gravity accelerated the dumbwaiter's downward progress. The cable sang as it slipped through my blistering fingers. Then came the part where our stomachs were in our throats and we seemed to be in a bottomless free fall, the dizzy, protracted prelude to the earthshaking clatter of our landing. The crash must have alerted the cooks in the basement kitchen of Ratner's Dairy Restaurant to our arrival; because, when I slid open the door, there they were: a surly lot in soiled aprons and mushroom hats, looking scornfully at the pretzel the Fefers had made of themselves. I appeased them as always with a jar of fresh manna, an ingredient (scarce in latter-day New York) they'd come to regard as indispensable for their heavenly blintzes.

If the plummeting claustrophobia of the dumbwaiter, to say nothing of its bumpy landing, hadn't sufficiently disoriented my charges, then the shrill Sunday brunch crowd I steered them through would have finished the job. I hustled them without fanfare out the revolving door into a bitter blast of winter barreling up Delancey Street from the river.

"Welcome home!" I piped, though the neighborhood bore small resemblance to the one they'd left better than three-quarters of a century ago. The truck horses and trolleys had been replaced by a metallic current of low-slung vehicles squealing and farting in sluggish procession; the pushcarts and garment emporia had given way to discount houses full of coruscating gadgetry, percussive music shuddering their plate-glass windows. Old buildings, if they weren't boarded up or reduced altogether to rubble, had new facades, as tacky as hoopskirts on dowagers. In the distance there were towers, their tops obscured by clouds like tent poles under snow-heavy canvas.

Myself, I'd grown accustomed to dramatic changes during my travels back and forth. Besides, I made a point of keeping abreast of things, pumping the recently departed for news of the earth, lest returning be too great a jolt to my system. But the Fefers, though they'd demonstrated a tolerance for shock in the past, seemed beyond perplexity now, having entered a condition of outright fear.

Gitl was in back of her husband, trying to straighten his crimped spine with her knee, so that he seemed to speak with her voice when she asked, "What happened to the Jews?" Because it was true that, while the complexions of the passersby ran the spectrum from olive to saffron to lobster pink, there were few you could've identified as distinctly yid.

I shrugged. "Westchester, New Rochelle, Englewood, the Five Towns they went, but for delicatessen they come back to Delancey on Sundays." Then I grinned through my remaining teeth and made a show of protesting, "No need to thank me," though who had bothered? I shook their hands, which were as limp as fins. "Well, good-bye and good luck, I got things to do . . ."

I had urgent business to attend to, didn't I?—brisses, famines, false prophets in need of comeuppance. All right, so "urgent" was an exaggeration. Also, I was aware that the ills of the century had multiplied beyond anything my penny-ante philanthropies could hope to fix. But I couldn't stand being a party to Feyvush and Gitl's five-alarm disappointment. This wasn't the world they knew; tahkeh, it wasn't even the half of what they didn't know, and I preferred not to stick around for the heartache of their getting acquainted. I didn't want to be there when they learned, for instance, that Jews had vanished in prodigious numbers from more places on the face of the planet than the Lower East Side. I didn't want to be there when they discovered what else had gone out of the world in their absence, and I didn't want to admit I made a mistake in bringing them back.

Still, I wouldn't send them away empty-handed. I gave them a pocketful of heaven gelt—that is, leaves from the Etz ha-Chaim, the Tree of Life, that passed for currency in certain neighborhood pawnshops; I told them the shops where you got the best rate of exchange. The most they could muster by way of gratitude, however, was a perfunctory nod. When they slouched off toward the Bowery, drawing stares in their period gear, I thought of Adam and Eve leaving the Garden at the behest of the angel with the flaming sword.

I aimed my own steps in the direction of the good deeds whose abandonment could throw the whole cosmic scheme out of joint. Then, conceding there was no need to kid myself, it was already out of joint, I turned around. Virtually invisible in my guise as one more homeless old crock among a multitude of others, I followed the Fefers. I entered the shop behind them, where a pawnbroker in a crumpled skullcap greeted them satirically: "Reb ben Vinkl, I presume!" (This in reference to Feyvush's outdated apparel and the beard that had grown rank on his reentering the earth's atmosphere.) But when he saw the color of the couple's scrip, he became more respectful, even kicking in some coats of recent vintage to reduce the Fefers' anachronistic mien.

There was no law that said Feyvush and Gitl had to remain in the old ghetto neighborhood. Owing to my foresight they now had a nest egg; they could move to, say, the Upper West Side, someplace where Jews were thicker on the ground. So why did they insist on beating a path through the shrieking winds back to Orchard Street, via a scenic route that took them past gutted synagogues, shtiblekh with their phantom congregants sandwiched between the bodegas and Chinese takeouts, the tallis shops manned by ancients looking out as from an abyss of years? Answer: having found the familiar strange enough, thank you, they might go farther and fare even worse.

As luck (if that's the right word) would have it, there was a flat available in the very same building they'd vacated a decades-long week ago. For all they knew it was the same paltry top-floor apartment with the same sticks of furniture: the sofa with its cushions like sinkholes, the crippled wing chair, the kitchen table, the iron bed; not that decor would have meant much to Feyvush and Gitl, who didn't look to be in a nostalgic mood. Hugging myself against the cold on the fire escape, I watched them wander from room to room until the windows fogged. Then someone rubbed a circle in a cloudy pane and I ducked out of sight below the ledge. But I could see them nonetheless, it was a talent I had: I could see them as clearly in my mind as with my eyes, peering out into a street beyond which there was no manicured pleasure garden, no Tree.

They went out only once. Despite having paid a deposit and the first month's rent, they still had ample funds; they might have celebrated. But instead they returned with only the barest essentials—some black bread and farfel, a shank of gristly soup meat, a greasy sack of knishes from the quarter's one surviving knisherie. Confounded by the gas range that had replaced her old coal-burning cookstove, Gitl threw up her hands. Feyvush hunched his shoulders: who had any appetite? Then they stared out the window again, past icicles like a dropped portcullis of fangs, toward a billboard atop the adjacent building. The billboard, which featured a man and woman lounging nearly naked on a beach, advertised an airline that offered to fly you nonstop to paradise.

Hunkered below the window ledge, I heard what I couldn't hear just like I saw what I couldn't see—Feyvush saying as if to himself, "Was it a dream?" Gitl replying with rancor, "Dreams are for goyim."

At some point one of them—I don't remember which—went into the bedroom and sat on the bed. He or she was followed soon after by the other, though neither appeared conscious of occupying the same space; neither thought to remove their heavy coats. The sag of the mattress, however, caused them to slide into contact with one another, and at first touch the Fefers combusted like dry kindling. They flared into a desperate embrace, shucking garments, Gitl pulling at her husband's suspenders as if drawing a

bowstring. Feyvush ripped open Gitl's blouse the way Cossacks part a curtain to catch a Jew; he spread her thighs as if wrenching apart the jaws of a
trap. Having torn away their clothes, it seemed they intended to peel back
each other's flesh. They marked cheeks and throats with bared talons, twisting themselves into tortured positions as if each were attempting to put on
the other's skin—as if the husband must climb through the body of his wife,
and vice versa, in order to get back to what they'd lost.

That's how they did it, fastened to each other in what looked like a mutual punishment—hips battering hips, mouths spitting words refined of all
affection. When they were done, they fell apart, sweating and bruised. They
took in the stark furnishings of their cold-water flat: the table barren of the
fabric flowers that once filled the place with perpetual spring, the window
overlooking a street of strangers and dirty snow. Then they went at it again
hammer and tongs.

I couldn't watch anymore; then God help me, I couldn't keep from watching. When the windows were steamed, I took the stairs to the roof, rime
clinging to my lashes and beard, and squinted through a murky skylight like
a sheet of green ice. When they were unobservable from any vantage, I saw
them with an inner eye far clearer than my watery tom-peepers could focus.
I let my good works slide, because who needed second sight to know that the
world had gone already to hell in a phylactery bag? While my bones became
brittle with winter and the bread and knishes went stale, and the soup meat
grew mold and was nibbled at by mice, I kept on watching the Fefers.

Sometimes I saw them observing each other, with undisguised contempt. They both shed the souvenir pounds they'd brought back from eternity. Gone was Gitl's generous figure, her unkempt hair veiling her pallid
face like a bloody rag. Her ribs showed beneath breasts as baggy as punc-
tured meal sacks, and her freckles were indistinguishable from the pimples
populating her brow. Feyvush, always slight, was nine-tenths a cadaver, his
eyes in their hunger fairly drooling onto his hollow cheeks. His sunken
chest, where it wasn't obscured by matted fur, revealed a frieze of scarlet
hieroglyphs etched by his wife's fingernails. So wasted were they now that,
when they coupled, their fevered bones chuckled like matches in a box.
Between bouts they covered their nakedness with overcoats and went to
the window, though not necessarily together. They rubbed circles, looked
at the billboard with its vibrant twosome disporting under a tropical sun;
then satisfied they were no nearer the place where they hoped to arrive,
Feyvush or Gitl returned to bed.

Nu, so what would you have had me to do? Sure, I was the great kib-bitzer in the affairs of others; but having already violated divine law by helping them escape from der emeser velt, the so-called true world, was I now to add insult to injury by delivering them from the false? Can truth and deception be swapped as easily as shmattes for fancy dress? Give me a break, the damage was done; human beings were not anyway intended to rise above their stations. The Fefers would never get out of this life again, at least not alive.

So I remained a captive witness to their savage heat. I watched them doing with an unholy vengeance what I never found the time for in my own sanctimonious youth—when I was too busy serving as a mighty mouthpiece for the still small voice that had since become all but inaudible. I watched the mortals in their heedless ride toward an elusive glory, and aroused by the driven cruelty of their passion, achieved an erection: my first full engorge-ment since the days before the destruction of the Temple, when a maiden once lifted her tunic and I turned away. At the peak of my excitement I tore open the crotch of my trousers, releasing myself from a choked confinement, and spat my seed in a peashooter trajectory over Orchard Street. When I was finished, I allowed my wilted member to rest on the frigid railing of the fire escape, to which it stuck. Endeavoring to pull it free, I let loose a pitiable howl: I howled for the exquisite pain that mocked my terminal inability to die, and I howled for my loneliness. Then I stuffed my bloody putz back in my pants and looked toward the window, afraid I'd alerted the Fefers to my spying. But the Fefers, as it turned out, were well beyond earshot.

I raised the window and climbed over the sill, muffling my nose with a fingerless mitten against the smell, and shuffled forward to inspect their remains. So hopelessly entangled were the pair of them, however, that it was hard at first to distinguish husband from wife. Of course, there was no mistaking Feyvush's crown of tufted wool for Gitl's tattered red standard, his beak for her button nose, but so twined were their gory limbs that they defied a precise designation of what belonged to whom. Nor did their fused loins admit to which particular set of bones belonged the organ that united them both.

My task was as always to separate spirit from flesh, to extricate their immortal souls, which after a quick purge in the fires of Gehenna (no more than a millennia or two) would be as good as new. The problem was that, given the intricate knot they'd made of themselves, what was true of their bodies was true as well of their souls: I couldn't tell where Gitl's left off and her husband's began. It took me a while to figure it out but ultimately I located the trouble; then the solution went some distance toward explaining their lifelong predicament. For the Fefers had been one of those rare cases where a couple shares two halves of a solitary soul. Theirs had indeed been a marriage made in heaven such as you don't see much anymore, the kind of match that might lead you to believe God Himself had a hand in it—that is, if you didn't already know He'd gotten out of the matchmaking racket long ago.

Romance

I.

The tale is told in my family of my mother's father, Eli Goldfogle, who was engaged at birth to his future wife, Esther, in the Old Country, what the immigrants called "the other side." Nobody believes the story; the married couple themselves could not have known the whole of it, which is to say they were in no position to pass it along to their children, who passed it on to me. But ours is a family of disappointed dreamers, many of whom, like myself, live alone, and it's our penance to carry such tales. This one begins at the end of the last century in the Byelorussian village of Utsk, when arranged marriages were à la mode. It was a mitzvah, a good deed, and an act of faith that families should pledge to each other, over honey cakes and brandy, infants born at approximately the same time.

Since the Goldfogles and Esther's parents—call them the Bluesteins, though nobody used surnames in those days; since the Goldfogles and the Bluesteins inhabited separate villages several rolling versts apart, Eli and his pledged one, his mash-kin, managed to grow up without ever meeting. There had of course been occasions when they might have, market days and celebrations when the communities converged. But while they were aware of a mutual fate, which they accepted the way the young accept their mortality, never really believing they will die, neither child was especially curious about the other. Each had more pressing interests, and as the marriage contract was an accomplished fact, what after all did it have to do with either of them?

Young Eli was in any case engaged in his studies. While he wasn't counted among the prodigies—he couldn't perform, like some, those dazzling feats of memory whose fame in the Pale of Settlement were equal to virtuosity on the violin—he was nonetheless a fervent scholar. From his tenderest years it had been the boy's ambition to become a Talmud khochem, "an uprooter of mountains," like the wise men who sat in their bearded serenity by the

synagogue's eastern wall. Like them he would devote himself to the Five
Books and their commentaries, and to a total adherence to the precepts
ordained therein. "Torah min hashamayim, the Torah is from heaven;
hashamayim min Torah, heaven is from the Torah." This was Eli's watchword, which he intoned with an earnestness that caused his unlettered father, Moishe the Pit (so called for his work in a quarry or his bottomless
appetite, take your pick), to scratch his head.

What he lacked in breadth of intellect, Eli made up for with his zeal and
fidelity to the letter of the Law. And if it didn't appear that, by such applica-
tion, he would ascend to the ranks of the saints, so be it; Eli had small patience with saints, who seemed to him in their mystical transports a largely
irresponsible lot. Under the benevolent eye of the sage Rabbi Ben Bag Bag in
the dilapidated study house, he had himself been tempted, through chanting
the words of certain texts, to fly clear of the rotting rooftops of his village.
But since such flights were not compatible with the social contract implicit
in his prayers, Eli, however reluctantly, stuck close to home.

His industry notwithstanding, Eli grew up ramrod straight, his cheek-
bones high and pronounced, with the fine hawkish nose and sable hair that
distinguished him from his rough-hewn tribe. His eyes, despite their severity, were large and doe-soft, dark as twin inkwells, which could weep—this
was his unspoken fancy—words of Holy Writ.

"Your son," the village marriage broker would sigh to Eli's mother, la-
menting a match already made, "a Daniel, a regular prince."

In her neighboring hamlet of Putsk, Esther Bluestein, Eli's betrothed,
had a bookish bent of her own. But since girls could not attend cheder, her
childhood reading had been necessarily confined to collections of Yiddish
proverbs for women, and to the fairy tales contained in the *Maaseh*, *Shmuel*,
and *Bovo* books. The last of these, Esther's favorite, recounted the implau-
sible adventures of the daring Prince Bovo, who courted the ladies even as
he confused his enemies with magic. As she grew older, Esther purchased
from itinerant book peddlers romances of historical thunder by the popular
author N. M. Shaikevitch, whose pen name was "Shomer." In them, Jewish
sons and daughters defied hypocrisy and overcame fanatical constraints to
seek their destinies in the world at large. Reading the books in fevered se-
crecy, Esther would later discard them, lest she be caught and accused of a
frivolous self-indulgence.

She was a pretty girl, Esther, small-bosomed and stately, with a waist that
might have been cinched by a velvet choker. She had olive skin, onyx eyes,

sparrow hands, cocoa brown hair that, when freed of its kerchief, floated in billows like the grain of finished mahogany. As a consequence Esther was not without her portion of vanity, which declared itself whenever she polished the solitary heirloom of her mama's samovar. Rubbing hard as if to release the burnished image of herself trapped in brass, she would step back admiringly.

"It's a maideleh fit for a hero," she'd say.

It was a time of great stirrings among the Jews of the Russian Pale; there was much talk of enlightenment, of impending revolution that would throw off for good and all the yoke of the czar. A new kind of Jewish hero was abroad in the land, not so much warrior as poet and idealist, young firebrands sacrificing themselves on the altar of their beliefs and getting exiled to Siberia by the trainload. That they never seemed to pass through Putsk, these heroes, didn't mean the village wasn't alert to their legends; and no one was more alert than Esther, who imagined that her star was crossed with one of these. No matter that her future was already fixed to that of her plighted husband, whose reputation for a drudge had preceded him to her parents' door. Still, Esther could dream, couldn't she? She could picture his handsome countenance next to hers in the cloudy samovar, his scholar's disguise laid bare to reveal the bold revolutionist. Then she would wish their wedding delayed a little longer, that his image might not yet have to come clear.

As it happened, the proposed date of the Goldfogle–Bluestein alliance was moved forward, due to its coinciding with Eli's call to appear at the induction center in Berditchev. There his eligibility for immediate conscription into the army of the czar would be reviewed. That he'd be taken was a foregone conclusion, since nothing short of a bribe far beyond the humble resources of Moishe the Pit could secure his deferment. Moreover, it was generally understood that the Russian draft, quite nearly a life sentence, spelled a virtual death sentence for a Jewish lad. If he didn't perish from abuse or exposure, he would suffer at the very least a spiritual death by separation from the community of Israel. This was especially true in the case of a boy such as Eli, who drew his very sustenance from the holy books.

Thus it was decided that the family Goldfogle would employ a strategy taken by so many in those days: they would scrape together the funds to pack their scholar off to America. The Utskers might be relied on for contributions, since, his zealotry having made Eli something of a local spoilsport, most would be eager to see him go. It was further decided that the prearranged nuptials would take place as planned, prior to Eli's departure.

That way, no longer a bachelor, he would be proof against the temptations for which America was famous, temptations he already considered himself a bulwark against. Once established in the Golden Land, he could purchase the shiffs-carte for his wife's passage over; and later on, when he became a millionaire, a relatively predictable stage in an immigrant's progress, he would send for the rest.

The wedding canopy had been erected in the courtyard behind the Bluesteins' ancestral hovel in their ditch-side village, to which half of Eli's own village had traveled for the event. Consisting of a prayer shawl that had once belonged to an illustrious ancestor, the canopy would be passed on to Eli after his nuptials. He'd often coveted it, convinced it had properties that rendered one impervious to sin. But as he stood beneath it on that soft night in the month of Nisan, surrounded by a mob of wedding guests holding candles, Eli took small comfort in the bequest.

Although the marriage had always loomed on his horizon, he'd given little thought to it until now. What, frankly, had he given thought to other than the books in Rabbi Ben Bag Bag's study house, which contained worlds? Granted, Eli had no special taste for the more fanciful portions of Torah, but if he'd ever yearned for exotic places, he had only to read descriptions of the flora and fauna of paradise. Should he feel the urge to travel, he read about the patriarchs, who'd done enough wandering to last the Jews for all time. Hadn't Joseph, torn from his father's house and thrust into alien lands, made such dramas redundant for future generations? But here he was on the eve of departing the Pale forever, a prospect that had thus far filled him only with dread—until tonight, when the dread was nudged aside by a secret thrill. Undignified though it was to be roused by circumstances outside scripture, Eli found himself looking forward to the journey; the wedding was an awkward formality he had to suffer through before taking flight.

As his old teacher and rabbi shpritzed the seven benedictions in his face, Eli could scarcely contain his impatience. He chafed in the top hat and stiff white kittl, which he had reason to think made him look like an ornamental saltcellar. It didn't help that he was center stage in an unfamiliar setting, at a spectacle catered by a wealthy merchant for his own greater glory, where one and all, be they relations or beggars, had been invited to witness the banns of a scholar and a reputed beauty—seeing whom Eli would believe. But there was something else that troubled him beyond the vulgarity, though he'd known all his life this night must come. After all, it was written, "It is the duty of every man to take to himself a wife, in order to fulfill the precept of propagation." Indeed, a Jew without a wife, without children, was not a Jew in the eyes of the community. Although wasn't it also written, "When one is deeply engrossed in the study of Torah, and is afraid that marriage may interfere with his studies, he may delay marrying, provided of course he is not lustful"? Too late did it occur to Eli that the wedding should have been postponed.

To try and filter out the proceedings, he mustered his powers of concentration to rehearse the midrash he intended to deliver at the wedding feast. In that way he managed to ignore the entrance of the bride and the ritual raising and lowering of her veil—which hadn't in fact revealed very much, since Esther, according to tradition, was blindfolded. She was furthermore positively giddy, enjoying herself hugely as her attendants led her in circles around her betrothed. For as long as she couldn't see anything anyway, she was free to erect a palace in the goat-reeking courtyard, to make a prince of the groom; or, forgetting the groom, imagine the wild yeshiva student from Shomer's *Hershele Hotspur* leaping over the trestle tables on horseback to steal the bride away. Then the scarf was removed from her eyes and Esther peered through layers of lace at the bridegroom, who might as well have been a figure behind a waterfall.

When he placed the ring on her finger, Eli had occasion to note its tapered slenderness, thinking, "He who gazes at even the small finger of a woman in order to enjoy its sight commits a sin." He might have quibbled as to whether he'd actually enjoyed the sight, from which he was in any case distracted by the rabbi's pronouncement: "Behold, thou art consecrated according to the Law of Moses and Israel." Eli squashed the goblet like an offensive bug.

At the banquet, though bride and groom sat side by side, neither found cause to turn toward the other. Flanked by their respective families, who talked animatedly over them to their counterparts-in-law, Eli and Esther kept their eyes fixed on the entertainment. The wealthy merchant, rather than embarrass the poor with overmuch prodigality, had provided well within his means. Beet soup and groats, which the merchant intimated were a concession to the toothless rabbi, comprised the main courses, chased by a paint-thinning kvass. The hired jester, too arthritic to climb on the table, advertised his sidelines—love philtres and abortifacients—even as he performed his shtik. He told a medley of tasteless jokes ("It's the wedding night and the newlyweds are packing their bags for the honeymoon, while the machetonim, the in-laws, they're listening through the wall. 'Let me sit on it,' says the bride . . .'' and so forth), after which he broke into sentimental song. The songs were accompanied by a skeleton orchestra of gypsy klezmorim: shrill horn, hammered dulcimer, a fiddle that set one's teeth on edge, a double bass that the musician seemed to be trying to saw in half.

It was a circus, thought Eli, arranged for his personal humiliation, whereas Esther was thankful for any diversion that put off a little longer the reckoning between husband and wife. Having summoned a composure befitting her newly elevated station, she received the blessings of her maiden friends; she nodded with regal approval at the festivities, clapping in time to the dancers—the men with men, women with women, mother-in-law in mock quarrel with mother-in-law, the old bubbeh swaying with a loaf of challah bread. Nor was she disappointed that the groom had foregone the custom of offering her an end of his handkerchief, following which they'd have been expected to dance a mitzvah tantz face-to-face.

During a lull between songs Eli rose to make his speech. Not wanting to invite more attention to himself than was necessary, he nevertheless felt obliged to lend some sanctity to an otherwise pagan affair. "If a man sets out to take a wife . . . ," he muttered, then cleared his throat and repeated the phrase like a call to arms. This was the passage from Deuteronomy to which Rabbi Simeon had applied a famous analogue, concerning a man who seeks something he's lost. But no sooner had Eli launched into Simeon's sermon than the wedding party applauded, the band struck up a quadrille, and everyone demanded he kiss the bride. Next to him Esther closed her eyes, but other than a zephyrlike stirring at the fringes of her still unlifted veil, she felt nothing at all. Then "Mazel tov!" and the pair of them were hustled from the courtyard, Eli prompting laughter with his protests that this wasn't Jewish; it was some goyishe sacrifice he'd been lured into unawares.

Left alone in the dark "bridal chamber," which was merely the close little room Esther shared with her younger sisters (chased out for the night), Eli was ashamed for his outburst. Determined to steel himself for what lay ahead, he tried to calm his stampeding heart, to curb his fingers from fanning the pages of imaginary books. In the dirty window the tilted ewer of a yellow moon spilled light onto the quilted bed, which Eli gazed at like a country spied from the gondola of a balloon. Waiting for Esther, who'd retired behind a gunny-cloth curtain, he reviewed what Rabbi Ben Bag Bag—Eli could feel the old man's whistling exhalations in his ear—had instructed him to think of as his duty. It was a distasteful business, but he believed himself more or less equal to the task. He was aware that some misguided souls were said to take delight in it, as it was written: "Since the destruction of the Temple, sexual pleasure was taken from those who obey Torah and given to those who transgress it." But Eli didn't think himself in any danger of succumbing to pleasure.

Naked behind the curtain for the instant after she'd shed the brittle silk dress (which both her mother and mine were also married in), Esther felt a warm flickering begin in her belly and travel to her extremities. Hurriedly she pulled on her muslin gown as if pouring water to douse a flame. She presented herself in shadows to the groom, whose silhouette in its unremoved top hat resembled a trembling beaker on the boil. If unstoppered, would he evaporate or explode? As she waited for him to speak—they'd yet to exchange a word all evening—Esther admitted to herself that he was perhaps no Prince Bovo, no valiant Yossel from Shomer's *The Convicted*, who fights a duel with the gentile count that made advances toward his sweetheart. But surely this Eli Goldfogle was *someone*, and Esther bit her lip in anticipation of who he might be.

However, as generosity had its limits, she presently judged his time to be up, satisfied that his silence had confirmed his nonentity. Taking the initiative, Esther was astonished that her first words to her husband should be a lie.

"I'm unclean."

"Ah," replied Eli, as if she'd imparted an interesting conversational tidbit rather than confessed herself ineligible for ritual immersion. The *Shulchan Arukh* was unequivocal on this point: One must never sleep with one's wife during her menstrual flow, as it was written: "The husband in that period should not touch her even with his little finger . . ." With heartfelt gratitude for his eleventh-hour reprieve from intimacy, Eli announced, "Then I'll sleep on the floor."

From what he knew of the mysteries of the female body, he pictured a bloody tide, a red sea upon which the Ark itself might have foundered. Happy to have escaped inundation, Eli pulled down the gunny curtain and made a pallet at the foot of the bed. He curled up like a weary castaway and praised God for making his marriage the minor interruption it had so far proved to be.

At dawn, when the sexton rattled his clapper to call the men to prayer, Eli rose, having slept not a wink. He gathered the stiff kittl about him so that its rustlings wouldn't awaken his bride, who lay with the covers pulled over her head. Shrugging, he stepped out into the grease-fetid hovel, where the men in their boots and patched caftans were already abroad. A rowdy bunch of mostly blacksmiths and beekeepers, Eli's in-laws greeted him with rough embraces and swept him off to shul. Along the way their ranks, and high spirits, were swelled by Eli's own father and uncles, mostly smugglers, who'd stayed the night at a local inn. They joked and made rude references to the marriage bed, the rudest emanating from Moishe the Pit himself, who made amends with his hardihood for his son's bloodless reticence. Services over, all returned to the Bluestein abode for a breakfast of pot cheese and blintzes, a standard fare for weddings and funeral wakes alike. It was served by bustling wives, one of whom, supposed Eli, his swimming head bent toward the table, belonged to him.

Afterward, while the machetonim made their noisy farewells, Eli climbed onboard the wagon to wait for his father, holding his breath lest someone should call him back. Although it was understood that he would return home immediately to start preparing for his journey overseas, he couldn't believe they'd allow him to make such a clean getaway. You might almost think Esther's family were as glad to be rid of him as he was to go. The caravan pulled into the ruts of the unpaved street, and Eli gave a look over his shoulder at a row of waving women like kerchiefed pears, again idly wondering which was his.

When they were gone, Esther finally came out of her room. All morning long, resisting her mother's pleading, she'd lain in bed imagining what might have been, but now she emerged as if nothing had happened. Her mama scolded her roundly and thanked God that the groom had not made a scandal by demanding she appear.

The next few days were filled with the flurry of arrangements surrounding Eli's departure. For the scholar himself, who'd made a curious peace with leaving his village, if not the entire continent of Europe, the preparations were simple: he had only to select what books to take along. Under his old rabbi's tutelage he learned the traveler's benedictions, which to say after having passed thirty cubits, which before traveling the first parasang, and so forth. It wasn't until the end of the week, when he was placed in the bed of his father's wagon and buried under a bale of beaver pelts, that Eli had doubts and, once more sensing the magnitude of the journey he was about to undertake, grew afraid.

He was spirited across the border by his father and his uncle Pishke, neither of whom (along with the rest of his family) would Eli ever see again.

Outside Bialystok he was disinterred and consigned to a good-natured peasant, in whose rattletrap droshky he traveled by easy stages to Poznan, thence on to Hamburg by train. There, thanks to the forged passport and papers that were the speciality of the Utsker scribe, the red tape was kept to a minimum. The swindling ticket agents, the doctors' prods, a rat-infested wharf-side quarantine, all took their turns at him, but insulated against torment and loneliness by his devotions, Eli endured. And one breezy afternoon in his eighteenth year, he found himself standing at the rusty taffrail of the S.S. *Gravenhage*, bound for the port of New York.

Watching the shoreline sink in the distance under an emerald swell, he asked aloud, "Ribbono Shel-Oylem, if it pleases You, what have I done?" and straightaway ducked into *The Ethics of the Fathers*. He recited his psalms with the intensity that some claimed would mend the rift between heaven and earth, though Eli had always disdained such notions. Hadn't Maimonides in his *Guide* inveighed against the illogic of viewing prayers as "holy aphrodisiacs," the chanting of which would hasten the birth of Messiah? They should be uttered, such prayers, with measured breathing, of the type Eli associated with that of the girl back home in the so-called bridal chamber.

But this was the stuff of forbidden texts, which made otherwise serious scholars into crackpots and would-be saints—the kind who might see, in place of, say, the rolling green ocean, Satan's own rippling cloak, its folds concealing biblical monsters and frogs sixty houses high. To allay such phantasms, Eli increased the fervor of his spiritual exercises; he fasted as well, which wasn't difficult given the weevil-ridden kasha served in steerage from a common pot. In his hunger he remembered the tale of Rabbi Fertig, called the Armrest of HaShem—how he was nourished by words of Torah, which, as he pronounced them, had both texture and taste. Although it smacked of arrogance, Eli decided that his case was much the same, or how else, on an empty stomach, should he have been so often sick over the rail?

II.

As she passed through the gates of the processing shed at Ellis Island, Esther muffled her face with her shawl against a blustering March wind. The shawl covered a wig, like a sat-upon ball of yarn, that in turn concealed her once-shorn hair, grown back in abundance since her marriage. What she hadn't been able to stuff into a canvas seabag, Esther wore, so that dresses ballooned about her slender frame. In a coat graffitied with chalk marks, bristling with tags, reeking of carbolic acid, she supposed herself indistinguishable from the other arrivals. How would he identify her, her husband, and vice versa? she wondered, although it was somehow the least of her concerns.

Outside at the head of the water stairs, in a roped-off receiving area, Esther saw what she mistook at first for a crowd of striking workers. Already begins the freedom, she thought. But their upheld placards, instead of radical slogans, bore the scrawled names of friends and relations they'd come to meet. Spying her own name in the stark Hebrew characters grown familiar to her over the years, Esther made her way toward the sign with modestly lowered eyes. She teased herself by prolonging the moment of mutual recognition with her husband, then wondered, when she didn't raise her eyes, if she'd missed forever the moment favorable for looking.

But if she didn't look at the man with the sign, who shouldered her bag in lieu of an embrace then led her up a gangplank into the steam launch, Esther took in everything else. Weary as she was from the voyage, eyes still smarting from an examination that turned their lids inside out, nothing was lost on her—not one tower among the fog-wreathed cluster, like a clutch of swords in a hand, rising before them as the ferry plowed the harbor toward the Golden Land. Later, when they'd boarded the Second Avenue Elevated at dusk, she noted the horse cars startled by electric broughams; she recorded a thousand rime-bordered windows framing a thousand beige repetitions of mother, child, and sewing machine. There was the man on a platform who might have been a fugitive masquerading as a consumptive tailor, the woman bundled on a fire escape banked with airing mattresses like alfresco madhouse walls. She saw bazaars lit by bonfires, a billboard advertising the Uwanta Pill, King of Cathartics, a theater marquee for *Lula, the Beautiful Hebrew Girl*.

If the man beside her spoke, Esther never heard him over the din of the screeching train, too absorbed was she in any case with getting an eyeful of America. How long had she fed her imagination on books alone? The shundromans printed by New York's Yiddish presses and exported abroad, hawked in the marketplatz of Putsk, all of them depicting the Lower East Side of that city, rather than Warsaw or Kiev or Siberian exile, as the international seat of heartbreak and romance? "You want heroes?" the peddlers would tease her. In America they came by the job lot—artists and actors, poets and playwrights, revolutionists who lived on air in the attics of skyscrapers, close to the stars and high above the Law.

"Shomer" Shaikevitch, Esther's old favorite, had himself relocated abroad, and now set his penny dreadfuls, replete with disguises and mistaken identities, in the teeming streets of New York. Then there were the traveling players. Although Yiddish theater had been outlawed in Russia, by cleverly germanizing the dialogue, wandering troupes had staged the dramas of Messrs. Hurwitz and Lateiner, Shomer's spiritual sons. On boards thrown over barrels in the market, they'd portrayed the ruptures and passions of the East Side ghetto—the wayward sons in conflict with unyielding fathers, pious daughters with cruel stepmothers, the wayward sons and pious daughters conceiving for one another impossible loves. The players also performed the lively songs of Tin Pan Alley, such as "Yiddle on Your Fiddle Play Ragtime" by Izzy Baline, now Irving Berlin. Eventually it had begun to seem to Esther as if life itself had emigrated to America.

True, she had at first been in no hurry to leave. Why travel so far to join a perfect stranger about whom she'd lost all curiosity? Nor was it easy to abandon one's family at a time when the shtetl was so threatened with government ukases, dispossessions, and peasant pogroms. Turn away, and before you turned back, the entire Pale of Settlement might be swallowed up by history like the sea swallows a mythical continent. So in the end her departure had less in common with leave-taking than escape. But as she made ready to exchange her old world for a new one, Esther had felt that, in a sense, she already enjoyed the best of two: she was, on the one hand, the honored spouse of a husband who'd made a place for her in di goldeneh medina, while on the other hand, she hardly felt married at all.

During the five years it had taken him to save the money for his wife's shiffs-carte, Eli had worked in a cloakmaker's loft on Rivington Street. It still rankled him that a scholar should have been reduced to a common wage slave, whereas on the other side they would have competed for his upkeep. Here the scholar was indiscernible from the ordinary shnorrer peddling door-to-door notions and secondhand clothes, bags of ersatz Jerusalem dirt. Here a "mister" must become a "shister," and even the most devout began to question whether or not the Almighty ever condescended to visit the Lower East Side.

"Golden Land," they scoffed, "some joke! No wonder they call it America—ama reka, which it means 'hollow people,' the disciples of Moloch."

But in time Eli had made a virtue of necessity, for as it was written: "Where there's no bread, there's no Torah." He became a Columbus tailor, one of the multitude who learned their needle skills in the New World. He even began to take some satisfaction in his handiwork, the neat stitchery that brought to mind the sainted Enoch, who, by sewing shoe leather, stitched together the upper and lower realms. When the shop foreman commended his labor, comparing it favorably to the inferior work of the young wags Eli's own age, Eli made no attempt to conceal his pride.

The wags in the cloakmaking factory had nicknames for everyone. Old Man Markish was the Goat for the way his pinking shears munched blindly at a bolt of chintz; Fischel the foreman was Polka Dotz, because the cough from his galloping shop disease speckled his garments in blood. Mrs. Grinspan, owing to a prodigious endowment of bosom, was Froy Two-Bags-Full, and Eli was naturally the Rabbi. Although no one escaped their raillery, Eli, who'd refused to trim his beard and persisted in winding his phylacteries at his sewing machine, posed a special challenge to his "oysgreened" coworkers. They teased him mercilessly, making certain he was in earshot whenever they vaunted their amorous escapades.

They congratulated one another on their conquests at the Nonpareil Dancehall, on heated encounters with soubrettes in red tights backstage at the Bowery burlesques. They spoke openly of affairs with the ethical-culture ladies in the progressive East Broadway cafés, of their dalliance among handkerchief girls under the Allen Street El. Aware that much of this talk was for his benefit, Eli sometimes doubted its veracity; after all, their jobs were no less toilsome than his. So where did they find the pep, let alone the spare time, for such degradation? Then he remembered that the yetser hora, the evil intention, was said to be an inexhaustible source of fortitude.

Generally Eli kept his own counsel as scripture prescribed, suffering a martyrdom that was its own reward. But as his silence only served to spur them on to more fiendish taunts, someone occasionally crossed a line beyond which even Eli couldn't hold his tongue. Such as the time Ari Baumgart lifted Sophie Gluck's skirt in front of him, asking his professional opinion of the picot stitch on her finespun drawers.

Scarlet to the gills, Eli rose to his feet. "Baumgart, shame!" he protested. "Are you not, like me, a married man?"

In fact, several of the young men had wives and families for whom they were theoretically saving money to import from the other side. But out of sight, their families were also out of mind, a condition that Baumgart illustrated, enlisting the help of his fellows in looking under pressing tables and bundles of cloth.

"Wife? I don't see no wife."

Then Eli had had to struggle against admitting they had a point. Over the years he'd been making regular, albeit token, weekly deposits at the draft and passage office, but the gesture had always seemed empty. Who was it exactly he was supposed to be sending for? Dutifully he had written to advise her of his progress, stiff and impersonal letters beginning: "I greet you, my esteemed and exemplary bride [he omitted using her name, which seemed too intimate] in accordance with Proverbs 5:18—'Have a joy in the wife of thy youth, etc. . . .'" Her replies were of an equal formality, in a hand like a water spider's tracings. But so neutral were the events she recounted that they might have belonged to anyone, and therefore invoked an image of no one in particular. Further, her letters suggested that she was no more eager than he was for their reunion, which vindicated the dawdling pace at which Eli saved for her fare.

Meanwhile he'd pursued his studies and ritual observances unimpeded, and with an increased sense of urgency. In the Old Country the Ark of the Covenant was synonymous with the Ark of the Flood, a vessel that kept the Jews perpetually afloat. But here in America the vessel had run aground, and Torah was a broken rudder you clung to for dear life. It was Babylon, this new world, where the Jews were no sooner off the boat than they shaved their beards and traded their shtreimels for narrow-brimmed fun hats. They haunted the blasphemous Yiddish music halls, the dancing academies, stuss parlors, and disorderly houses operated by Jewish gangsters celebrated in the ballads of the day. They made journeys on Shabbos to a city erected for the sake of pleasure at Coney Island, and took trains into the mountains to worship flowers and trees.

One had always to be on his guard against such enticements—a worthy enterprise, reasoned Eli, since resistance to temptation had no value where temptation was not tempting. As Rabbi Yohanan of blessed memory once said, "A bachelor who lives in a great city and does not sin—the Holy One Himself daily proclaims his virtue." No matter that, technically, Eli was not a bachelor.

Twice a day he attended the storefront cloakmaker's shul on East Broadway, where he davened with a handful of bare-boned relics who still adhered to old ways. On Friday nights he treated himself to a seat in the opulent Eldridge Street synagogue. After hours, fatigued though he was from his daily labors, he pored over his tractates and commentaries by guttering lamplight. The cramped quarters of the Widow Winkelman's Ludlow Street apartment, where he boarded, was not conducive to the task, nor were his fellow boarders sympathetic to Eli's diligence. Waxman, the dipsomaniacal fruit peddler, would comment on it by means of a musical sphincter that corrupted the air as he fitfully dozed; and Fiedler, a freight handler and voluptuary, complaining that Eli's murmuring kept him from sleep, would abandon his own bed for the widow's, whence was heard a raucous frolicking through the wall. But Eli persevered.

He lived with the utmost frugality, as how could he not on such meager wages? His only expenses beyond his room and board, and the pennies he socked away toward the steamship passage, were the books he bought from the Essex Street stalls. He deemed them essential, since not only did he require them for study, but they afforded him a measure of privacy—this by virtue of the parapet he stacked them in to separate his cot from the bed shared by the other boarders. And if the purchase of books meant that it took a bit longer to save for his wife's ticket over, where was the harm? Better she should find him steadfast and faithful, still girded against wickedness by word and deed.

At length Eli had begun to expand the base of his scholarship, which is not to say that he ventured into the secular—far from it. But along with the intensified rigor of his prayers had come a new development: a concentration so heightened that Eli often experienced what could only be called ecstasy. It was a sensation that had at first embarrassed him, then prompted an inquisitive itch that made him look beyond the purely halakhik, or legal, dimension of his studies. He became interested in the kinds of texts that one was discouraged from reading outside the covenant of marriage—the otherwise forbidden books found in obscure and cavernlike shops presided over by shriveled ancients in dusty gabardines; books that some called "sacred pornography," though Eli thought the term far-fetched. Still, the books did sometimes embrace unorthodox concepts, such as casting the union of heaven and earth in the respective roles of husband and wife. Thus it was said that God engaged with His creation, personified as the Holy Shekhinah, the feminine aspect of the divine, through the medium of physical love. In his own rapturous meditations Eli, clutching a book to his breast, might believe he held the shimmering Shekhinah Herself, wearing only Sophie Gluck's ash-gray drawers.

It was hard to know which had exacted the greatest toll, work, study, or prayer (never mind loneliness—who was lonely?), but Eli was aware that he'd aged. He'd aged considerably more than five years could account for. Barely twenty-three, he walked with a stoop from the arduous hours of bending over his machine. His hair was thinning, his beard grizzled, brow creased, eyes red-rimmed and clouded by the cheap spectacles he bought off the Hester Street carts. His spare frame was racked with nameless aches, not all of which could be ascribed to his job. Some might have said he'd acquired character, though one thing was clear: he was no longer the fresh-faced *bocher* of Utsk. Which made Eli wonder if his wife, whose advent he'd put off for as long as his conscience allowed, would even recognize him when she arrived?

She was to work for the Widow Winkelman, whose parlor was transformed by day into a pillow-making sweatshop. Alongside the other girls in the widow's employ, Esther would stuff the pillow slips with feathers for a nominal salary; in addition she would help with domestic tasks to defray her board. Later on, when their combined incomes permitted, the wedded couple would take a flat of their own, or so Eli assumed. But for the time being—Waxman having been banished to the parlor sofa; Fiedler having moved in with the widow, neither of whom bothered to make a pretense of chastity anymore—husband and wife would have the second bedroom to themselves. It was a situation in keeping with the general depravity of American life, but that wasn't what aggravated Eli most. As the widow, a generous woman for all her salaciousness, welcomed Esther and showed her to her room, Eli realized with a sinking heart that he'd looked forward to her coming. Having deferred the event for half a decade, he'd found himself counting the days until her arrival, and now, God help him, he thought he knew why.

That evening, to commemorate Esther's disembarkation, the widow had the supper table dragged into a space designated as the parlor. Separated from the kitchen by a curtain, the parlor was no less crowded, its bins of eiderdown spilling over in drifts about the pier glass and the potbellied stove. It was as if a stuffy New York tenement had been invaded by its occupants' homesick dreams of the snowy steppes. That was anyway Waxman's sodden observation made for the benefit of the new arrival, whose attentions the freight handler also competed for. His bluff spirits enlivened by the widow's savory brisket and a growler of beer sent up from Max Schure's saloon, Fiedler outdid himself. He stroked his mustache like a music hall villain, suggesting that Mrs. Goldfogle was the toothsomest dish at the table; while at the same time he played footsie under her chair with their hostess, who cackled throatily. Eli, who'd yet to lift his head since saying his benedictions, might have felt more ashamed for the others had he not been so ashamed of himself.

Having identified the source of his anticipation, he was mortified to discover that its name was not Esther but "sexual intercourse." Eli tried to dismiss his feelings as merely the natural impulse, so long restrained, to perform the mitzvah of making children, but who was he kidding? Call it what you will, he knew he was guilty of wanton desire, and that intercourse—as the Reverend Joseph Caro strenuously asserted in the *Shulchan Arukh*—must never be entered into to satisfy desire. It must only be performed in the fulfillment of the obligation of one's conjugal duty, like paying a debt. As the sages said, "A man has a small organ; if he starves it, it is contented, but if he pampers it, it is hungry." The sages also said flatly that a man should avoid women, and it was immaterial to Eli, who still didn't feel like a husband, that such precepts did not apply to man and wife.

Albeit the lumpish woman he'd met at the Immigration Bureau, her face hidden in her shawl, hadn't exactly been the type to inflame the loins; Eli's ache was of a less localized nature. That she'd changed into a contoured pearl shirtwaist, her face scrubbed to incandescence, the tendrils of cocoa hair peeping out from under her sheitel wig, made no difference. For lest she read his thoughts in his eyes, Eli never raised his head. Nor did he look up when the widow, mistaking Esther's abstraction for an eagerness to be alone with her man, said complicitly, "Faygeleh, you're tired. Gay shlufn already, go to bed." Esther's voice, as she excused herself, sounded to Eli a touch melodic, recalling the maxim "It is forbidden to hear the voice of a woman singer, or even to gaze at her hair."

He put off the inevitable for as long as he could stand, but having endured a surfeit of unsolicited advice from the boarders, Eli finally removed himself from their company. In the bedroom the turned-down gas flame shivered like a distant blue star. The window giving onto the air shaft was also blue, ice like silver foil at its edges, a woman's garments hanging limply from the elbow of a stovepipe that impaled a corner of the room. In the sagging brass bed vacated by its former tenants, a slight form relieved the covers, and Eli felt the scalding urge to crawl in and possess it. Embracing it, he would inhale its attar of earth, warming his blood, which had suffered from poor circulation of late. After all, as it said in *Pirke Avot*, "A man may do with his wife what he pleases." Though it said elsewhere that it was forbidden to share a bed except for the purposes of procreation, out of the question before the woman had attended to her ablutions, and so on. She in any case appeared to be sleeping, and Eli's thoughts were not fixed on the purpose, and it was moreover forbidden to do this and forbidden to do that . . . So he lay down on his cot, surrounded by the books like the sandbags around a soldier's redoubt.

Neither husband nor wife slept that night. Eli chanted to himself the psalms intended to exorcise impure thoughts, wondering at the character of the king who'd conceived them, a man driven by lust even into his dotage. Esther, in a counterfeit repose that left her alone with her impressions, lay cherishing every sound. The air shaft contained a babel of voices the way a shell contains an ocean; but it was possible, if you paid attention, to discern now a curse, now a pleading endearment, a child bawling beyond the thin tenement walls. Somewhere a gramophone played "Nyu York kokht vi a keslgrib, New York bubbles like a pot . . ." A cough rattled, a siren wailed, a ferry moaned, the frozen clothes creaked on the lines, and Esther listened, committing noises to memory like the words of a lullaby.

In the morning, despite her vigil, she rose refreshed, though not until she was certain her husband had already set off for the cloak factory. The Widow Winkelman, in her billowing house wrapper, greeted Esther with a suggestive wink and introduced her to the other girls as they arrived. They were standoffish at first, suspicious of the pretty greenhorn, but Esther's artlessness soon won their assurances that they would take her under their wing. The work was tedious but not difficult, and once she'd gotten the hang of pillow stuffing, the inverse of the chicken flicking she was used to since childhood, Esther enjoyed the lively conversation. When they weren't advising her about the stylish shops on Grand Street, or describing a dance (which they called a "racket") at the Teutonia Hall, the girls talked of love. One spoke candidly of her Litvak fiddler, another of a young professor at the Alliance night school, with an open affection that would have scandalized Putsk. But here they seemed to feel, as Esther had known they must, that love was their due. Conducted mainly in Yiddish, their talk was peppered with American phrases, such as "bloff" and "fifti-fifti" and "vanemakerz depodmn stor," conjurations Esther made note of for future reference.

In all things, especially affairs of the heart, the girls deferred to the widow. She was a gentle taskmistress who pretended not to notice when her employees made a game of their labor, sometimes flinging more feathers at each other than they stuffed in the cases. Instead, as she fed the pillow ticking to her droning machine, she would recall for their instruction the landmark events of her past. These usually began with the example of her dead husband Jakie, peace on his soul, and advanced through a number of subsequent amours. Frequently, however, she waived personal experience in favor of keeping her girls abreast of the complicated liaisons of local celebrities: of stars like Tomashefsky and Rudolph Schildkraut, Adler the Eagle, Madames Liptzin and Kalish, the poet Leivick, the playwright Peretz Hirshbein.

On that first morning, stirred to intoxication by the mention of such legendary names, Esther had interrupted the widow's narrative to exclaim, "It's a dreamland, I think, this America!" Smiling from their worldly vantage, her companions patiently corrected her: Dreamland was a place you went to by the Coney Island Ferry on Saturdays. But the great moment came when, in late afternoon, the Widow Winkelman asked Esther to accompany her to the market. Later, when she'd accustomed herself to the neighborhood, she could go alone.

That same day at the cloakmaking loft on Rivington Street, Eli's coworkers gave him no quarter. Aware of his bride's arrival and remarking the deeper circles under his eyes, they made coarse allusions to marital monkeyshines. "So when do we get to see her, your Queen Esther?" they needled, posing the question Eli might as easily have asked himself. In the evening he lingered overlong at his prayers and, on his return to Ludlow Street, walked past the widow's building without stopping. He wandered the neighborhood, buffeted by a spectacle impervious to the chill and inclement weather. Boys fed broken kegs and mattresses to the flames of a cremated truck horse, around which couples in storm coats practiced their two-step. Peddlers hugged themselves behind naphtha-lit carts. A crowd on a corner abandoned a speaker indicting the capitalist cockroaches to chase after a runabout rumored to contain Anna Held. Saloons and pawnshops blazed; pianos rolled. On Allen Street painted girls in loose kimonos beckoned from open windows, their breath rivaling the plumed exhalations from manhole covers.

When Eli entered the dark bedroom, his wife was already asleep. He lit a lamp and took up a book, *The Palm Tree of Deborah*, a mystical text that ordinarily would have provided him the means to transcend his dismal predicament. But tonight such an ascent seemed inaccessible, not to say inappropriate under the circumstances, an ethereal seduction Eli would do well to resist. Instead he opted for the *Yesod Yosef*, grounded in its sober legalities. He forced himself to focus on an especially thorny passage, which debated whether laughter on a fast day constituted an excess of joy, to the

point of exhaustion. His eyes grown heavy, Eli lay back on his cot, thinking that things might be worse: so long as he and the woman kept to their
tacit agreement that neither existed for the other, life was tolerable. But no
sooner had he started to doze, lulled by the rhythm of her breathing, than
Eli succumbed to a sweetness beyond reason. Immediately he woke to the
realization that he had spilled his sticky seed.

"Master of the Universe," he appealed, "I have done this unwittingly, but
it was caused due to evil musings. Erase this iniquity and save me from sin-
ful thoughts, so may it be Thy will!"

After that, Eli's path was clear, outlined as it was in detail in the *Shulchan
Arukh*: he must endeavor whenever convenient to have circumcised infants
on his lap, increase his donations to charity, be the first to arrive at the minyan and the last to leave, and rise every midnight to lament the destruction
of the Temple. As for his wife, accessory though she was to his pollution, he
must not look her in the face until his heart was pure.

As the widow's particular pet, Esther received the lion's share of her sympathy. "Your husband that he's in heaven a saint already," the landlady would
repine. "Which it makes you almuneh like me, a widow." Though she sometimes said aguneh, abandoned wife. In either case Esther would heave a
wistful sigh, acknowledging the hollow charade of her marriage, but the
truth was that she couldn't have been happier. Dreaming was after all her
element, her true native country the land of heart's desire. Having spent her
days in a diaspora of longing, what more could she ask than to have found
herself in what she took to be the capital of dreams?

It was a conviction she reaffirmed each afternoon, when, dispatched into
the East Side streets to do the marketing, Esther was set free. Veteran of
countless traffickings among village peddlers, she was unintimidated by the
Hester Street throngs. With a practiced eye she distinguished the fresh from
the festering among the noisome chicken coops and herring tubs, confident
that her bargaining skills had traveled well. In this way Esther made short
work of the shopping, which left her time to linger awhile in the neighborhood before she was missed.

She took a daily excursion through what the widow called the Yiddish
Rialto, up to Second Avenue and down along the Bowery, where there were
palaces built for the adoration of dreams. There were nickelodeons and automatic one-cent vaudevilles, a life-size mock-up of David Kessler under

the Thalia marquee, brooding over a skull in *Hamlet, the Yeshiva Boy*. There was the great Jacob Adler tearing a passion to tatters on a poster for *God of Vengeance* outside his playhouse at the corner of Chrystie and Grand. No matter that Esther had yet to set foot inside one of these theaters; she was content to bide her time in anticipation of the day, just as she'd savored her coming to America. Then there was the fear that what went on in the theaters might fall short of what she'd imagined; it might pale by comparison with the continuous drama of the streets.

She made a loop through Seward Park past black-sleeve photographers and balladmongers performing topical songs—here an ode to the victims of the Triangle Fire, there a hymn to the heroism of Ida Strauss, who went down with her financier husband onboard the *Titanic*. She walked past the offices of the Yiddish dailies on East Broadway, then farther along past the cafés, which Esther saved for last. This was her destination, the end of the avenue where romance was run to ground, the very cradle of dreamers. And there they were, congregated in the Café Royal and Glickman's Odessa Tearoom, the writers indistinguishable from the creatures of their own invention—poets, revolutionists, renegade scholars in threadbare cutaways, their frayed collars upstanding, hair fallen in crescent forelocks over their face. They crowded around the tables as if ideas were dice in a crapshoot; as if they were surgeons and the muse was a patient under the knife. Wild-eyed, they gesticulated with monocles and Russian cigarettes, their animation a thing that could only have been borne of valor, or so Esther believed. They were a species not to be witnessed this side of the pages of books; though these, she had to remind herself, backing away from the plate-glass windows with a mortal shudder, these were flesh and blood.

Sometimes, before returning to Ludlow Street, Esther might pause to watch the ordinary men, toiling to and from the sweat factories in their molting alpacas, and wonder if one of them might have been her husband. She was grateful beyond measure not to know.

But ultimately there came an afternoon in early spring when the looking was no longer enough. Or rather, it seemed to Esther, leaning forward to peer through the sun's reflection on the window of Glickman's Odessa Tearoom, that she'd lost her balance and fallen in. How else would she have found the nerve to hide her market basket (into which she'd stuffed her wig) under a neighboring stoop and enter the café? At a corner table she ordered a glass of tea, stirring in the amber honey and discreetly eavesdropping.

"What you call art, I call it shmaltzgrub. Put Chekhov's pince-nez on Jacob Gordin and he's still another son of Esau."

"Libin and Kobrin—feh! Better Weber and Fields. By act two of *Prince Lulu* I had already calluses on the brain."

"Cross your social Darwinist with a Tolstoy vegetarian and what you get is—"

"Di gas?"

"From your mouth to Trotsky's ear."

Among the assembled there were girls Esther's age, clever girls unafraid to vie in irreverence with the men. They made daring remarks ("For her Yom Kippur penance she's shtupping Harry Fein at the Labor Bund picnic") and performed variations on the personals column of the *Arbeiter Zeitung:* "I'm a young man with a good job that's got only on the back a slight hump, which it will bring, so they tell me, much mazel to my bride . . ." A pair of them sang in chorus: "We get our knowledge from the College of the Circumcised Citizens of New York . . ."

Vacillating between shock and envy, Esther determined to stay seated until she felt at home. Then she observed that some of the younger men were trying to catch her eye, and brought to herself, she abruptly rose and fled the café. So flushed was she on her return to Ludlow Street that her landlady hinted she must have had an assignation. Coquettishly, Esther neither affirmed nor denied, feeling that, in a sense, it was true, and afterward the glass of tea at Glickman's Odessa became a part of her daily routine.

Insomnia having compounded Eli's anguish, no amount of prayer and mortification could calm him down, or help to reduce his desire. He was further galled by the incessant jibes in the cloakmakers' loft, convinced that his co-workers were encouraged by the benighted thoughts writ on his brow. They could read in his features how the sound of his sleeping wife's breathing blew through his head all day like a desert wind. So why not just get it over with and consummate the marriage? Eli reasoned. It was after all his sacred obligation—though he saw through his own sophistry. What he contemplated was nothing other than the means to an evil end, to the satisfaction of his lust, and it was written that children born of such unions were tainted; they were the offspring of the left-hand side.

As part of his atonement, Eli forbade himself the mystical texts that might have released him awhile from despair, and concentrated exclusively on legal tractates. Instead of saying his benedictions at his sewing machine, he now attended afternoon services at the cloakmakers' shul. Since time in the factory was measured not by hours but the number of garments one made in a day, he was forced to stay later at work, which also suited his program. On his afternoon walks to and from the East Broadway shtibl, Eli had to pass the cafés, the kibbitzarnia, where he was irked at the sight of so many idlers talking through their noses. He marveled at their license, these apikorsin, these heretics, who had no use for guilt, let alone God Himself. Art, they claimed, was their God, or idolatry, to call it by its rightful name. So why was it they who had all the robustness of spirit, while Eli had only his shame?

What was it about these lumpen do-nothings that made them so fascinating to Jewish daughters, though such daughters as one would wish on no pious father! For these had discarded modest apparel for loose blouses and un-corseted waists, skirts with peekaboo pleats; they'd exchanged cowls and wigs for jaunty bonnets, for hair streaked with henna and braided like the devil's own challah, when not allowed to flow free. They smoked cigarettes, these sisters of Lilith, and insinuated themselves into arguments, striking adventurous poses. As he observed them through the window of Glickman's Odessa, one of their more infamous haunts, Eli's heart would irately rattle the cage of his chest. His custom was to walk away in disgust, though today, an especially sultry late May afternoon, he stood his ground; he told himself he needed a closer look, if only to prove he could face provocation with self-command. Then doing the unthinkable, Eli entered the café and ordered a glass of tea.

He glanced about with contempt at his surroundings, the framed chromo of Theodor Herzl, the broadside above the buffet advertising last year's Yom Kippur Ball. The air was caustic with pickle brine, thick with the names they conjured with: Kropotkin, Zhitlowsky, Zola, Beilis, Cahan . . . , all of whom meant nothing to Eli. What interested him was the aggressive behavior of the young women, whose every gesture, while pantomiming devotion to this or that cause célèbre, was an enticement. Neither was Eli deceived by their faces, whose engaged expressions thinly veiled a wantonness bred in the bone. Though there was one, seated alone over her tea in an adjacent corner, whom he excused from his general assessment. This one had a dignified beauty that needed no extravagant airs, a smooth olive complexion and searching onyx eyes. Her cocoa hair, strands of which had come loose from a tidy bun, was as undulant as the grain in dark mahogany. Obviously out of place here, she might have been a young rebitsin; she had the look of a fit companion for a Torah scholar, were that scholar—a hammer fell in Eli's head—not already married.

Still he was unable to take his eyes off the girl. Sipping this tea, he drank the elixir of her presence, which warmed his vitals and tickled his brain, and presently he felt he wanted her more than anything on earth. Here was a desire that knew no remorse, a passion that purged the mind of all impurities. He sat studying her face as intently as he might have a page in *The Book of Mirrors*, and experienced rapture. Lit from within, he was convinced that beams shot from his every orifice; a radiance escaped his eyes, ears, and nostrils as if the moon were captured in a helmet full of holes. This was a higher order of lasciviousness; call it love, which emanated from the supernal realm, its beguiling physical complement notwithstanding. A holy delirium was upon him, in the throes of which Eli understood that this was the woman he'd been saving himself for. Then he noticed that she was observing him with an equally unflinching stare, and dropping his eyes, he paid his bill and left the café.

On her way back to Ludlow Street Esther may as well have been sleepwalking, so thoroughly had the image of the young man in the tearoom displaced everything else in her consciousness. She was drawn to his solitude, the melancholy that set him apart from the rest, the haunting quality of his inkwell eyes. Those eyes, so sunken and limned in red, possessed a molten sadness that belied their best efforts at severity. They belonged to a poet who lived alone in a drafty attic near the river and stayed awake nights composing verses to one such as her. It was a hero's face, the gaunt face of a martyr to dreams, whose details came clearer in his absence: the furrowed cheeks and untrimmed beard, the side locks twined about the temples of his lopsided spectacles. Then he'd removed the spectacles, as if to show how the badges of his bookishness failed to repudiate the sensuality of his eyes.

Had she known about the tripartite soul—the nefesh, ruach, and neshomah—Esther might have concluded (as had the learned Eli with respect to her) that the young man completed her neshomah, her highest soul, which meant that they were destined for each other.

That night, as she undressed for bed, Esther felt she was waiting for him; she'd been waiting for him all her life. And so, when the door opened and he entered, her expectancy was at such a pitch that she was hardly surprised, only thankful that she'd thus far kept herself pure and inviolate. There was a moment when she thought the visitor might be her husband; she had a husband. But the gas lamp, dim as it was, suggested the striking visage of the young man from the café. Besides, it was a certainty that her husband could never have embraced her so impulsively, never "taken" her—a thrilling notion!—without a thousand preliminary rites. He could never have cried out, "Ikh vil ayk ufesn! I want to eat you up!" so that the whole household must have been alerted, but who cared? Let them listen at the door if they must to the groaning bedsprings, the straw mattress crackling like flames, Esther's heated assurances that she was his.

For a time Eli held her tightly, the way a rabbi hugs his scrolls on Simchas Torah: dveikuss, this was called, a cleaving in ecstasy to the sublime. Then he drew back and lifted her muslin gown. A fragrance as of moist clay tinged with cloves went to his head, and in his dizziness Eli had to close his eyes. With his fingers he explored the sloping expanse of her hip, the trough of her abdomen, the close-pored dunes beyond—the geography of a new world whose shores he'd reached after years of voyaging. He pulled the ruck of her gown from beneath her chin as if unfolding petals, opening his eyes to find her face. The kiss that she so hungrily returned was the kiss of the Holy Shekhinah, which rendered powerless the Angel of Death and allowed one to enter paradise alive. It was the kiss that sealed the union of a soul cleft in two in heaven, prior to birth, and reunited in the lower world with its other half.

Afterward, remembering the words of the masters, Eli invited regrets. "Do not suppose," said the masters, "that only he who commits the act with his body is called an adulterer. He who commits it with his eyes is also considered unfaithful." And they said, "If a wife is alone with her husband and is engaged in intercourse, while her heart is with another man she met on the road, no act of adultery is greater." Surely this applied to the husband as well, Eli conceded, rolling desolately out of bed to resume his former place on the cot.

Relieved to be alone with her musings, Esther sighed in the afterglow of passion and imagined that her lover had left her bed before her husband's return. Unable to contain his inspiration, the poet had gone back to work at his poems.

III.

At first Eli had to force himself to avert his eyes whenever he walked past the café, but after a couple of months the habit had become second nature. He'd continued to go doggedly through the motions of his three-part regimen, but of work, study, and prayer, only work could still hold his attention.

Otherwise he remained in a walking stupor, wondering at the exquisite felicity attached to sin. Then there was a day toward the end of summer, as he
plodded along the sidewalk toward his afternoon minyan, when thoughts of
the girl had momentarily slipped his mind, and Eli chanced to look through
the window of Glickman's Odessa. She was seated at her table, looking out,
sullenly watching him watch her.

Riveted to the pavement, Eli was seized by a sudden recklessness. Here
I stand a fallen creature, he brooded, who, having already lost heaven, has
nothing else left to lose. So why shouldn't he take some pleasure on this
side of the grave? He might as well step into the tearoom, state his case, and
let the chips fall where they may. "Shalom, my name is Eli Goldfogle and I
adore you." Hesitating, Eli allowed his gaze to caress her perfect cheek, the
not-so-slight curve of her breast, her waist, where he noted a subtle difference: despite its tightness, her corset had failed to confine a telltale swelling.
She belonged, it seemed, to another, and carried his child. She was heavy
with the get of some unwashed scribbler, he would wager, a ragged pipe
dreamer, blind to her condition, who tilted with windmills all night in a gar-
ret room. But was this really any of Eli's business? Her life was something
alien, probably wicked, which he could never in any case enter into, and so
there it was—she could never be his.

Of course, it shouldn't be forgotten that Eli had a companion of his own,
a woman named Esther with whom he'd had relations that tarnished them
both for all eternity. It was a situation that, beyond dissolute, was more
than the Law allowed. How could he have strayed so far from the path of
righteousness—such a distance that, should his holy books ever speak to
him again, he wouldn't hear them?

He returned to the loft on Rivington Street where he pumped the treadle
so furiously that his machine traveled several feet across the floor. Quipped
the wags, "The rabbi is racing his chariot." That very evening he was advised
that the ailing old Polka Dotz Fischel had finally succumbed to a bout of the
white plague. Since none of the other young men in the shop were half so
conscientious as Eli, the boss, Leyzer Cohen, designated him the foreman's
successor, with a substantial raise in salary. The position was his provided he
discontinue the practice of nipping out for afternoon prayers, a stipulation
to which Eli readily agreed.

He moved himself and his expectant wife into an apartment of their
own in a railroad-style tenement on Cherry Street. It was a grim building of
baleful odors and thunderous toilets, even shabbier than the Ludlow Street

flat, but it had a parlor that might also function as a nursery. It had a cook-stove, black and solid as an anvil, on which Esther could prepare the Widow Winkelman's tempting recipes. Liberated from the pillow-stuffing sweatshop, Esther's time was now her own, which meant there was more of it to spend in the East Side streets. Never again, however, was she disposed to go back to the tearoom. Since the day she'd watched her young man walk away, she'd mourned him, but Esther nonetheless accepted as inevitable the end of their affair. It was enough to have participated in a tragedy that elevated her above the commonplace. Although regretful, she was serene in the knowledge that, in a place deep inside her only he had touched, a child was growing.

She'd begun to cultivate a long-dormant fondness for domestic pursuits. Employing talents she came by naturally, Esther took pride in her ability to, for instance, judge a capon's kosherness by pinching its intimate parts. In time, having driven hard bargains with the contract peddler, she'd cozily feathered her nest. She acquired a pier glass and a china cabinet, and de-termined that, when the baby (a boy, Nathan) was old enough, they would have a piano. From the sweet compotes and noodle puddings she plied her husband with to fatten him up, Esther also put on weight, its ballast serv-ing her well in her "pig market" campaigns. Become formidable, she was fiercely protective of her little Nathan, a difficult child whom she spoiled like a prince.

After my uncle Nathan, whose excessive pampering left him a petulant parasite all his days, came others: my malcontent maiden aunt Millie, whose favorite wish (gleaned from Talmud) was never to have been born; and my mama, the bedeviled Sara Rochel, whose bedroom games drove my milque-toast father, a grocer, to an early grave. (She was forever goading him—or so says Aunt Millie the Tongue—to make believe he was, alternately, Adolphe Menjou, Dutch Schultz, and Clifford Odets.) There was my scapegrace uncle Shmuel, the bluebeard, who told me this story in exchange for the loan of a couple of bucks. But for all the energy she devoted to her homemaking, my grandmother Esther still found time for the back-numbered romances of "Shomer" Shaikevitch and his ilk. She read them openly now, without embarrassment, titles such as *The Secrets of the Czarist Court*, which nudged from the shelves the sacred texts her husband had relegated to a closet.

Sometimes, of an evening, Eli would look up from his *Daily Forward*, which he preferred to the less progressive *Tageblatt*, and shake his head over his wife's lifelong addiction to fluff. All the same, he dutifully saved her the section containing Mrs. Bronstein's popular serial, "Woman in Chains."

Handing it over, he might wonder when it was he'd first begun to look at her, this dowdy balebosteh who kept his house in such apple-pie order, who raised the offspring that would pray for him after he was gone. When had she not been an indispensable part of his world? Then he would resolve to take her out one of these nights to the theater, and afterward for tea and pastries on Second Avenue. When his eyes were again lowered, Esther might steal a glance at her slump-shouldered man with his stubbled chins, his paunch like a pet in his lap, and smile inwardly, resolving that her children would marry for love.

Avigdor of the Apes

What ails you now, that you have gone up entirely to the roofs?
—The Zohar

Avigdor Bronfman, an indifferent scholar, made his way across Orchard Street at twilight, on his way home from his Talmud Torah class. He sidled between the vendors of nickel spectacles, celluloid collars, and cotton waists, and avoided a shrill woman in the process of slapping a peddler with his own stinking carp. He skirted a starving draft horse with ribs like hood louvers dropping a steaming pile into the gutter, and stepped onto the opposite curb. Mounting the stoop, he entered a cabbage-rank tenement beneath a sign in Hebrew characters advertising the second-floor occupant's profession of circumciser. That was his father. The boy climbed a flight of stairs, opened the door to a stuffy apartment wherein his bearded papa stood swaying in his prayer shawl, his mama pumping her sewing machine, and tossed in his books. Then he closed the door and continued his ascent up the five remaining flights to the top of the building, where he pushed open a tin-plated door onto the tar-papered roof. Crossing the roof he shed his reefer jacket and hopped onto the low parapet, stood a moment admiring the salmon-pink sunset, and plunged into the crisp autumn air.

His flights had begun soon after Avigdor and his friend Shaky Gruber went to a Shabbos matinee of *Tarzan of the Apes* at the Grand Street flickers. The film starred Mr. Elmo Lincoln in the role of the ape-man, an actor so gross and lumbering that even when battling an authentic lion—a mange-ridden beast whose drugged movements were even clumsier than those of its human prey—he failed to convince. Nevertheless, while his pal Shaky snickered irreverently, Avigdor was transfixed. Sunk in the plush seats of the dark picture palace, a sanctuary from the clamor and menace of the neighborhood streets, he experienced a kind of savage freedom. He was a scrawny kid, Avigdor, tethered to a claustrophobic household in the sump of the East Side ghetto, and the progress of an orphan raised to manhood by anthropoid apes struck a chord in his pigeon breast. It was not so much Tarzan's brute power and ferocity that thrilled him—though such attributes were nothing to sniff at—as his ability to maintain a largely aerial existence, navigating the lush canopy of the Congo high above the earth without ever having to come down.

Excited as he was by the film, Avigdor was not immediately moved to emulate its hero. Raised in an atmosphere where sedulous study was valued above action, he first visited the Seward Park Library, where he obtained a copy of the novel by Edgar Rice Burroughs from which the photoplay had been adapted. He read it in secret, since his pious papa regarded all secular literature as obscenity. Then he found himself doubly spellbound, the exploits of the boy adopted by a tribe of great apes further validated by their translation into print. The son of a mohel, a ritual clipper of infant foreskins, Avigdor had been the object of countless jokes at his own and his father's expense, as well as a frequent victim of bullies. He knew he was the unlikeliest of candidates for a transformation from yeshivah bocher to jungle denizen, but on the strength of his fascination with the ape-man he determined to reinvent himself.

"Grow up already," sneered his friend Shaky Gruber—himself no model of maturity—when Avigdor confided his resolution; and ambivalent until then, Avigdor was briefly inclined to agree. Then he surprised himself by dissolving his friendship with Shaky on the spot.

Soon after, on an early March evening, he climbed to the windy roof of his six-floor tenement. He'd been there before, on sweltering nights when his family joined others escaping their ovenlike apartments to bed down beneath lusterless stars on the so-called tar beach. But at those times Avigdor had felt uncomfortably vulnerable, lying awake amid alien bodies emitting rude noises and crying out from troubled dreams. Now, as he surveyed the scene, he had to admit that the rooftops of the Lower East Side had little in common with the dense arboreal expanse of equatorial Africa. Except for a few scraggly plane trees over in Seward Park, there were no boughs to perch on, no luxuriant creepers or lianas to swing from. The realization came almost as a relief, since now he could dispense with the passing compulsion and resume his ordinary life. But look again with less tellurian eyes and there was no end of purchases and footholds, of aeries and swallows' nests and lofty towers affording panoramic views. There were ledges, catwalks, drainpipes, and lampposts, an urban skyscape with any number of features that a sprightly young primate might employ in eluding predators.

But how to proceed? You could beat your chest with your fists gorilla-style—which Avigdor commenced to do; and the gesture did lend him a certain Dutch courage, not to mention giving a vibrato quality to his yawp. But after that it seemed incumbent on him to perform some feat of simian athleticism. Avigdor had never before demonstrated the least hint of athletic ability; until now his body had been a rickety construction wherein he was forced to dwell for lack of a sturdier container. Then he invoked a passage from the novel, which he recited under his breath like a portion of scripture: "He could spring twenty feet across space at the dizzy heights of the forest top . . . ," after which Avigdor made a dash for the surrounding parapet. Bounding onto it he launched himself with cycling legs over the air shaft onto the neighboring roof. The distance was not very far; other boys routinely cleared the shafts flat-footed, the taller ones able almost to step across. But something happened as soon as Avigdor felt himself airborne: his apprehension dissolved, his brain ceased its caviling, and he became a pure expression of the physical. Instinct supplanted self-consciousness and his limbs assumed an integrity of their own.

So it seemed to Avigdor he had a gift, which he straightaway began to nurture, developing it along with the strength he needed to enhance his prowess. Over time his gaunt body acquired a tough and sinewy armature of muscle, a tempered vitality he augmented with various devices either scavenged or manufactured by his own hand. From modest monkeylike efforts at swinging, leaping, and vaulting, he graduated to circus-grade acrobatic feats. For these he was not above consulting library books on gymnastics and even the physics of leverage and balance. But while the information might be useful to some, the boy found the technical language a distraction, calling his attention back to the pedestrian plane, and in the end he left the books behind in the world where they belonged.

On any given afternoon, abandoning his studies, Avigdor might step to the edge of the roof and throw himself off, perhaps catching hold of a clothesline fastened by pulleys to an adjacent tenement wall. Then he would "brachiate" arm over arm along the sagging line above a flagstone courtyard, where far below a mother patsched a whining child's tushy and a vendor of sheet music intoned a music hall air. He might drop neatly onto the fire escape of an opposite building and clamber up a ladder to the roof, where he fetched from under a pile of rubble beside a spinning air vent a rope tied to an iron hook. He would twirl the rope lasso-fashion above his head in ever widening circles and release the grappling hook, watching it arc over Ludlow or Essex Street to clank onto a scaffold or wrap itself serpentlike around a balcony rail. He might swing out over the jostling thoroughfare and let go before smashing into a wall, free-falling ass over elbows to land plump in the tent of a consumptive erected on the pebbly roof of a candy store. (So what if the tent collapsed, traumatizing the invalid inside? The law of the jungle made allowances for such damage.) He might land in an awning or a canvas tarp stretched over a seed frame and bounce back into the air like a shot from a sling.

In lieu of vines Avigdor scaled walls of jutting masonry—"He could gain the utmost pinnacle of the loftiest tropical giant with the ease and swiftness of a squirrel . . ." Reaching the top, he might locate a limber flagstaff hidden in a cache of scrap lumber, and making a run across the tar paper, plant the pole and vault over an alley; or hurl himself feetfirst against a bulkhead and, shooting his legs like a jack-in-the-box, catapult himself onto the pitched roof of a rowhouse several stories below. Clattering down the shingled slope he might leap onto the top of an omnibus, dropping into a seat beside a startled passenger. The bus would turn a corner into Orchard Street, forging like a pachyderm lumbering upstream through hordes of hawkers and market wives, passing under a hanging ladder that the ape-boy would then grab hold of, hoisting himself onto a fire escape where he opened a window and tumbled inside.

As he rolled onto the creaking floorboards, his pear-shaped mama, placing a dish of stuffed derma beside his place at the table, would ask him, "Where's your jacket?"; while his papa, already seated with a napkin tucked under his chin, called him apostate and invited him to say the prayer over breaking bread.

You might ask what became of his fear, for he'd always been a timid kid. But once he'd overcome his trepidation through blind faith, Avigdor discovered that the ghetto's higher plateaus had been his element all along. Swarming over the rooftops he remained in a state of pure rapture. The rest of the time—forced to sit in dusty classrooms and run the gauntlet of his discordant neighborhood—he regarded as misspent. It was true that his new physicality had toughened his frame, making him a less objectionable companion, but Avigdor shunned the society of his peers, whom he'd yet to forgive for ridiculing him as his father's son. Now he lived only for the moment when he could climb above the choking warren of the Lower East Side. Down below, amid the mercantile crush, he endured the monotonous passage of days, while above he dwelled in a timeless space where he would never grow old. He liked spying on the ethereal activities of his neighbors: the women kneeling to spread their freshly washed hair over a skylight to dry, the pigeon fanciers wielding their hooples shaped like snowshoes to shoo the birds back into their coops. Blind children performed calisthenics on the caged roof of their academy on Pitt Street; artists erected their easels atop the Educational Alliance on East Broadway.

Ultimately, however, he felt the pull to range farther afield. There were towers that beckoned with their Babel-like altitudes, roof gardens where orchestras played for tea dances and gentlemen waltzed slinky ladies about the upper reaches of the metropolitan night. You had rooftops where grass grew and barnyard animals grazed, rooftops with whole parlors under awnings, penthouse terraces designed to resemble the decks of ships. There were kite fliers and laundry thieves whom Avigdor furtively observed, lovers entangled in trysts among flapping sheets. In Herald Square there was a giant billboard in the shape of a windmill on whose turning arms you could ride. All this he viewed through the eyes of a curious young savage looking onto a strange civilization, its inhabitants aspiring to the heights while remaining anchored to the terrestrial world.

Sometimes the boy felt sorry for them. So freighted were they with their worries and piecework, so bound by the shackles of their phylacteries, that they could never know his high-flying freedom. While they required so much to sustain the little they had, Avigdor needed next to nothing—only an occasional taste of his mother's soup afloat with medallions of fat to keep him nourished, and his dexterous limbs to give him access to a city that had become his own personal jungle gym. Still, it was a solitary life, and there were times when he might feel sorry for himself as well, a sentiment that actually sweetened his life aloft.

Summers swelled the population of the ghetto's elevated real estate, and Avigdor occasionally confronted gangs of other boys in his wanderings. As the Jews were likelier to remain earthbound, these were typically Irish lads in their floppy caps or Italians east of the Bowery, youth auxiliaries of the older gangs that were the strong arm of Tammany Hall. When they spotted a sheeny trespassing in their territory—Avigdor's beak was a dead giveaway—they were quick to give chase across the sticky tar paper. The boy exulted in these encounters even to the extent of seeking them out, nor was he above baiting his enemies in a Yiddish as exotic to them as the language of apes:

"Putzim mit oyren," he might shout, "pricks with ears," hopping up and down on a chimney pot.

Then he would turn a backward somersault over a gap between buildings and lead them on an obstacle course across the housetops. At first they followed in a threatening mob, though their ranks would soon thin. Those who persisted were brought up short by the sight of Avigdor, atop a facing tenement, reeling in the ladder he'd just danced across. Then he would run up a plank he'd left slanted against a trestle and weighted at its foot by a keg of nails. The yammering plank, which served as a springboard, would toss the nimble yid onto some far-flung height, where he turned to raise his fist and voice a victory cry:

"Kish mikh vi di yidn hobm gereet, kiss me where the Jews reposed!"

And while he still wore his shopworn sweater, knee pants, and tramping shoes, he imagined himself prancing in a loincloth—"his brown, sweat-streaked body glistening in the moonlight, supple and graceful among the awkward, hairy brutes about him."

Occasionally it occurred to Avigdor that he might stand and fight, that with his "mighty thews" he might tear out their hearts as Tarzan did to Sabor the lion and Horta the boar, but it was frankly more fun to lead them on a merry chase. Eventually, though, they wearied of the sport, after which he would have to egg them on, pelting them with insults and standing on ledges to pish on their games of alley craps. When the weather began to turn and the roofs became less tenanted, he sorely missed their cat-and-mouse games.

By then he'd become something of a legend in the neighborhood, the feats ascribed to him including aspects of the miraculous. (The more credulous spoke of flying carpets and wings.) Though he never made any effort to disguise himself in his flights, no one on the ground ever confused the ape-boy with the son of the mohel who remained the butt of jokes: "Whaddaya call Reb Bronfman's toolbox? A bris kit." But the fact of his double identity only added spice to his zeal for aerial exploits.

With the return of cold weather, however, Avigdor sometimes found it a stretch to sustain his fantasy, so incompatible were the frosty altitudes with his vision of the jungle's verdant humidity. His fingers and toes stiffened, his frigid scalp chilled his brain, and occasionally as he scrambled up a stone facade or swung from a rope above an arcade, the lemony light from a window might beckon him back indoors. Sometimes, however much he might judge himself to be of another species, Avigdor missed the life of the tribe. But always his exhilaration renewed itself, and winter had its virtues: the clotheslines, for instance, bereft now of garments and coated in ice, gave the passenger—dangling from a walking stick hooked over them—a streamlined ride at breakneck speed. Though once, while zinging above the courtyards via this mode of travel, the brittle line snapped from his weight, and unable to arrest his forward momentum Avigdor was thrust headlong through the flimsy frame of a tenement window.

He crashed into the railroad flat in a cataclysm of splinters and glass and went sprawling onto the floor of a kitchen, where a woman stood dusted to the elbows in flour from a kneading trough and a girl sat naked in her bath. The woman—face like a pomegranate in a lopsided wig—came at the boy with her upraised rolling pin as he attempted to get to his feet. The girl in the inclined porcelain tub covered her breasts with her arms and shrieked hysterically; but Avigdor, lacerated head to toe, was deaf to the sound, insensitive to everything but her radiance, which shone through the lather that festooned her pink flesh like surf. A mermaid, thought the boy, frozen in his enchantment until the rolling pin descended on his skull. Lightning struck a baobab tree in his head as he crumpled onto the floorboards again.

He came to in a paddy wagon from which he was unceremoniously hauled through dank corridors and tossed into a holding cell in the Tombs. With blood crusted like war paint over one whole side of his face, he climbed the bars and rattled his cage, uttering guttural cries—until he noticed that he wasn't alone in the long cell. A number of desperate-looking parties in equally gore-stained attire sat slumped against the walls frowning at his antics. Their censure had an inhibiting effect on Avigdor's outbursts, and realizing that he ached exquisitely in every fiber and joint, he satisfied himself with gingerly thumping his chest. At length he was allowed to send a message to his family, whereupon his father, who for all his piety understood how the system worked, paid a visit to the Honorable Max Hochstim in the back room of an Essex Market saloon. Mr. Hochstim, local ward heeler and trafficker in Jewish girls, had a son at whose bris Reb Bronfman had presided, and at the request of the distraught mohel he appealed to the Tammany boss Big Tim Sullivan, who saw to it that Avigdor was released from captivity.

"Now you going to be a good boy?" Reb Bronfman inquired of his son, whose head was swathed in gauze bandages; and the chastened Avigdor assured him that that was the case. But no sooner did his wounds begin to heal than the boy, heeding once more the call of thin air, took again to the roofs.

But instead of traveling by leaps and bounds to remote destinations about the city, Avigdor kept close to his own native quarter; close, to be precise, to a railroad tenement on Attorney Street, whose unmended window was covered with a dingy gray blanket whipped by the wind. Perched on a ledge supported by stone gargoyles, whose squat pose the ape-boy duplicated, Avigdor maintained his vigil, waiting for a glimpse of the girl in the tub. Not that he expected to see her naked again. In fact, he was a little ashamed of having first viewed her in her natural state; for despite the tension that troubled his heart and loins, Avigdor still respected her modesty. In anticipating a second sighting, he clothed her in his mind, though not in the drab shirtwaists and buttoned boots of her peers. Rather was she wreathed in spindrift, hobble-skirted in rainbow scales, a creature of the sea as he was a creature of the air. That was the vision that had surfaced in his brain to displace the vertiginous throbbing left there by the rolling pin. It was a vision that vied with the dominion of the riotous jungle canopy that had lured him so far from the commonplace, an image he'd seen not just with his eyes but with organs of perception that Avigdor could not even name—and he knew that every nerve in his body would sing out when he saw her again. So he watched from a neighboring ledge and sometimes dropped onto her fire escape to peer through windows, all to no avail. He spied the pomegranate-faced woman at her breadboard and a bald man reading a Yiddish newspaper at a table, rocking a cradle with his foot, and a daughter occasionally moving among them to perform chores; but how could she, who resembled so many others, be the same girl whose rosy essence permeated his waking dream?

From time to time Avigdor's restlessness would get the better of him. Now that the season was milder, his body revived its involuntary agenda, and he was compelled to turn circles about a horizontal flagpole or shove off on a housepainter's ladder, riding it like a giant second hand across an alley. He might skip over an avenue on the tops of the cabs of trucks as if across the armored backs of a herd of rhinoceros. But always he returned to his perch to watch for her, aware that "in his savage, untutored breast new emotions were stirring." He wanted to rescue her from jungle cats and mamba snakes, from the sharklike youths in yellow spats who preyed on pretty Jewish daughters. "He knew that she was created to be protected, and that he was created to protect her." Scrutinizing the girls on the sidewalks or at school, he wondered if he was missing her among them, so much had he come to distrust his own senses at street level. On earth he was only the son of a poor father who wore a suspensory and muttered benedictions into a beard so strewn with scraps you could boil it for soup; whereas aloft . . . but aloft was not where she lived.

Then came an afternoon in late April when the wind started up, the drizzling rain gathered into a cloudburst, and a girl appeared on the tenement roof to take her turn among the women bringing in laundry from the lines. From his roost Avigdor watched her struggling to stuff the billowing garments into her basket in the downpour: how her ginger hair was plastered to her forehead and cheeks, her white frock drenched until it clung to the contours of the sylphlike form beneath. So dizzy with desire was the boy that he nearly pitched head foremost from his perch; for this one he recognized as his rusalka, his seaborne maidele and destined mate. The other ladies had abandoned the roof, leaving the girl still wrestling chemises and sheets, while Avigdor mounted the terrace behind him. Impervious to the driving rain, he stepped onto a cedar plank arched over the fulcrum of a railroad tie, which was wedged under a water barrel at one end, lashed with ropes at the other. He took up a fireman's ax he'd left propped there for the purpose, and bracing for the release of tension that would fling him over the chasm between buildings, severed the ropes at a stroke. But nothing happened; the wet plank retained its warp—his devices were growing outworn from neglect. So he forsook the mechanism and hurtled the abyss on his own steam, clapping hold of a ceramic drainpipe on the opposite wall. He shinnied up its slippery length and sprang onto the roof in time to place himself between the girl and the door to the stairs.

"Then Tarzan of the Apes did just what his first ancestor would have done. He took his woman in his arms and carried her into the jungle," and Avigdor, believing he'd detected a hint of compliance in her attitude, made to follow suit. He grabbed her arm with a force that caused her to drop the basket and pulled her to him, intoxicated by his own strength. Trying his best to ignore her panic, he looked about for the readiest route of absconding with the girl. He saw walls whose irregular bricks he might ascend spiderlike with his burden, chimneys he could bound across like stepping-stones, a distant bell tower that might provide a temporary nest. There he would deposit her after she'd come "to trust this strange wild creature as she would have trusted but few of the men of her acquaintance." He would make her a bed of ferns and grasses and leave her to sleep in the leafy bower while he lay across the entrance to keep watch. In the morning he would bring her coconuts, and when he lifted her up and offered to return her to civilization, she would throw her arms about his neck and unashamedly declare her love.

But that was not how things fell out. Furiously beating her fists against his chest, she cried, "Lemme go!" in a voice whose stridency froze his bones. When he relaxed his embrace, she tore herself from his grasp spitting curses—"Boolvan! Idiot!"—while he remained at a loss for words, having ruled out the language of the great apes as inadequate. Recovered enough to take up her basket and make for the stairwell, she hissed, "A cholera in your guts!" as she swept through the bulkhead door.

Standing there with the rain buffeting his upturned face, he declared, "I'm Avigdor, Lord of the Rooftops," then asked of the closed tin door, "What's *your* name?"

It was Fanny, Fanny Podhoretz, but he wouldn't learn it for a time. For a time he continued lurking in the vicinity of her building, squatting on elevations that afforded him an unobstructed view of her roof. But if she appeared at all (and it was seldom), it was in the company of other girls, as she was clearly not of a mind to risk solitary exposure again. Though she wore the same calicos as her companions and seemed to share in their conspiracies, Avigdor could now discern that, wet or dry, she was a creature composed of pure light. By summer, when he spotted her beating a rug or feather bed with her companions, or braiding another girl's hair, he wondered if she even remembered their encounter. Forgetting it would be in his favor, though the thought also filled him with regret. There were occasions when he saw her eyes stray from their occupation to scan the rooftops, and although at those times he read a certain uneasiness in her expression, he also believed he saw something else—which gave him cause to hope. Nurturing that hope, he would station himself on a cornice or atop a water tower so that, when she looked up, she might observe him hunkering there. But if ever she caught sight of him, she quickly averted her glance. Of course Avigdor continued his aerial sorties, but he no longer plummeted and soared for the sheer animal sport of it; always now he liked to imagine she was watching, that he was showing off his agility for her sake. Such self-consciousness had already in some degree compromised his freedom, or so Avigdor supposed, even as he despaired of ever seeing her alone again. Then early one evening in June, as dusk stained the sky a plum purple over the river, there she was by herself on the roof taking clothes from a line.

And before she could release the corner of a hanging pillow slip, he was standing right in front of her.

The clothespin fell from between her clenched teeth as her jaw dropped open. "Meshuggeh ahf toit!" she cried, taking a step backward with a hand to her breast; but that was the extent of her retreat. Perhaps she'd had a change of heart, or was she merely too frightened to flee? In either case Avigdor felt encouraged, but while he knew better than to try and abduct her, he was still unable to find his tongue. How after all did humans pay court? Then it seemed to him a great mercy that she was the first to speak, demanding in her unladylike voice:

"What are you, a man or a monkey?"

The question demanded an earnest answer and the boy hung his head to consider. "Both?" he replied at length.

"You can't be both," she insisted almost angrily.

He did not contradict her.

Then she cautiously submitted, "You look more like a monkey."

Again he let the statement stand.

She shrugged as if having determined his harmlessness and began hurriedly to fold a sheet that was dragging the tar paper, dropping it into her wicker basket. "In monkeys I ain't innerested," she snapped, but unless he was mistaken, there was a trace of coyness in her tone. Emboldened, Avigdor rallied all the courage he had at his command, which wasn't much—it was only the untried courage of a callow youth, which had little in common with the fearlessness of apes.

"In what then you innerested?" he asked.

She gave another tug at the clothesline on its pulley, causing a tendril of russet hair to come loose from its bun. It spiraled, thought Avigdor, like an auger that could drill to the core of your soul. "I tell you what I ain't innerested; I ain't innerested in talking no more to you. You're bughouse."

But she made no effort to depart, dropping another item of clothing into her basket, an unmentionable article at which Avigdor saw her blush. He felt again the urge to snatch her up and swing aloft with her, to feel her supple body in his arms. He wanted to battle the rogue anthropoid Terkoz over her. An ape-boy had many options unavailable to the son of a mohel. Then she blessedly took the initiative again, uttering somewhere between an insult and advice:

"Go walk up a wall, why dontcha? What are you always spying on me?"

"Because"—in his mind he let go of a vine with no notion of what he might next catch hold of—"I love you."

"Feh!" She made a disgusted face, pulling another scanty item from the line, stuffing it into the basket without folding it as she turned on her heel. "Bughouse!" But the next evening she was on the roof alone again.

He offered her the celestial altitudes and she assured him that the roof of Number 76 Attorney Street was lofty enough for her, thank you very much. He told her that with him she could fly and she said there was nowhere she was going that she couldn't get to on the Third Avenue El. Thus disparaged, he had the presence of mind, once he got around to introducing himself as Avigdor, to insert a "formerly" before "of the Apes." She sniffed and said she was Fanny of the Lower East Side Podhoretzes, her father the proprietor of Podhoretz's Foundation Garments, one of a dozen such hole-in-the-wall establishments on Orchard Street. Then she told him in no uncertain terms that rooftop rendezvous were not her style; they were the kind of thing that could give a girl a reputation, and personally she preferred being closer to the ground. If he wanted to see her again—which wasn't to say that she wanted to see *him*—he could come calling at her family's apartment like a regular person. As she spoke, Avigdor became a student of her emerald eyes set slightly aslant in the cameo pink oval of her face, and realized he was hopelessly torn. To be with her would mean coming down from up above, a bodeful prospect for a youth who had no other prospects in the world of men; and to present himself as a candidate for Fanny's hand he must have prospects.

So, with a heavy heart, he temporarily abandoned the roofs in order to indenture himself to his mother, whose finished piecework he delivered to the rag trade jobbers after school—school having become a place where his attendance seemed daily less imperative, while the cheder was already history. Neither of his parents was especially troubled that his tasks abetted his truancy; both were already resigned to the fact that scholarship would not save their son from the life of a wage slave. At first Avigdor thought he might make short work of his deliveries by taking aerial routes to the uptown emporiums, but given the bundles he had to carry, that method of transport proved impractical. And so he became a shlepper, identifying more with the native bearers the Lord of the Jungle viewed from the treetops than the Lord of the Jungle himself. Still, he was making a salary, if only a pittance, and with his inaugural pennies he purchased a bouquet of chrysanthemums, brilliantined his hair, and turned up with palpitations at the threshold of the Podhoretz flat. He was relieved when, opening the door, Fanny's mother failed to recognize the interloper who'd crash-landed on her kitchen floor, though he still had to submit to what amounted to an inquisition from her father. Once it was established, however, that the merchant Podhoretz and the ritual circumciser Bronfman both hailed from the Ukrainian town of Drogobych—once determined that, un-Jewish musculature notwithstanding, Avigdor was an ordinary kid from the neighborhood—Fanny was allowed to step out with the reformed ape-boy.

They went to a candy store with a fountain on Delancey Street, where Fanny had a charlotte russe, Avigdor a phosphate, and overcoming his disappointment at finding her less siren than sensible Jewish daughter, Avigdor asked her to marry him.

"Behave yourself," simpered Fanny, licking her spoon with a tentacular tongue, but the boy had developed no talent for small talk. In fact, he had no facility for conversing with a young lady in any conventional fashion, when by all rights they ought to be frolicking among branches reached only by the most intrepid of tropical birds. But as he sat there at the marble counter looking out onto the sidewalk, aswarm with toilers and lunch-bucket drones, the jungle, beyond inaccessible, seemed merely a childish dream.

Fanny pointed through the plate-glass window toward a sad-faced capuchin monkey tethered hat-in-hand to an equally dour Italianer's barrel organ. "Maybe you could get his job," she teased.

Among Avigdor's airborne attributes that failed to translate to sea level was his aptitude for playfulness. "I got already a position," he replied, and was instantly ashamed of having adopted a contrary tone with his beloved. But while the shlepping might foot the bill for an occasional excursion to the nickelodeon or the candy store, he knew perfectly well it could never support a wife and family. So what was the alternative? Should he apprentice himself to his father and look forward to a future paved in infant foreskins? His distaste for the profession aside, he was aware that inflicting the bloody sign of the covenant on newborn pishers earned the mohel little more than a dubious local prestige. He supposed he might join the legions of cutters, basters, and pressers that swelled the district's sweatshops, but even these occupations required a modicum of skill, let alone the fetters they imposed on the worker. Or—and here Avigdor had a vision of trapezes and midair arabesques above cheering crowds,

"Maybe I could join a circus?" he proposed.

"Maybe," responded the girl with a coquettish wink, "my papa will give you a job."

The two families met in the rabbi's stuffy chambers in back of the Beit Emunah sanctuary on Stanton Street, where a heavy-lidded Rabbi Iskowitz officiated over the signing of the ketubah, the marriage contract. The Bronfmans and Podhoretzes were courteous to one another, though both families were clearly skeptical about the alliance. After all, their children, barely out of diapers, had bypassed traditional channels in their haste to pledge themselves to one another; and while Fanny was a good girl with a practical nature, Avigdor had only recently shown signs of overcoming a lifelong fecklessness. As they toasted the occasion with thimblefuls of kiddush wine, Reb Bronfman repined with a shake of the head, "Amerikaner kinder," upon which Mr. Podhoretz placed a hand in sympathy on the dandruff-dusted shoulder of the mohel's gabardine: "At least we robbed from the marriage broker his fee, eh, Bronfman?" Their wives—respectively moon- and fruit-faced—assured each other that this was how things were done in the New World, where tradition was trumped by something called love.

For all his giddy emotion, Avigdor was uncomfortable with the business-like atmosphere surrounding the contractual arrangement; while on the other hand he was pleased to be regarded as a person of substance, a grown-up if you will. He felt a measure of gratitude toward his prospective father-in-law (whom he couldn't yet bring himself to call Leon, not that Mr. Podhoretz invited the familiarity) for offering to take him on as an employee in his shop. True, his salary would not amount to much more than his shlepper's wages, but Podhoretz also owned rental property on Rivington Street and had promised to provide the newlyweds with an apartment, rent-free, as a wedding gift. It was a tiny apartment in a dilapidated Old Law building, but even for that Avigdor was thankful, since its condition somewhat salved his feelings of being in the merchant's debt. Still, he was a little breathless from the speed with which events had proceeded: was he in fact about to swap his secret life for a domestic one he was wholly unprepared for? But the important thing, the thing to remember, was that he'd found his bashert, his fated one; that, astonishingly, Fanny had made up her mind to accept him, albeit with some reservations.

"You got potential, Avi," she assured him, poking a forefinger point-blank in his solar plexus, "but you got yet to be a man." Which estate seemed to preclude his simian high jinks.

On strolls past the East Broadway shmooseries or along the Second Avenue rialto in the weeks preceding the wedding, she allowed him certain liberties, but always at a price. The held hand required the promise of some newfangled appliance or, say, a Brussels carpet; the pecked cheek a baby boy. As he listened to her recite the plans for the wedding—echoing her father's anxiety over the rent for the hall, the cost of the catering, the bridesmaids' bouquets—Avigdor felt again the sense of having entered into a business transaction that he'd experienced in the rabbi's chambers. He longed for spontaneous displays of affection, the heated embrace that she would return with a fervent will, her "surrender"—though he wasn't entirely sure what that would entail. But mostly he contented himself in the knowledge that it was her appreciation of his animal grace that had won her; she understood that he was not your garden variety Orchard Street son. So Avigdor kept his passions in check, though it seemed to him dishonest that he should have to suppress them. Also he resented how, the more time you spent on earth, the more the earth's ills flocked about you. The papers harped on the events of the day: the war in Europe, the threat of Spanish influenza, the lynching of Leo Frank. Such incidents from the so-called civilized world had not much concerned him in his days aloft, but now they infected him as if contaminating his blood with lead.

He and Fanny went one night to the picture palace on Grand Street, where they saw Douglas Fairbanks in *The Thief of Baghdad* leaping from onion dome to minaret, and Avigdor felt the charge along his sinews that announced his impulse to soar. He missed the days, already growing remote, when he'd longed for the girl with such keen devotion from an airy distance. ("His thoughts were of the beautiful white girl; they were always of her now. The ape-boy knew no god, but he was as near to worshipping his divinity as mortal man ever comes to worship.") He needed to see his Fanny that way again, from a vantage clear of the poison creepers of commitment that had begun to hamper his limbs. So he climbed walls and vaulted over air shafts and alleys onto her roof, where he lay across the skylight above her landing waiting for a glimpse of his betrothed. She emerged that very evening from her family's flat with a pair of her girlfriends, while her fiancé, feral instincts in play, regarded her through a pane whose dustiness lent a halo to her ginger head. And again he wanted to snatch her up and carry her off without ceremony: the ways of these white men, these Jews, were not his. Watching as she and her friends disappeared down the stairs, he was impervious to the groaning of the window frame (which might have been the rutting of pigeons) as its slats sagged under his weight, then collapsed, so that he plummeted willy-nilly onto the landing below, shattering his leg.

At the wedding he leaned on a crutch like some crippled beggar invited out of charity to partake of the feast, as the veiled bride encircled him seven times. Over her finger he placed a silver ring, purchased on credit, that would often see the inside of pawnshops in the coming years; then he nearly lost his balance while trying to lift a leg to stomp the goblet before he settled upon smashing it with his crutch. During the catered meal that followed the ceremony the wedding bard cut capers that seemed a deliberate mockery of the acrobatics Avigdor had once performed so effortlessly overhead. The spidery badhkn in his boxy skullcap and tailcoat made crude references to the groom's wooden third leg and lampooned his father's profession in the style of the boys at school: "Reb Bronfman was careless on the job and got the sac." A three-piece orchestra serenaded the company and the bard did a kazatski, the mothers-in-law a mekhutonim à deux, but the groom was unable to dance. Fanny had insisted on the goyish tradition of a honeymoon, so they took a train to the Catskills Mountains, where they could not afford the price of a hotel. They stayed in a rundown bungalow colony whose noisy neighbors made of the place a lumpen annex to the ghetto itself. There Fanny tried her hand with mixed success at cooking, while Avigdor, graduated from crutch to mahogany cane (the same he'd once hooked over telephone wires), hobbled about the yard gazing at the dense forest that blanketed the mountains. Then he bounded up a slope, grabbed hold of a low-lying limb, and, hoisting himself into the upper branches, swung from tree to tree until he was beyond the observation of anyone in the known world. Having thus imagined his flight, the bridegroom concluded that undomesticated nature, which he looked upon for the first time in his life, was rather forbidding; whereas Fanny's freckled pink and alabaster body under her modest blue gown—a place she now welcomed him to without conditions—was home.

He ate her rubbery farfel, listened to her dreams of pier glasses and carpet sweepers, and entered her bed with a trembling gratitude—and by winter the stem of her waist had begun to swell with the ripening fruit of their union. By then Avigdor had become more or less accustomed to working in his father-in-law's shop. It had not been an easy adjustment; retail sales demanded of the clerk a healthy measure of convivial talk, which Avigdor did not come by naturally. The ladies, mostly zaftig wives grown heavy with the cares of their middle years, had to be coaxed into feeling comfortable when purchasing intimate garments—garments whose very nature had at first given Avigdor acute distress in handling. He would have liked not to handle them at all, to perhaps offer them to the customers on the end of the snatch pole used for retrieving out-of-reach merchandise. But Mr. Podhoretz, text-book in his methods, told him in no uncertain terms that he must learn to "seduce" the ladies into purchases. The word made Avigdor's skin crawl. But in the end the son-in-law overcame his discomfort and learned to present the corsets and corset covers with deft fingers that tickled the ladies as if they were wearing the garment he teased in his hands. He cultivated the ap-propriate patter ("... your patent bust improver modeled on the one by the famous Venus de Milo ...") and displayed the more compromising items, such as abdominal supporters and uterine trusses, in a manner requiring the utmost discretion. In the end his clientele warmed to the young man with his stringy muscles grown slack from want of exercise and his pronounced limp; for his leg, improperly set, had never truly mended. By the time the child was born—a difficult birth that injured the mother, precluding any further offspring—Avigdor had made himself a virtually indispensable as-sistant to his father-in-law, whose largesse he had more than repaid.

Taking partial credit for her husband's satisfactory progress, Fanny proudly declared one evening as he slouched into the apartment, weary from the day's labor: "You're housebroke, Avi," and Avigdor had to pause to remember a time when he was not.

The boy, Benjamin, named after Fanny's zayde (who'd died of dysentery during the passage from Hamburg), was himself an anemic and often sickly child, doted on by his mother to the exclusion of almost everything else. Before Benjy's conception, Avigdor and his wife had gamboled like young animals in their conjugal bed, whose galloping incited the neighbors below them to bang on the ceiling with brooms. In their transports they'd attained heights from which they were granted an angel's-eye view of their canoo-dling, their hilarity approaching a dangerous pitch. Sober-minded by day, at night Fanny could be adventurous in ways that shocked and delighted her husband; but once she'd become pregnant, adventures ceased, as she concen-trated her energies on the child that filled her womb—which no longer had room for anyone else. Avigdor of course honored her humor; it was after all only temporary; he worshipped at the shrine of her melon tumescence. But after Benjy's delivery, during which the girl had suffered complications that would make intimacy painful in any case, Fanny had no interest in reviving their passion. "If it don't lead to babies, Avi," she stated with a finality that caused her husband's soul to shrink, "it's a sin."

Her body, as if to consolidate her disposition, lost its girlish shape, never again shedding the heft of her pregnancy, while the freckles that stippled her cheeks and chest seemed smeared into blotches and stains. In the meantime Benjy grew at his unsteady pace, still frail and subject to a cavalcade of childhood diseases. These he endured in his convertible bed in the corner of the crowded parlor, reading Bible stories and later the novels of Baroness Orczy and Rafael Sabatini, leading the cosseted life his mother facilitated. She was protective of him to a degree that seemed sometimes to protect him even from his father, who adored him as well—though he nourished an anticipation that the boy's reading would lead eventually to notable deeds. To Avigdor's private dismay, his son was also an acrophobe, who shunned the fire escape and threw tantrums when his parents tried to take him onto the roof to sleep. As a consequence, the family was confined on summer nights to the furnacelike atmosphere of an apartment cluttered to nearly impassable with its Windsor range, davenport bed, and Brunswick Vibrating Shuttle sewing machine; for Fanny would have her distaff accessories. Then she would have a larger apartment ("I got a hashek for a real home, Avi") and had begun to extol Brooklyn as the Promised Land. To please her Avigdor took his wife and child on an excursion out to Brownsville by subway to inspect the mushrooming subdivisions in their uniform lots. Such a move was not out of the question; Podhoretz's Foundation, thanks in part to Avigdor's good offices, was prospering. Mr. Podhoretz had bought the failed haberdashery next door and knocked down the wall between them, expanding his premises as well as his inventory— which now included a new line of queen-size vests and bloomers, and fancy French underwear. Then just as Avigdor was about to close the deal on a two-bedroom duplex in Brownsville, a series of calamities befell his family.

They started when a pair of two-bit extortionists in their fedoras and pencil stripes began dunning Mr. Podhoretz for protection gelt. Edged out of competition with the local bootleg syndicate, the thugs had fallen back on strong-arming East Side shopkeepers, and were naturally attracted to the thriving garment mart with its increased stock-in-trade. But Leon Podhoretz, a stiff-necked man of commerce, a landlord and wise investor whose son-in-law's yeoman service permitted him to contemplate an early retirement, remained obstinate in the face of threats. Avigdor, however, was worried, worry having become a recent avocation. The stock market had crashed, and the old ghetto, in its proximity to the epicenter of the collapse, was especially rocked by the seismic shudder. Pleased with their Yankee-style speculations, Mr. Podhoretz along with his brethren of the Kaminsker Landsmanshaft had lost their shirts, but despite Avigdor's counsel to the contrary his father-in-law still pooh-poohed the underworld menace. The fire that consumed the Podhoretz gesheft spread to the businesses that flanked it on either side, so that a great gray cavity like a meteor crater smoldered in the middle of Orchard Street. The property was of course heavily insured, but the insurance company protested the owner's claim, alleging arson, which was epidemic on the Lower East Side. Thus began a lengthy period of litigation that exhausted what remained of Mr. P.'s savings, while his unemployed son-in-law was forced to apply for jobs that he was eminently unsuited for.

With his lame leg bedeviled by various -itises that flared from activity as from an infestation of fire ants, Avigdor was officially handicapped. Nevertheless he made the rounds of the local shops, limping on his walking stick, canvassing situations that had dried up in any case in a rash of layoffs. He turned out faithfully for the predawn shape-ups (which now attracted multitudes) in Seward Park and at the fish market in South Street, where his disability ruled out his selection for work. A little relief came from an unlikely quarter, since Reb Bronfman's profession turned out to be Depression-proof, and his destitute son, beyond humiliation, had no choice but to accept his papa's handouts. He used the pennies to purchase from a Delancey Street wholesaler tin cups, potato mashers, and shoelaces, which he peddled, in the absence of a pushcart, door to door. But the competition was stiff and few had the wherewithal to buy; never mind that the drag-of-foot peddler, appearing with his sack like a troll out of a grandmother's tale, did not present an appealing countenance. While he might scrape together enough to keep the family in bad herring and stale farfeloons, he continually failed to make the rent they owed under the building's new ownership, since Mr. Podhoretz had had to sell off his holdings. For that Fanny had to take in sewing, restoring spent gathers and orchid folds in worn knickers, stitching needle-run lace to the hems of old petticoats, demonstrating a talent that who knew she had for rejuvenating secondhand apparel. Still they lived week to week in jeopardy of being dispossessed. Then Reb Bronfman, despite a flushed face that some took as a sign of health, dropped dead of a stroke, and Avigdor's fretting over the fate of his bereaved mother supplanted the grief he might have spared for the mohel.

With his wife he discussed his intention of moving the Widow Bronfman into Rivington Street, where her piecework operation combined with Fanny's furbelow trade would comprise a regular cottage industry. But Fanny pointed out that this was a physical impossibility.

"Tahke, so she can sleep in the closet?"

But even as he understood there was no room, Avigdor resented what he perceived as his wife's selfishness. Selfish? She was taking in work by the bushel without complaint, bartering for cracked eggs in the market, sometimes returning home with a chicken under her dress that her increasingly dumpling anatomy helped to conceal. All this she managed while shielding her delicate Benjy—whose diet consisted mainly of milk of magnesia—against the depredations of hard times. If he harbored any lingering spite on account of her frigidity, Avigdor was not aware of it, since his chronic fatigue (and her dowdy figure) had neutralized all carnal thoughts. Still he accused her: "Fanny, a heart you ain't got." But when the tears started in freshets from her eyes, Avigdor wept along with her, and his mother—who had no wish to come between husband and wife—accommodated the children by conveniently passing away herself.

In his woeful distraction Avigdor remembered Shaky Gruber, the friend of his youth, with whom he hadn't communicated in over a decade. Gruber had become a floorwalker at Wanamaker's Department Store, a sharp dresser with the haughtiness of one gainfully employed while the rest of the country waited for F.D.R.'s alphabet agencies to save them. At first Gruber mistook his diminished old chum for a panhandler, until Avigdor, who'd staggered up to him outside the store at the corner of Broadway and Eighth, identified himself. "Guess you don't do much running through the jungle these days," quipped Shaky, though Avigdor didn't seem to know what he was talking about. Once he heard his old friend's appeal, however, Shaky Gruber tugged his lapels and made noises like he might have an inside track; and while he promised more than he could deliver, he was ultimately able to secure Avigdor part-time work as a stock boy, for which the petitioner embarrassed the floorwalker by kissing his hand. Most of the labor went on behind the scenes, on the loading dock and in the stockrooms where the merchandise was sorted and stored—sometimes on shelves that involved climbing ladders upon which Avigdor experienced bouts of vertigo, to say nothing of the constant aggravation in his leg; but often he was called on to move garment racks through the various departments of the mammoth emporium. Then the freight elevator gate would open like a mouth debouching him into gilded halls lined with jewelry in glass cases, aisles of mechanical toys and luxury items in galleries overlooking a cathedral-size atrium. It was during one of these forays, while rattling through Ladies' Furnishings, that Avigdor happened to spy a salesgirl at a loss for words before a customer who insisted on returning an "underbelt corselette."

"The thing makes me look in my chemise like I'm wearing a canary cage," she complained.

"I'm s-s-sorry, madam," stammered the salesgirl, evoking a clearly much rehearsed phrase, "but store policy prohibits the return of discount items . . ."

Looming over the diminutive girl, the woman was demanding to see her supervisor when Avigdor, without thinking, abandoned the garment rack and trundled forward to volunteer his expertise. Later on it would seem to him that he'd stepped from a towering height into a void.

"Excuse me," he said, "but you have every right to complain. However, the new Corslo-silhouette, which it's just in from Paris that I have samples of on my rack, offers a combination of bust bodice, hip belt, jupon, and pantalon—the fabric so flimsy if you eat a grape it will show. We have them in satin and apricot crepe de chine . . ."

The salesgirl stood open-mouthed as the stylish lady listened attentively to Avigdor's shpiel; then she recovered herself enough to protest the stock boy's temerity, only to be shushed by the customer. Actually stomping her foot in indignation, the girl was further chastised by her supervisor, who'd come from behind a counter upon witnessing the scene. A matronly woman squinting through a tiny lorgnette, the supervisor had sized up the situation and, having determined that the crippled stock boy, albeit a male but otherwise innocuous, was the better spokesperson for their merchandise, promoted him on the spot and dispatched the inept salesgirl to the bargain basement. And that was how Avigdor found a safe harbor in intimate apparel, just as the Japanese bombers demonstrated to the nation that no harbors were safe.

But even then he felt uncommonly snug in his new situation, where he remained unruffled in the presence of the ladies who sometimes teased him as they might have a eunuch with whom they felt perfectly at ease. He was a balebos, a householder and provider again, and it wasn't until his bookish son Benjy received his conscription notice that Avigdor's worries, briefly dormant, were recalled to life. This was soon after the Bronfmans, having waited their turn on a long list of intensely vetted applicants, had moved into an apartment in a recently completed housing development near the

East River. The apartment had two bedrooms, steam heat, a tiled bath, and a balcony with a view of the Brooklyn Bridge; and though the news from Europe was dire, it seemed to the Family Bronfman that they had arrived on a friendly shore after a storm. Their son, still prone to infirmity, had just earned his high school diploma and was being courted by colleges looking to fill their Jewish quotas with whiz kids. Vain of his academic accomplishments, Benjy was coy in fielding their invitations, having yet to decide on a particular area of study; for he'd excelled in every subject in the curriculum other than gym. The apartment was full of his awards and citations, and his parents' pride in his achievements was a place where they still found common ground, though they sometimes differed in their ambitions for the boy: Avigdor imagined he might build rockets and cure pestilence, while Fanny preferred he take an easeful seat on the Supreme Court. She was concerned, however, that the stress of high office might tax his weak constitution. Given his continued poor health, it had always been assumed that, even in wartime, the boy would be deferred from the draft. He was a special case and it was unthinkable that his fate should be cast among the rank and file. Then it seemed even more inconceivable that after his induction, rather than assigned to some administrative (if not counterintelligence) desk, he was sent instead to the front, where he was shot by a sniper in the snow-deep forest of the Ardennes.

Now, thought Avigdor, there was nothing left to worry about; the worst had happened. Now there was only his trying to imagine the magnitude of the fear his son must have known in the chaos of battle, and as it turned out he was very good at imagining; it was an exercise that caused the chronic pain in his stiffened leg to resonate in his heart. Then the fear, assuming volume and weight, would come to occupy the spaces where the boy had been, supplanting the ache of missing him and the regret over having neglected him when he lived. Nothing on earth was untainted by it; naked fear emanated not just from the Bomb or the Reds or the execution of the Rosenbergs, not only from the evidence of a continent toiveled of Jews, but from the diaphanous fabrics he handled in the emporium and the doll-like women who bought them. It emanated from the coffee-skinned strangers who'd begun to invade the old neighborhood. By the time the fear had subsided enough for Avigdor to notice her, his wife had languished too long in the bed from which he'd banished himself. From the first he'd resented the way she hoarded all the sorrow, leaving him to absorb the dread, but in time the situation started to seem like a fair enough bargain. It was only when her body (which in wasting away had reverted to its original spindliness) began to fail her that Avigdor wondered why, though he no longer loved her, he should be so afraid of her passing. Nor did his apprehension die with her, when after a regimen of pills that left her sleepwalking when she wasn't prostrate, Fanny finally gave up the ghost. Or was it that the ghost she'd become surrendered the heartsick Fanny? In any event the world now seemed almost too frightful a place to visit anymore, notwithstanding Avigdor's fear of being alone.

His old friend Shaky Gruber tried to remind the shop clerk that the world was wider than the blighted Lower East Side. Shaky himself had made a killing through shrewd investments in the postwar real estate boom and had moved his family into a house on Ocean Parkway in Brooklyn. He came into the neighborhood on Sundays to buy delicatessen, when he would deign to treat the sad-sack Bronfman, not much stouter these days than his own walking stick, to cheese blintzes at the Garden Cafeteria. Grown venerable in his prosperity, Shaky would assure Avigdor that the earth was still full of a number of things.

"Such as," Avigdor humbly conceded, "the murder of a young president and a brand-new war—or is it just the continuation of an old?" For the shop clerk caught only vague references to such things between episodes of *Mr. Ed* and *I've Got a Secret*, and reruns of *The Honeymooners* on the snowy screen of his rabbit-eared TV.

Shaky dismissed his friend's rotten attitude with a harrumph. "You must've accumulated what, maybe a decade's worth of vacation time? Why don't you make a holiday?"

"Where would I go?" wondered Avigdor, whose whole life, come to think of it, was circumscribed by the vanishing ghetto. The journey by bus from Grand Street up to Broadway and Eighth was far enough for him, thanks all the same. (He'd since curtailed his junkets to a home for the aged in Greenwich Village, where Fanny's little sister, grown up and married to a doctor, had installed her parents; for the Podhoretzes had made it clear they regarded their son-in-law as somehow complicit in their daughter's demise, a judgment with which the son-in-law guiltily concurred.)

"I dunno, Bronfman." Shaky stopped chewing, one varicose cheek stuffed with blintz. "Visit the Fiji Isles, go to the moon. Maybe you should get in with the Hasids that got a shuttle service between East Broadway and paradise . . ." He was alluding to a community of fanatical Munkatsh refugees who had taken up residence down the street, their little shtibl sandwiched between a bodega and a Puerto Rican social club. "If you don't want a woman, you can get religion instead."

Shaky himself was a big shot at a showcase temple out on the Parkway, and he recommended that Avigdor get involved with a local congregation if only for the sake of fellowship. Avigdor respectfully rejected his advice out of hand, prompting Shaky to ask, "Why do I bother?" Then he stopped bothering and more years passed, bringing more universal enormities, some of which bled uncensored into the shop clerk's companion TV. Meanwhile Wanamaker's had changed hands, though Avigdor, as much a fixture as the model home on the furniture floor, managed to hang on to his job; but his increasingly clunky demeanor no longer inspired confidence in his clientele. Moreover, he'd grown uneasy with recent trends in the undergarment industry, squeamish in the face of their vulgarity. So when it was not so subtly suggested that he'd outworn his usefulness, he took the hint and retired on a modest pension; he rented a small apartment in a lower-income development and became for all intents and purposes a shut-in.

His television, however, remained a poor filter for the incursions of history, and even *Bonanza* and *The Beverly Hillbillies* were haunted by images of torched villages and cities in flames. Then the retiree, harried from his isolation, would find himself toiling along once familiar streets such as East Broadway, where, in lieu of the talkers' cafés and Yiddish journals, there was tropical music even in winter and the Chinese had commandeered a beachhead in the old Forward Building. On this particular early evening, in a sudden blue flurry that rivaled the staticky reception on his TV, Avigdor heard issuing from an eroded fieldstone townhouse the sounds of inharmonious prayer. He hadn't been in a synagogue since his dead papa had circumcised his son with a palsied hand in the vestibule of the Stanton Street shul, its doors since boarded up. But shivering in his threadbare overcoat, he told himself he was only seeking warmth rather than heeding some elemental call. He trudged up the steps and pushed open the door of the Munkatsher shtibl, surprised that no one prevented his entry; because it seemed to Avigdor that he should have been forbidden what he witnessed: a minyan or more of Hasidim, like a crowd of black mantises, their forelegs resting on each other's shoulders, shuffled in a circle about an old man who stood on a stepladder (in place of a bima) hugging the sacred scrolls. With his thin beard curling like smoke from a lamp, his narrow face lifted in ecstasy, the old man maintained a precarious balance on the ladder's middle rung. "Kadosh, kadosh . . . ," warbled his disciples, raising their raucous singsong a decibel or

two as their rebbe ascended another step. Their voices swayed the chandelier
and caused plaster to waft from the ceiling, as the rebbe, in his gymnastic
rapture, mounted the ladder's summit then stepped further onto an invisible rung. Was Avigdor dreaming or did the holy man, his white-stockinged
ankles a visual echo of the Torah finials, hover in midair an instant before
plunging into the arms of his disciples? It was in any event the moment
when the retired shop clerk, having seen more than enough, fled the roomful
of lunatics.

Safely returned to his apartment, he switched on the television set, which
as luck would have it was on the blink. This was no great loss, since the thing
had recently become nothing more than a cabinet of proliferating horrors.
But left to his own devices, Avigdor, still trying to catch his ragged breath,
realized that he had no devices left. There was little to distract him amid the
sparse furnishings of his compact abode, scoured as it was of any mementoes
of his marriage—which made the small shrine of his lost son's books, on their
shelf atop a wheezing radiator, so conspicuous. Avigdor could not remember
the last time he'd read a book, nor had he ever been tempted by these, which
were mostly dry academic texts. But among them was also a handful of dog-
eared novels that Benjy had abandoned in early adolescence: adventure sagas
by Delos Lovelace and Jules Verne, a volume by Edgar Rice Burroughs entitled
Tarzan of the Apes. Taking the latter tentatively in hand, Avigdor could feel his
follicles tingling, though he couldn't at first have said why; but when he opened
the book and perused a random passage ("None more craftily stealthy than he,
none more ferocious, nor none who leaped so high into the air in the Dance of
Death"), his heart released a sob that left it deflated.

Collapsing into an armchair, he concluded after a while, "Whatever time
I got left, it's wasted on me," and thereupon resolved to end his miserable
life. Months passed, however, before he was able to stir himself to the task.
The bones of his crooked leg seemed as if replaced by a fiery brand, which
did little to assuage the chill that pervaded the rest of his meager frame; so
it wasn't until a soft morning in April that he felt mobile enough to put his
plan into practice. He nibbled some toast dipped in tea, bundled himself in
his overcoat despite the warm weather, and began his halting progress toward Orchard Street, obeying a sentimental impulse to locate his childhood
tenement and fling himself from the roof.

The building was still standing, its dim stairwell still dense with a pa-
limpsest of odors that included, beneath a veil of peppery spices, an ancient
cabbage stench. The water-stained walls were riotous with spray-painted

graffiti like prehistoric glyphs on the walls of a cave. Having slogged to the head of the stairs, his lungs and joints howling, Avigdor nudged open the unlocked door, inhaled a deep draught of noxious ozone, and fell into a coughing fit. The brick bulkheads were also emblazoned with gang insignia, the defunct water tanks with Day-Glo portraits of murdered boys. As the cripple made his way between the rotting frames of untended gardens, he was aware of trespassing, of perhaps being watched by the tribes that oversaw these heights. Exhausted past his capacity for being afraid, however, he approached the parapet and, with the aid of his cane (which he relinquished thereafter), hoisted himself onto the knee-high wall, its width broadened by an ornamental molding. He stood totteringly erect and thought he could see, beyond the skirmishing antennae and huddled towers, continents swarming with ignorant armies butchering their own. Their distant cries mingled with those of the immigrant merchants shmeikeling cheap leather goods in the street below.

Then a memory insinuated itself into his weary brain: of being taken as a child to the East River wharves by his parents on the Jewish New Year, where he was instructed to toss his fledgling sins in the form of bread crumbs into the murky water. Could a person release the burden of his years in the same fashion? he wondered; but Rosh Hashanah was months away and Avigdor could not at any rate imagine how to discard his sins exclusive of himself. So, as a breeze fluttered his coattails and caressed his cheek, he stepped from the ledge and dropped like a stone. But no sooner did he find himself plummeting toward the pavement—which was rushing up to slap him into oblivion—than he realized that the wounds of past decades were nothing compared to what he'd suffered at the hands of the mountain apes Bolgani and Kerchak. Instinctively he snagged an electrical cable with the same strong arm that had slain the brute Terkoz, and felt his body whipped into a sudden jackknife from which—once he'd adjusted himself to the empty air—he unfolded into an impeccably executed swan dive. He caught hold of a wrought iron sign pole that jutted out above a shop and swung around it, hesitating at the apex in a momentary handstand, enjoying his view of the world turned upside down. Then he spun in a giant revolution once, twice, three times before letting go, confident that in flight he would find something else to grab hold of . . .

Heaven Is Full of Windows

Had Gussie Panken looked up from her machine, a movement that could get her salary docked a dollar, she would have seen what the lazy Sadie Kupla saw in the window overlooking Washington Place. The late-March breeze was causing the orange curtains to billow, the serrated orange curtains, though the open windows along Washington Place had never had any curtains. Then the wisps of orange turned into waves, a rumbling swell that poured over the sills into the shop, engulfing the bins of scraps, torching the bales of unfinished waists heaped atop the oil-soaked tables. By the time Gussie had turned to see what Sadie was screeching about—her shrieks echoed in a chorus all up and down the long rows of worktables—the fire was advancing like a mob of ragged hooligans. Gussie's first impulse was to do nothing; she was tired and this wasn't the first time she'd been the victim of hooligans. Hadn't they driven her family out of their home back in Dlugacsz, forced them to cross an ocean to a rat-hole flat on Broome Street, where she lived with a crippled father and her bed-wetting little brother who must nevertheless be honored as a prince? She felt her charging heart secrete a poison that paralyzed her limbs, but only momentarily, until she too was swept up in the hysteria that harried her fellow seamstresses from one end of the shop to the other, like sticks in a box tilted this way and that.

At the door to the Greene Street stairwell, which opened inwardly, the knot of workers rushing to escape was stalled, and unable to squeeze through the narrow gap they began in the thickening smoke to claw and flail at one another. Then the crowd had reversed itself, stampeding through eddies of flame past wicker baskets combusting in horse-fart poofs, and Gussie found herself carried along in the tide. At the door on the Washington Place side of the shop, which was always kept locked by management for reasons known only to them, a burly fellow with a handlebar mustache hurled his weight against the metal plating, leaving it concave though the door never budged from its jamb. Others pounded the door with their fists, a shuddering that reverberated in Gussie's gut until she retched, sinking to her knees. From the floor, her eyes smarting, lungs beginning to wheeze in pain, she groped among the remnants on the table above her for a swatch of lawn to cover her face. Showers of sparks seemed to blend with the curses and cries for help like flights of hornets making an eerie drone. Windowpanes above a nearby air shaft splintered in popgun bursts, and a party of workers swarmed through their ruined frames out onto the fire escape. Then in seconds the whole rusted structure had pulled away from the wall, and the people, releasing a noise like a sepulchral moan, dropped out of sight as on a raft sinking below waves.

"Mama," said Gussie, unable to hear the sound of her own voice, not beckoning her mother so much as scolding her for having died of diphtheria three years ago back in Dlugacsz.

Somehow she was on her feet again, blundering blindly alongside the tables on top of which the more athletic girls hopped and jigged in an effort to elude the saw-toothed conflagration. Rearrived at the Greene Street vestibule just in time to see the freight elevator descending, she blinked through stinging tears at what was at once real and not real: a clutch of employees who hadn't made it on board the elevator thrust aside the accordion grate and, licked from behind by tongues of flame, plunged after the departed car into the yawning shaft. She saw a pretty girl spinning like a top to try and unravel the fiery helix of fabric she'd wound about her for protection, and another with a torch in place of her hair. One shouted something in broken English about having to meet Gaspar behind Bottle Alley; another crooned idiotically in Yiddish: "Ev'ry little movement has a meaning all its own." Unaware that her own skirt had started to smolder, Gussie now wanted only to breathe. A wall of fire flapped like sheets on a line, then blew apart in a dragon's exhalation that chased the seamstress back toward the windows along Washington Place. In each of them were figures silhouetted against the failing afternoon light, who disappeared only to be replaced by others who also instantly disappeared. Jostled and caromed against from all sides in the choking atmosphere, Gussie half-stumbled, half-fell in the direction of the tall windows. Unconscious of having made a decision, she avoided the casement in which the girls tussled as if vying with one another to board a packed trolley; the window from which a tangle of girls tumbled like a flickering pinwheel over the ledge. Instead she elected to mount the sill upon which a young man in a waistcoat stood helping the girls to step one by one into space. With sleeves rolled he bussed them tenderly on the cheek, then lifted them under their arms, as in a dance, before letting them drop.

Now it was Gussie's turn and with the aid of the gallant young man she had mounted the sill, stepped onto the ledge, and stood vaguely aware of the sirens, the roar of the multitude below, their howls of alarm indistinguishable from cheers. She saw the ladders extending several stories shy of the ninth floor, the plumes of water spraying so far from their marks. Letting go of the lawn hankie, which the wind carried over the sooty skylights and water tanks etched against a cobalt sky, Gussie imbibed the cool evening air of her oblivion, and felt her fear abruptly dispelled. In its place was pure rage.

Plain Gussie Panken, born to be a spinster, dried up and unshtupped at twenty-three: "What did I have? Mama's carbuncle brooch when it wasn't in hock, and her dog-eared copy of *The Duties of the Heart*. Freda Fine has a beau plus a book signed by the theater idols Tomashefsky and Kalish, and my pious papa tells her, 'Our Gussie will get in paradise her *Duties from the Heart* autographed by God.'"

Over her shoulder the shop was a garden of flame, every flywheel, driveshaft, and burning maiden limned in undulant gold. "Ptui on God," spat Gussie, feeding the blaze.

It came then, the gingerly peck on the cheek from the young man, a fresh-faced boy really despite his tarnished brow, with downcast eyes and a shock of sable hair; he kissed her and endeavored to lift her under her sweat-soaked arms. "That's it?" she asked, still immovable. Then wiping the drool from her lips, she clapped her hands over his cheeks and kissed him full on the mouth: a scandal! She grinned at his astonishment, impish Gussie, who also blushed, then heaved a sigh over the ineffectual husband he would make—a pisher who stole kisses from ladies in extremity. She sighed as well at the dingy hall they would rent for their wedding, the tallis shop they would open on Orchard Street and later set fire to for the insurance, the hungry baby mauling her breast and the dim one lolling underfoot on the greasy floorboards, the extra weight she'd put on fore and aft that added to her burden, the shoes she had to cut slits in to relieve the pressure on her bunions, the silver hairs that would come to signify this frustration and that disappointment and the joys (surely there would be a little joy) that she'd survived. Then Gussie, decked out now in an incandescent gown, wrapped her fingers—perforated by a thousand needles but still very strong—about the hand of the chivalrous boy and leapt from the ledge without the help of anyone on earth.

A cop covering the broken bodies with a tarpaulin noted the half-incinerated girl with her goggle eyes and crooked mouth holding hands with a dark-haired lad, and observed ironically to his mate, "A match made in heaven."

III

EUROPE

Yiddish Twilight

for Howard Schwartz

Before he became a dissolute wanderer and corrupter of children, Hershel Khevreman was a devout student of Talmud. Son of an impoverished poulterer known as Itche Chicken in the Galician village of Zshldz, he'd far outdistanced the local scholars and soon after his bar mitzvah had set off on foot in search of a higher learning, landing eventually in the court of the Saczer Rebbe in the remote Carpathian outpost of Stary Sacz. There, beyond the diseases and rampaging Cossacks that plagued his native Zshldz, beyond the reach of his dowdy parents, Hershel flourished; he earned a reputation for scholarship that in turn brought him to the attention of Reb Avrom Treklekh, a prosperous distiller of fruit kvass, who offered Hershel his daughter's hand in marriage. Despite his youth (he was barely sixteen) and his absorption in the study of the Law, Hershel was no fool, and he anxiously looked forward to assuming his portion as a rich man's son-in-law.

On the Monday night before the wedding (Tuesday weddings were considered propitious because God had said thrice, "It is well" on the Third Day), Hershel and his fellow scholars were gathered in the besmedresh for an informal celebration. With its timeworn benches and sagging shelves of books, their weathered pages as scalloped as cockleshells, with its burbling samovar atop a barrel-shaped stove, the study house was more than a classroom; it was parlor, dining hall, and dormitory to the majority of yeshiva boys. Outside, the early autumn wind was indistinguishable from the howling of wolves on the heights above the town; while across the steppes below swept the armies of an emperor, a kaiser, a czar, for whom the zhids were cannon fodder or target practice. Below their mountain fastness were blood libels and legal pogroms, a night distinctly unfriendly to the Jews; but despite (or because of) the dangers, the house of study remained for its occupants as snug as a humidor.

For the eve of Hershel's wedding, the scholars, penniless all, had nevertheless managed to stockpile some refreshment: a little herring, zweiback and sour pickles, a couple of bottles of Shabbos wine. This they did more out of a sense of tradition than from any love of the groom, whom they largely considered an arrogant prig. If they had anything to celebrate, it was that the self-styled Talmud chochem, the wise guy, would soon be moving in under Reb Avrom's ample roof, and hopefully out of their hair. Still, unaccustomed to excess, the lads found themselves growing festive with drink, the friskier among them teasing the groom in a spirit that betrayed their jealousy.

Velvl Spfarb, for instance, a fat boy who fancied himself a serious challenger to Hershel's standing as resident genius, raised his glass to propose: "If the shekels are there, the groom will appear." Meant to suggest Hershel's mercenary intentions, it was a hypocritical dig, since who among them wouldn't have liked to be in the scholar's shoes? Then Shloyme Aba, ungainly in peaked cap and patched gabardine, a permanent leer across his foxy face, went Velvl one better. "The uglier the piece, the luck will increase," he declared; because the truth was that Hershel's betrothed, Shifra Puah—Hershel had hardly noticed her at the contract signing, so beguiled was he by the uncracked books in Reb Avrom's study—was not a very prepossessing young woman. In fact, just thirteen, with a body like an empty pillow slip and a pinched face the hue of a biscuit dipped in borsht, she was not a woman at all.

Seated stiffly in the place of honor at the head of a scored oak table, Hershel chafed at their disrespect. A proven prodigy who'd bested them all in the toe-to-toe pilpul discourse, he didn't like being used with such familiarity. Moreover, observing an obligatory prenuptial fast, the bridegroom was forbidden food and drink, which made it doubly hard to appreciate their sportive mood. Still, Hershel reminded himself that, given the degree of good fortune that had lately befallen him, he could afford to be a little indulgent. After all, what did he want beyond the leisure to pursue a lifelong exploration of Mosaic Law? And if that pursuit was sustained by the generosity of in-laws in a house like a Venetian palazzo, then how manifold were his blessings; and how small a price to pay for them was the sniping of his less accomplished peers.

The drudge, Muni Misery, shoulders drooping from what he liked to claim was the weight of history, offered this observation: "A wedding is like a funeral but with musicians." He was seconded by Yukie Etka Zeidl's, ordinarily a taciturn oaf but moved to speak up tonight: "A man goes to the bridal canopy alive and returns a corpse." More proverbs equating marriage with death were tendered as toasts, after which the boys took another sip of wine.

Then Shloyme Aba, the closest to an authentic wag the yeshiva could boast of, bounded onto the table to pose a riddle like a wedding jester. "Why," he asked, extending a finger from the ragged wing of his sleeve, "does a stretcher have only two poles while a wedding canopy has four? Because—" He was interrupted before he could answer himself.

"Because, with a stretcher you bury only one person"—it was Hershel, unable to suffer in silence any longer—"while with a wedding canopy you bury two." Risen to his feet, he displayed the assurance that made him both the bane and envy of the other students.

There was a hush while the gathering fumbled for some common attitude toward Hershel's intrusion, though none were perhaps more surprised than the bridegroom himself. Had he, by participating, given his blessing to these unseemly goings-on? An asthmatic wheeze from Shloyme Aba signaled the others that the guest of honor had at last entered into the spirit of the occasion; raising his glass, he proposed another toast, this one more or less sincere. "God send you the wife you deserve!" Hershel, at some expense of dignity, forced a smile.

As the company joined in the toast, Shloyme Aba hopped down from the table and launched into an impersonation of their teacher, Rabbi Asher ben Yedvab, the Saczer Rebbe. Rattle-boned, with a nose like a spigot, Shloyme was eminently suited for the role. He bent his back, fluttered an eyelid, fidgeting a mock-palsied hand at the level of his crotch; while Velvl Spfarb, who'd done yeoman service in assisting the actual rebbe, stepped forward to lend his support to the sham. The hammerheaded Salo Pinkas took Shloyme Aba's other arm.

"P-place a drop of blood on the t-tip of a sword," he intoned in the rebbe's reedy stammer. "The instant it t-t-takes the drop to d-duh-duhhh [Salo Pinkas slapped him hard on the back] to divide into two parts, that is t-twilight."

It was a fair approximation of the Saczer's fanciful pronouncements, and the students cackled their approval. Goaded by the laughter, Shloyme Aba further exaggerated the rebbe's galvanic tics and spasms, joggling so that his supporters could barely hold on. Then he turned toward the eastern wall of the study house, where a ponderous piece of mahogany furniture stood. This was the hall tree the rebbe had brought with him on his journey from Przemysl over half a century before. Since the study house had no vestibule and the thing itself looked nothing like a tree—was in fact a tall, thronelike structure with a seat and a large oval mirror circumscribed by coat hooks—it was a constant source of amusement to the yeshiva boys. Especially amusing to them was their otherwise ascetic rebbe's attachment to his hall tree. He addressed it with a reverence typically reserved for the Ark in the synagogue, wherein the scrolls of the Law were kept. This made Shloyme Aba's prayerful convulsions, body flapping like a shutter in a gale, all the more risible to his audience.

Even the haughty bridegroom succumbed to the comedy, which, fueled by drink and the zeal of his fellows, wildly exceeded Shloyme Aba's ordinary mischief. Having stooped to make an adjustment, he now turned back around to show a limp sock dangling from his fly—unbuttoned flies being one of the rebbe's frequent oversights.

"Rabbi Ishmael ben Yose's member was the size of a wineskin of nine k-k-k-kav," he proclaimed. "But Rav Papa himself had a shwantz like the b-baskets of Hip-hip-areenum . . ."

While most still hooted their encouragement, some of the younger boys had fallen silent, perhaps sensing that Shloyme Aba had crossed a line. Hershel, who for his part had never shared the others' unconditional affection for their rebbe, applauded the imposture. He had always been irritated by Rabbi ben Yedvab's overheated romance with Torah, an attitude he deemed lacking decorum and courting indecency. ("Like the s-sex of the gazelle is the Torah," the rebbe was wont to say, "for whose husband every t-t-time is like the first.") He disapproved of how the old tzaddik used scripture as a stimulus to ecstatic transports. If scripture was meant to be a stimulus for anything, thought Hershel, it was to inspire practical interpretations, such as Maimonides's *Mishneh Torah* or Rashi's commentaries—texts the scholar tended to prefer to the Pentateuch itself.

So when Shloyme Aba, whose performance was approaching the feverish, began reciting the betrothal benedictions, Hershel—reasoning that the burlesque was after all in the nature of a rehearsal—stepped up beside him. Velvl Spfarb, as if seized by conscience, backed furtively away, but Yukie Etka Zeidl's took his place, and together he and Salo Pinkas, in lieu of a wedding canopy, raised a threadbare caftan over the bridegroom's head.

"Mi adir al ha-kol b-b-biddle-bum . . . ," chanted Shloyme Aba, having faced the hall tree again; as over his shoulder Hershel took the measure of himself in the cloudy mirror. With his interest generally fixed on the abstract, the prodigy had seldom concerned himself with appearances—why should he care what kind of figure he cut in the tortured alleys of Stary Sacz? But tonight, no doubt infected by the high spirits of his companions (he hadn't thought of them as "companions" until tonight), Hershel felt peculiarly at home in his body, and noted that he wasn't a bad-looking chap. Slender as a taper, he stood remarkably straight for a boy who spent his days bent over books. His cheeks, still beardless, were unblemished by the eruptions afflicting so many other students; his nose was imperially aquiline. Ginger curls boiled from under his skullcap; his earlocks were like scrolled ribbons, his eyes echoing the emerald of the mirror glass. All in all, Hershel thought he made quite an affecting bridegroom.

As Shloyme Aba completed the nuptial formula, Muni Misery, never so antic, placed a goblet near Hershel's foot for him to stomp. A stickler for protocol, however, Hershel came suddenly back to himself.

"How can I crush the glass," he wanted to know, "before I put the ring on the finger of my betrothed?"

The question was calculated to abort the ceremony, which to Hershel's mind had gone far enough; and since he was confident that the ring remained in the safekeeping of his future father-in-law until tomorrow, he assumed the horseplay was at an end. But Muni Misery again rose to the challenge. He presented Hershel with a loop he'd fashioned from a tuft of fur belonging to the perpetually molting study house cat. (A brindled and querulous animal whom the rebbe suspected of being the reincarnation of Menachem Mendl of Kotzk.) Hershel, for whom the charade was effectively over, received the loop a little impatiently, but having committed himself thus far, he accepted his cue to proceed. He began to recite, albeit halfheartedly, the sacred kiddushin: "Harai at mekudeshet lee, b'ta-ba-at-zu, k'dat Moshe v'Yisrael. Be sanctified to me with this ring in accordance with the law of Moses and Israel." Then he placed the loop over the crooked brass finger of a coat hook.

The boldness of the gesture made him shudder, the shudder reverberating around the room—because no sooner had the ring encircled the coat hook than the surface of the mirror began to stir.

Hershel wondered if the vinous breaths of the other bochers had distorted his own perception, inducing a dizziness that blurred his image in the glass. He momentarily lost his balance, stepping on the goblet, which made a sound like a jaw munching bone; but more fascinated than frightened, he steadied himself, observing how the rippling glass resembled watered silk in a breeze. He watched his image begin to fragment and dissolve in the murky oval—as if a reflection on a pond were being replaced by a body floating to the surface. Then the body acquired dimensions that contradicted the flat face of the mirror, assuming the form of a young woman, tall and lean, with billowing midnight hair. She was wearing a loose cambric shift that clung to her sinewy limbs as she stepped from the mirror onto the swept clay floor.

With the exception of Menachem Mendl, screeching as he arched his back, screeching louder as he singed his fur on the stove, no one had the wit to utter a sound. Taking flight, they climbed over one another in their frantic efforts to escape through the solitary door. The slew-footed Yukie Etka Zeidl's stumbled at the threshold and was trodden upon by his cronies; Velvl Spfarb, already backed against the far wall, squeezed his girth through a narrow casement and tumbled out headfirst. Hershel himself would doubtless have been in their number had not the woman—she seemed for all practical purposes a woman, of about eighteen in human years—had she not taken his hand in her own, which was brackish and cold.

"My pretty husband," she said, her voice as tart as prune compote, "shalom."

Your garden-variety yeshiva scholar was never known for his discretion. So routine were his days that the least irregularity—one fainted from hunger, another suffered a nocturnal discharge—was likely to trigger a rash of loshen horeh, of gossip. Any deviation from the usual was subject to scrupulous inquiry; this was their habit. But what the boys had witnessed in the study house tonight so far surpassed their tolerance for abnormality that it confounded their ability to carry tales. Too prodigious and frightful a burden to pass on, this one was better left alone.

The few who boarded in town fled to their hosts; the rest sought sanctuary across the compound in the little stone shul. Despite the protests of Fishke the shammes, who reminded them that the small hours were reserved for the dead, they insisted on saying penitential prayers. Most remained in the synagogue—its haunted atmosphere notwithstanding—throughout the night, though some, more curious than chastened, girded themselves to return to the besmedresh. There they found Hershel Khevreman, naked but for his ritual garment, huddled on the seat of the hall tree with unfocused eyes.

Nobody dared to interrogate him, nor did Hershel, absently accepting his trousers from one, his waistcoat from another, offer any enlightenment. He said nothing to counter their unspoken pact to forget this evening's incident altogether. Only Velvl Spfarb, who'd turned around after diving through the window and lost his smugness for all time—only he reported the story, first to the rebbe and again many years later, after Hershel himself had long since passed into legend. Then Velvl told how the paralyzed scholar had submitted to the woman's toying with his ritual fringes, her unfastening of his suspender buttons, the stroking of his chest; how she'd hunched her shoulders to let the shift slither down her tawny length, pooling like fog at her feet; after which they'd admired each other in the glass. And when, having touched the mirror to no purpose, Hershel turned to touch her umber flesh, she let loose a cry—like a sound that had traveled through three twists of a devil's shofar to rattle the study house walls.

(The "three twists" were a bit of embroidery Velvl permitted himself despite the families who reproached him for recounting such an unsavory tale. Already sick with fear in a crowded boxcar clattering toward Gehinnom, why should their children be further abused by the phantoms of a windy old man?)

When they'd expended enough guilty solicitude on him, the students nudged Hershel out the door, pointing him in the direction of the clockmaker's shop where he boarded. Tottering through the switchback streets of the Jewish quarter, the prodigy attempted to apply his talmudic logic to what had transpired, but found that once reliable faculty in sad disrepair.

With a borrowed key he entered the shuttered shop, its interior as alive with ticking as a field of locusts. Last week had been Kalman Tsensifer the blacksmith and his ringing anvil, the week before Falik the cobbler and his last; this week was Yosl Berg the clockmaker with his ticking, his wife with the swinging pendulum of her broom. Thus did the shtetl keep time with a pleasing monotony to the rhythm of Hershel's days. Parting a curtain, he slipped into the close compartment that served as parlor, kitchen, and bedroom for the Bergs. He crossed the floor, his footsteps muted by the clocks and the stormy snoring from behind a burlap screen, then climbed a short ladder to the loft above the ceramic tile stove. There, amid the risen odors of goose fat and human gas, he stripped to the flannel gatkes (it was cold for the month of Tishri) and crawled into the quilted cavern of his featherbed.

Raised on mealy potatoes by a lumpish mother, herself potato-shaped, and a father festooned in feathers like a flightless bird, Hershel had conceived, since coming to Stary Sacz, a fondness for creature comforts. He liked clean linen, warm rooms, and bakery goods. In fact, his affection for featherbeds might rival on occasion his passion for the conundrums of the Law. But such pleasures marked the limits of Hershel's indulgence. The wayward thoughts and temptations the rebbe described as the reverse side of the scholarly virtues seldom disturbed him. To resolve some thorny legal problem—the culpability, say, of a family into whose home a mouse brings unleavened crumbs on Passover, or how much farther to rend a garment upon the death of a near relation than of a friend—this was meat and drink to Hershel; of the commentaries of the Oral Torah, he could say along with the psalmist: "How sweet are Thy words unto my palate!" Nothing in the larders of the households on whose charity he depended had ever beckoned him more.

But all that was changed in an hour by a lady who stepped out of a mirror—which was of course impossible. It was a phenomenon that defied the rational categories, a thing that would never have been credited in the pandects of Maimonides or the Vilna Gaon. The Jews of Stary Sacz, Hasids and mitnagdim alike, might be prone in their unworldly isolation to superstition. They might observe their watch nights, shooing demons from a baby's crib on the eve of his bris, incanting in the chamber of women in labor: "Womb, lie down!" But Hershel Khevreman, who had no patience with magic, discounted all irrational expressions of faith. He discounted them so fervently that he sometimes wondered if faith itself was not irrational. Wasn't God, when you thought of it, a somewhat absurd proposition? This was a line of reasoning Hershel rarely followed any further, always returning to a conscientious exegesis of texts. Study, that was his ruling impulse, overruled though it had been tonight.

So where had she fled to? For as soon as the boys began to creep back into the study house, she was gone, leaving him to crumple in a heap against the hall tree. To ask himself again if she was real was to belabor the question, for hadn't he already dismissed her as a figment, a dream—though it's said that "a dream is one-sixtieth of prophecy," and this one he recalled with uncommon lucidity. There were, for instance, all the things she had that, l'havdil! he did not: such as the hair in its abundant black whorls that could founder a frigate, the nipples that stood to attention with a look, the fluted ribs, the close-pored hollow where her navel should have been, her laughter like a glockenspiel . . .

According to the rebbe's precious Kabbalah, of which Hershel was deeply skeptical, one must yield to sin before attaining the higher status of penitent. But Hershel had argued from tractate Berakhot that "at the place reserved for penitents, no righteous man may stand," and surely he, by virtue of diligent study, was a righteous man. So what was he thinking? Only that, real or not, the lady from the mirror had awakened in him a desire that—God forbid!—he would trade Shifra Puah and all the bounty that came with her to realize.

Then it occurred to Hershel that the only logical explanation for what had taken place tonight was that he'd lost his mind. Coincidental with this conclusion the ladder creaked; it creaked once, twice, the planks giving gently, a body with a pungent odor (its flesh mingling fire and ice) sliding next to him in his goose-down cocoon.

"My man"—her breath kindled his brain like an ember in a warming pan—"we got yet unfinished business . . ."

Around the same time the old bachelor rebbe, Asher ben Yedvab, was awakened by a knocking at the door of his cottage adjoining the besmedresh. Wearing only his nightshirt and talis koton, a shawl pulled over his scurfy head, he allowed himself to be tugged by an excited Velvl Spfarb into the study house. There he detached himself from the gibbering student and proceeded in his jerking progress—elbow, pelvis, and knee each attempting to go its own way—toward the hall tree. With the cat twined fretfully about his ankle, the Saczer struggled to maintain his balance as he inspected his trophy. He removed the loop of fur from the coat hook, held it a moment in his twitching palm, and smacked his bearded face, leaving the loop stuck in his eye like a monocle. Then he peered into the mirror whose surface had cleared of mist, which permitted him to see straight through to the other side.

"Come down, Hershel Khevreman!" Reb Yosl summoned from below. "The kloger rattled the shutter already. Would you be late for morning prayers on your wedding day?"

Torpid from too little sleep, Hershel opened a bleary eye, letting the phrase "wedding day" resonate sweetly in his head. He yawned luxuriously, stretched, extending his left arm from beneath the quilting, and endeavored to stretch his right—which was pinned beneath a breathing form. "Oy!" he cried, starting up from the pallet in consternation, as a hand gently squeezed him between the legs. He made a grab for the hand, and found there instead the warm head that had slid from his chest to burrow in his lap. Hershel wondered a panicked instant if he was giving birth.

"What's the matter?" called the clockmaker.

"Nothing!" Hershel chirped. "I banged my head on a rafter."

Rigid as the carved wooden figures that hourly emerged from the face of his clocks, Reb Yosl told him to hurry it up, he moved like a fart in brine.

"Go ahead," stalled Hershel, the hand having abandoned its hold to a pair of moist lips. "I'll catch up with you."

"Basha Reba," Yosl protested to his wife, who seldom spoke; although the fragrance of the tea she was brewing caused the prodigy's stomach to churn. Despite the circumstances, he still remembered that he was hungry; all his appetites, it seemed, were wide awake. "Basha Reba," complained the clock-maker, "it's a sluggard we got under our roof. Reb Sluggard, come down, you'll start your honeymoon tomorrow."

"Dawhahefing," said the voice from beneath the cover with her mouth full. ("That's what he thinks.") Her hair filled the scholar's lap like spilled lokshen noodles, her mumbling jaw made him whimper aloud.

"What's that?" asked Reb Yosl. "Basha Reba, what's he saying?"

"I'm coming!" cried Hershel with more emphasis than the situation called for, commanding all the heartsunk strength he had left to pry himself free.

He swarmed down the ladder still pulling his pants on, prompting the clockmaker's wife (who disapproved of young men on principle) to throw her apron over her vinegar face. Her husband squinted in puzzlement through cockeyed spectacles, suggesting "Shpilkes?" and pretending to chew his nails, as their boarder bolted past him for the door.

If he'd hoped to lose himself among the felt caps and gabardines crowded into the study house for the morning service, Hershel was soon disabused of the notion. Already distinguished for his status as khasn, bridegroom, he was made even more conspicuous by the presence of his prospective father-in-law. Chief elector of the merchants' synagogue—the ornate cedar pile behind the marketplatz—Reb Avrom had condescended, for the khasn's sake, to pray this morning among Rabbi ben Yedvab's Hasidim. For their part the Hasids, devoted consumers of Reb Avrom's merchandise, fawningly acknowledged the honor. Throughout their semisilent articles of faith, they winked at the brandy distiller, expressing their shared amusement at the bridegroom's nervousness.

They snickered at how Hershel had managed to entangle himself in his own phylacteries, as if—he feared—they could read his mind. Perhaps they perceived that, fatigued and famished from his unending fast, aching in every part, he was helplessly reliving the episode of the night before: when, after the first great wave of passion had subsided, he'd wished her gone. And when she refused to leave him, somewhat heartened by the unbroken snoring from the householders below, he'd summoned the courage to ask her, "Who are you?"

"I'm the black neshomah, the soul below the belt," she whispered, a sulfur moon through the dormer aglint in her teasing eye. "I'm the naughty intention. Three groschen worth of asafetida I can eat on an empty stomach without losing my skin. Take a chalice from the smithy, fill it with pomegranate seeds, circle it with roses, and set it in the sun, and you got only an inkling of my beauty . . ."

Then she said she wasn't a woman at all but a succubus, a daughter of the demon Lilith named Salka, who'd been trapped in the mirror over half a century. This was owing to a spell invoked by none other than the Saczer Rebbe himself, with whom she'd attempted to interfere during his own student days. But unlike Hershel he'd resisted her charms. He'd tricked her into admiring herself in the mirror of a hall tree in the home of the wealthy merchant where he took his meals. Then he'd uttered a swift incantation and *presto!* Salka found herself confined to the other side of the glass. But rather than abandon the hall tree, the young rabbi had purchased it, over his host's insistence that he accept it as a gift: let it be included as part of the dowry attached to the merchant's unwed daughter. But the youth, who'd developed a twitching that rendered him incompatible with domestic tranquillity, took the hall tree instead of the girl; he lugged it over the mountains from Przemysl to Stary Sacz, where he installed it in a prominent place in his "court."

"And that's where I waited for you to release me, my fated one," said the succubus, nibbling the lobe of Hershel's ear.

He'd wanted to prove he was done with her, that his will was as strong as any apprentice tzaddik's; he wanted to disbelieve in her altogether—but he'd nevertheless responded to her touch with a blind urgency. And now, as Hershel watched the Saczer davening fitfully on the dais, his torso like a runaway metronome, he wondered why he should feel so jealous of such a comical old man.

After prayers the men dispersed, causing Hershel further annoyance with their conspiratorial pinches and backslaps. Reb Avrom, distributing noblesse oblige left and right as he departed, paused to chuck the prodigy's chin. "Torah is the best of wares," he announced, as if bestowing sound business advice. Then, while the room reverted back to a yeshiva, the boys, saying hasty blessings over milk-boiled groats before pairing off to pursue their studies, each stole private glances at the bridegroom. To avoid their scrutiny, Hershel took a seat at the end of a bench and buried his head in a volume of Talmud.

"If a fledgling bird is found within fifty cubits of a dovecote," he read, hoping to solace himself in the old familiar way, "it belongs to the owner of the dovecote. If it is found outside the limit of fifty cubits, it belongs to the person that finds it. But Rabbi Jeremiah asked: If one foot of the fledgling is within the limit of fifty cubits, and one foot is outside it, what is the law?"

Hershel thought the question unbelievably stupid. Clamorous dialogues were developing all around him; children ushered into the study house by the melammed had begun reciting their alef-bais to the beat of his leather knout. Again Hershel addressed the text, trying to decipher it with a speed that outran his critical judgment, let alone his gnawing anxieties. Had Basha Reba discovered the creature in the loft and run shrieking into the street? Salka was nothing if not elusive, but she was also unpredictable, a quality he admired at the risk (he supposed) of his immortal soul. Unable to concentrate, Hershel asked himself when he had ever before been unable to concentrate.

Then a shadow fell across the page and Rabbi ben Yedvab, supported in his quivering by an abject Velvl Spfarb, stood before him. Hershel was aware of being the object of all eyes.

"I see your t-text is the B-b-bava Batra," said the tzaddik, his facial tics signaling the commencement of a standard catechism. "So tell me what three things ch-ch-ch-changed in the days of Enosh b-ben Seth?"

Hershel began his response with characteristic aplomb: "Corpses putrefied, men's faces turned apelike, and . . . ," he faltered. Was it possible that his memory had lost its steel-trap fidelity overnight?

"D-demons," reminded the rebbe, with alternately blinking eyes, "demons became free to work their will upon them. Hershel, it's your wed-d-ding-ding"—Velvl dutifully swatted him on the back—"your wedding day. You should visit the bathhouse."

Hershel straightened in his seat, wondering if his teacher, remarkable for his own rancid odor, could smell her salty essence on his person. Of course it was customary for a khasn to visit the bathhouse, not for purification—that was the bride's imperative—but to prepare himself through meditating on the estate he was about to enter. Still, he was distrustful, feeling almost belligerent toward the wintry old man, his shifting features as difficult to read as a map in a storm. Also, while tradition demanded that the groom not be left alone on the day of his marriage, was such a mob of attendants really necessary? Most of the key participants from last night's burlesque—Shloyme Aba, Salo Pinkas, Muni Misery—had zealously volunteered to accompany Hershel, and waited for him now with the air of hired strong-arms.

But having apparently no choice in the matter, Hershel rose and delivered himself up to his chaperones, resenting them nearly as much as he hoped they would stick by his side.

The bathhouse stood at the end of the butchers' shambles, its roof slates sprouting tussocks, its fissured brick walls breathing steam like a sleeping dragon. Serving on odd days as a mikveh for ritual immersion, the decrepit building was presided over by Moshe Cheesecloth—so-called for a skin condition resulting from his years of exposure to the sodden environment. It was to Moshe's good offices that the boys handed over the bridegroom, reluctant now to leave his protectors. Hershel also worried that the attendant might find, in checking his body for shmutz, marks left there by the talons of a lady demon. Never especially thorough, however, Moshe was too busy measuring the level of his rainwater cistern, fanning the copper furnace with a rawhide bellows, to make anything but a cursory inspection of Hershel's fingernails. Then he issued the scholar soap and towel, a birch broom to flog himself with, and sent him into the dressing cubicle off the entry.

Naked beneath the towel wrapped about his shoulders, Hershel padded into the humid tub room. He skirted a stack of smoldering rocks and, shedding the towel, lowered himself from the slippery platform into tepid, chest-deep water. He stirred the bilious green pool (in accordance with the precept against viewing one's own parts) and chased from his mind the water's resemblance to the surface of a certain looking glass. Then, leaning against the moss-grown tiles, he allowed himself a sigh. Gone for the moment was his apprehension at being left alone, the events of the night before having again withdrawn to the distance of dream. This was weariness, of course, but with it came a resurgence of hope regarding his imminent marriage. He had the feeling he might be only a short nap away from the knowledge that his future was yet in place. Yawning, Hershel turned to climb out of the tub and collapse on one of the cots that lined the walls, when a hand took hold of his ankle and dragged him under.

He fought his way sputtering back to the surface, taking deep gulps of the muggy air, frantically rubbing open his stinging eyes: to find her also risen from the turbulent pool, lit by an amber shaft from the bull's-eye window overhead. Her damp hair was strewn like a cat-o'-nine-tails across her laughing face, her coral-tipped breasts jigglingly upheld by the water.

It was unconscionable that she should have appeared in broad daylight, however clouded in vapor. Clapping his hands over his face, Hershel recited the pertinent passage from the *Shulchan Arukh*: "Semen-is-the-vitality-of-a-man's-body-and-when-it-issues-in-abundance-the-body-ages-the-strength-ebbs-the-eyes-grow-dim-the-breath-foul-the-hair-of-the-head-lashes-and-brows-fall-out . . ."

When he peeked through his fingers, she submitted in a voice whose music thrummed his vitals, "Did I tell you that Salka is short for *rusalka*, a mermaid?"

"For God's sake," pleaded Hershel, "will you leave . . ."—forcing a whisper that was half a shriek—". . . will you leave me alone!" Her presence in the mikveh was an affront to all things sacred, a violation of every law on the books.

Salka gave a careless shrug and began to pull herself out of the pool, the sleek, elongated S of her spine like a stem to the onion bulb of her glistening tush. Hershel wanted to tell her, "Demon, good riddance!" but a dreadful longing choked the words in his throat. Groaning, he threw his arms around her waist and squeezed mightily, hauling Salka back into the clammy water. He covered her with kisses so voracious that he felt they must constitute an untimely breaking of his fast, not that it mattered to a soul so already lost. A blessing came to his lips: "Praise God who permits the forbidden!" which was the phrase once invoked by the false prophet Sabbatai Zvi to excuse his sins. Afterward Hershel couldn't remember whether they'd made love above or below the surface of the bath.

Outside, the bracing autumn breeze, laced with a bouquet from the slaughter yards, did nothing to lift the weight from his spirit. Weak-kneed and shame-faced, Hershel fell in among the ranks of his waiting comrades, but felt no safety in their numbers. Why, if sent by their teacher to guard the groom against his evil impulse—for how else explain their presence?—why had they even bothered to respect his privacy? Why hadn't they charged into the bathhouse, interrupting what he would never have forgiven them for? And to think that only yesterday Hershel Khevreman had been a master of logic. Yesterday all he'd needed to complete his contentment—the dowry of a rich man's daughter—was in easy reach; now the distance between him and his wedding lay before him like a no-man's-land he feared to cross alone.

Huddled around by bodyguards, he nonetheless felt dangerously exposed. As they straggled across the open expanse of the market square, raucous with vendors hawking dried fish and caged fowl, Hershel wanted to take shelter in some obscure commentary. A virtual orphan since leaving Zshldz, he reasserted under his breath his credo that the Book was his home, its many branches his family tree; Rashi, Nachmanides, the Rambam—these were his real mishpocheh, the only company in which he felt truly secure. Then a glance beyond the academy caps of his fellows, and Hershel was granted a sight that made him shrink even further, retracting his neck into his shoulders turtle-style.

For over the way, Reb Avrom's road-muddied Panhard touring car, complete with liveried chauffeur, had pulled up before the lime-washed facade of Berel Schnapser's inn. In the backseat were a pair of passengers: one a scarecrow in an undersized rug coat dusted in feathers, the other a stolid, potato-shaped woman holding a carpetbag. Hershel recalled how, at the contract signing, Reb Avrom had offered to bring them to town for the wedding, but the groom had argued that his parents didn't travel well. "Nonsense!" replied the distiller, who couldn't do enough for the boy whose scholarship guaranteed his in-laws a share in Kingdom Come. And while he knew he couldn't postpone the meeting indefinitely, Hershel figured his afflicted conscience would scarcely register another offense: so for the present he gave Itche Chicken and wife a wide berth.

In the meantime, too depleted to do otherwise, he surrendered himself wholesale to the custody of his peers. They in turn saw to it that the scholar remained upright through afternoon prayers, then—though he reached for a scriptural codex like a drowning man—hustled him off to be outfitted for the ceremony. Practically asleep on his feet, Hershel was conducted by a growing convoy of students through streets thick with the aromas of baking kugel and potted meat. The entire quarter, it seemed, was busy making dishes for the nuptial feast, while the youth on whose behalf they labored swooned from hunger, begging his beleaguered senses to let him be.

His escorts, on the other hand, seemed to have recovered something of their mood of the night before. Putting aside their watchful solemnity, they grew livelier as the hour approached. They were jaunty as they marched the bridegroom through Reb Yosl's tiny shop, which (as Shloyme Aba observed) ticked like an anarchist's basement in Lodz. In the apartment behind the shop they twitted Basha Reba on the scythelike movement of her broom; a few made as if to steal the almond torte left cooling on an upended washtub, while the rest led Hershel behind the fabric screen. There they attired him—Salo Pinkas holding him erect while Shloyme Aba and Yukie Zeidl's manipulated his arms and legs—in the silk plus-fours and ankle-length black kittl that the distiller had provided. They crowned him with the beaver-trimmed turban and drew him around to face a tarnished pier glass to admire his finery, but having lately conceived a phobia of mirrors, the groom turned his head.

It was left for Muni Misery to describe what he was missing with a philosophical wistfulness: "All grooms are handsome, all the dead are holy," he said, prompting Hershel to steal a sidelong look. What he saw resembled a folded parasol, its tip through a wheel of cheese gone furry with mold. But so relieved was he to find himself alone in the mirror that his nerves relaxed their grip on his insides, and he had abruptly to excuse himself.

In the yard in back of the shop he pulled to the latchless door of the privy; he raised the stiff garment, dropped his breeches, and plunked his bare bottom on the splintered wooden seat. Given his empty stomach, Hershel wondered what was left to purge, unless—settling himself for a restful interlude—he might look forward to the emptying of his unquiet mind. Then the door swung open and the succubus swept in, lifting her shift to straddle Hershel's naked knees, entwining his tongue with her viperish own.

"Mmphlmph!" protested Hershel, fighting to retrieve his face. "Please, Salka, not here!" It was all so unspeakably degrading.

But the creature rocked her hips as if in a shukeling prayer—and despite his exhaustion and the fetid surroundings, despite everything he'd previously deemed to be decent, the scholar responded to her beckoning movements. For some moments he clung to her, sucking the pastille of a nipple through the thin cambric bodice, anticipating as best he could her fluid rhythm; until, with a cry that was equal parts rapture and shame, Hershel let go, experiencing a seismic release both fore and aft. Then, slumped in humiliation against the still-heaving torso of the demoness, he wept guilty tears.

"Such an emotional boy," she breathlessly rebuked him, reaching for a cob from the pile on the floor: "Here, let me help you."

That's when Hershel heard the music, and once he'd determined that it originated on earth, that it came in fact from the street in front of the shop, he thought it might yet herald his salvation. Heedless of personal hygiene, he got to his feet, causing Salka to slide sprawling from his lap onto the spongy boards. "Impetuous!" she accused him even as he stumbled over her, snatched up his pants from around his ankles and staggered out to join the parade.

The groom's procession, led by one-half of Reb Dovidl Fiddle's klezmer ensemble, wound its way into the unpaved yard behind the Hasids' listing stone shul. Although the date had been favorably fixed between the Days of Awe and Sukkot, it was late in the season for outdoor weddings. A brisk (if fair) afternoon, it would be nippy in the shaded court toward sunset. But bonfires would be lit to reduce the chill and—along with the garlands of garlic brandished by the guests—frighten the sheydim, the demons, away.

Ill-smelling and nearly insensible, jerked between the rebbe's dancing disciples (who'd hooked their arms through his), Hershel reminded himself he didn't believe in demons.

A path opened up for them through the crush of guests surrounding the canopy erected on four slender poles. In this way Hershel was made to run a gauntlet of shtetl society, from the crutched beggars on the periphery through the artisans, students, and Hasidim, to the machetonim, the in-laws, seated just outside the chupeh in straight-backed chairs. Among the in-laws (sitting together but for the aisle dividing men from women) were the bridegroom's own parents, whom Hershel hadn't seen face-to-face in almost three years. He acknowledged them now with what little filial deference he had left: a polite bow; and they returned his greeting with stony, befuddled nods, clearly uncertain of why they'd been asked to come. Hershel waited for the embarrassment to set in, and for the remorse that followed embarrassment, but the pair of rustics seated before him were strangers, people of the chicken and distaff, not the Book. They had no real connection to the prodigy about to make a brilliant match with a rich man's daughter; and for all his debilitation Hershel felt reassured.

He took in for the first time the magnitude of the gathering, indicative of the wedding's great significance; he remarked the string of lanterns, the trestle tables awaiting platters of stuffed goose necks, the cauldrons of golden soup and calves' brain puddings as large as drums. Neither ghosts from the past nor the nightmares of a treacherous present, he concluded, could lay claim to him here, safe in the bosom of his community.

Opposite Hershel, his erstwhile teacher, the Saczer Rebbe, had already begun his desultory benedictions, every feature of his face asserting its independence. Leaning on the humble arm of Velvl Spfarb, he nodded to the bridegroom, also bolstered by attendants, so that the two of them teetered like pugilists in a ring. Then came another flourish of fiddles and horns, as the other half of Reb Dovidl's orchestra ushered the bride's entourage into the compound. Flanked by her maids of honor, the kallah, the bride, came forward enshrouded in silk and brocade, her face mercifully concealed by a veil. Her venerable parents sashayed just behind.

When the bride had taken her place next to her intended, the music ceased and the rebbe curtailed his prayer. The guests shushed one another, as Rabbi ben Yedvab, his ceremonial sable as moth-eaten as his beard, was helped forward to perform the ritual lifting of the veil. Here was a moment Hershel had not looked forward to, when the kallah's face would be revealed for his eyes only; for although entitled to call off the marriage if the face displeased him, he knew perfectly well what he must do: he must give his unqualified approval to the mousy, pinched ponim of Reb Avrom's daughter.

But the face beneath the mignonette veil, which the rebbe raised like the lid of a covered dish, bore small resemblance (if memory served) to Shifra Puah's. This one stunned Hershel with its narrowed onyx eyes and kittenish grin, the sooty ringlets spilling from under her pumpernickel loaf of a wig. Then the veil was lowered again, though not before the succubus had taken the opportunity to wink.

Involuntarily Hershel winked back, satisfied that he must be hallucinating. Fine, he thought, let it be *her*: then last night's unholy wedding would be consecrated before Israel and all set right in the eyes of God. A shudder racked Hershel's frame as he woke up to what he was thinking: he was contemplating his final disgrace, the mortal blow. The rebbe chanted the betrothal benedictions ("Who is m-m-mighty over all . . . ?"), and Hershel told himself this was the authentic piety—the kind that scourged the devils that haunted the mikvehs and privies but would never, in any case, dare to venture in public. But despite his wishful silent endorsement, Hershel still thought the rebbe's performance less convincing than Shloyme Aba's spoof of the night before.

Then a commotion was heard from the courtyard, and all heads turned to see the distiller's daughter, a twig in a rumpled chemise, trailing rope from her ankles and wrists as she flailed through the crowd.

"Papa," bawled Shifra Puah amid universal imprecations against the evil eye, "she tied me up!"

Madame Treklekh, clattering jewelry and flapping jowls, bustled head-long to her daughter's side, as her husband rose puffing from his chair. "Rabbi ben Yedvab!" he bellowed, his whiskers repeating the scimitar curve of his pointed finger. "What is this?" The rebbe looked ruefully from Shifra Puah to her usurper, and frowned; then with a swiftness that belied his frailty, he again removed the bridal veil, silencing the crowd with the savage beauty he exposed.

"S-s-s-s," stammered the Saczer, until Velvl respectfully smote him between the shoulder blades. The old man caught his teeth in his hand, shoved them back into his mouth, and clicked them once to ascertain their working order. "Salka, sweetheart," he said tenderly, "you have to go back."

She'd assumed a defiant stance, arms folded over her breasts, shaking her head with a vehemence that dislodged the wig. Tresses tumbled from beneath it like unspooling yarn.

"Hartseniu"—the rebbe was more sorrowful than threatening, a rare steadiness sustaining his speech—"don't make me have to lower the boom."

Visibly skittish, Salka sniffed and continued to stand her ground. Then liltingly for one so hoarse, the rebbe began to intone: "Return, return, O Shulammite, for love is strong as death, jealousy as cruel as the grave . . ."

Having expected some species of antidemonic humbug, Hershel was puzzled to hear the rebbe reciting snatches from the Song of Songs—and these in a throaty rendition that sounded less like a conjuration than a lullaby. It was evident, though, from the set of her damson lips, the exaggerated lift of her chin, that the words were making the demoness ill at ease. Had her brazen masquerade somehow proven a miscalculation? In none of their tumultuous encounters had Hershel detected in Salka the least hint of vulnerability; and seeing it now, as she stood there defenseless before the gawking multitude, he was filled with conflicting emotions. Desperately he tried to displace his feelings with sober concerns: How-does-one-determine-the-kosherness-of-apples-grown-on-a-tree-in-a-yard-where-a-pig-was-slaughtered? How-assess-the-property-value-of-a-tower-floating-in-air? But it was no use. Once again he was inflamed with desire, only this time the fire in his loins, try as he might to douse it with reason, reached his heart.

"Who is she that looketh forth as the dawn," warbled the rebbe, "fair as the moon, fierce as an army with banners . . . ?"

Salka folded her arms more tightly, hugging herself.

Good, thought Hershel: whatever their sentiments, the tzaddik's words were having the proper effect; soon the creature, assaulted by righteousness, would be banished forever from their midst. Then he thought what he dimly recognized as sheer madness: I can save her.

"Salkeleh"—the rebbe was personal again, stationary and unstuttering—"the boy isn't for you. This one's destined for a teacher."

"Then," she countered, the tremor in her voice betraying her agitation, "let first the teacher learn to be a man."

"He's not your type. In the flesh he ain't interested."

Hershel coughed and Salka, for all her extremity, managed the shadow of a smile. "A man who's too good for this world is no good for his bride."

"This one belongs to the Book," the Saczer insisted—and Hershel's head, swiveling back and forth between the tzaddik and the daughter of Lilith, stopped at Rabbi ben Yedvab's ruined face. Never had it appeared so exalted, almost a young man's wearing the transparent mask of an old.

Then the creature spoke, so softly that she might have been inquiring of herself: "If he don't know from temptation, how will he know what to resist?"

His eyes having shifted back to her chastised radiance, Hershel could no longer contain himself. "I don't want to resist!" he cried, stretching his arms toward the object of his obsession. "Salka, I'm yours!" But instead of accepting his proffered embrace, she stiffened, confusion distorting her features, the last of her composure crumbling in the face of his need. It was as if, in disdaining the rebbe, Hershel had assumed his power over the creature, a daunting influence he had not sought. She shrank a step backward, her dark eyes aflicker with fear.

"Salka, don't worry, I'll save you!" declared Hershel, though he hadn't a clue as to what that might entail.

"Stay away from me!" she cautioned with out-thrust hands.

". . . Behold thou art fair," the rebbe had revived his chant, "thy navel like a rounded goblet, thy thighs the links of a golden chain . . ."

"But Salka," said Hershel, bewildered, "what are you saying? Aren't you . . ."—he had first to swallow—". . . my wife?"

". . . Thy teeth like a flock of ewes . . ."

"I'm nobody's wife, you amhoretz, you idiot! I'm a demon. All you did was break a spell, and that you didn't even do on purpose."

"But Salka, it's your Hershel! What are you afraid of?"

"It's you I'm afraid of."

"Salka, I love you!"

"Feh!" she spat, and was gone. She made a sudden reckless dash across the courtyard toward the tin-roofed study house, the guests parting before her like reeds.

Hershel turned back to the rebbe, who himself seemed abruptly deflated, requiring the aid of the faithful to raise his bony shoulders in a shrug. "It's love she c-c-c-can't stand," he said.

Suppressing an impulse to do the old man bodily harm, Hershel asked him, "How would you know?"

Again an assisted shrug. "Because I once loved her t-too." He explained that love had kept her trapped in the mirror, while desire brought her forth again. "But s-s-sometimes desire itself becomes sublime, and this the succubah-bahh"—smack—"the fiend cannot endure."

Aware of the intensity with which he was being regarded, Hershel stared back at the ogling assembly—at the row of would-be relations among whom the Treklekhs were trying to comfort their mortified daughter; at the poulterer and his wife, who sat watching so complacently that they might have been enjoying a Purim shpiel. To them he felt oddly grateful: they were like some cozy couple who'd raised an imp the sheydim had substituted for their own lost child; and now the moment had come for the imp to return to his kind. Looking the rebbe full in his flinching face, Hershel reaffirmed the temptress's angry farewell: "Feh!" He shook off the groomsmen who tried to restrain him, picked up the skirts of his kittl, and flung himself after his bride.

Accompanied by students, disciples, and assorted wedding guests, Rabbi ben Yedvab entered the study house, finding it empty but for a petrified cat. He inspected the hall tree, then shakily (because he'd begun to twitch again), removed his tallis, kissed it, and draped it over the mirror, as in a place where someone has died. No sooner had he done this, however, than the glass exploded in a hail of flying slivers and the prodigy crashed through the mirror from the other side. Tangled in the tallis, Hershel plunged into the arms of the rebbe, who fell backward in turn into the open arms of his retinue.

Helped to his feet, the old tzaddik (muttering a blessing over broken glass) sought to help a disoriented Hershel, pulling the blood-flecked cloth from his head. His lacerated face, framed by lank silver hair, was utterly strange, an arcane text his one-time rival Velvl Spfarb endeavored the rest of his days to construe. What he gleaned from the scholar's expression was the story he repeated years later, though nobody listened, in the shadow of the chimneys belching yellow smoke: how the bridegroom had discovered that yenne velt, the other side, was identical to this one, except that the ghosts there had more substance than the living. The echoes there were louder than their original noises, and the ancient history of the souls you encountered was more vivid than their current incarnations. Beauty there had a density of meaning no scholar could penetrate—a terrible beauty that had stopped Hershel Khevreman in his tracks; and frightened of his own ignorance, having lost the object of his pursuit in the dusky distance, he'd turned around and beat a path back to the world. Only to find that the house of study and the town on the Carpathian heights were too desolate now to accommodate his longing. There was nothing left but to continue the chase, charging out the open door and following to its logical conclusion the route already taken by his heart.

The Ballad of Mushie Momzer

My mother took a dump and out I came, more or less. It happened like this: I was conceived when my brother Doodya, who was also my father, sat in the privy behind the family's hovel in Vidderpol playing with his shwantz. This is what they told me, and the Jews loved telling me at every least opportunity. My mother, fat and blind, eyeballs like soft-boiled eggs, had lumbered into the outhouse to move her bowels. She hoisted the skirts of her tent-sized shift to squat over the hole, where she felt herself impaled on an alien organ as it spurted its load. When she shrieked, Doodya opened his eyes and, bellowing like a gelded calf himself, shoved my mother onto the outhouse floor. Then pulling up his moleskins, he trounced through the muddy yard scattering fowl, gathered his patched caftan and phylacteries from a hook, and vanished from the earth as surely as the Ten Lost Tribes. My mother, Breyne Dobish, was too bloated to show her pregnancy, and dull-witted, she may not even have known she was with child. But when she finally dropped me, her husband, the hod carrier Velvel One Lung, who hadn't shared his bed with her in years, drove her out of the house. She went begging for a season along the highways, but as her story had preceded her the Jews were not inclined to be charitable—though a few generous souls insisted that the rumor of my birth was unfounded, and from the look of me (pink eyes, harelip, jug ears, no chin), I was more likely the child of the demon Asmodeus, who was known to hang around privies. Eventually my mother, infected with cholera, fell down dead in a bog, and I, Mushie Breyne's the momzer, was sent to the poorhouse, which also served as a foundling asylum. I dwelled there and elsewhere awhile—some five or six decades all told—then died in desolation by my own hand.

While I lived, I was outcast even among the wretched. My earliest years were spent largely in the stable yard pecked at and nibbled though mostly ignored by browsing livestock. I was also ignored by the humans that haunted that yard. In winter I crawled atop the stove and hugged the samovar till

I was scalded; but I was often evicted from that coveted spot by other orphans, who scrambled over the sooty shelf like shipwrecked refugees clinging to a raft. I was attended to like some drooping houseplant whenever it was remembered that I required a measure of nourishment to survive, though there must have been those who questioned whether I ought to survive. Still I grew, if somewhat erratically, since my bones had the ungainly look of limbs that had been broken and improperly reset. As the bastard child of an unholy union, I suppose I should have regarded myself lucky that anyone bothered to keep me alive, but I wasn't especially grateful; I never saw much advantage to having been born.

The poorhouse was a hybrid structure consisting of stable, kitchen, and dormitory loft, with a shit hole out back, which my fellows were fond of reminding me was a shrine to my nativity. But little lower than the angels—as they assured us in cheder on those days when we weren't farmed out to labor (I preferred the labor)—we slept on straw pallets just above the jackasses and goats. While most of the orphans slept in a knot of pretzeled bodies for warmth, I was generally shunned for my unhappy features and the peculiar stench that emanated from my person owing to my chronic bed-wetting. Yakov Fetser, who managed the asylum, a man whose carroty eyebrows appeared to be in flames, loaned us out to the families of the Duyanov community for a nominal fee. Our own reward, in exchange for emptying slops, sweeping sawdust, scrounging the bones, bark, and cow chips that were fed to the cookstoves in lieu of coal, was perhaps a fistful of groats in sour milk. No wonder that, when I was old enough, I stole whatever I could from the market stalls. Never a skillful thief, however, I was commonly hauled before the elders, who caned me to within an inch of my life. There were times when, as I vomited up the radish or piece of dried herring I'd bolted, I wished they had gone the extra inch.

When not indentured for the day or herded with the other boys into the tin-roofed study house, I was left to my own devices—what devices? The only pastime I had a passion for was sleep. I had no friends, since my cleft palate discouraged communication, though I was occasionally pestered by Yahoodie, called the Angel, another orphan who from time to time took pity on me. He should piss green worms, the draikop: I was perfectly capable of feeling sorry for myself without anybody's help; though truth be told, the Angel's sympathy was indiscriminate. A frail, fiddle-shaped kid with a shock of ginger hair half-concealing his shaigetz-blue eyes, he was the pet of the shtetl; even the bullying butchers' apprentices indulged him for his vaunted innocence. Call it innocence if you want, but frankly I thought he was nuts.

"Mushie," he would confide; he took liberties with everyone's given name, though "Momzer" was how I was generally addressed. "Mushie, everything is alive."

Despite myself I would look around to see what he was talking about. Our town with its rat's-nest houses, a quarter of them charred to cinders from former conflagrations, was sunk to its shins in mud; it reeked from the stench of slaughterhouse and tannery beneath a leaky leaden sky. Its inhabitants were no less crooked and weather-worn—such as Laibl the Kaddish, as nearly petrified as the listing tombstones he took alms to pray among; or Falik the belfer, a scarecrow upon whose head and shoulders the children perched like blackbirds en route to the beit midrash; or Shpindl the whore, whose apiary wig was routinely snatched by the wags. There was the rattle-boned Balitzer Rebbe in his long gabardine girdled with silk at the waist to separate his holy upper half from the lower, which the rebbe had no commerce with. It was therefore speculated that his organ was as shriveled as a pope's nose. They all performed their civic and liturgical functions dutifully, but could you really call them living? Then there was me, Mushie Momzer: if folks judged their own unfortunate circumstances as accidents of birth, then what of one whose very birth was an accident? Could I still lay claim to being completely alive?

"Ngh shgngh!" I spat at Yahoodie, which was as close an approximation to "Narishkeit!" as my disfigured lips allowed. Still the fool would persist in indicating miracles: a ram with a hennaed fleece and single horn, the perpetual ruby beacon of the forge. No doubt all the God talk in cheder had addled his brain. If an early flower burst through the earth's crust in an April thaw, he took it so personally you'd have thought he'd achieved a heroic erection, the kind the older orphans—lowering their trousers—liked to flaunt in your face. Everything fueled the Angel's awe: from floating eiderdown to the girls with their swinging braids, their pinafores kilted in the riverbed where they washed their clothes. The more he admired, the more I resented, since everything he deemed beautiful seemed a personal affront to my ill-favored self. Especially the girls with their lilac and vinegar scent, whose tittering at my expense disturbed me in ways I couldn't yet explain. The thimblewit, he even saw living beings where there was nothing but thin air; for wandering souls, he maintained, were resident in every riven tree and polluted well.

Sometimes I goaded him: "Ngh onfen ngh . . . ," meaning, "Our town is a toilet and life a rehearsal for Gehenna." But he shrugged off my barbs, admonishing me, "Mushie, you got no imagination," as if imagination was the key. He told me that, wondrous as this world was, it was only a veil behind which was an even more wondrous world, the real Promised Land. Though it hurt me in my heart to laugh, I laughed heartily. "Ngh ngh . . . ?" meaning, "Veil? What veil? The whole earth is a splayed carcass exposed to plain sight." Another time, in a moment of weakness, I asked him amid the bedlam of the beit midrash, "Fonfen . . . ?" meaning, "So, Yahoodie, did God make me?" But I was overheard by Reb Gargl, our treble-chinned melammed with his knockwurst shnoz, his ritual garment stained with borscht or blood, who was also a seasoned interpreter of my hobbled speech. He whacked my head with a pointer and assured me, "Sometimes HaShem, may He be blessed, has his little jokes." Funny man.

It was a relief when he died, the Angel. For such a good-natured sap, you'd have thought his entrails pooped wildflowers, but in fact they refused to void anything at all. Though I seldom saw him eat—he seemed to live on the doting affections of the Duyanovers (who also plied him with sweetmeats)—he suffered from an unending constipation. "It's like the Akedah," he repined, comparing his humiliating condition to some fable he'd learned in the study house. "It's the binding of Isaac all over again in my kishkes." Eventually, when he swelled up and turned blue, Fetser called in Genendel the enema lady, who brewed some toxic concoction in her gutta-percha bag that she squeezed through a tube shoved up the Angel's ass. It turned out he'd been full of shit all along, for once the evacuation started it never stopped, and Yahoodie found himself marooned atop a rising tumulus of night soil. In the end he expelled his soul along with his insides, and as the light departed his eyes, the Angel seemed shocked to discover the secret that his sunny disposition had kept from him throughout his days. Good riddance, thought I; the burden of my existence was hard enough to bear without that flea in my ear.

Just before I was kidnapped and sold for a Cantonist conscript in place of some shopkeeper's son, a troupe of Yiddish actors passed through Duyanov. They performed on a makeshift scaffold erected over hay bales flanked by green benzine flares in Shmulke der Keziker's cow barn. The play cost a couple of kopecks at the door, but I slithered in under the splintered wall in back of the stage where the props were stored. It was a shpiel about a happy-go-lucky scamp who, for the sake of filling the village quota, is tricked by the local kahal into volunteering for the army. After a number of japes and songs—some of them scurrilous—on the part of the ragtag company, the scamp's sweetheart dies with much hand-wringing of a broken heart, and his blind old mother, tearing her sheitl wig and beating her meal-sack breasts, loses her mind. Then the recruit, no longer so devil-may-care, hangs himself from a rafter by his tallis, his lolling tongue the complement to his coxcomb hair.

I was interested to see that, unlike ordinary experience, make-believe did in fact make a kind of sense, which I deeply resented; I didn't like that I should be made to feel bad on account of a bunch of costumed players. Nevertheless, I was consoled by the notion that you could exit this life whenever you chose. Since I scarcely mattered, I wouldn't be missed, and there was little I would miss in return. So I watched with insouciance as other boys my age, the sons of merchants and artisans, were solicited by marriage brokers who offered them the dowries of young girls. While I pulled my putz with a fervor usually reserved for wringing the necks of geese (a tradition that apparently ran in my family), other lads were already honoring the injunction to be fruitful and multiply. The idea of multiplying my misbegotten self was as offensive to me as it was to everyone else, and when Mendy Elefant, our resident khapper, stuffed me into a potato sack and bound it tight, Nu, I thought, wherever he's taking me can't be worse than here.

Not that my capture came as any real surprise: unless you were crippled or your family had the gelt to buy your exemption, you were destined in those days of Czar Nicholas (the Jews called him Haman the Second) to fall victim to the Rekrutshina Edict. Wasn't Duyanov full of children whose fingers and toes were hacked off, their ears lopped by parents who sought to save them from the draft? They were already nine-tenths ghosts, those mutilated children—to say nothing of the ones who'd disappeared, burrowing out of sight in cellars and forest caves. You never saw them until some informer disclosed their hiding place and they were hauled off kicking and screaming to the induction center, only a few versts away in the market town of Slutsk. As for us orphans, we were viewed as a pool of ready substitutes for the sons of gentlefolk.

It was the dead of winter when it happened, and I was shivering inside the sack that Mendy, a drayman in a leather apron by day, had tossed onto the bed of his horse-drawn sledge. As we rattled along the icebound highway, I felt myself nudged by other sacks wriggling in close proximity to mine, all of them sidling against one another for warmth. At one point we hit a bump and Mendy's contraption was briefly airborne, bouncing me clear out of the rackety sledge. I hit the road and rolled down an incline into a ditch that ran alongside, where I came to rest. Then it struck me that, bruised but otherwise undamaged, I was free, a concept that had little meaning, unable as I was to escape the tightly lashed sack. To lie still for long, however, would mean freezing, and as there was room in the sack to raise myself into a stoop, I managed to scramble by awkward stages up the side of the ditch. While the burlap seams were wide enough to see through, the falling snow blotted out the dark landscape; still I had no option but to keep moving. I stumbled blindly forward, slipping on patches of ice and struggling back to my feet, becoming aware in my clumsy progress of sporadic laughter. As the blizzard began to abate and a full moon appeared, the laughter swelled to a noisy hilarity, and through the stretched seams I could now observe that I wasn't alone. There were other upright potato sacks in front of me toddling like ninepins in an impromptu parade as we entered the outskirts of Slutsk, greeted by the guffaws of the gathered onlookers. It was a moment when I felt like a witness as well, as if I were watching an entertainment in which even Mushie Momzer had a part, and I came that close to laughing myself. But just as the howling of the Slutskers approached hysteria, we were scooped up by deputies of the kahal, who tossed us over their shoulders and carried us through the market arcade to the recruitment station.

They dumped us onto a tile floor that sloped toward a drain as in an abbatoir, in a low-ceilinged room where a flag emblazoned with a two-headed eagle was mounted on the wall. The potato sacks, rather than unfastened (Mendy's knots being inextricable), were slit open with knives so that we tumbled out as from a generous womb. That was anyway how it was put by a boy in a crocheted skullcap with serpentine earlocks, who looked nothing at all like the Angel: this one was well fed and apple cheeked despite the difficult journey. "This is for us our second birth," he pronounced. "Only here we are born into Sitra Achra, which is the wrong side of the mirror." He talked like that, even more spookily than Yahoodie; he said we were like Joseph sold into slavery by his own brothers, but I knew he was speaking rubbish. We were nothing like Joseph, whose plight I knew from a Purim shpiel, and it galled me to hear us compared to stories in which events made a modicum of sense. In this world nothing made sense and, despite the stories they force-fed us in cheder, the greatest sin was to pretend that it did.

I was relieved when an officer with no face—only scar tissue like a papier-mâché mask—rose from behind the heavy desk and peremptorily stove in the kid's skull with a saber hilt. Good riddance.

There was some question in my mind as to whether my defective condition would render me ineligible for the army, but one look at the faceless officer in his frogs and epaulets dispelled my doubts. For my incapacity to answer questions intelligibly—doubly handicapped as I was by my harelip and an ignorance of the Russian tongue—I was soundly thrashed, after which I was promptly inducted into the cadet corps. More manhandling ensued: we were hustled across a courtyard and thrust into quarters where malevolent barbers shaved our heads so poorly that we resembled peeled oranges. We were draped in pocketless greatcoats that dragged the ground, issued pants with a rough canvas lining infested with lice and coarse leather boots whose straps practically reached our hips. Further saddled with ungainly knapsacks—which contained among sundry items black dye for the mustaches we were still too callow to grow—we were dispatched in a tottering lockstep flanked by mounted soldiers over a bridge leading into the forest surrounding Slutsk. This was the point of departure for a forced march that was to take us across the frozen steppes beyond the Pale of Settlement to the garrison city of Archangelsk far to the north.

Along the way our ranks were substantially thinned. At the outset the boys that weren't crying for their mothers recited the traveler's prayer, only to be abruptly silenced by our mounted escort. Then, as if prayers were threads connecting them like marionettes to heaven, they dropped the sticks that doubled as rifles from their shoulders and crumpled to earth. Others, rejecting the unkosher swill we were offered—mostly cabbage soup afloat with lard or a freshwater insect called a crawfish—fell from malnourishment. Accustomed to hardship and having no convictions to constrain me, I adapted to the putrid fare. This isn't to say I didn't suffer, but since I already felt I hardly existed, death to me seemed almost superfluous. In the villages we were billeted with families who used us as cruelly as those to whom I was sent on eating days back in Duyanov. (Once I was housed with a lunatic who lowered me down a chimney I was supposed to purge of demons, then chased me with a brickbat for a demon myself when I emerged from the hearth covered in soot.) We were transported on one leg of the journey by a barge attached to the stern of a steamboat, but the Neva was so clogged with ice that we spent more time on the riverbank towing the boat by hawsers coiled about our waists. Some suffered from a frostbite that mercifully caused them to lose their fingers and toes, but more died outright of exposure. As the weather grew warmer, the fleas seethed in our uniforms until our skin felt as if on fire from stinging nettles, and I cursed my own instinct for survival, my apparent immunity to a medley of diseases.

By the time we reached Archangelsk, centuries later, we were a meager handful of herring-gutted Tom Thumbs; nor did the uncaulked barracks we were quartered in offer much respite from the journey's ordeal. Most of the plank beds were already occupied by older recruits, so that we were forced to sleep beneath the berths, facedown so as not to inhale the bedbugs and dust. It was nearly Passover, which coincided with Easter, when the priests were especially compelled to convert us. They came into the barracks in their rosy vestments and plaited beards carrying icons. "Only submit to baptism," they enjoined us, their words translated into Yiddish by a mincing convert, "and you will no longer menstruate; your dorsal appendages will drop off and you will lose your foetor judaicus." They were accompanied by a boozy lance corporal who threatened to pound us to blood pudding if we didn't forswear our faith. Those who resisted were made to run the gauntlet, throttled with leather straps soaked in brine, forced to sweat on the seventh step of the steam bath until their brains began to boil. Some, who finally conceded to be led to the water's edge and baptized, refused—once immersed—to resurface from under the river. Some managed to drown in cauldrons of bean slops and barrels of kvass.

Ordinarily my inability to talk was deemed a virtue, but while I presented myself as a willing candidate for conversion, I couldn't make myself understood. Nasal snorting aside, I was illiterate and largely considered to be an idiot, so no one realized when I proclaimed myself geshmat: "I'm a Christian, okay?" They tortured me anyway, and when I made gestures that argued my sincerity, which included crossing myself, they thought I was mocking them and stepped up the abuse. In the face of similar persecution, some of the boys opted for kiddush ha shem, for martyrdom. They cut their own throats and hanged themselves, thus stealing my thunder, so that if only to avoid becoming a copycat, I stayed alive.

We were told that, since we were technically underage, the battalion to which we were attached would function as an academy; we would be educated and given military instruction until we reached our majority and were admitted into the regular army. But education consisted of being roused at dawn and lined up in the yard to sing hymns and recite the czar's family tree;

instruction meant splashing in full battle gear about the rain-soaked parade ground for hours. Then we were issued our quarter pound of black bread with salt and sent to peel potatoes, knead dough, and (a specialty of mine) clean spittoons in the officers' mess. We were assigned along with parties of convicts to dig canals and break stones for breastworks and barricades, and if ever I heard a reference to building pyramids, I spat three times. They christened us Sergei or Anastasy so that we no longer had any relation to our former identities, no great loss as far as I was concerned. The seasons changed like moods; I was cold, I was hot, the whiskers sprouted on my chin, the fur around my parts, but did I care?

Then a Polish uprising along the western border made it necessary to deploy all available troops for active duty. I remember the Balitzer Rebbe saying that the purpose of life was to perpetuate it, but in Maykop, Krapivno, and Stawatycze an opposite corollary obtained: the purpose of life was to end as much of it as ventured into your purview. Who you didn't kill, you at least tried to maim, be they soldier or civilian, and some of us—those that didn't soil themselves or faint dead away in the heat of battle—took a bisl joy in the slaughter. Myself, I felt neither joy nor fear. I already understood how this world was, so to speak, death's vestibule; so why shouldn't the earth be carpeted in corpses? I was made to dust them in quicklime, and when the charnel wind blew back in my face, I was covered in the powder myself, so that my fellows took me for a walking dead man. In combat, while my brain was befogged, my body followed its own agenda. This involved aiming my musket in the direction of the enemy and pulling the trigger, of skewering him like shashlik at close quarters on the end of my bayonet. For all I know I might have demonstrated some skill as a marksman; I believe I murdered my share of Poles, to say nothing of the Zhids who suffered collaterally at the hands of Fonya's army. After a skirmish the defeated village was torched, its population savaged, shops looted, women raped—that was the drill. I was an indifferent participant in the killing and plundering of goods, though in the violation of women I took an interest.

I was human, I had appetites, albeit they were usually limited to victuals and sleep, commodities never in any great abundance, but on occasion I had a yen for female flesh. Seeing my comrades in arms—Zaporozhians, Circassians, Tatars, some of them nearly as dogfaced as me—seeing them bum-basting women bent over saddle horns and the railings of galleried inns gave me ideas of my own. I dimly recalled how Yahoodie the Angel, who never touched himself (never mind the maidelekh), would talk about love: a holy mystery, the poor man's tikkun olam, and so on. Curious, I chose a woman, a button-eyed girl really, with dishwater hair and a birthmark like a spider's shadow over her left cheek. She was a slip of a thing whose resistance would be negligible, and I dragged her into an alley beside a church. I shoved her down among the wagon ruts and told her, "Ngh onfen nghsh," meaning that she was my sweetheart and I cherished her forever. She responded to my overtures with an expression of dumb horror, even as I began to demonstrate my affection, lifting her petticoats and tearing her dirty drawers at the crotch. I dropped my trousers and made to implant the standard of myself, though I had to hammer away at her with my hips until her maidenhead collapsed. Then I was inside her and a star burst in my skull, the warm sparks like a school of flickering minnows swimming through my lungs and loins. The more I labored, the more she exuded her intoxicating scent of dread, and the more I loved her, feeling that my devotions were building toward some rapturous truth. I was also vaguely aware that we were surrounded by a cohort of Cossack irregulars who'd begun to cheer me on. But just when I thought I might melt or burst into flame, I was rudely separated from my neshomaleh, hauled by the ankles from between her spindly thighs. Someone planted a boot heel in my spine while the others took their turns with the girl, until she stopped screaming and went limp from exhaustion or death.

Then they told me, "Zhids got no business defiling our women." I tried to explain that I wasn't a Jew, I wasn't anything, but as usual my animal grunting went unheeded and I was further refuted by the evidence of my bald schlang. They carried me into a cottage whose rush roof was being nibbled by a horse, and swept a stiff off a table to stretch me out on. As my muddy parts were already exposed to a spirit lamp, the deed was soon done. The pain of the incision was superseded by the pain of the cauterization, but just before I lost consciousness, I felt them fold into the palm of my hand my own swollen beytsim. "A souvenir," said someone in the vernacular I now understood. "Like scarlet doves' eggs." Had I not been their comrade, my testicles would have been used to replace the eyes they'd neglected to gouge from their sockets.

When I could walk again, I was released from a field hospital where I'd squirmed in delirium for an indefinite time. I was told I was fortunate the infection had left my membrum virile intact, not that I had much use for the thing anymore. The loss of my manhood was no great concern, since I'd never been judged much of a man; and it was good to be relieved, give or take the odd phantom spasm, of the desire for intercourse. I had little taste left now for even the most basic of needs, and there were days when I wanted for nothing on earth.

In the shtetl the years passed, while time (simultaneous with the Flood and the Exodus from Egypt) stood still; whereas beyond the shtetl, out here in history, time flew, while the years were all of a piece. I was sent back to my battalion, which was transferred to another garrison somewhere in the Caucasus southeast of Kiev. There was a period of servitude and then another war, in which I figured as a cipher with blistered feet; I was a musket and ramrod in an infantry corps that belonged to a battle group that was part of a regiment attached to an artillery division joined by other divisions of grenadiers, fusiliers, sappers, and light cavalry. Our bivouacs stretched across whole valleys into the rolling uplands. Arrayed in the field with the sun glinting off helmets and shako plates, off the polished brass of gun batteries and caissons, we sprawled like a titanic dragon with myriad scales—or so said some purple tunic soon to be shot from his steed. As a unit of the rank and file, I could be further reduced to my constituent parts: forage cap, greatcoat, chamois pants, cartridge pouch, rifle sling, hobnail boots. Relieved of them, I was skin that was itself a map of historic stations: the canister burns across my belly that I'd received at Balaclava (where the British used a windmill for a missile to hit our powder magazine); the smallpox scars I'd acquired during the siege of Sevastopol. There we scuttled ships of the line to block the harbor, their lanterns extinguished like dying fireflies as they sank. I saw a company of hussars fall in unison from their starved horses (which were later eaten) when their surcingles could no longer be drawn tight. Then a salvo from siege guns caused a hail of slain bodies to descend upon me where I hunkered in a redoubt on the Fedyukhin Heights. By the time I was disinterred, days had passed, and pulled from beneath that warm canopy, I was declared to have been absent without leave. Due to the general outrage over our humiliation at the hands of the British alliance, goldbricks and malingerers, or those perceived as such, were shot on the flimsiest of excuses. I was stood up against a wall and made to strip off my tattered uniform, my sodden underwear and footcloths rank as Stilton cheese. It was a frosty morning and a long moment elapsed before it was realized that my empty sac wasn't shriveled because of the cold. "He's a fucking eunuch!" they cried, regardless of the contradiction (and the secondary insult that I was circumcised)—at which point it was concluded I wasn't worth shooting. Thereafter I was regarded as a virtual slave.

Soon I was old, my wattles and wisps reflected like silver drizzle in the bottom of a copper kettle licked clean of kasha. Obsolete, I was discharged from the Imperial Army with a promised pension I never received. Where would I have received it? I had no fixed abode. I wandered the roads scrounging from town to town, sleeping in study houses and barns. Once in a blue moon I stole a plum compote cooling on the sill of peasant hut, but mostly I dug turnips in the fields and, when desperate, peeled the bark from trees like a goat. Usually the children threw stones, or at best I was treated as some harmless domestic beast and fed scraps accordingly; I was offered lentils in exchange for showing my horns and cloven hooves. What made them think I was a Jew? Meanwhile the empire was ailing, its hamlets quarantined from typhus, inundated by floods, sows floating in the waterlogged streets like capsized dinghies; hamlets destroyed by government ukases and pogroms. On occasion, when my documents were in dispute, I was hauled into jail for a piyamnike, a vagrant, and then I would have a roof for a couple of nights. One day I entered a ruined town and saw, upheld by disciples at either elbow, a papery patriarch in a brittle capote whose vermin-ridden beard struck a chord. The chord thrummed in my aching head, its vibrations dislodging other landmarks from my dormant memory: the wooden synagogue wrecked by carpenter ants and Cossacks, the warren of the poorhouse given over to swallows' nests. Duyanov had always been something of a ghost town, but now most of the ghosts had fled. In the beit midrash, which was missing a wall, I inquired of the other beggars, "Nghlsh onfen ngh?" and was understood, since mine was the only question anyone ever asked.

"They went to the Promised Land," the beggars answered, explaining that to each Jew his own goldeneh medineh. Some had gone to America to become millionaires, others to Palestine to drain swamps, others sent to Siberia for fomenting the revolution that would transform Mother Russia herself into a promised land. A representative of the Society for the Resurrection of the Dead, himself a skeleton, offered me charity, which only reminded me that my tenure on earth had been for some time a postmortem affair. Anyway, I was tired. I remembered when the Angel told me about the gilgul, how if you died without having performed the 613 mitzvot (not one of which I recalled), you must return for another round. With the assurance that he was crazy, however, I rose early the next morning; I borrowed a rope from a tethered ox and tossed it over a rafter amid the debris in Shmulke der

Keziker's cow barn. I stood on a spongy scaffold erected upon rotten hay bales and, while the cock crowed and the shnorrers snored, stepped into thin air. My stringy neck stretched but didn't break when the rope went taut, so I dangled until I strangled.

Death, as it turns out, is even lonelier than life. I found myself in a dimly lit area that I took to be the backstage of a theater, though I'd never set foot in a theater before. Sandbags hung from the rigging, cables extended from catwalks like the strings of an enormous harp, their ends wrapped around belaying pins. Theatrical properties were stored against the walls: a twelve-pounder unicorn battery, a cat-o'-nine-tails, a cartridge pouch, a scroll, a bandolier. There were painted flats depicting fortifications, a tilting outhouse, a village cemetery with a headstone beyond its wall, and there was a dark drop curtain that appeared opaque at first glance, but look again and it proved to be a diaphanous scrim. On the other side of the scrim a performance was in progress. I pressed my nose against the gauzy fabric and saw a spectacle illumined by a row of radiant footlights: a beetle-browed priest assisted by devils was trying to wrest from the harried hero his immortal soul. He was a funny-looking hero, who seemed to set no great store by his soul ("What soul?"), but I knew its value, as did the rowdy audience, who mourned his persecution, grieved aloud for his apostasy, and wished he could somehow be saved.

If I scooted left along the boards, the hero was younger, a wild orphan filching live carp from a tub in the marketplatz, the carp flopping out of his pants as they were lowered by elders about to lather him for his sins. The audience groaned at his punishment and laughed despite themselves at his abduction by a bogeyman in an agitated potato sack; for he was after all an antic figure, the hero, with the face of a rueful rodent. If I moved to stage right, he was older, crawling across a smoky battlefield dusted in the pollen of sunflowers, sequined in the brains of his comrades, and I thrilled with the audience to the danger and the distance he'd traveled from his quaint beginnings. I worried over his terrible wounds. But the worst of it was that I seemed to know what was coming, and wondered if his fate could be altered. Hadn't I heard that even centenarians had taken December brides and gotten from them sons to say Kaddish for them after their passing? Scurrying back and forth along the gossamer curtain as far as the wings at either end, I sometimes overshot the production and saw the events that framed the play: abominations and exiles on the one side, enormities yet to come on the other. Then the life of the hero seemed an incandescent moment fraught with possibilities, a space between past and future as between parted waters, in which passions might culminate through exquisite suffering; and I wished I could step onto that stage and slip into his skin.

I pawed frantically at the curtain in search of a seam, a place where the fabric was worn thin enough to be torn. Eventually I located a patch no more substantial than cobweb and felt my heart drumming its martial rhythm throughout my frame. Gripping the scrim with trembling fingers, I ripped open the membrane between one world and another; I stuck my head through the hole, lost my balance, and tumbled straightaway out of a sack onto the tiles of the recruitment center in Slutsk, where all the benighted years stretched hopelessly ahead of me.

The Man Who Would Be Kafka

"Finally," said Professor Felix Meltzer in response to his students' efforts to view it positively, "there is no room for hope in the work of Franz Kafka."

A slender man whose physique had retained (despite sedentary habits) something of the suppleness of his athletic youth, Meltzer stood with his back to a row of open windows. The windows overlooked a square named after a student who'd set fire to himself in protest against the Soviet invasion. Beyond the square was the river, and beyond the river—like a prow cresting waves of red roofs—Prague Castle and the lacy twin spires of St. Vitus Cathedral.

"With that in mind—"

"Excuse me, Professor," interrupted Yossel Tchernobler, the know-it-all, slouched against the wall in his outlandish garb, "but isn't this the same Kafka who said, 'There are only miracles'?"

An unkempt young Lubavitcher Hasid transplanted from Brooklyn, Yossel was Meltzer's self-appointed nemesis, and in their competition to determine the direction of the classroom discourse, the professor was on the verge of conceding defeat. He was weary of the fanatic's relentless campaign to claim the famously unbelieving author for some species of rabbi. If Meltzer presented, say, the story "Josephine the Singer" as an ironic take on the role of the artist, Yossel countered with some perceived parallel to the idea of the tzaddik, a Jewish saint. He subverted and judaized Kafka at every opportunity, turning the writer's uninterpretable ambiguities into neatly resolved Hasidic allegories; and in his own zeal to defend Kafka's universality, Meltzer had perhaps overstated the case, to the extent that he was losing his class.

He frowned at the students and was met by a wall of intransigence, especially palpable among the women—the younger ones anyway, with rings through their flaring nostrils and discreet tattoos on their shapely calves.

But tempted as he was to surrender to the Hasid's version of the troubled author, rather than admit contradictions Meltzer rallied with yet another quid pro quo.

"Yes, Mr. Tchernobler," he replied, betraying a hint of smugness, "but this is also the Kafka who said to his friend Max Brod, 'You want the impossible while, for me, the possible is impossible.'"

On his first night in Prague Felix Meltzer, tenureless assistant professor of literature, sat in a monastery orchard overlooking the city and judged his whole life to have been a mistake. This was not a new assessment. But as he took in the dazzling city, its domes and turrets tumbling out of a blanket of terra-cotta roofs, the river aglint from the setting sun, he conceived a fresh perspective on his past. He included among the elements of his thirty-five-year blunder his obsession with the writer Franz Kafka, which was a paradox he thought the misfit author might have appreciated.

Tired and disoriented from his transatlantic flight, the professor had nonetheless set out from his pension on Maiselova Street to explore the city. It was a place he was already so familiar with from books that visiting it seemed almost superfluous. Didn't he have its points of interest by heart? Still, he could kill a few hours attempting to locate some of Kafka's former addresses. Who knew but it might be a pleasant exercise, nosing about neglected thresholds the author had once crossed over. But once Meltzer had set foot on the cobbled expanse of the Old Town Square, thronged with tourists sporting jesters' caps and sloshing tankards of beer, his worst fears were confirmed: the bashful genius had already been run to ground.

Everywhere he looked there were images of the late author. The stalls devoted to tourist kitsch displayed Kafka postcards, stationery, coffee mugs; T-shirts bearing his silk-screened likeness hung on racks and the slumped shoulders of youths. A bronze head, fixed to the corner of a building where Kafka was allegedly born, exaggerated his features: the jug ears stretched to satanic points, the soft eyes rendered piercing as a mesmerist's, the forehead receding to a vampirish widow's peak. Look left and you saw a Kafka museum, right and there was the Kafka Bookstore & Café. Young men, wearing bowler hats and competing with one another in anemic dissipation, held placards advertising Kafka walking tours.

"God help us," lamented the professor, "my Franz has become the Elvis of Prague."

He had of course heard rumors that, since the fall of the regime, this notoriously somber city had assumed a carnival atmosphere—but who would have guessed a Halloween party at which Kafka was the mask of choice?

Addled by the spectacle, Meltzer was ready to retrace his steps to the pension, but taking a wrong turn he was swept up in the tide of sightseers. He stumbled along streets flanked by ancient houses, some squat as toadstools, others narrow as the spines of books, with signs bearing mythical beasts over their doors; he trudged through lanes as twisted as funhouse corridors. "Like the configurations of the human brain," was how the fin de siècle decadents had characterized the streets of Prague. At the river he was carried along with the rubbernecking multitude over the statuary-studded Charles Bridge, into the streets of the Little Quarter on the other side. Trams rattled past the cafés in front of which languid women conspired over Turkish coffee; baroque saints on the eaves of churches trembled from the sepulchral organ strains within.

Meltzer might have been sleepwalking, so unreal was the impression the sights left on his overcharged mind. He passed a monument to here a martyr, there a plague, passed a palace sandwiched between the facades of tilting houses in one of whose gables a girl combed her hair. He toiled up the inclined streets of Malá Strana to a height where the crowds had begun to thin out. The immense yellow walls of Prague Castle loomed on his right, and on his left a gravel path led into a secluded glade of apple trees, toward a solitary bench upon which the professor collapsed.

Towers and steeples bobbed among the rolling rooftops; sparks winked from oriel windows as the sun sank behind a perimeter of lavender hills. Head reeling, Meltzer supposed it was all very beautiful, though for beauty he'd never had overmuch tolerance, at least not since his first encounter with the author of "The Metamorphosis."

That was back in high school when a progressive, somewhat bohemian (and soon to be dismissed) teacher of English in the tidy Long Island village of Sagahasset had introduced a class of bewildered adolescents to Kafka's fable: the one in which a commercial traveler wakes one morning after fretful dreams to find himself transformed into a bug. The class snickered and pulled faces, while young Felix, sensitive as any to the mood of his peers, nevertheless recognized a voice like a warning in the nick of time. Franz Kafka, it seemed, had spoken Felix Meltzer's own heart's hidden truth.

Previously he'd found truth, insofar as he'd sought it, in the tall tales of Edgar Rice Burroughs or the historical romances of Rafael Sabatini. There was a kind of truth in the skill with which he performed on the tumbling mat and flying rings, his prowess approaching that of a circus acrobat—which vocation he'd sometimes thought he might like to pursue. Truth was also in the angel faces of the local girls, whose heads he'd begun to turn. Of course there had been some uneasiness, some guilt over his father's accusation that he was betraying a tradition of nebbish Meltzers dating back to the Babylonian Exile. Then, at his introduction to the segmented belly and wriggling pincers of Gregor Samsa—the cracked carapace wherein lodged the apple that Gregor's own father had hurled for spite at his son—the scales fell from Felix's eyes. One day he'd been a clean-limbed youth, the unlikeliest candidate for conceiving an identification with vermin, the next he was stricken with an awful knowledge: the human condition was hopelessly compromised, his family a bourgeois abomination, their religion a sham. The world, which had seemed so full of promise, was now a forbidding place; it was an airless labyrinth, its inhabitants subject to a cosmic bureaucracy whose laws were as merciless as they were inscrutable. Moreover, his own life, Felix realized, had been fundamentally too good to be true. And on the evidence of Kafka's fiction, he understood that in fact it wasn't true; that hiding behind the masks of scholar, athlete, and dutiful son was an insect, cowering and alone.

Thereafter an acute self-consciousness set in. Things that were once second nature, such as performing on gymnastic apparatus (come to resemble in his mind the cruel machinery of "In the Penal Colony") or mingling with his fellows, hobbled him with guilt and fear. Since he'd been bitten by the Kafka bug, so to speak, Felix's world had shrunk to the confines of his own thin skin, and never once had he looked back—until now.

He'd come to Prague at the invitation of the Comp Lit Department at Mermelman College in Old Binstock, Massachusetts, the seat of Meltzer's undistinguished career. Mermelman was coordinating a program of month-long seminars at the Charles University, currently celebrating its 650-year anniversary; and Meltzer, who enjoyed a reputation for his particular interest in the works of Franz Kafka, had been asked to lecture there. (Though it was generally noised that Felix Meltzer was less an interpreter of Kafka than his impersonator.) At first he politely declined the offer on the basis that "I don't travel well," his little joke. The truth was he didn't travel at all, obedient to Kafka's dictum: "If you are to keep madness at bay, you must never go far from your desk; you must cling to it with your teeth."

Not that the professor had done much of consequence at his desk. His résumé was meager, consisting only of a volume of essays on Kafka, which he'd edited, and an uncompleted monograph. The latter had been an attempt to place Kafka's work in a Jewish context, an uninspired task since Meltzer had little real relation to his own lapsed faith. In the book, whose subject was synonymous with Prague, he'd attempted to find a thread connecting the sixteenth-century mystic rabbi Judah Loew and his legendary golem to Kafka and his guilt. Ultimately though, the project was abandoned, the slender thread having snapped midway through the slender text. So it was not so much for his currency as Kafka "specialist," he assumed, but as a sop for his not earning tenure that Meltzer was asked to take part in the Prague seminars.

His initial refusal had exhilarated him: once again he'd resisted temptation in order to nurture regrets in solitude. Of course, there was the lingering suspicion that the failure of his book, so steeped in the city's culture and lore, may have stemmed in part from his failure to visit Prague. Then, too, the word "pilgrimage" had lately begun to turn up in his otherwise stay-at-home lexicon. In the end, the professor shocked himself by swallowing his small portion of pride and asking if it was too late to change his mind. The invitation had acquired the weight of destiny.

But no sooner had Meltzer arrived than he was appalled by the city's shameless exploitation of its own past. To say nothing of the sobering perspective he'd experienced that first night in the orchard atop Petřín Hill. Thereafter he'd tried to reconstitute as best he could his Mermelman routine, leading as circumscribed a life in the bosom of Kafka's "little mother with claws" as he had at home in Old Binstock. He met his class in the late afternoons, avoided his colleagues, and dined on something called "modern gastronomy salad" in a drab vegetarian café. He returned early to his rooms in the pension, kept scrupulously clean by Mrs. Vodičkova, the varicose-cheeked concierge, then read himself to sleep with a book pertaining to his area of presumed expertise. In the mornings he breakfasted on fruit and cheese, prepared for class, and took a stroll, if only to prove his immunity to the charms of latter-day Prague.

Still, after only about a week and a half of teaching, Meltzer had come to dread entering his dusty classroom in the Philosophy Faculty, where his

Kafka seminar had turned mutinous. It was a modest-sized group composed largely of American undergraduates, tousled boys and stylish girls from prestige schools. Bleary-eyed in the aftermath of their previous night's debauch, they were nevertheless of a thoughtful turn of mind. Among them were also a smattering of inquisitive spinsters and retirees on an educational holiday, and Yossel Tchernobler, expatriate provocateur. Most of the class were Jews, and whatever their reasons for coming to Prague in the first place, once arrived they'd begun (as Meltzer cynically observed) to go native. It was as if the very absence of a once prodigious Jewish population obliged them to overcompensate. At night they might sample the Euro-decadence, but by day they toured the Jewish quarter and made trips to the former transit camp at Terezin, in search of lost identities. As a consequence, whatever enthusiasm they'd originally brought to the course was tempered by their celebration of heritage, and they began to resent having their faces rubbed daily in Kafka's fatalism. They resisted their teacher's enforced reverence for the author who "invented the twentieth century," his constant reminders that completeness was impossible in a world bereft of meaning.

In the ensuing tension between students and teacher, Yossel Tchernobler, the anti-Meltzer, had emerged as the people's champion. With his blinkered, one-note relation to history, he blithely explained the phenomenon of Kafka in terms of a thousand years of internalized Jew hatred; he made a virtue of the author's self-loathing, translating it into the cozy folk tradition of the Diaspora. Rather than a milquetoast who considered himself less than nothing, Yossel's Kafka was the staunch advocate of Yiddish theater, the avid reader of Hasidic tales, the one for whom writing was "a form of prayer."

Today the class was to discuss Kafka's famous "Before the Law" parable. This was the tale told by a priest to Joseph K toward the end of *The Trial*, about a man who comes from the country to gain admittance to the Palace of the Law. He's forbidden to enter by a doorkeeper, the first of a succession of doorkeepers, each more fearful of aspect, who will bar his entry should the first fail to do so. Having believed the law was open to all, the man is surprised by this condition; but he waits patiently outside the door, sitting year after year on his bench, making small talk with the doorkeeper, whom he bribes to no avail. Eventually, old and near death, he observes a radiance streaming through the door, and asks the doorkeeper why no one else has come to this entrance to seek admittance. The doorkeeper tells him, "This door was intended for you alone—and now I am going to close it."

"The theme of twentieth-century literature," pronounced Meltzer, a touch antagonistically, "has been our fundamental inability to enter the palace." For effect he turned his chin toward the window, beyond which the castle was veiled in mist. "In this parable Kafka strikes a chord that resonates . . ."

"So why," interjected the gadfly Tchernobler, his feet propped on a table in front of him, arms folded across the ragged bib of his ritual vest, "why couldn't you just crawl under the legs of the doorkeeper?"

"What?" said Professor Meltzer, incredulous, while the class began to stir from its general torpor.

"You couldn't make a dash beneath the legs of the doorkeeper—who's a Goliath, no? They're all Goliaths? So you scramble beneath their legs, snatch the scrolls of the Law, and jump out a window, mirtsishem."

"What are you talking about?" Meltzer took a handkerchief from the pocket of his funereal suit coat and wiped his brow.

"I'm talking Hershel Ostropolier, the Yid trickster, or maybe even the prophet Elijah himself—he dodges the doorkeepers, storms the palace, and rescues the hostage Torah . . ."

"What Elijah? What Torah? The parable doesn't say anything about Torah!"

"Nu, so I made a midrash on the text."

The class, in an unruly chorus, offered words of encouragement: "Good one, Yossel!" "Righteous, bro!," the lot of them opposed to the professor's dispiriting message. Running a hand through the ebbing tide of his slate-black hair, Meltzer blinked and saw a mob. He coughed once, twice, in an effort to salvage his foundered authority.

"Kafka isn't scripture, Mr. Tchernobler"—injecting a note of long-suffering patience into his voice—"he's literature. 'I have no literary interest,' he once said, 'but am made of literature . . .'"

"L'havdil," said Yossel, "and we are made of standard issue flesh and blood."

"What's that supposed to mean?"

Yossel shrugged. "What am I, a philosopher?"

The tension broke as the room erupted in laughter. Fools, thought Meltzer, doubly resentful since, through no fault of his own, his course was lending fuel to their willful ignorance.

"Listen, Professor," continued Yossel in a tone of appeasement, looping an oily elflock around a dirty ear, "come meshiach zeytn, come the Messiah, every man in Israel will read Torah according to the meaning peculiar to the root of his soul. This is also how Torah is understood already in Paradise."

Meltzer was livid: once again the upstart was making Kafka out to be some kind of Kabbalistic Rorschach—it was a dangerous naïveté. Determined to have the last word, the professor testily proclaimed, "Let me remind you that, when asked what he had in common with the Jews, Kafka declared, 'I have hardly anything in common with myself, and should sit quietly in a corner content that I can breathe.'" But the quote sounded like nothing so much as false modesty.

Walking home from the Faculty that evening, Meltzer wondered why his outrage always dissolved into self-pity, and why self-pity gave him such an appetite. Too impatient to wait for service at his customary vegetarian restaurant, though it was only blocks away, he stopped at a street vendor and bought a garlicky, sausage-filled potato pancake. Disposed as he was to dyspepsia and constipation—a condition known as "Jew's stomach" in Kafka's day—he nevertheless devoured the pancake with relish. It was greasy, rubbery, and delicious, and eating as he walked, Meltzer had the perverse notion that he was taking a sacrament. He headed back to Maiselova Street, trying to invoke as usual the pathos of loneliness. "Like Kaspar Hauser?" a friend of Kafka's had once inquired of him, attempting to gauge his companion's sense of isolation. "Much worse," said the writer. "I'm as lonely as Franz Kafka."

"I'm as lonely as Felix Meltzer," Meltzer tried on for size, but found the fit a bit large.

When he entered his rooms at the pension, there was Mrs. Vodičkova, stocky and good natured in her late middle age, scrubbing his bathroom—it was a warm night—in her peach bikini underpants. Blushing to the marrow, the professor apologized for having barged in on her, and, while she showed not a trace of embarrassment, backed out the door.

Maiselova Street was itself a chief artery of the Josefov district, locus of the original ghetto. Of course the ghetto was long gone, razed at the turn of the century to make way for Parisian-style boulevards and art nouveau flats. Afterward, with only a handful of Jewish sites left standing, no one was proof against nostalgia, not even Kafka, who said, "In us all it still lives—the dark rooms, secret alleys, squalid courtyards, and sinister inns. The fetid old Jewish Town within us is more real than the hygienic town around us. With our eyes wide-open we walk through a dream, ourselves only a ghost of a vanished age . . ."

But the Josefov, as Meltzer had judged on first impression, was now just another branch of the thriving kitsch industry. By day, sightseers from all nations swarmed over concessions flogging Jewish tchotchkes—menorahs, mezuzahs, ceramic golems—the way Indian villages sold tom-toms and tomahawks. Among the guided tours led by stout ladies wielding umbrellas, you might spot the odd yarmulke, but resident Jews were nowhere in evidence. The professor was well aware that this was the district the Nazis had designated for their Museum of an Extinct Race, which was more or less what the ghetto had become. The clock on the Jewish Town Hall, true to the logic of its Hebrew numerals, ran backward in an enticement to enter the past, but the tourists had chased all the ghosts away.

This was Meltzer's feeling as he stood on that soft summer night outside the locked gate of the old Jewish cemetery. Behind the bars a cat prowled the listing monuments, which looked in moonlight like a swaying congregation turned to stone by a Vesuvius of molten years. There were, Meltzer knew, twelve strata of souls buried in that heaving ground, the last interred long before the Jews of Prague, declared vermin, were banished to places from which they never returned. They were buried before the toppling of the medieval warren, back when the hovels still maintained a respectable squalor; when the grandparents of ritual slaughterers, merchants, and market wives could still remember a golden age: the very rich hours of the Emperor Rudolf, who invited the first citizen of the ghetto, Rabbi Judah Loew, the Maharal, to visit his cabinet of curiosities.

All this Professor Meltzer knew; but unlike his students who blindly embraced a murky, distant heritage, he (with eyes wide open) was marooned in his own sad century.

Slouching away from the graveyard, he paused on a corner adjacent to the Altneushul. This was the absurdly named Old New Synagogue, the tent-shaped Gothic centerpiece of the Jewish Town. Light slanted from its narrow apertures, the steep-pitched naves appearing to shiver from the chanting within. True, it was Friday night, Shabbat, but with the closing of the buildings comprising the Jewish Museum, the streets of the Josefov were virtually deserted. So where in Prague would you have found a minyan of Jews, let alone a group large enough to rock the walls of the ancient shul? Then Meltzer was startled by a familiar voice beside him, uttering an intrusive, "Gut Shabbos, Professor."

He turned toward the scrawny young man dressed as an old (an old young man?) in his tatty gabardine suit and wide-brimmed fedora. The thick glasses on his beaky nose were crooked, pimples peeping through his sparse beard like candy corn, the unshorn hair at his temples spiraling his ears.

"Gut Shabbos," said a vexed Professor Meltzer for perhaps the first time in his life, "Mr. Tchernobler."

"The tourists, they make a joyful noise and everything's just dandy, no?" said the Hasid, ruefully alluding to the synagogue's full house. "Abracadabra, the Jews survived."

Meltzer was a little surprised by the young man's tone. "I thought you were an optimist, Mr. Tchernobler."

"For the genuine article I reserve my faith," announced Yossel. "A yid bin ich un a yid vil ich blaybn. About Meshiach's imminent arrival I am confident, though not so much about the Jews' readiness to receive Him. So, Professor Meltzer, would you like to lay tefillin?"

Meltzer stiffened as if he'd been made an indecent proposal. He hadn't known Yossel to be one of those pushy Chabad boys who made nuisances of themselves accosting tourists, asking them to put on phylacteries and pray. ("Are you Jewish?" they would needlingly inquire, prompting crises of conscience for so many passersby.) Flustered, Meltzer started clumsily to demur, when Yossel let him off the hook.

"Relax, Professor," he chuckled. "Didn't you know we don't do tefillin on Shabbos?"

Stung by the tiresome kid yet again, Meltzer was eager to call an end to their exchange, but the zealot, seeing his teacher's discomfort, had swapped his teasing manner for one more confidential—which made the professor cringe nonetheless.

"You know he's still there."

"Who's where?"

"Him, di goylem—tahke, he's still in the attic." Yossel gestured with his scruffy chin toward the crenellated nave, where Meltzer noticed what he hadn't before: a steel-runged ladder climbing like staples up the side of the building toward a small metal door near the tip of the roof. "You know goylem?"

"Of course!" the professor fairly barked. Hadn't he immersed himself in the stories while researching his book: how the scholar-rabbi Judah Loew, to protect the ghetto from reprisals following the accusations of ritual murder, had created from the clay of the Vltava embankment a silent, deathless android—a golem. Then once the creature had laid waste to the enemies of the Jews, outwearing its usefulness (and becoming unmanageable to boot), the rabbi removed the parchment Name of God from its tongue, rendering it inanimate. Afterward the limp body was placed for safekeeping in the synagogue loft until it might be needed again. But the legend had endured in books, plays, films, and never-completed monographs by untenured professors. Even Kafka had succumbed to its allure, undertaking in his diary a description of the monster's genesis.

"Our people," boasted Yossel, "they broke the lock," as if to say they broke the mold. "You can climb up and see for yourself."

To what sounded less like an invitation than a dare, Professor Meltzer said, "Thanks all the same." Then, anxious to get away from this screwball, he made his excuses: "Glad we had this little chat, Mr. Tchernobler. See you in class."

As he reached the pension again, Meltzer thought to himself, Home free, but a restlessness—why was it his brushes with the fanatic always left him restless?—urged him past the tall double doors. In the Old Town Square he threaded the milling crowds and ducked into one of a number of random passages. The passage wound beneath vaulted arcades into a blind alley that, after a turn, miraculously regained its sight. Here was the heart of magical and romantic Prague, all lamplight and shadow, a cityscape like a set out of *The Cabinet of Dr. Caligari*—which was about as authentic as it seemed to the professor. Then it occurred to him that the fault lay not in the city but in himself: he was jealous of his students' guileless capacity for magic and romance; how they took for granted the very synthesis of past and present that had eluded Meltzer in researching his abandoned book.

The insight gnawed at him, even as he stepped out of the crush into a blue-rinsed tavern with a sgraffitoed facade. Having little tolerance for alcohol, he nevertheless ordered the native lager, which came in a tall, fluted beaker. He sipped first, then drained the glass and ordered another. It tasted frankly ambrosial, putting him in mind of the potable gold of the alchemists, with whom the city was associated in its Habsburg heyday. Leaving the pub, Meltzer carried on walking, having acquired the hint of a spring in his trundling step.

He passed under the arches of a Gothic tower that marked the boundary of the Old Town, and crossed another broad and populous square. Beyond the square was a dimly lit avenue whose faded Victorian buildings offered a reprieve from the theme park burnish of the medieval precinct. Entering it, Meltzer noted, here and there along the sidewalks, unescorted ladies lingering alone or in clusters, teetering on platform heels. Most had faces as garish as painted ponies, while a few, perhaps embarrassed by their own extravagant beauty, were unadorned: almond-eyed women under streetlights revealing, through translucent fabrics, the medallions of their nipples, their intricate underwear. With regard to their sex the professor had, as in all things, followed Kafka's example, cultivating an ambivalence that tended to abort relationships before they were properly begun. Franz Kafka was the model, though tonight Meltzer couldn't kick the nagging suspicion that the dead author was merely an excuse.

He remembered the master's parable of the sirens, how they couldn't help it if, talons and sterile wombs aside, their laments sounded so seductive. Then the professor stopped beneath a lamppost wreathed in fireflies, clutched his heart, and pulled an uncracked guidebook from his jacket pocket. Checking his whereabouts against the map, he looked to see on his left the cast-iron hulk of a railway station. Catty-cornered to the station, under a cement marquee in a shabby huddle of nondescript buildings, was another landmark, identified by the buzzing neon in its plate-glass window: the Café Arco. Despite its ordinary appearance and the absence of any commemorative plaque, the guidebook corroborated: this was the one-time habitat of the Arconauts, a literary circle whose members had included Max Brod, Franz Werfel, Egon Kisch, and occasionally Kafka himself. Hesitating only long enough to ask himself why he should hesitate, the professor went in.

Acrid smoke and raucous conversation, overwhelming the bass throb of the jukebox and the knock of billiard balls, assailed his senses. He took one of the few available tables against the wall, and too self-conscious to hail a waiter, sat waiting to be asked for his order. When no one did, he looked away from the predominantly male clientele—some of whom, in their dirty neckerchiefs and mismatched plaids, had turned to observe him—and pretended to admire a water stain on the wall. At a nearby table a stunted fellow in a floppy golf cap, his nylon running suit as loud as a jockey's silks, was quarreling with his deadpan lady companion. At one point he thrust an arm across the table to slap her cheek. Though her head snapped sideways, her drugstore face remained expressionless, as if the incident were part of a seated apache dance.

Taking refuge in his guidebook, Meltzer discovered that the once renowned Arco, having seen better days, had become the resort of the so-called Havel's Children. This was the label given the felons that the playwright president, in a gesture of democratic largesse, had amnestied after his election. Freed from prison and evicted from their former haunt of the railroad buffet, where they regularly fleeced the tourists, they had regrouped in the dilapidated Arco across the street—which, as the guidebook advised, had become a vipers' nest.

Peeking over the edge of the book, he tried to picture the place as it had been, the klatsch of writers speculating on the end of empire, on the war that would usher in a modernity culminating, eighty years later, in characters as feckless as Felix Meltzer. He imagined the young Kafka seated among them, quietly attentive, speaking only to utter some gnomic non sequitur ("We are forever stumbling through unfinished suicides"; "We are nihilistic thoughts in the mind of God") that would stop conversation cold. Then a voice diverted the professor from his musing. He lifted his head to see a moon-faced young woman, one cheek still flushed from having been slapped, seated adjacent him at his table. Her face was rouged and mascaraed to an almost clownish degree, her teased hair (dark at the roots) dyed a toxic yellow shading toward green. Her thin, sleeveless cardigan revealed round shoulders; her nose was wide, eyes large and glazed with a boredom that discouraged further exploration of their amber depths.

"What did you say?" asked Meltzer, stuffing the paperback into his coat pocket.

"You want to potty?"

The professor was confused. "No," he replied uncertainly.

She became more specific, saying in a fair approximation of English, "You like . . . emmm . . . blow job?," pursing her poppy petal lips.

His second "No!" was in a higher register and could be heard above the surrounding din, prompting several surly faces to turn his way.

She rested her arms on the table and leaned forward, bunching her breasts behind the stretched seams of her half-buttoned sweater. "How about . . . emm . . . to fuck with me?" Meltzer sputtered in place of an answer, giving her further entrée. "You reech Americky, no? Reech Americky got . . . emm . . . beeg deek?"

Her voice was bland, conversational, nearly uninflected but for the tentative lilt at the end of each sentence. Since he remained speechless, the girl—which was what she was, cosmetic mask notwithstanding—took further advantage of his chagrin to tell him, "You don't got to be shy with . . . emm . . . Astrid?" As if she were unsure of her own name. Meltzer was unsure as well, thinking Astrid a name for some sylphlike ingenue, not this one with her stolid features and candy-floss hair. This one looked more like a Ludmila.

"Please, leave me alone," he appealed. "I'm not interested."

"In what then you interested? You want . . . emm . . . spanky? You want I will tie you up?" Saying which, she winked an eye, the lid descending as heavily as a visor. Then she turned to a passing waiter and requested "Dva slivovitzy, prosim?" The professor, seizing the opportunity of her momentary distraction, attempted to rise, but he was arrested in his effort by her fingers under the table, which had begun to walk spiderwise up his thigh. Then the waiter returned to place two foggy glasses of a kerosene-colored liquid in front of them. The whore lifted hers, indicating that the professor do the same. In need of fortification, since his earlier pot valor was spent, he ignored her toast ("To the . . . emm . . . sexual intercourse?") and tossed back the drink. The afterburn made him gasp, upon which the whore leaned across the table and pounded his back. When he recovered, he found that the drink had left him with a pleasantly humming brain.

"So . . . Astrid, is it? Ad Astrid per aspera," he said idiotically, then clearing his throat, "So how did you learn to speak English?"

"I swallow much the . . . emm . . . jissom? from Americky." It was impossible to tell if this was intended ironically. "Now we will to the fuck?" Rising abruptly from her chair, she glanced toward her golf-capped mishandler of moments ago. He sat toad-faced at his table nursing his schnapps, signaling openly with stubby fingers. Turning back to the professor, she announced, "One thousand . . . emm . . . fumfty crown?"

This is reasonable, thought Meltzer, instantly banishing the thought. He rehearsed words of protest in his head, which he stood to deliver, but all that escaped his throat was an anxious, "Where?"

"In toilety?"

"Eh?"

"Toilety? Emm . . . the double-you see?"

"I don't see," he replied, though the truth had begun to dawn in his muzzy brain. He'd imagined perhaps a tidy room upstairs, a scene not unlike Kafka's first time with the shopgirl—Kafka's nafkeh, Tchernobler had called her—about which the author had written in his diary: "It was charming, exciting, and disgusting." A toilet was beyond disgusting, it was depraved. So why was he helplessly following the blockish girl past the waiter, who stopped him to ask that he pay the check, and the leering patrons?

In a narrow corridor at the rear of the bar the whore tried the grimy door marked WC, and found it locked, a labored groaning from within. She was patient a moment, then began to shout without a hint of the interrogative, "Proçvamtotakdlouhotŕva!" Eventually a chesty woman in a Cleopatra wig exited the restroom with a drooping elderly gentleman in tow, and she and Meltzer's whore exchanged words. Meltzer asked himself if this could be any more sordid, and had his answer when the alleged Astrid hustled him into the cramped lavatory.

She locked the door (lest he try to escape?) and asked for her money, which the professor perfunctorily handed over. The stench was ripe, the plaster walls discolored by mildew and worse, but due perhaps to the absurdity of the situation (and the effects of the slivovitz), Meltzer felt strangely impervious. He watched from what seemed like a lofty distance as the girl stooped to open his belt buckle and unzip his pants. To his fascination, his organ sprang to attention at her first touch, which caused the girl to recoil as if from a spitting snake. Then cautiously, she reapproached him and squatted to take him into her mouth, thus ending his detachment. After a reflexive thought concerning vagina dentata, the professor experienced a profound gratitude.

Tenderly, as if coaxing a kneeling subject to rise, he pulled the girl to her feet. Along the way she shoved his trousers to his ankles, then sat him down on the toilet seat. "Sticky," he remarked, though the whore showed no willingness to indulge him in further conversation. As she fished in her purse for a condom and began to unwrap it, Meltzer missed their faltering rapport of the barroom table. He was touched in any case to see that the condom was lime-green in color, matching her brief vinyl skirt, stiff as a megaphone. Having unrolled the rubber with clinical dexterity over his erect member, she hoisted the skirt above her ample hips, and alternately lifting her dimpled knees, peeled off the pantyhose and underwear with a practiced ease. Then she proceeded, squirmingly, to settle herself astride Meltzer's lap. She pushed up her sweater, raised her bra, and shoved a plump breast (tasting faintly of vinegar) into his mouth. The professor nearly swooned. To prolong the event, and retard his headlong slide toward release, he invoked a contrary sentiment of Kafka's: "My life has dwindled dreadfully," he whispered under his panting breath, "nor will it cease to dwindle. Nothing else will ever satisfy me." But satisfaction was clearly at hand. Having entered Astrid's body, Meltzer had taken leave of his own melancholy mind; he was a carnal engine, bouncing the girl's jiggling buttocks on his organ as if he meant to inflate a world. Watching her face—which remained implacable, eyes wide open though focused on nothing—he wondered how he could feel so intensely what she apparently felt not at all. Determined to make her aware of him, he squeezed her fleshy bottom and rose up from the toilet seat, lifting her with him. She was forced to scissor her legs around his spine, as Meltzer enjoyed a strength he hadn't realized since his acrobat days.

Then came a sensation like a swarm of bees escaping the hive of his testicles through the tip his penis, spilling warm honey (spiced with all the corruption of his soul) into the latex sheath. "Oyyy!" he cried triumphantly, as the girl slid from his wilted person and dismounted. Though the separation instantly curtailed his pleasure, the professor knew better than to try and impede her. When at last he opened his eyes, she had already readjusted her clothing and was standing at the cloudy mirror freshening her makeup, raking a comb through her crackling chartreuse hair. Moved by her ministrations, Meltzer shuffled forward, pants still around his ankles, to touch her shoulder. She flinched, failing even to turn her head. He pulled off the soggy condom like a mournful circumcision and tossed it into the toilet bowl, then hoisted his trousers and staggered out of the pungent stall.

All that weekend Meltzer waited for the remorse that did not come. The incident at the Arco was humiliating; it was ugly and degrading to both parties, but the truth was that the professor was more ashamed of not feeling ashamed than of what he'd done. Toward the girl he felt only a wistful regard, sometimes thinking (granted, irrationally) that he actually missed her. But frustrated by the memory of her impassivity, he wished he'd been able to evoke in her some human response; he wished he had fucked her so deep that he'd nudged her heart, and he wondered if he might ever have another chance.

By Monday, however, Meltzer was himself again. After a weekend spent summoning enough guilt to cancel the thrill of his Friday night aberration, he was able to face his afternoon class with composure. Gazing over the rows of desks, he was aware that some of the younger men and women—holding hands across the gaps between chairs—had paired off during the past two weeks. Previously solitary seniors sat in couples as well: Mr. Rosen the autodidact, throat like the gut-strung neck of a violin, having sidled next to the demure Widow Kupferberg; Ms. Thigpen cackling every time the lickerish Dr. Bloom called her "shikse." All of them were slumped in a collective languor that might have been interpreted as postcoital afterglow.

It offended Meltzer, their brazen show of intimacy, like a deliberate affront to the themes (lovelessness, desolation) that were his own stock-in-trade. He also took personally, though with some tincture of relief, the absence among these honeymooners of the Hasid Yossel Tchernobler, whose chair against the wall was conspicuously vacant. Today's Kafka portion was "The Hunger Artist," the archetypal tale of deprivation, which the professor viewed as the author's signature story. He looked forward almost sadistically to citing its maddening central paradox: that the hero had made an "art" out of fasting because he couldn't find the food he liked. Then how, he would ask (for once without fear of interruption), how can you call it "art," what for the protagonist is also necessity? Never mind that, while art is so typically assumed to be life affirming, the "artist" in the story embraces death as his crowning achievement. But as soon as he opened his mouth, a hand shot up at the rear of the classroom; the zealot, as it happened, was not absent at all but merely out of place.

"So what if the hungry artist got bored with dying?" Yossel wanted to know, his wooden chair rampant against the paneled back wall.

"What are you doing back there?" blurted the professor.

"I came in late," said the Hasid. "God forbid I should disrupt the class." Which prompted general laughter. "So what if the hungry artist . . . ?"

"It's hunger."

"Wha?"

"You said hungry artist," Meltzer corrected, possessed of the weird sensation that the script was already written, and Yossel its author. "It's hun-*ger*, not hun-*gry*."

"Nifter shmifter, a leben macht er," said Yossel dismissively. "Anyhow, what if he got bored with dying, the hun-*grrr* artist?"

Meltzer wanted to tell him, Don't be absurd, boredom doesn't enter into it. If Kafka had wanted him bored, he'd have written him bored. But just as he recognized the predictability of his answer, so could he predict— afflicted suddenly with clairvoyance—Yossel's response, which he decided to preempt. "Nu," he began, mocking his student's artlessness, "if he got bored, he would probably climb out of his cage, right? Nobody ever bothered to lock him in. So he'd climb out of his cage and follow the spectators who'd abandoned him for the other sideshow attractions." Meltzer had begun to enjoy his sacrilege, seeing clearly now the thing he described, his risen voice approaching conviction. "A stick man with a birdcage for a chest and a rag about his loins, a pathetic survivor, he would join the crowd ogling the panther—whose coat is as glossy as a jackboot and bursting with vitality . . ."

Then he stopped, wondering what dybbuk had gotten his tongue— and since when was *dybbuk* a part of his working vocabulary? The class too had fallen silent, including Yossel, who'd righted his chair and lowered his hand to half-mast. Everyone seemed duly chastised by Meltzer's image of the wasted artist admiring the robust creature that would ultimately replace him. But no one was so chastised as Meltzer himself, who felt ashamed at having stolen the Hasid's thunder. Moreover, he was sorry for subverting Kafka's fable and liberating the hunger artist, thereby exposing him to such indignity; better to let him rot in his cage.

After their initial consternation the class began venturing comments on the professor's little homily—his midrash, as Yossel would have called it. They seemed willing, for the sake of argument, to entertain the possibility that Meltzer was right: Kafka's ironies were inescapable; the neurasthenic author was for better or worse the conscience of the age. But for Meltzer the damage was done. The period was over and the students, wanting to continue their dialogue in the cafés, for once invited the professor to come along. He courteously declined, noting as he did that Yossel Tchernobler was grinning at him from the back of the class.

Fleeing the Faculty, Meltzer boarded the Metro to make a journey that was long overdue. He rode to the suburban stop at Želivského, where he exited (as the guidebook prescribed) into a residential street bordering the New Olšany Cemetery. It was after-hours and the gates were already locked, but the professor, surveying the spiked iron palings, was oddly undiscouraged. Walking down Izraelska Street, he came to a spot where a linden tree, growing inside the cemetery grounds, overhung the sidewalk. Turning his head in either direction to ensure the absence of onlookers, Meltzer leapt for the dipping limb; catching hold, he grappled hand over hand—brachiation, they called it among apes—to the top of the fence. From there he dropped neatly to the mossy earth and stepped into a graveled avenue.

It was dusk, and he wandered awhile in the cool primrose light among headstones and monuments, past an untended urn grove and an ivy-choked ceremonial hall. At length the professor arrived at a wooden signpost pointing in several languages toward the grave of Franze Kafky, Plot 21. Following the arrow, he came upon a flared granite obelisk, missile-shaped in its beveled top-heaviness, bearing the name of Dr. Kafka along with his parents' names—whose cramped company he had not escaped even in death.

So this was his shrine, the prophet who'd announced toward the end of his truncated life, "I myself cannot go on living because I never lived; I remained clay. I have not blown the spark into fire, but only used it to light up my corpse." The golem could not have put it better, thought Meltzer, who knew himself to be neither golem nor insect nor rodent nor mole. So what does that make me but a lousy Kafka wannabe? He remembered the writer's claim that he was "trying to communicate the incommunicable, explain the inexplicable," which he then felt obliged to qualify: "Basically it is nothing but fear spread to everything—fear of the greatest and of the smallest, fear of change . . ." But here at the terminus of his pilgrimage, the professor wondered why he'd come to Prague if not in search of change. Where Kafka'd had to overcome his devils in order to write, Meltzer had to overcome, well, Kafka in order to live.

Facing the six-sided stone, surrounded by the scattered blossoms of scribbled tributes, Meltzer acknowledged aloud his betrayal of the master. "Forgive me," he said, "for not being you." He took a pebble from the path, placed it alongside the regiment of others at the base of the monument, and recited as much of the Mourner's Kaddish as he could remember. Then, retracing his steps, Meltzer took once again to his tree.

The Arco was as packed with undesirables as it had been on his previous visit, though this time, as if he'd already become a regular, Meltzer turned no heads on entering. He found a table in the midst of the commotion (which tonight included a gypsy accordionist with a mastiff) and, catching the waiter's eye, ordered a beer. Along with the beer arrived one of the ladies who circulated throughout the tavern, this one with bird bones and coral hair, batting lashes the size of harem fans.

"American?" she inquired, taking a seat without being invited, and when Meltzer replied in the affirmative, asked him, "You like the blow job?" as if it were the specialty of the house. Then she reached under the table and grabbed the professor ungently between the legs. Pulling her hand from his crotch the way one might pluck a sand crab, he asked if Astrid was around.

She sniffed, blowing cigarette smoke in his face. "We all Astrid, dollink." But just then the girl herself appeared, entering the café in midaltercation with the bullnecked dwarf Meltzer assumed was her fancy man. They were some striking pair all right: he in his floppy golf cap and running suit of many colors; she in a scarlet tube top and patent leather skirt that cinched her thick waist, causing her midriff to pooch like custard between ladyfingers. With a sinking heart, the professor conceded that they probably belonged together, these persons of the evening, the incubus and his thrall. Still, their persistent squabbling, as they took their seats at a nearby table, offered hope;

and to the annoyance of the woman at his own table, who hissed what must have been unkind words, Meltzer stood and approached them.

He planted himself patiently beside their table, where her procurer was shaking Astrid by the shoulders, her head bobbling like a bulb on a stalk. Noticing the intruder at his elbow, the pimp ceased manhandling the girl—whose flat expression and electric hair remained unruffled—long enough to spare the professor a quizzical look. Astrid also turned her head and, at a poke in the arm from her partner, emitted an obligatory, "You want to potty?"

"Don't you remember me?" replied Meltzer, injured.

"Oh sure," she said without a hint of recognition in her sleepy eyes. "You the one got . . . emm . . . beeg deek?"

He decided not to pursue this line of inquiry. The pimp jerked his chin in Meltzer's direction and Astrid rose to ask the professor if he would like a blow job, et cetera—while he searched her face for the woman behind the mask. She was as artificial in appearance as one of the numberless mario-nettes Meltzer'd seen in shopwindows all over Prague, and he was possessed of the Gepetto-like impulse to make her real.

"Come home with me to my pension," he implored.

She asked his address, which she repeated aloud, glancing at her associ-ate, who tapped a cigarette significantly on the back of his hairy hand. She turned again to Meltzer and quoted a price.

"Were it above rubies," he replied.

In the taxi to Maiselova Street the professor was talkative. He confided to the girl that this sort of thing was new to him; she should understand he'd been for many years a virtual shut-in. He confessed he'd never been any great shakes at tomcatting—"Title my memoirs *No Fun Intended*, ha ha." Then he asked, begging her pardon, if she'd ever read Kafka. But while she remained silent, rigid but for the occasional glance out the rear window, Meltzer had faith, as at the bed of a coma victim, that at some level she took in what he said.

At the pension he escorted her up the stairs from the courtyard, past the landing where Mrs. Vodičkova poked her head out her door to give her blessing. Unlocking his rooms, the professor was overtaken by an antic no-tion, and sweeping the hefty girl into his arms, staggered with her across the threshold.

"You will . . . emm . . . please to put me down?" she said, as he'd shown no signs of doing so. Restoring her to her feet, the professor hoped for some acknowledgment of his vigor and spontaneity, but Astrid remained strictly business. Meltzer forked over a wad of cash at which she nodded, saying, "Now you can yourself . . . emm . . . to make comfortable?"

After the moment it took him to comprehend the euphemism, Meltzer obliged. Starting mechanically, he then began to enjoy what he turned into a slow striptease: removing the unseasonable suit jacket, the skinny necktie and age-yellowed white shirt (exposing first one shoulder, then the other), the pleated trousers, all with a tantalizing deliberateness. Down to his shorts, he thought he detected something like a flicker in Astrid's listless eye, indicating perhaps an appreciation of his trim figure. When he'd shucked the last garment and sat on the bed in a state of virile anticipation, she walked over to the door presumably to lock it.

"I did that already," Meltzer informed her, as she turned the key and stepped aside, allowing her runty, stubble-jawed accomplice to burst into the suite with pistol drawn. "Astrid!" cried the professor in a seizure of disappointment, pulling the bedsheet over his lap.

"Who?" said the whore.

The pimp had crossed the carpet to rummage through the pants Meltzer'd thrown over an understuffed armchair. Securing the wallet, he rifled and pocketed its leftover contents, then snarled something at the girl, who retreated the rooms without a backward glance. At her exit Meltzer, swaddled in his sheet, endeavored to rise from the bed, but the pimp, charging forward to cut short his effort, clouted him over the head with his revolver.

"I fell back on the bed, gripped my aching skull with both hands," said Professor Meltzer to his seminar, "and realized the adventure was over."

It was the day they were to discuss Kafka's celebrated novella "The Metamorphosis," and Meltzer—sunlight framed like bullion in the open casements behind him—had begged his class's indulgence: would they allow him to offer a personal gloss on the text? Then, to their bewilderment, he'd launched into an account of the events of the previous night.

"The adventure was over," he continued, "for last week's Felix Meltzer, who wouldn't have been in such a fix in the first place—though could he have imagined it, he'd have said it served him right. But today's Meltzer"—seated atop his desk in his shirtsleeves with folded arms—"this one knew he wasn't finished yet with the girl. I shook my head clear of loose sprockets and got unsteadily to my feet. I gathered the sheet around my loins and pulled a flap between my legs, which I knotted like a diaper as I flung myself out the door.

"The pimp was in the process of tugging the girl toward a double-parked car halfway up Maiselova. I reminded myself this was not an abduction, that the two of them were in cahoots to swindle a foreigner; she didn't need to be rescued. But I knew what I wanted, and shouting 'Astrid, please wait!,' I gave chase. Overtaking them in the street, I leapt astride the pimp's back and pulled his cap down over his eyes. Uncommonly strong for his size, he whirled about, hurling me to the pavement. Then he shoved back the bill of his cap, manipulated the muzzle in his pocket, and released a string of epithets, which Astrid volunteered to interpret . . ."

"Otakar say," came a girl's timorous voice from a chair in the front row, "'What are you . . . emm . . . crazy fucker?'"

The class strained for a glimpse of the sulfur-haired newcomer, powder runneled like melted icing on her florid face. She was wearing, along with her scarlet whore's ensemble of the night before, what she must have considered a concession to her day in school: a pair of frilly white anklets and open sandals below her barked shins.

"Risen to my knees I pleaded, 'Astrid, come with *me!*'" continued the professor without missing a beat. "Then more venom from Otakar . . . ," winking at the visitor.

"Jedem ty dušu"—the girl was expansive—"prosive plemeno židi . . ."

"Which Astrid duly translated . . ."

"He say you are Jew dog? and he will cut from you your *pžiroženi* . . . emm . . . your cashews? and feed to swine."

"That was my first experience of the famous European anti-Semitism," confessed Meltzer, "and God help me, it gave me a flutter. Then the pimp spoke what were perhaps his only two words in English—'Piss off'—and grabbed the girl's arm to haul her into the car.

"'Only if she tells me,' I said, having regained my feet—at which Astrid turned her head to pronounce . . ."

"Piss off?" said the girl.

"I nearly took the hint," admitted Meltzer. "Clearly they were wed to their mutual dependency, she addicted to his chronic abuse. But it was too late to take no for an answer. Once again I started for Otakar, who drew the revolver from his nylon pants—this despite the little knot of spectators who may have thought they were witnessing street theater, you tell me."

For several members of the class, including Mr. Rosen, Mrs. Kupferberg, and Yossel Tchernobler, had been out for the evening discussing the impact of Kafka on their lives.

"Anyway, I had the sense to stop and raise my hands. Meanwhile my makeshift breechclout had slipped around my hips, and when I reached to pull it up, Otakar cocked his pistol. I shut my eyes and heard a familiar question—"

With eyes shut Meltzer pointed conductor-style toward the wall against which Yossel, grinning goatishly, sat in his tilted chair.

"Are you Jewish?" he said on cue.

"I looked to see that Mr. Tchernobler had whipped out a phylactery cord and, stepping up to Otakar, wound it with amazing swiftness around his gun-toting wrist. He pulled tight and the pimp dropped the pistol, which Mrs. Kupferberg, I believe it was . . . ?" Meltzer squinted in her direction, evoking a blush that was half a rash on her wrinkled cheek. "Which Mrs. Kupferberg picked up and stuffed in her handbag." The old widow produced the gun from a crocheted handbag, held it out like a bad herring before placing it on her desk: Exhibit A. "That's when the impossible happened," said Meltzer. "That's when Astrid tottered forward to take my arm, asking . . ."

At her desk the girl allowed the faintest suspicion of a smile. "You reech Americky? You will . . . emm . . . take me back with you Time Square, America, for buying me t'inks and to make for me beeg fun?" She relaxed her shoulders after the exertion of such a speech.

"Otakar was struggling with Mr. Tchernobler, who'd managed to bind both the pimp's wrists in a regular cat's cradle of leather thongs. 'Why not?' I replied, as Astrid tugged at my hand to lead me away. We'd already advanced past the doors of the pension before I thought to turn around—just in time to see Otakar, who'd succeeded in furiously tearing off the tefillin, reaching to lift a flick-knife out of his sock.

"Astrid was stalled and I feared for a moment she was having second thoughts, but she'd only paused to kick off her ungainly heels. Then holding hands, we ran for it, and I was impressed at how, for a full-figured girl, she was fleet of foot, her face set with determination, her soles slapping the sidewalk in time to my own. But the pimp, pumping his bandy knees to the level of his chest, was gaining on us. And I thought: here I am nearly naked with a woman I stole from an angry flesh peddler, sprinting across Široká past the Jewish Town Hall, where Kafka once said, 'People of Prague, you know more Yiddish than you think . . .'"

There were requests from the class that Meltzer stick to the subject.

"By the time we'd reached the Altneushul, Astrid was puffing exhaustedly and Otakar was quickly narrowing the distance between us. Then remembering something a Chabad boy had told me about the shul"—he nodded toward Yossel, who clenched his hands above his head—"I had an idea. 'Come on!' I urged the girl, dragging her forward over the road between a pair of parked Škodas. When we'd arrived at the base of the whitewashed synagogue, I jumped into the air. The first time I missed the ladder, but on my second try I caught hold; I pulled my knees up over the steel rung and, hanging upside down, yanked off the sheet and lowered it to the girl.

"'Astrid, grab hold!' I called down to her.

"She hesitated—at least until Otakar, spewing curses, lurched from between the Škodas with knife upraised. Then she said . . ." Meltzer prompted her with a look.

"Ludmila," the girl declared breathily. "My name is . . . emm . . . Ludmila?"

That, the professor had thought, was more like it. He told her he was Felix and to forgodsake hurry up!

She gripped the sheet and he hoisted her—the veins branching in his straining arms—to a height where she could take hold of the ladder; then he dropped the sheet, which settled like a collapsed canopy over the head of the irate pimp. Still hanging from his knees, Meltzer boosted Ludmila by the cushiony soles of her feet, which enabled her to clamber over him to find a purchase—a process that stirred him to an inappropriate arousal. He sat up in midair, seized the ladder with one hand, and began to shove the girl with the other, until they'd both reached the higher rungs. At the top of the ladder was a small tin door, where Meltzer had a momentary lapse of faith, but the Hasid had been as good as his word: the padlock, sprung from its rusty hasp, was dangling from a hook in the wall. He had only to tug once, heartily, before the door creaked open and he could push Ludmila by her dumpling tush into the synagogue loft. Then he followed; while below, disentangled from the bedsheet, Otakar railed at them both.

But the darkness of the loft, only slightly diminished by moonlight through the open door, dampened the couple's sense of sanctuary. As their eyes adjusted, a hill of relics became visible under the rafters: tarnished menorahs and Torah crowns, rotting cedar chests bulging open with outworn scrolls. There were ram's horns, empty velvet mantles like headless dolls, a heap of moldering prayer books as high as a funerary mound. The attic itself, rigged with cobwebs and reeking of age, further oppressed them with its stuffiness. Although the professor had taken Ludmila's hand, he found himself helpless to console her, sharing as he did her presentiment of dread.

Ludmila, lacking Astrid's insouciance, squeezed Meltzer's fingers in return, communicating a vulnerability that seemed to ask, where had he gone, the reckless gymnast of minutes before? Then Otakar, who must also have had some qualities of a human fly, exploded through the door of the loft, growling despite the switchblade clenched in his teeth. Spitting the knife into his hand, he lunged toward the professor, who rolled with Ludmila instinctively out of harm's way. The downward arc of Otakar's blade stabbed the air, striking the pile of books—which straightaway began to stir. Ludmila and Meltzer looked on in dumb fascination as the pimp attempted to retrieve the knife he'd buried to its the hilt among the tumbling siddurim.

His capacity for wonder stretched beyond reason, Meltzer pointed at the shifting books and whispered, "It's him."

"Who?" asked the girl.

"The golem. He's awake again."

Then the books fell away and the thing beneath them was in sudden precipitous motion, carrying Otakar (who clung facedown to its armored spine) across the sagging floorboards. It stopped dead at the door to the loft, where the pimp, losing his grip on the knife hilt, was jettisoned backward into the evening air. A thud followed by a howl of pain was heard from below.

In the small opening the oval moon revealed the creature responsible for Otakar's defenestration, at the sight of which the professor's panic abruptly subsided. For this was not the ill-omened automaton formed by a sorcerer rabbi in some dim occult epoch, but rather an enormous bug with searching antennae and half a dozen wizened legs. Ludmila let out a shriek, while Meltzer, intrigued, crawled on his hands and bare knees toward the attic door. Placing his fingertips on the insect's (cockchafer? dung beetle? the scholars had debated its species for generations) brittle shell, he looked down at the pimp, his leg at an unnatural angle as he writhed in the limbs of a privet hedge. Sirens wailed in the near distance, and Professor Meltzer, grasping the bone-handled knife (think of young Arthur removing the sword from its stone), cleanly extracted the blade; and while he was at it, he searched the silvery carapace for other wounds and imperfections. Ultimately he found what he was looking for: Herr Samsa's final insult, which looked now like a barnacle imbedded in an otherwise lacquered shell. With the point of Otakar's shiv Meltzer prized out the foreign object, whereupon the creature squealed like a very old squeezebox; then it scuttled immediately backward, burrowing into the books until it could no longer be seen.

The sirens were just outside now, flashing red lights vying with the shadows in the synagogue attic—a hubbub swelling, authoritative voices shouting up at them. Still sobbing, Ludmila rocked herself on her haunches. The professor pitched the knife and crawled back to her, delighted at how little he missed his clothes. He wrapped an arm about the girl's quivering shoulders and pressed into her hand what she accepted with some trepidation, eyeing it as if he'd brought her the gift of a trod-upon heart.

"It's all right," he assured her, folding her fingers around the ancient apple.

In the classroom, having removed it from her purse, Ludmila tossed Meltzer the object in question, which the teacher placed beside him on his desk. Meanwhile Yossel Tchernobler, his chair balanced precariously on its hind legs, was wagging his hand in the air. Heaving a sigh, Professor Meltzer yielded to the fanatic the final word.

"It's all right, got su danken," said Yossel, picking up where the professor'd left off. "It was only Gregor."

On Jacob's Ladder

"Spin, little spider, spin," the corporal called down in his guttural sing-song. He was attempting—to no effect whatever—to twirl the rope with which he'd lowered Toyti into the chimney. Braced against the warm walls of the flue, the boy ignored Corporal Luther's efforts at sabotage; he was after all harmless, the corporal, a laughingstock among his fellows, and his lame jokes and taunts were merely the way he tried to disguise his fear of scaling the smokestack. It was on account of his cowardice and generally unfit condition that Untersturmführer Stroop had assigned him repeatedly to this exercise in humiliation. Then other guards and even kapos would gather to observe his fat rump toiling up the iron rungs behind his charge, whose nimbleness was a torment that the tub-of-guts Luther took as a personal offense.

The little yid should by all rights have been dead already—hadn't the corporal lost a small fortune in wagers on that score? The shelf life, so to speak, of climbing boys in the camp was ordinarily measured in minutes, but this one had survived, even thrived at the task; which was why Luther, smug in his use of a Jewish locution, had christened him Toyti. And Toyti—since he was no longer able to remember his real name—was who he'd become. There was in fact a whole world he no longer remembered, though bits of it sometimes came back to him like objects under water that never surface far enough to recognize. The guards called him Toyti as well, as did the other prisoners, who viewed him as a creature whose intimacy with the machinery of death gave him the status of an honorary corpse. He took a peculiar pride in his status, which endured long after so many of his fellow inmates had disappeared. Generations of them had joined the ranks of the officially dead, their torched bones pulverized and sprinkled over the gardens and orchards beyond the high-voltage fence, while Toyti continued to master the game of survival.

"Hey, little spider," shouted Luther, still asthmatically panting, "you know how the sausage makers of Rott—*hunh*—they claim to use every part of the pig but the oink? Well, here we use every part of the yid—*hunh*—but the oy." His wheezy laugh like a trodden concertina reverberated in the square chimney shaft.

Toyti had heard the joke before ad nauseam, to say nothing of the endless threats and complaints that accompanied their climbing excursions. He knew that Luther looked forward to the day when the stunted sweep would be overcome by the heat and fumes, and instead of hauling up a spider he would reel in a dead fish. That was after all the purpose of the rope, not to protect the boy but to prevent his becoming an obstruction. Hence the wire ruff like a ballerina's skirt that encircled his chest along with the rope, so that in the event he was no longer capable of scraping residue from the tiles, his very body could still serve as a cleaning instrument. It was another example of the efficiency for which Luther and his kind had such affection, but Toyti had cheated them all by making the chimneys his element.

By now he'd descended far enough into the flue that Luther's barbs were barely audible anymore. The bloated corporal was in any case an amateur at abuse compared to the death's-head soldiers that supervised the work details to which Toyti had been attached before his transfer to the crematoria. His back still bore the stripes from their quirts, his head the ache from the heels of their patent leather boots grinding his face into the mud. Their dogs had sunk their fangs into his ankles as he shoveled drek from a latrine overflowing from a thousand cases of dysentery; they snapped at him as he dragged stumps and lugged stones to no purpose other than breaking a body in which the spirit no longer resided. For these endeavors he was rewarded each evening with a bowl of soup abob with drowning vermin and a mealy potato from which even his empty gut revolted. His eyes drooled a murky sap, his limbs brittle as twigs, and during that notable morning selection when the oberführer called his number, he groaned in relief that he would soon be delivered from the onus of his days. But rather than sent to the gas he was dispatched (owing no doubt to his pint size and advanced puniness) to sweep the chimney of one of the incineration centers. At the time he would have preferred to lie down and die. But when he was hoisted by the disgruntled corporal onto the rusted rungs that protruded from the smokestack wall, something happened; because his spent limbs, never athletic or especially strong, seemed to welcome the opportunity to clamber up the ladder. In no time at all he had risen to an altitude at which the poison stench of the camp was dispersed by crisp breezes, and the jaunty marches the slave orchestra played were no longer a mockery. He could see beyond the barbed wire and the towers to the woods and cultivated fields, the feather-soft rolling hills, but even more pleasing than the view from the crown of the chimney was the sense of safety he felt once he was lowered into the shaft.

So it seemed that Toyti had a vocation. The work was of course no less taxing than the drudgery he had previously endured, but it was essential. If the flues were not regularly scoured of the crust of chemical condensation that the burning bodies deposited on the ceramic tiles, the chimneys were in danger of catching fire, and such an event could have devastating consequences for the otherwise seamless operation of the camp. Therefore, diminutive boys saddled with an ungainly utility belt—from which depended a whisk broom, putty knife, and hammer—boys wearing the ridiculous wire collar and the rope wound beneath their arms were dangled like plumb bobs into the smoky conduits. There they had to chip, scrape, and dust with a feverish activity in order to complete the job before succumbing to the heat and the choking atmosphere. It was true that the furnaces were extinguished during the cleaning, but the work of the crematoria was a twenty-four-hour-a-day enterprise, so the Reich could not afford to take a building out of commission for very long. As a result, the flues were never given time to cool. Such conditions had caused the asphyxiation if not the roasting alive of his predecessors, and Toyti himself was scalded head to toe; his charbroiled flesh—where it wasn't uniformly coated in soot—had turned the color of coral, and only vestigial patches remained of his ocher hair. (It was a startling countenance that had the virtue of discouraging the kapos from using him as they did the other boys.) But Toyti's aptitude for sweeping chimneys, and his peculiar habit of outliving the task, had earned him a semipermanent situation in the lager.

Transferred from the lice-ridden barracks, he was given a berth above the incineration hall, in an attic room penetrated by pipes like pneumatic tubes through which the gas pellets were dropped from the roof. His rations were improved: he was allowed a quarter loaf of black bread a day along with a dollop of coal tar margarine, and on Sundays fifty grams of wurst. He was careful, however, to eat only enough to assuage his hunger, since any increase in the size of his spindly frame could result in his becoming ineligible for an occupation Toyti lived to resume.

Why? "Because I'm ensuring the Jews a clear passage to heaven," he told himself, though he never believed it for an instant.

Due to the constant accumulation of creosote and fatty deposits, the cleaning rotation was ongoing, but there could be lapses between of several days. During that time Toyti was expected to lend his energies to facilitating the business of cremation, though his assistance in that area was negligible. He was negligible, he understood, in everything but his function as sweep. Still he helped sort the clothing that the victims left behind on numbered hooks in the undressing room, often finding scraps of food that could be bartered for various indulgences. He found jewelry secreted in their shoes and the folds of their garments, treasures that must be turned over as property of the Reich on pain of being tossed into the furnaces oneself. With a rag masking his face, he moved among the tangled bodies, pink and dappled with seagreen spots, that were brought up in the lift from the basement chamber. Often they had to be pried apart like braided cheeses, and once Toyti had seen, between a lady's legs, the just emerging head of a child. He sheared off the hair of the women, which would be woven into socks for the crews of submarines, and cracked the jaws of the deceased to extract their gold teeth; he removed rings from fingers and sometimes, when the rings were stubborn, the fingers themselves. He stood beside the pit where the corpses were burned when the furnaces became glutted, while the guards laughed at the rude noises the pyre emitted, how the men's penises came to attention in the flames. He hosed out the blood and shit from the artificial showers, their walls stained an azure blue from the Zyklon gas, like a mural of the sky that someone had begun and abandoned. But for these tasks anyone would do, and whole units of Sonderkommandos had come and gone since Toyti had been reassigned to the killing centers. He knew well enough that it was only for the sake of his skill in the chimneys that he was kept on this side of oblivion.

Far above Luther was shouting something about a spider tangled in its own web, something about the cold, to which Toyti paid no special heed. But as he scraped, brushed, and chiseled toward a depth that was the point of no return for so many before him, he encountered an obstacle in his way. This had never happened before. While the sludge that caked the insulation could often be bulbous and dense, there was never so much of it that it interfered with his descent; but this was something else, an authentic obstruction. The sulfurous square of light high over his head gave no help in identifying the blockage, but as Toyti holstered his tools and ran his hands along the dry, lathlike surfaces, he was satisfied that what lay in his path were bones. It was a skeleton, curled up but—as best he could judge—wholly intact and belonging to a creature no larger in fact than himself. Blindly he described with his calloused fingers the human-shaped configuration of limbs, stroking here a knotted knee joint, there a vertebra, a collarbone. As he proceeded in his inspection, he discovered an irregularity beyond the skeleton's natural frame, from which jutted a pair of appendages composed of a cartilage as fragile as jackstraws. Toyti handled the twin protrusions, one of them crimped to accommodate the shaft's right angle, the other unfolded to allow a fully extended wing.

He recoiled, thinking he'd come upon the upshot of one of those monstrous experiments the doctors performed on the inmates of Block 10. But how could it have gotten lodged here in the flue? Gingerly Toyti began again to trace its contours, feeling a warmth suffuse his body that had nothing in common with the residual heat from the furnaces. This was a warmth that inspired visions: a clockwork marionette wobbling across a damson carpet in a room whose walls were lined with books. He stroked a shinbone and saw a slender lady seated at a crow-black piano; stroked a rib and felt the silken tongue of a spaniel lapping his chin in a garden where he hunted snails; he touched a knuckle and saw, as if lit by lightning, a bearded gentleman in a top hat cradling a scroll. The bones were an instrument for evoking images and sensations, the sensations causing a stir in the pit of his stomach, which curdled and convulsed until Toyti had to undo his trousers and empty his bowels on the spot. Then his head was light as a bubble and floating, his body dangling like a jellyfish in the inky air. He jammed his feet and spine against the tiles to catch himself and shuddered from a vicious impulse to kick the thing from its perch. When the impulse passed, he pulled the rope off over his head and looped it in turn around the skeleton's rib cage, pulling it tight. What a joke this will be on Luther! thought Toyti. But who was he kidding? Having resolved to salvage the bones at whatever cost, he feared that the joke was on him.

He yanked at the tether, which was the signal for the treble-chinned guard to begin hauling up his burden, but instead of becoming abruptly taut, the rope tumbled down the shaft on top of him.

"Corporal Luther?" cried Toyti, but there was no answer.

Ordinarily such an event would not have greatly concerned him. Agile in his narrow domain, he could inchworm his way up the vertical duct with relative ease. Of course today's ascent would be somewhat encumbered by his new acquisition. Then there was a further development: for as Toyti embraced the skeleton with the intent of lifting it out of the chimney's throat, the heat from the furnaces below, which were supposedly inoperative, had begun to intensify. Moreover, though he struggled from his nearly upended attitude to dislodge the bones, they remained obstinately wedged in place. Toyti tried again to wrench them free from their station, while the thickening smoke caused his lungs to constrict, his smarting eyes to flood with tears. He coughed and gasped for air, yowled from the scorching tiles, so hot now they'd begun to blister his flesh. Then he made his mightiest effort yet to wrestle his prize from its fixed position, and this time he did manage to jar it loose, but its weight—who would have thought that such a small parcel of bones could weigh so much?—tugged Toyti from his own precarious purchase, and losing his balance he pitched headlong after the angel into the abyss.

Down below Corporal Luther, a fat baker tending his oven, opened a muffle to see if all the clattering meant that his strategy had met with success.

IV

THE CATSKILLS

The Wedding Jester

As for me, who called myself sorcerer or angel,
I have now returned to the earth, with a duty to look for
and a rough reality to embrace. Peasant!
—Arthur Rimbaud

As he drove her toward the wedding in the Catskills, Saul Bozoff's aged mother told him yet another of her stories.

"...so Lolly Segal wouldn't go with the girls to see *Chorus Line* at the Orpheum last week..."

While Saul, who wondered why he should care, withheld as long as his conscience allowed a halfhearted, "Why not?"

"I don't know," Mrs. Bozoff expressed her own bafflement. "She said her nipples ached."

Saul glanced at the crepe-hung little woman, her bosom like a sat-upon ottoman, and tried to blame her for his life. Hadn't he adopted his own rueful nature as a protest against her relentless sanguinity?—which he knew to be only skin-deep.

Her he blamed for his feeling that, at fifty-three, he was not even successful at failure. An author, the books of his middle years (there had been no books of his youth) had earned him a small audience in what he considered "the ghetto." His fiction, full of exotic Jewish legends translated to contemporary settings, had been well received among a generation that was already half legend itself, and a handful of a generation that was tediously born again. Among his peers Saul Bozoff had no currency at all.

Of course, if he were honest, Saul would have to admit it served him right. Sometime in his early forties, after a protracted and largely fruitless literary apprenticeship, he'd been seduced by "heritage." But for a handful of short-lived absences (school, Wanderjahre, artists' colony), he'd spent his life in an unlikely town in the Mississippi Delta, wishing he were somewhere else. He'd taken a job—one in an endless series of temporary positions—doing clerical work at a local folklore center, transcribing interviews with Baptist preachers who'd taught their hogs to pray, blind blues singers with half a dozen wives, a pawnbroker who'd sold the young Elvis Presley his first guitar. During this latter interview the retired usurer had alluded to a transplanted Old World community on North Main Street where he was reared; and Saul, recalling that he too was Jewish, made a pilgrimage to take a look.

What he found was a desolate street of crumbling buildings and weed-choked lots, a junkyard, a bridge ramp, an old synagogue converted into a discotheque of ill repute. But blink and there were ghosts—the immigrants crying hockfleish and irregular pants, pumping their sewing machines like swarming hornets in the tenement lofts, braiding Yiddish curses into their yellow challah bread. Not ordinarily given to ecstatic transports, Saul was as struck by the timelessness of his vision as was another Saul on the road to Damascus. Never much at home among the living (in whose company he'd managed only to botch a marriage and squander an education), he resolved to take up residence among the dead, whose adventures he was convinced made good copy.

Saul reported their picturesque antics in a book of stories that earned him a modest reputation, which he parlayed into a teaching job at a small New England college. (North Main Street being portable, Saul was hardly aware of the change of scene.) Noted for its Jewish studies program, the college was a place where Saul felt he could go native, immersing himself in a tradition he'd previously ignored. No longer confined to his Mississippi River outpost, or attached to any particular moment in time, he dwelled in the place where history and myth intersected; he was the contemporary of prophets, martyrs, and exiles, whom his spirit (he felt) had expanded to accommodate. From that vantage he sent back dispatches in the form of two subsequent books, each more saturated in Jewish arcana than the one before. Heedless of the tradition's rational ethos, he populated his tales with every species of its folklore, every manner of fanciful event—a labor that kept him occupied for about ten years. Then, just as abruptly as the spell had come over him, it lifted: Saul's vision of Yiddishkeit everlasting reverted back to rubble and unsalable real estate.

"What possessed me?" he wondered, astonished to find himself in his sixth decade the author of books cataloged as *Fiction/Judaica*.

Still, he mourned the loss of his yenne velt, his other world. It was cruel that spiritual afflatus should have abandoned him at an age when he had also to suffer so many other desertions: like muscle tone and a formerly thick head of wavy auburn hair. (Saul would have liked to draw a parallel with Samson, but such references now seemed distant echoes of a once joyful noise.) And things better abandoned, such as libido, had begun after a dormant period to reassert themselves. So, when his eighty-something-year-old mother asked him to accompany her to a wedding at a Catskills resort, Saul surprised himself by saying, "Why not?" Maybe a trip to the buckle of the Borscht Belt, the famed Concord Hotel itself, would be just the thing to revive his lost inspiration.

He'd forgotten, however, his mother's gift for reducing him to a childish petulance with her gossip, which Saul judged a poor substitute for an unlived life.

"So Wednesday night the women are playing canasta in Harriet Fleishman's apartment when Millie Blank can't get up from the table . . ."

His moody silence giving way to surrender: "Why not?"

"Oh, honey," replied his mother, "she was dead."

Mrs. Bozoff had flown into her hometown of Boston from Tennessee, where she'd remained despite the passing of her husband two decades before. Picking her up at Logan Airport, Saul had driven the Mass Turnpike into "the Mountains" of southern New York, wondering, what mountains? Because Sullivan County, heart of the Jewish Catskills, was nothing but gently rolling hills. The renowned autumn foliage had already flared and expired, leaving a scorched landscape of gray and tobacco brown. Then there were the towns, which in their heyday had supported conspicuous Jewish populations, boasting scores of kosher butchers and delicatessens; not to mention the hemlock-shaded boarding houses, bungalow colonies, cochelayns. Now their facades, where intact, were mostly boarded up, strangled in wisteria vines: providing backdrops for the local unemployed, who loitered in front of them as on blighted city streets.

Spotting a single hoary Hasid beside an ash can, Saul thought to himself, Reb ben Vinkl: he went to sleep in the golden age of the Mountains and woke up to this. "Looks like we're too late," he observed.

"What?" The battery of his mother's hearing aid was conveniently rundown.

"I said it looks like we're too late, all the Jews are gone."

Mrs. Bozoff smiled in serene denial.

The hotel was no less a disappointment. A good forty or fifty years out of fashion, the Concord was a cluster of boxy buildings, their rusting exteriors as forbidding as the Pentagon. Once inside, there was the sense of corridors measureless to man, though the acres of oriental sofas in flammable fabrics, the showy fixtures out of Belshazzar's salon, were faded, the enormous mirrors as shot through with cracks as with veins of gold. None of this was lost on Saul as he lugged their bags in a snail-like progress alongside his mother; while she, preceded by the clanking third leg of her metal cane, exclaimed, "It's like another world!"

Here and there you saw a woman with cat's-eye glasses and flashy jewelry, her husband in plaid pants, sporting the hairpiece that could double for a yarmulke; but these were far exceeded by the decidedly gentile presence of a regional convention of emergency medical technicians. They were welcomed by a banner that spanned the lobby and eclipsed the bulletin board, which announced (among other weekend functions) the Supoznik–Shapiro wedding. Identifiable by their insignias, the paramedics also shared a generosity of girth—men and women alike wearing T-shirts bearing life-affirming logos stretched across medicine-ball midriffs. Parking his mother on a circular sofa surrounding a fountain, Saul resented her fixed smile, the rheumy eyes whose vision was as selective as her hearing. Had she even noticed the mixed clientele, which in this kosher-style establishment was the equivalent of mingling dairy with meat?

But he'd no sooner checked them in than Saul turned to find that his mother had become a rallying point. She was beset by what must have been mishpocheh—a host of relations she had perhaps not laid eyes on since migrating south with Saul's father over half a century before. Each was protesting that the others hadn't changed a bit.

Approaching them, Saul could hear Mrs. Bozoff unburdening herself— "You know I lost my husband"—like the event had occurred only yesterday; and one or two of her listeners looked about as if Mr. Bozoff, a weary merchant who'd gone much too gently into his good night, might only have been misplaced.

Saul was introduced to a pint-sized character in bubble spectacles whom Mrs. B. referred to as Uncle Julius, and his wife, Becky, a head taller though bowed by a sizable dowager's hump. There was a trio of thick-ankled maiden ladies with a neutered-looking fellow in tow, his trousers hoisted to the level of his pigeon breast. These were relations once, twice removed, hailing from places like Larchmont and New Rochelle, names that for Saul had a fabled resonance. And judging from the way they greeted him, making a perfunctory show of civility before dispersing wholesale, his name must have had some significance for them as well.

Back home, owing to his fecklessness, Saul had enjoyed the reputation of a confirmed (if harmless) black sheep. Writing books had only aggravated the perception, since most assumed without reading him that he'd merely graduated from private to public disgrace. That his notoriety should have preceded him to such far-flung parts was in some way flattering, lending a slightly outlaw cast to an otherwise lackluster career.

"Help me up," his mother was entreating, sunk in the sofa's upholstery like a reclining Michelin man. Saul gripped her pudgy fingers and made a token effort to raise her, complaining that his back was sore from the drive. But even as he warned her she might have to sit there the entire weekend, a woman unsolicitedly grasped Mrs. Bozoff's other hand. Together she and Saul hauled his mother to her feet.

"Thanks," muttered Saul under his breath. "I thought I might need a forklift."

"Wise guy," replied the woman, who Saul noted was nevertheless sizing him up with a heavily mascaraed eye.

"Thank you so much," panted Mrs. B. with the excessive gratitude of a person pulled from the jaws of a beast. "I'm Belle Bozoff and this is my son Saul," who perhaps needed further explaining: "the author."

"Oh?" said the woman, circumflexing a plucked brow. The information seemed to have rung a bell. "Haven't I heard of you?"

"See," kvelled Mrs. Bozoff to her son, "everybody knows you," and to the woman: "He thinks he's a failure."

Clucking her tongue in sham sympathy, she introduced herself as Myrna Halevy and offered her hand.

Saul took it reluctantly, avoiding her eye. "Any kin to Judah?" he inquired in a pedantic reference to the Hebrew poet famous for declaring, "The air is full of souls!"

"Whodah?" asked Myrna. "Myself, I'm from the Great Neck Halevys. You maybe heard of Halevy's Fine Furs? That's my papa, the retired fur king, that dashing character over there—Isador, short for 'is adorable.'" She pointed to an ancient party in a sport coat the hue of a putting green, his ginger-gray hair back-combed over a freckled pate. Tall and ramrod stiff, he was prominent among his cronies in their various stages of decrepitude.

As for his daughter, Saul thought he could read her history at a glance, though she was a type he'd seldom encountered outside of books and film. She was a "girl" in her forties trying hard to hide the fact, no doubt divorced and living on generous alimony. Her painted face was somewhat vulpine, her snuff-brown hair (highlighted with henna) puffed high and as sticky with spray as candy floss. She was thin to the point of appearing malnourished, probably due to a diet of white wine and pills, though her breasts, which proffered themselves as on a platter, were disproportionately large. She wore an ocelot top and a tight leather skirt, below which—Saul had grudgingly to admit—her legs in their patterned stockings and heels were good.

She gave him a sidewise smile as if to ask if he was finished looking, and Saul flushed, adjusting his collar. A decade's hermetic devotion to dreams and outré texts had left him sensitive in the area of desire, and he resented that this aging princess, bracelets clattering like a Kristallnacht, should chafe him there.

"Is your mama with you?" Mrs. Bozoff was asking, to which Myrna replied that her mother had passed on some years ago; and accepting Mrs. B.'s condolences with a dismissive wave, she assured her she'd always been Daddy's girl.

Saul's mother sighed. "You know my husband, Mister Bozoff—"

But Saul intervened, having realized that his mother, like the Ancient Mariner, might never stop buttonholing wedding guests to tell her tale. Clearing his throat, he piped, "I don't like to break up the party, but there's a tired old bellhop waiting to take up our bags."

Myrna Halevy gave him another appraising look, from which Saul recoiled. "Are you in the bride's party or the groom's?" queried Mrs. Bozoff, and when Myrna said the groom's, Mrs. B. pooched her lip to signal an incorrect answer. "We're in the bride's," she stated with regret, "but it was nice to meet you anyway."

With his mother safely installed in her room for an afternoon nap, Saul was free to inspect the premises looking for ghosts. This was what he'd been anxiously waiting for. He strolled out under a leaden sky past a drained swimming pool the size of an inland sea, venturing onto a desert golf course called the Monster. Everything seemed to suggest that a race of giants had once walked these hills. But the visionary gift that had served him so well on North Main Street remained inactive on this brisk afternoon.

"Come back, Eddie Cantor singing 'Cohen Owes Me Ninety-Seven Dollars,'" Saul beckoned softly. "Come back, Sophie Tucker, Sid Caesar, Fat Jackie Leonard, Danny Kaye né David Daniel Kaminsky; come back, Mister Wonderful, Little Farfel, Eddie Fisher, Totie Fields . . ." Come back, the mamboniks, the mothering waiters named Shayke ("Boychik, you want heartburn? Go ahead and order chop meat"), the bungalow bunnies, the busboys from City College chasing the garment czar's daughter, the porch clowns doing Simon Sez. Saul could call the roll of all the talents that had their start in the Mountains, the gangsters and boxers and nabobs who'd watered there—he'd read the literature; he could trace the lineage of Yid personalities from the lion tamers, conjurers, and strong men of the Old Testament through the wedding jesters of the Diaspora, the shpielers and singing waiters of Second Avenue, right down to this late chapter in the long-running pageant entitled "the Catskills."

What hadn't he missed growing up in the Delta? Poverty and diseases notwithstanding, he coveted the Lower East Side; Nazis, he'd missed, and Cossacks, Inquisitors, Crusaders, Amalekites. At least there would have been some compensation in summers spent hustling tips in the Mountains, oppressed by flighty hoteliers and drunken chefs. But no: born at the wrong place and time, Saul Bozoff had been forced to abuse himself these fifty odd years.

Later on, trudging beside his mother (through a herd of paramedicals) toward the rehearsal dinner, Saul wondered why he'd agreed to come. What did this tacky terminus to the dream of a golden America, this Jewish waste-land, have to do with him—a lover of the "old knowledge"? Life prior to the discovery of North Main Street—the dead-end jobs, the brief dead-end marriage to a woman he scarcely remembered, who'd blamed him (as he blamed her) for its barrenness—had been a largely somnambulant affair. He'd had to wake up in order to dream. But now, bereft of the company of his wonder rabbis and hidden saints, Saul deplored his banishment to the ordinary world. What identity did he have beyond that of a dilettante, all passions spent? A bachelor professor of a certain age, squiring his mother to a faded resort half a century past its prime.

"So Kitty Dreyfus wouldn't go to her husband, Moey's, funeral . . . ," Mrs. Bozoff informed him to the beat of her clanking cane. (All her gossip was homegrown within the walls of Ploughshares Towers, a geriatric high-rise wherein the Angel of Death—Saul surmised—kept his own efficiency.)

Said her son, reflexively, "Why not?"

"She said he wasn't her husband; sixty-five years they never, what you call it, consomméd the marriage."

On their way past the neglected closet of a hotel chapel, mother and son were abruptly halted by the sight of a young woman leaving the ladies' room in disarray. In completing her business inside, she had carelessly tucked the hem of an indigo cocktail dress into the waistband of her underpants. The panties, Saul could not help but notice, were a satiny eggshell white, scarcely visible (but for the ticktocking cleft at their center) against the cream of her perfect tush.

"Oo oo!" exclaimed Mrs. Bozoff, pointing. "Saul, tell her before she makes an embarrassment."

"I can't tell her!" he objected. "It's not my place."

"Excuse me, dear!" his mother had begun to shout at the girl, when Saul clamped his palm over her mouth. At that moment the girl was met by several others, one of whom saw the problem and corrected it discreetly with a sweep of her hand. A crushed velvet curtain dropped over the girl's bottom, concealing the stockings that made her look as if she waded in blue water to the thighs.

Her friend whispered, giggling, to the girl, who turned to see who might have observed her: only a trundling old woman and her round-shouldered, middle-aged escort, neither of them apparently worth wasting a blush on. So why was it that Saul, removing his hand from his mother's sputtering mouth and assuring her he didn't know what had come over him—why did he feel as agitated as an elder who'd spied on Susanna? And why, even more than her fanny, should her face—distinctive for its cameo pallor among the artificial tans of her sisterhood—set his vitals vibrating like a tuning fork?

The cavernous Calypso Room, with its undulant walls and glittering terrazzo floors, reverberated with the noise of happy reunions. Everywhere families and friends reclaimed prodigal members and long-lost acquaintances to draw them into the larger fold. To ensure his own exclusion from such scenes, Saul had contrived to leave his name tag in his room. At his mother's request that he go back for it, he complained to her much tested patience that such badges invoked for him bitter racial memories. It was in any case a relief to see how his mother, once again an object of warm regard, drew the attention away from him.

Seated next to her at their appointed table, Saul had assumed an expression so arch as to forbid anyone's attempting to engage him in conversation. The strategy was effective enough that he began in a while to feel sorry for himself; nor was he heartened by the notice of the Halevy woman, who fluttered her fingers at him from a nearby table. He nodded without altering the set of his jaw, and inwardly groaned. She was a cultural cliché, wasn't she?—the spoiled New World Jewess, her life organized around excursions to boutiques. The room was lousy with her tribe. Still, as a caricature, she seemed to Saul slightly larger than life—a condition in the face of which he was duly humbled.

Mrs. Bozoff was confiding to a lady with hair the blue of a pilot light (something about a nonagenarian neighbor no better than she should be), when a tinkling of silver on crystal was heard from the head table. A youthful rabbi with a neatly trimmed Vandyke was begging indulgence to perform, as it was Saturday evening, a brief havdalah service. Pushing back the cuffs of a sharkskin jacket as if to show he had nothing up his sleeves, he lit the candle, tasted the wine, and thanked the Lord for holding the line between the secular and the sacred. The guests amened, some with mouths full of chopped-liver salad, then pitched into the beef flanken à l'anglaise and the roast stuffed breast of veal with peach garni. They were gnashing asparagus spears, slathering baked potatoes in sour cream, when the crystal tinkled again.

This time a prosperous-looking gent, his spun-silk suit shooting asterisks of light, had risen to his feet. He introduced himself (unnecessarily for most) as Irving Supoznik, father of the bride. Deeply tanned, he was endowed with a regal nose and a two-tone head of hair—sandy on top and fluffy gray at the temples, like an inverted cotton boll. Observing him, Saul was troubled to note that, for one thing, he and the bride's father were approximately the same age, and that the daughter seated next to him was none other than the glimmering girl of the visible tush. Saul realized he'd been leering at her all along.

"You're probably wondering why I asked you all here," said Supoznik, waiting for the laugh. Someone called out, "A tummler you'll never make!" to which he replied, "Very cute. Who let Milton Graber in here? Will the ushers please escort that man from the hall?" Then confidentially, "Milt's still POed about last night's pinochle game. Anyway, I hope you're enjoying your nosh because I'm in hock to the eyeballs over this little soiree." Again polite laughter, while their benefactor assured them that, really, the house of Supoznik was in no immediate danger.

"Now if Nate Pinchas there can stop stuffing his face for a minute—I know the kishke is good, Nate, but this is my moment, okay? Gertrude, control your husband! But seriously, I'd like to thank you for traveling so far for this shindig. Everybody told me, who has weddings in the Catskills anymore? So call me sentimental, but when Ilka and I got married here thirty-two years ago, the place was lucky for us, and I'm betting some of that luck will rub off on these kids." With his pocket handkerchief he dabbed the corner of an eye.

Graber, the wag, shouted, "Shmaltz we had already from the herring!"

"You didn't blubber like a baby at your Tracy's wedding last spring?" challenged Supoznik, to which Graber said, "That's because she married a bum," knuckling the burr head of the lad beside him, who good-naturedly shook a fist.

"But all kidding aside," continued Supoznik, "I'd like you to join me in a toast to the happy couple." He lifted his glass. "Have I got naches or what? You young people maybe don't know naches?—that's when your daughter brings home a fine, clean boy like David Shapiro"—he bestowed a smile on the bridegroom at his left, a curly-haired, fresh-faced youth with a Clark Kent forelock, his blazer displaying a fraternity crest—"who's about to graduate Yale Law School with a job waiting for him already at the firm of Klein, Klein, Klein—"

"Goes the trolley," sang Milton Graber.

"And Levine!" proclaimed Supoznik, ignoring his heckler. Young David, showing ivory teeth, clenched his hands in mock triumph over his head. Irving Supoznik then turned to his daughter, his tone becoming worshipful. "And now I give you our doll, our treasure, our Shelly—mwhaaa...!" He kissed his fingers, which inspired more needling from Graber. Saul asked himself if the literature of the day hadn't already done these people. Shouldn't they have been retired like old stage props? But for all that, he couldn't take his eyes off Irving Supoznik's languid daughter. Her fine-boned beauty seemed a bit out of place among the solid, aerobically contoured girls of her circle, her tranquil features opposing their constant animation. Her blue-black hair, whose lustrous profusion she'd tried to arrest with ribbons, tumbled over a milky brow. Occasionally she parted the tendrils to peer with dark eyes from behind them, but, the pert tilt of her head notwithstanding, she seemed drowsily unimpressed by what she saw. Here, thought Saul, was the meeting in one girl of Marjorie Morningstar and Trilby; for Shelly Supoznik appeared as if under an enchantment, her secret inaccessible even to one who'd spied the secret of her bottom drawer.

Having divested himself of platitudes ("Like they say, love is sweet but better with bread"), Irving Supoznik offered a health to the bride and groom. Saul sighed, trying to remember the last time he'd been intimate with a woman. During his driven years, abstinence was never an issue; so sated was his spirit that his physical self was a virtual irrelevancy. But now that his spirit had flagged, hadn't his flesh begun to go the same way? Although a restlessness in his pants argued to the contrary, he needed further assurance. What he needed was some fey creature like Shelly Supoznik to help him achieve, through the medium of his baggy body, the restoration of his soul.

"What am I thinking?" Saul asked himself, feeling that he ought to be ashamed. But while others fed on sponge cake, halvah, and petits fours, he nourished himself on fantasies of stealing the bride away.

Then Myrna Halevy, in a form-fitting, strapless tube dress that seemed to be made of mirrors, approached the table shadowed by her planklike father, whom she introduced to Mrs. Bozoff. Mrs. B., for her part, removed the napkin from under her chins and—a touch coquettishly if Saul wasn't mistaken—invited Mr. Halevy to sit down. Myrna said they were on their way to the Imperial Room to see the bygone teen idol Frankie somebody, whom Saul had supposed long dead.

"Maybe you"—she turned briefly from his mother to give Saul what he wanted to believe was an involuntary tic, but was clearly a wink—"maybe you and your son would care to join us?" He lowered his eyes, only to see himself dizzily multiplied in the scales of her gown.

"Oh, Saul," shrilled his mother, "let's go! It'll do you good."

Still preoccupied with thoughts of romance, Saul nonetheless wondered what she meant by "do him good." More curtly than he'd intended, he told her, "Go ahead, you'll have more fun without me," then conceding to universal objections, agreed to join them later on. First he needed a little air.

He made a wrong turn outside the Calypso Room and ended up in a dimly lit cul-de-sac. A dumpy couple plastered in paramedical emblems were in midtryst beside a faux-marble cherub, rubbing noses Eskimo fashion. As it was too late to back off unnoticed, Saul asked them foolishly, "How do you get outside?" The man scratched his muttonchops: "You mean this place has an outside?" his moonfaced companion bursting into titters.

Eventually he found an exit that delivered him into an uncomfortably chilly night whose fine mist was turning to drizzle; though, insulated by his visions of Shelly Supoznik, what did Saul care? But out there in the elements it wasn't so easy to pick up the thread of his imaginings. Still he tried: reviewing precedents from *Blood Wedding* to *The Graduate*, Saul endeavored to picture himself snatching the girl from the altar; but who was he kidding? What he felt had more in common with a pedophile attraction than heroic passion. He turned up his coat collar against the October wind, cursed the rain pelting his unprotected head, and supposed he ought to be inside among the guests. But inside he would doubtless want to be out. After all, what did he have to say to the young go-getters and their fathers who had already gone and gotten? From the worldly world Saul had long since de-camped for the society of his phantom Jews. Now, excluded from their num-ber, he was neither here nor there, inside nor out. Neither past nor present was hospitable, and his people were not his people, and there was nowhere on earth that Saul Bozoff belonged.

He decided it was time to go and check on his mother, since what reason did he have for being here other than looking after her? Suddenly Saul was resentful that others should have presumed to usurp his role. But as he was about to enter the lobby under a massive porte cochere, whom should he encounter but La Myrna leaning against a stuccoed column. With a scarlet lambskin jacket draped like an opera cape over her scintillating dress, a ciga-rette wedged between talonlike nails, she was a thing of smoke and mirrors. The Dragon Lady, thought Saul, hoping to get past her with some minimal courtesy, but the question she posed brought him up short.

"So, are you getting good material or what?"

He uttered a querulous, "Come again?"

"Admit it, we're all just kitsch for your mill."

Saul thought he caught her implication: she was confusing him with writers of a more acerbic bent, the kind that made satirical hay out of affairs such as these. Not wishing to disabuse her, however, he replied mysteriously, "The mills of kitsch grind slow but exceeding fine."

"What's that supposed to mean?" she asked.

Saul shrugged. "You tell me. Look, I'll level with you, Miss . . . ?" He pre-tended to have forgotten her name but sensed she wasn't fooled. "I never draw from life."

"Then what do you draw from"—Myrna exhaled a plume of smoke with all the éclat of the caterpillar in *Alice*—"death?"

Saul coughed. "You never heard from the imagination?" he said with un-disguised condescension.

Myrna was thoughtful. "The what nation . . . ?"

"Now who's the wise guy?" asked Saul, irked with himself for having been lured into an exchange with this ridiculous person.

Then Myrna abruptly changed the subject. "Your mama's enjoying her-self," she said, taking—as it seemed to Saul—credit for Mrs. Bozoff's good time.

"My mother always enjoys herself. She doesn't know any better," he apprised her, then attempting to beg off, "If you'll pardon me . . ."

"You got something against enjoying yourself?" asked Myrna.

Said Saul, "I have a very low fun threshold."

"I think you've seen too many Woody Allen movies," she submitted.

"Oh, very astute," replied Saul—was there no end to the woman's presumption? "Look, Miss . . . Halevy was it?"—summoning patience. "You might think you know me, but you don't know me."

Then came what was probably supposed to pass for a Sibylline remark: "Everybody's disappointed, sweetheart."

Sweetheart?

"You want disappointed, you should see the crowd in the Imperial Room," continued Myrna, upon which she threw down her cigarette and ground it with studied precision under a spiked heel. Suddenly frisky, she stepped forward to take Saul's arm. "C'mon, I'll show you."

"I'm not disappointed," Saul lied, reclaiming the arm. "I'm just damp from walking in the rain. I want to get out of these clothes and go to bed."

Myrna arched her brow, and Saul feared for a second she might offer to help him undress. "Naughty boy," she accused him, "you made a rendezvous with some college cutie, didn't you? Your type doesn't waste any time."

Would it were so, thought Saul, who allowed himself for the briefest instant to believe he was a ladies' man. Of course, Myrna Halevy was only teasing him, wasn't she? She had about her, seasoning her character of the Long Island parvenu, a touch of the demoness. Shelly Supoznik, he knew, would never tease him; though Shelly Supoznik might not have the wit. In any case, rather than give the woman the pleasure of witnessing his chagrin, Saul adopted what he imagined was a roué's demeanor. He smiled enigmatically, made a careless little salute, and swept back into the hotel alone.

He woke the next morning racked with guilt over his mother, whom he'd neglected to see to her room the night before. To get even with her for having deserted him, never mind that the opposite was true, he'd gone straight to bed. There he tried again to conjure erotic scenarios featuring himself and the spectral Shelly, though images of Myrna Halevy kept intruding. Oddly, Saul had been nonetheless aroused. In vain he'd attempted to defuse his lust by recalling Hasidic folktales, a proven remedy for insomnia in recent years. There was the one, for instance, about Rabbi Elimelech, whose seed, spilled in his effort to resist the temptations of the she-devil Lilith, turned to glow-worms at his feet.

Dressing on the run, Saul hurried to his mother's room, separated from his own by two flights of stairs. (The hotel had been unable to provide adjoining rooms, for which Saul was much obliged.) He knocked at her door, called her name, and receiving no answer, began to pound. Had she died in her sleep or—unthinkable prospect—spent the night somewhere else? Aware that neither circumstance was likely, Saul still couldn't shake his unease and, as there remained no response from within, made a dash for the elevator. The lobby was full of medical conventioneers, to whom Saul in an irrational moment considered appealing, when he saw his mother shuffling toward the dining room. She was flanked by the Halevys, father and daughter, which gave him the impression she was being abducted.

Catching them up, Saul had it on the tip of his tongue to exclaim, "Thank God I found you!" but got hold of himself in time to utter a glib, "Remember me?" Myrna turned to greet him with a wry and knowing, "Hello, sleepyhead!"

Said Mrs. Bozoff, "We didn't want to wake you, tateleh," and Saul wondered who was this *we*? but vowed to keep his own counsel until he'd had his coffee.

At breakfast he was still wrought up. Why was he so wrought up? After all, his mother was well taken care of—she was regaling Mr. Halevy (who nodded either from compassion or palsy) about a friend's uterectomy and subsequent malpractice suit. They were in the common dining room, where the wedding guests, though legion, were outnumbered by paramedics. Many of the latter said grace before eating, ending their devotions with "in Jesus' name, amen," but none of the Jews seemed aware of any menace. Instead, beyond an air of mutual tolerance, there was even a shared preference of attire among wedding guests and medical fellowship alike—namely, the nylon warm-up suits as brilliant as jockeys' silks. Dining, it appeared, was a friendly athletic competition.

Puerto Rican waiters brought groaning trays of food to the table, excess having remained a constant over the years. There were Danishes, jelly blintzes, bagels with lox, nova, and whitefish, baked herring, cream-cheese omelets. In light of such abundance Saul had ordered, perversely, a poached egg and toast. When it arrived, Myrna, wearing a shoulder-padded jumpsuit that looked like commando issue (but with spangles), leaned over to shovel some of her bounty onto his plate.

"Essen un fressen," she invited, taking the further liberty of unfolding a napkin and tucking it into his collar. Saul removed it, flinging it down like a gauntlet.

"That's it, isn't it?" he asked rhetorically. "That's all that's left, *essen un fressen?* The language of Mendele, Peretz, and Sholem Aleichem, Halpern and Leivick—poor consumptive Leivick, who came to the East Side via Siberia, and had to check his paperhanger's ladder at the box office before attending the debut of his play, *The Golem.* The language of Itzik Manger, Moishe Kulbak, and Israel Rabon, who crawled out of the corpse-strewn trenches at the Polish front to write *The Street*, then hung on long enough to be slaughtered by Nazis and tossed in a mass grave. The world's most resilient language, it survives every worst calamity of the past ten centuries, only to dribble its last on the lips of a pampered Long Island minx at a Catskills hotel. O essen un fressen yourself, and despair!"

Myrna batted her fake lashes the size of bats' wings. "I also know gai kuckn in yam . . ."

He stared at her with a sanctimony that crumbled in the face of her taunting admiration, then lowered his eyes. They lit on the lavender kerchief round her neck. Myrna followed his gaze, touched her throat, its tendons taut as bowstrings.

"You like the scarf?" she asked. "It's got sentimental value. I strangled my first husband with it."

Saul took a breath, odors of stewed prunes and cologne vying in his nostrils, taking him to the brink of a sneeze, which he suppressed. "Myrna," he said—it was the first time he'd used her given name—"can I ask you a question?"

"I'm all ears, kiddo," replied Myrna, bending an ear from which dangled a pendant like a loaded key ring.

"With all due respect, just what is it you think you're doing?"

She gave him a kittenish smile. "I'm throwing myself at you, can't you tell?"

Saul's mouth must have been hanging open, because Myrna took the occasion to stuff into it a thick piece of whitefish. He chewed tentatively, eyeing her like she might be Lucrezia Borgia, then succumbing to its savoriness, swallowed the fish, and took up his fork to skewer another piece from her plate.

Mrs. Bozoff was struggling to rise from her chair. "I'm gonna plotz," she jovially announced, and, suggestible, Saul had a brief panicked vision of his mother's exploding. "Let me help you," offered Myrna, getting up to take

Mrs. B.'s free arm, and together they made their way toward the powder room.

Left alone at the table with Mr. Halevy, Saul felt obliged to break the heavy silence between them—while on the other hand, given the paces his daughter was putting him through, why should he pay court to her tight-lipped old man? If this was a standoff, Saul was damned if he'd be the first to fold.

Although you had to hand it to the geezer: he was certainly fastidious—his hair spread like tortoiseshell tines over a sun-speckled poll, his close-shaven cheeks (thanks to cracked capillaries) in perpetual blush. His safari jacket was complemented by a Hawaiian print shirt whose collar was tucked neatly outside the wide lapels. It was a nattiness, though, that didn't quite conform to Mr. Halevy's mummylike deportment; and it dawned on Saul that the old guy's spruce aspect might be owing to the fact that his daughter dressed him.

Then Mr. Halevy's mouth had started working, distorting the stony dignity of his features—his fierce eyes asquint, face twisted from the effort, noises that scarcely resembled speech burbling up from his diaphragm.

"Your m-m-m-m, m-m-m-mah . . ."

"My ma?" guessed Saul. "My mother?"

The old man nodded. ". . . is whhh, a w-wha . . ."

Saul found himself mouthing the syllables by way of encouragement. "W-whaaa . . ."

A Watusi? This was awful. "A woman?"

Again a nod; two out of two. "My mother is a woman . . . ," Saul restated what he'd gleaned thus far, but just as he felt he was getting the hang of it, the game was over: an ancient engine, Mr. Halevy's voice had apparently required a few false starts.

"Your mo-ther," he said, the words coherent if agonizingly deliberate, "is a whole lot of w-woman." And with what sounded slightly tinged with hoarse reproach, "K-character she got, and heart."

Then it was Saul's turn to nod, wondering was this an idiot or a madman? Or more sinister, were the alleged fur king and his daughter some kind of confidence team, gigolo and gigolette, who worked weddings and bar mitzvahs to fleece the unsuspecting? If so, it was clear that Mrs. Bozoff had fallen into their clutches past redemption. This was unfortunate, and while Saul wished he could help her, already lost, she would surely want him to save himself.

"Excuse me," he said, rising from the table and pointing to his slightly distended belly, "the fish isn't sitting too well." The phrase sounded inscrutable in his own ears.

The wedding was not until late afternoon, but according to the handouts there were meanwhile no end of activities to amuse and distract. There were organized water aerobics in an indoor pool with someone called Gilda, a cosmetic makeover workshop with Carol, a hair-replacement lecture, a lecture on "the sensuous spine," shuffleboard and horseshoe-pitching tourneys. There were gold clinics, investment clinics, bingo, duplicate bridge, instant art with Morris Katz, complimentary tango lessons with Mike Terrace on the promenade . . .

What, wondered Saul, no practical Kabbalah with Rabbi Naftali? Still nursing the distress he'd brought away from the breakfast table, he felt disoriented to the point of nausea, whose antidote (he decided) lay in the pursuit of boredom.

He nosed about the shops, wandered past the solarium where off-season sunbathers lolled behind glass as in a human zoo. Leery of running into Myrna, he nevertheless tried to comprehend why the woman, any woman, should have set her coif for him: a mediocrity manqué. Though hadn't he once been a kind of poor man's Prospero? They were probably wondering where he was at that very moment, Myrna soothing his mother's worries by offering to go and look for him; and Saul supposed there were worse things than being found. But after a time it came to him that he wasn't so much eluding Myrna as seeking the sylphlike Shelly Supoznik.

She too might be wandering aimlessly, entertaining second thoughts. He would come upon her lingering before a wall of celebrity photos—Red Buttons, Jerry Lewis, Jan Peerce—and step up to recite their pedigrees: "Aaron Chwatt, Jerome Levitch, Pinky Perlmut . . ." They'd chat, establishing their distant cousinhood, and once he was technically no stranger, the girl would begin to confide in him. "The future seems so predictable," she'd admit, and Saul would delicately suggest it didn't have to be. She'd insist that she wanted the life her husband wanted, and Saul would ask who was she trying to convince, him or herself? Then he'd tell her of the timeless world he'd discovered and lost, but might locate again with her help; and she would lift her Dresden face, open wide her sleepy eyes to behold a man . . .

When he came back to himself, Saul had strayed beyond the confines of the hotel proper; he was outside under a breezeway connecting the main building with the covered tennis courts. Entering on impulse, he was thrust into the big-top atmosphere of the emergency medical technicians' showroom. Here was an even greater density of conventioneers than he'd seen at large in the hotel. Scores of them milled about the exhibits of helicopters and streamlined ambulances with computerized instruments for monitoring every vital sign. Sirens sounded, some in ear-splitting squawks, some in arpeggios like Good Humor mobiles. Broad-beamed men and women modeled the latest in emergency medical fashion, from insigniaed windbreakers to double-knit fatigues, their hips girded in utility belts worn with a military flair. Like stage magicians they demonstrated their ventricular defibrillators and blood-gas apparatus on live volunteers. A few diehards clung to hands-on procedures: artificial resuscitation and Heimlich maneuvers; but the majority seemed to glory in the use of their whirring and blinking machines. It was a technology, to judge from the reverence the paramedical community paid it, that put miracles in the shade; that rendered outmoded the devices of a Prophet Elijah or a Baal Shem Tov when it came to raising the dead.

Moving furtively among them, Saul felt like a trespasser who'd penetrated some forbidden holy of holies; he was thankful, once he was out of there, to have escaped (as he saw it) with his own wounds still unstanched. Making for his room, he dove between the covers of a recent translation of the mystical text *Palm Tree of Deborah*, but couldn't fathom it. For a couple of hours he alternated between dozing fitfully and longing for Shelly Supoznik, until it was almost time for the ceremony; though why he should bother to attend he didn't know. But knotting his tie—a task he hadn't performed since his own nearly forgotten wedding day—Saul experienced a vague twinge of anticipation, which he had actively to dispel. On the way he stopped by his mother's room, knocked fatalistically, and was surprised to find her in.

"Isador?" she called, a name Saul didn't answer to.

"Oh, Saul!" Mrs. Bozoff greeted upon cracking the door, delighted to see him. She had a sense of time like a house pet, her zeal as fervent after an hour as a year. "I don't know why I thought you might be Mister Halevy—he said they would save us a seat at the wedding. Oh, we had a lovely day; we played bingo and I won seven dollars, and Mister Halevy . . ." She clucked her tongue, shook her head in fond sympathy. "The poor soul, you know in Great Neck they won't let him sit in a minyan."

Saul heaved a sigh. "Why not?"

"They say he had too many insides replaced with artificial—he's not a man anymore but a machine. So can you tell I'm wearing a girdle?"

Her dress, its material shimmering like an oil slick, was shapeless; it looked as though, to fill it, she'd been inflated to nearly life size. Punch her and she might reel backward, only to bob up again still smiling. Her rouged cheeks stood out like strawberry stains in oatmeal.

"You look fine," said Saul.

"So tell me, what did you do all morning? Myrna was worried you weren't enjoying yourself. I told her you never let yourself relax. You know she's crazy about you, don't you?"

Under his breath Saul muttered, "She's just plain crazy."

Mrs. B. tapped her hearing aid. "What's that?"

"I said Myrna Halevy has got a screw loose!"

"Oo oo," exclaimed Mrs. Bozoff, who could not abide unpleasantness.

Saul fairly shouted that he hadn't meant to shout, which elicited one of his mother's conciliatory non sequiturs.

"You know, Saul, we're more like good friends than mother and son."

Downstairs, as they inched along the corridor, Mrs. B., but for the clanking of her cane, was unusually quiet. She seemed to be pondering something, though since when did she ponder? When at last she spoke, it was to inquire experimentally of her son, "So how would you like a new papa?"

Saul ceased his forward progress. Incredulous, he would have liked to borrow her tactic of pretending she hadn't heard, but the question wouldn't go away. "You must be kidding!"

Mrs. Bozoff hunched her shoulders as if to say maybe she was and then again maybe she wasn't.

"But you only just met," gasped her son, thinking surely he could do better than this.

"Sometimes," replied his mother, reciting from what seemed the only available script, "these things happen." And on further consideration, "Maybe it's this place—don't you think it's sort of, I dunno, magical?"

"Magical?" The bite of his fingernails into his palms would leave fossil-like traces till doomsday. "This is the place where magic died!" Then making what he deemed a superhuman effort to control his emotions, Saul adopted a breezy tone: "Okay, fine, if you want to be the bride of Frankenstein, go ahead. So what if my father's not even cold . . ." His father was twenty years in the grave, but who was counting?

Then it pleased him to see how readily his mother acquiesced. "You're right," she said, her lower lip beginning to quiver, face clouding over, "I was just being selfish." Her eyes behind their fishbowl lenses were already aswim with tears, and pulling a tissue from her purse, she gave herself up to sobbing.

Having unmasked her for the forlorn thing she was, Saul tried to savor his triumph. The punishment, he told himself, fitted the crime. For, after all, hadn't she betrayed their unspoken contract, that they should each remain solitary and disconsolate throughout their days? But as he watched her brittle smile collapse before the deluge, Saul's victory began to turn hollow, and ashamed of himself, he wanted to take it all back.

"I didn't mean it," he declared. "It's just so . . ."—discarding *ludicrous* and its fellows—". . . sudden."

More to conceal their spectacle from the guests than to comfort his mother, Saul steered her between a potted rubber tree and the wall. There he enfolded her with arms whose circumference at first barely touched her. Then bracing himself, he put a hand in Mrs. Bozoff's crisp, silver hair and pressed her injured face to his chest.

The unsettling warmth of her tears seeped through his shirt. Patting her back, Saul asked himself why, after her years of carrying tales, shouldn't she be allowed to become an item of gossip herself? Just because he lived with ghosts didn't mean she had to as well. But the truth was, he didn't live with ghosts, and he couldn't live without them, and but for the fact that his narrative fund had dried up while hers remained bottomless, he was every inch his mother's son. Her misery having awakened his own, Saul too surrendered to a quiet blubbering.

At length he managed to swallow the lump in his throat (it sank into his heart, increasing its burden) and make an effort to humor his mother: "Mama, why don't you tell me a story."

Still snuffling, Mrs. B. disengaged herself from her son's embrace, corrected her lopsided glasses, and blew her nose. Her pout dissolved the moment she began to talk. "Did I tell you Sally Blockman asked to be buried in her apple green nightie, but her husband Myron, the momzer, said not on your life . . ."

"Why not?" asked Saul, wiping an eye with his jacket sleeve.

But before the mystery of Sally's nightie could be disclosed, they were apprehended by Myrna Halevy, nudge extraordinaire. "Where have you two been?" she said, appearing as if out of the mushroom cloud of her own hair. "Do you want to miss the show?" She hooked her arms through those of Saul and his mother, coaxing them in the direction of the converted nightclub.

As they entered, Myrna quipped, "Look at us, we just met and already—" "—we're strolling down the aisle," Saul dryly co-opted her remark; and to further cover his vulnerability, when Mrs. Bozoff exclaimed, "Oh, isn't it beautiful!" he responded,

"Sure, if you like beauty."

Transformed yet again, the Calypso Room was a bower, its capaciousness reduced to almost cozy by the long wine-red curtain dividing it. Rafts of flowers in unnatural shades of yellow, pink, and blue decked the walls and trimmed the stage that doubled as an altar; flowers overwhelmed the wedding canopy like a garden gazebo, suffusing the air with their sickly perfume. It was a scent made audible by the cloying strains of a Broadway musical that Mrs. Bozoff identified as *Phantom of the Opera*. She allowed that she'd always loved the music of Andrew Lloyd Wright.

Ignoring the business of bride's side versus groom's, Myrna conducted the Bozoffs into an aisle where her father sat poker-stiff beside three empty chairs. Mrs. B. was deposited next to Mr. Halevy, Saul plunking himself down beside her, while Myrna took the folding chair to his right. Thus hemmed in, Saul was interested to see how his mother took the furrier's hand in her own: how, laced together, their gnarled fingers looked as if they held between them a liver-spotted brain.

In his ear Myrna buzzed unrelentingly, "Don't they make a nice couple?"

"Yeah," said Saul, "like the Trylon and the Perisphere."

"I bet that's very witty," replied Myrna, and gave him a playful elbow in the ribs.

Saul made a face at the woman, her shoulders and glossy legs left exposed by her bustiered jack-o'-lantern of a frock, and thought she didn't look half bad. Then he wondered, was he losing his mind, or had the generations of love matches inaugurated at the Concord contaminated the atmosphere? How else account for the ease he'd begun to feel in his adversary relation to this impossible female?

"Myrna," he said, to try and sink their intimacy, "why me? This place is full of millionaires."

She narrowed her eyes in a burlesque of indignation. "So that's what you take me for, a gold digger? Well, I can assure you, sweetie"—lifting a hand to let the bracelets rattle down her forearm—"I don't have to dig."

Saul backpedaled, lowering his voice in the hope that Myrna would do the same, for heads had turned. "All I'm asking is, what the hell do you see in me?"

She looked at him as if amazed he didn't know. "You're the author," she informed him, giving the word the romantic dash of, say, *scourge of the Spanish Main*.

Saul struggled to keep from glimpsing himself through her eyes—God forbid she should lend him any unwonted self-esteem—and remembered that he knew her type: Hadn't his wife been one of them? Women who believed the cure for what ailed him was to show him a good time? Well, he didn't want to have a good time.

He was about to give her reasons why the title of author no longer applied, but when he opened his mouth, she put a finger to his lips and said, "Shah!" The theme from *Exodus* had started up over the public address, which was apparently the cue for the wedding procession to begin.

First the groomsmen then the bridesmaids marched in in double file, their full-dress ensembles repeating the pastel floral scheme. A crinolined toddler strewing rose petals waddled behind them, herself followed by a boy in a Tom Thumb tuxedo bearing a ring on a cushion. In their wake came the bride, escorted by her father—and the sight of her gliding over scattered petals, her breasts nestled dovelike in the empire bodice of an alabaster gown, her face tantalizingly obscured by a chiffon veil, chased every other consideration out of Saul's mind.

Her intended waited at the altar, imperially handsome, his slender frame flattered by the white cutaway with its crimson boutonniere. Beside David stood his own flushed father, potbelly corseted in a silk cummerbund, looking either smug or pickled in his capacity as best man. Giving his daughter a melancholy kiss, Mr. Supoznik handed her up the steps to the altar before taking a seat next to his wife. There the girl was greeted with a wink by Rabbi Lapidus, rocking on his heels at the center of the chupeh. Smart in a madras dinner jacket, the rabbi clutched something Saul at first took for a staff of office, but turned out to be a handheld microphone; for once the participants were in place under the canopy, the wedding suite fanning out behind them like a choir, the rabbi brought the mike to his mouth with a practiced panache.

"Barchu haba HaShem adonai...," he crooned, while Saul wondered why such a showbiz production should even bother paying lip service to tradition. Of course, he didn't know Hebrew himself, nor had he set foot inside a synagogue since the confirmation of his sixteenth year—an ecumenical affair that in the Reform movement replaced bar mitzvah. Saul had not been bar mitzvahed: his Jewishness, like his connection to his mother's family, was several times removed. But for a brief bibliography of fables he felt increasingly had been written by someone else, Saul regarded himself an artificial Jew. So what made him think that his presence among this company should have anything to do with Providence?

The first sign that something was wrong occurred after the second benediction, when the rabbi invited the couple to drink alternately from a goblet of wine. The Shapiro kid took a modest sip, but the bride, when her turn came, upended the cup and greedily slaked its contents to the dregs; then she emitted a most unladylike belch and wiped her mouth with the back of her hand. A shocked murmuring rose up among the guests, subsiding only after they'd assured one another (at least those in Saul's hearing) that Shelly was just a little high-strung.

The ceremony proceeded on a note of tension, which relaxed a bit as the groom began to recite, after the rabbi, the marriage formula: "Blessed art Thou, O Lord our God, Who hast made man in Thine image . . ." Vows were exchanged, the bride's with an especially breathy deliberation; then the groom, receiving the ring from his father (who, to the delight of the crowd, rifled his empty pockets before remembering the ring bearer), tried to place it on the tapered finger of his betrothed. But before he could succeed in this, the girl snatched the ring from his hand. She threw back her veil, disarranging a complicated black braid, and examined the stone through the loupe she made of her fingers; then wresting the mike from Rabbi Lapidus, she blurted in a Yiddish-inflected voice that bore no resemblance to her own,

"You say rock, I say shlock—let's call the whole thing off," nevertheless dropping the ring into her bodice.

The wedding guests collectively forgot how to breathe.

Turning toward them, Shelly Supoznik appeared for all the world like some callow ingenue with stage fright, though the words that came out of her conveyed no hint of trepidation.

"Maybe you heard about this fellow started a line of maternity wedding gowns?—un iz geshvoln zayn gesheft!" The room was deadly silent. "I said, you should see how his business is growing!" Not a sound, though the girl, or rather the voice that had borrowed her, remained undismayed. "It's not every line can bomb twice," it declared. "So Ethel and Abie are discussing Einstein's theory of relativity. Explains Abie to Ethel, 'All this means, every-tink is relative. It's like this but it's also like that, it's different but it's the same, farshteyst?' 'Neyn,' says Ethel, 'give to me an example.' 'Okay, let's say I shtup you in the fanny. I got a prick up the fanny and you got a prick up the fanny. It's different but it's also the same. Now you understand?' 'Ah,' says Ethel, 'but I got only one question: from this Einstein makes a livink?'"

The party onstage, but for Mr. Shapiro, who guffawed, remained frozen in place, while the only movement among the folding chairs was from seniors reaching for pills.

"The doorbell rings at a nafkeh byiss," continued the bride, who was not herself: her body rigid, a helix of hair dangling over one eye. "You know nafkeh byiss, dear? A whoorhouse. So the madame answers and finds there a poor soul with no arms or legs. 'What do you think you can do here?' she asks him. The cripple says, 'I rang the doorbell, didn't I?'"

Standing on either side of her, the groom and the rabbi traded glances of stunned bewilderment, both of them afraid to touch the girl. A susurrus of murmurs was again heard throughout the cabaret.

"Don't laugh so loud, you'll start a landsleit, I mean startle the landslide, a nechtiker tog . . ." None of the mordancy escaping Shelly's lips was expressed in her face. The bridal veil trailed like vapor from her inky tresses which—though she'd yet to move a muscle—seemed to have grown even wilder; her gown had fallen off a pale shoulder. "Gornisht helfn," said the voice, "we got here tonight the undead. So what should I say to make friends? I want to sleep with each and every one of you, and I mean sleep! I ain't had a moment's rest since I croaked . . ."

The murmuring had swelled in volume to the hum of an aerodrome.

"But seriously," the voice went on, "it's great to be here in the bosom of Shelly Supoznik—and such a lovely bosom it is. Forty years I'm in the cold, I can't find shelter to save my soul, and believe me, I wasn't so young when I died. When I was a boy, the Dead Sea was only sick." The hand she lifted to quell the laughter that wasn't forthcoming looked as if raised by a puppeteer. "But this one, this maidele, so delicate, so graceful like a gazelle, so . . . empty. I mean, hello?" The girl knocked mechanically at her temple as the voice echoed from within. "Is anybody home-mome-ome . . . ? But don't you think I ain't grateful. Who else can accommodate a whole extra person without doing a time-share? Oy, Shelly Supoznik, such a princess! Ever see her eat a banana?"

Pretending the microphone was a banana, the bride made-believe she was peeling it, then placed a hand behind her head to force her open mouth toward the fruit.

Gasps of revulsion greeted the pantomime, the bridal party beginning to break ranks. Mr. Supoznik, having mounted the altar, appealed to the rabbi to for God's sake do something; while Rabbi Lapidus, checking his watch, replied that the episode was outside his jurisdiction, then screwed up his face as if to ask himself what he meant. Infuriated, Supoznik gave him a shove, which jarred the rabbi into asking if there was a doctor in the house.

A half dozen or more men and women got officiously to their feet and began to make their way toward the altar spouting conjectures: "Cataleptic dementia," "paraconvivialis," and "Trepuka's syndrome" among the infirmities heard bandied among them. Consequently, before they'd reached the foot of the stage, the neurologist, the psychoanalyst in her stretch-velour original, the hidebound osteopath dredging the bowl of a pipe—each identifiable by his or her respective theories—were at an impasse. Fixed on diagnoses peculiar to their own areas of expertise, they were stalled by their differences, quarreling before any had bothered to examine the girl.

As other guests weighed in with their theories ("Her mouth you should wash it out with soap!"), Mrs. Bozoff turned to her son and said, "Nu?" Saul shifted in his seat and conceded that they were certainly witnessing a one-of-a-kind event. On his right hand Myrna Halevy leaned a spongy breast into his shoulder, the teasing tone as ever in her voice.

"This is up your alley, no?"

"No," Saul denied unequivocally, then sheepish: "What makes you think so?"

"Your mama gave me one of your books."

Saul didn't know which was more surprising, that his mother carried around his books or that Myrna could read. Moreover, he was aware that she was aware he was lying: for wasn't he familiar enough with the sources, both canonical and apocryphal? S. Ansky's classic drama and Paddy Chayefsky's heretical spin-off; he'd read Scholem and Steinsaltz, *The Path of the Name*, *The Booth of the Skin of Leviathan*. He might be a dunce when it came to observance, but ask him about King Solomon's necromancy or the properties of an herb called *flight of the demons* from Josephus's *Antiquities*, and he'd give you an earful. He understood, for instance (though he was much too agitated to say so), that the girl was possessed of an alien essence, a dybbuk, and that this one was the restless spirit of a dead Borscht Belt comedian—whose name, as it introduced itself following the gangbusters opening, was Eddie Romaine.

"My parents changed their name to Rabinowitz when I went into show business." Eddie's voice waxed nostalgic. "Ach, I played them all, Kutscher's, the Nevele, the Concord, the Pines—this was back in the days when you came up from the city by the Derma Road. I started in the Mountains eighty years ago at a place called the Tamawack Lodge. This was a bungalow colony run by a Jewish farmer famous for mating a Guernsey cow with a Holstein to get a Goldstein—instead of moo it said, 'Nu?' The Tamawack was just thirty miles from here, and look how far I came in this business"—nostalgia giving way to resentment—"thirty farkokte miles! This is the end of a career, ladies and gentlemen; on your way out leave a stone afn meyn kop . . ."

Under the canopy David Shapiro, his forelock dripping sweat, pleaded with his bride to admit she was having a joke—wasn't she? (Though not even her father, in his recital of her virtues at last night's banquet, had counted among them a sense of humor.) Chastised by Supoznik, David's dad had buried a rufous nose in the bib of his shirt, trying unsuccessfully to choke down his wheezing laughter—this while his counterpart, Irving Supoznik, tore the hairpiece from his own head and, inconsolable, stood wringing it in his hands as if strangling a rodent.

"Anybody helps her can have her!" he cried out in his desperation, which brought his wife in her yards of sequins and tulle to her feet.

"Irving, what are you saying?"

Again Myrna tickled Saul's ear with the feather of her breath. "Go ahead, Mister You-Don't-Know-Me, I dare you."

Saul turned to her in annoyance—she had a nerve! Though on the other hand, with all his yearning after the supernatural, wasn't he at least partially to blame for this visitation? Wasn't Eddie Romaine in a sense Saul's guest, and therefore, in a manner of speaking, his ghost to lay? Although he fought it, his vexation with Myrna fizzled into gratitude; he was beholden to her for calling his bluff.

Still he sat chewing his lip, emotions battling in his heart like cats in a bag. Who, after all, was Saul Bozoff, flash in a pan whose sheen had since rusted, to imagine himself the hero that saves the day?—to say nothing of a fundamental conflict of interests: because how could he not help feeling a certain sympathy for the dybbuk, who like himself was stuck between this world and another? Wavering, he asked himself where he got off even contemplating such a trespass, or for that matter even believing that this could happen. But somewhere between not wanting to seem a coward to Myrna and the growing conviction that he'd been elected, that no one else could release the girl from her spell, Saul stood up.

Instantly he felt it was too late to sit down. Exactly what he was going to do he didn't know, but excusing himself to his mother and Mr. Halevy

("Nature calls"), he slid past them, hearing nothing but the hammering of his heart in his ears. Between him and the girl the physicians debated, Mrs. Supoznik, breaking a heel, stumbled to all fours as she clambered onto the stage—all of which appeared as in a dumb show to Saul. He was conscious of little else but the babbling bride and his stinging left buttock, where Myrna had pinched him to speed him on his way.

"The Concord, gottenyu," repined Eddie Romaine from his situation inside the girl. "Today I don't know, but forty years ago the Concord was swank, the barbershop so deluxe you had to shave before entering. I said, you had to shave before entering, bada bum. You would eat like there's no tomorrow, check into the hotel as people and check out as freight. We had a waiter in those days, Shmuel—a k'nacher. 'Shmuel,' you'd say to him, 'what do you get with the brisket?' 'Severe vomiting and diarrhea,' he'd tell you. Ask him, 'Shmuel, you got matzoh balls?' he'd say, 'No, I walk like this from my arthritis.' Ask for Russian dressing, he'd bring you a picture of Stalin putting his pants on . . .'"

Under cover of the general disorder, Saul passed virtually unnoticed up the aisle, taking the stairs to the altar at a couple of stealthy bounds. Mr. Supoznik was busy dragging his rumpled wife to her feet, David Shapiro handing over his father—whose hilarity was now indistinguishable from sobbing—to the long-suffering Mrs. Shapiro, who'd come up from the floor to lead her squiffy husband away. Solacing one another as at a graveside, some of the bridesmaids wept openly, as Saul warily approached the girl.

Possessed by another, she appeared to him more desirable than ever. Her ebony eye, the one not hidden behind her hair, remained moist but unblinking despite the fingers he waved in front of it. Her gown had slipped low enough on one side to reveal a breast, the aureole of a nipple just visible above the lace of her Wonderbra. Attempting to cover her, Saul gingerly lifted the strap of the gown to her shoulder, though it instantly slipped down again. Sighing aloud, he made a mighty effort to subdue the tremor in his voice and address the dead comic inside her.

"Mister Romaine," Saul greeted respectfully, and was ignored.

"It was a regular sexpool in those days, the Concord. We had this house dick, you'll excuse the expression—Glickman; he was all the time kicking in doors. He hears shouts: 'Murder! Fire! Police!' so he kicks in the door. How's he to know it's only Sadie shouting, 'Furder, Meyer, p'lease!'?"

Clearing his throat to summon what was meant to pass for forcefulness, Saul tried again. "Excuse me, Mr. Romaine."

"You got to love a wedding," declared Eddie, who began pensively recalling his own wedding night. "I'm strutting my stuff in the buff in front of my new wife: 'Look by me,' I say, 'one hundred fifty pounds pure dynamite!'"

"Mr. Romaine, you have to leave this girl."

"'That's right,' says the wife, 'and with a three-inch fuse . . .'" Then Shelly's head swiveled in Saul's direction, the movement drawing with it the attention of the entire room—upon which the commotion died down.

"What is this, audience participation?" The dybbuk's delivery was arch. "Did I ask for a volunteer? Do I look like Mezmar the Great? All right, you're in my power: quack like a duck. No? Then quack like a chicken, I don't care." The voice becoming oily, "Gib a keek on this nice gentleman, so young, God bless him, he's just getting his hair. Nice gentleman, buttinsky, what's your name?"

Saul cautioned himself to stay on his guard, but for all his shuddering saw no reason why he shouldn't tell her, or him, or it, who he was.

"Okay, Mister Bozo, buzz off," said the dybbuk, "but first repeat after me: 'The sight of her behind . . .' What are you waiting? 'The sight of her behind . . .'"

"Pardon?"

"C'mon, be a sport. 'The sight of her behind . . .'"

Hesitating, Saul was nonetheless conscious that this was a beginning: he was involved in a dialogue with an undisembodied spirit; it was a step. Gathering courage, he forced himself to look past the violated beauty of the bride to the job at hand. He even found the temerity to propose a condition. "If I repeat, will you leave the body of this girl?"

"Sure, sure," replied the dybbuk. "Now say it"—holding the microphone up to Saul's jaw: "'The sight of her behind . . .'"

Uneasily, "The sight of her behind . . ."

"Forces Pushkin from your mind. Then you say: 'Forces Pushkin, Mister Romaine?'"

"Forces Pushkin, Mister Romaine?"

"Pushes foreskin, Mister B."

Shelly's expressionless head swiveled back toward the guests, some of whom chuckled, only to be met by a barrage of angry "Shahs!"

"How do you like that?" said the voice. "We're a double act—Weber and Fields, Sacco and Vanzetti . . . Of course our people ain't had a pipputz, what you call a foreskin, for three thousand years, which reminds me of a story. A guy's watch has stopped, so he goes into a shop with a giant watch hanging outside . . ."

Saul was squeamishly aware of his kibbitzers. The groom and the Supozniks, man and wife, had edged close to him and the girl, themselves pressed from behind by members of the bridal suite on tiptoe. Wiping the incipient grin from his face (for God help him, he'd taken pleasure in the exchange), Saul made an attempt to dispel any hint of complicity, exhorting the dead jester, "Now will you leave this girl?"

"Was that the shortest partnership in history or what?" remarked Eddie Romaine. "Anyhoo, the guy asks the shopkeeper to fix his watch. Shopkeeper says, 'I don't fix watches.' Guy says, 'But you got a big watch hanging outside . . .'"

"Will you leave her?" Saul reiterated with warmth.

"Shopkeeper says, 'I know, but I don't fix watches—I'm a mohel, a circumciser.' 'So why do you have a watch outside?' 'Tahkeh,' says the mohel, 'what should I have?'"

Saul started again. "Will you—?"

"No!" roared the dybbuk, its attention once more engaged, then sweetly, "but you can come in too if you like—there's plenty of room."

"What about our deal?" asked Saul, who knew better than to ask.

Said Eddie, "I lied."

No longer able to contain themselves, Mr. Supoznik and the bridegroom erupted simultaneously: "What do you think you're doing!" / "Shmuck, get away from her!"

Saul held up a placating hand and tried to explain that he was there to help.

"Help? You call this funny business helping?" said Supoznik, mopping his brow with the rug that he flung down in disgust. His wife begged him to remember his blood pressure.

"Listen to me," pleaded the intruder, "I'm Saul Bozoff," which made no impression whatever, and grasping at some straw of a credential, added, "the author." Then speaking hurriedly lest he be interrupted: "Your daughter Shelly has been occupied, that is possessed, by the spirit of a dead comedian. What she needs is—"

Inserted Eddie Romaine, "an enema."

"What she needs," insisted Saul through gritted teeth, "is an exorcism."

Voices of outrage and disbelief were raised from all quarters, the shrillest emanating from the girl herself.

"Nisht gedugedakh!" shrieked the dybbuk, mimicking the shock of the assembly. "We shouldn't know from it!"

In the hush that followed Eddie's outburst, Saul tried to reassert himself.

"With all due respect, I believe that with your help"—steering a tricky course between humility and resolve—"I can expel the uninvited spirit from Shelly's body." Again a stirring in the room. "Rabbi," appealed Saul in an effort to curry favor, "you know better than I what's required."

Rabbi Lapidus, though he raised his anointed head, showed no signs of having a clue, nor did he seem especially disposed to indulge Saul on the subject.

"A rabbi?" asked the dybbuk, perhaps repeating Lapidus's own thoughts. "This is a job for a nice Jewish boy?"

"Of course," continued Saul with forced optimism, "we'll need a quorum."

"Nonsense!" barked Supoznik, and through Shelly's coral lips the dybbuk voiced its hearty accord.

"I know what I'm talking about," argued Saul, though he was frankly riddled with doubts; and had an unexpected party not come forward in his defense, he might have been persuaded there and then to give up the cause.

"Irving," submitted Mrs. Supoznik, tiara askew, "my mama from the Old Country and all of them, they believed in dybbuks and the evil eye. Who knows but this Bozoff is maybe right?"

Saul lifted his weak chin like a prow.

Others from among the gathering, all admittedly in their twilight years, began to mutter their solidarity with Mrs. Supoznik: Bozoff should be given a chance. Her husband rolled his eyes. "Ilka, you're playing dice with our daughter's welfare," he warned, but moved by the urgency of her plea and otherwise stymied, he asked the rabbi if it wasn't worth a try. Rabbi Lapidus remained sullenly unresponsive, but from the floor the stretch-velour psychoanalyst opined that, in some cases, ritual could have dramatic results; though she cautioned it should only be used in the last resort.

"If the Concord ain't the last resort," shouted the joker Milton Graber (without irony) from his third-row seat, "I don't know what is."

In the meantime a dwarfish old man with one blind and one basilisk eye, whom Irving Supoznik greeted as "Papa," had begun a slow ascent up the steps to the altar. He was aided by an equally aged peer, head bald and veined as a marble egg, the two of them followed in turn by an assortment of antiquated gentlemen. Among them, in defiance of the Great Neck interdict, was Mrs. Bozoff's suitor, Isador Halevy. Why his presence should've mattered so much, Saul couldn't say, but at Mr. Halevy's arrival he felt a surge of confidence—the kind he suspected sorcerers must feel upon creating a golem.

Still it was daunting how these alter kockers, constituting a quorum and then some, had so readily placed themselves at his disposal. What if he should disappoint them? But once he'd recovered his tongue, Saul impressed himself with the poise he now seemed to have at his command.

"We'll need the Torah scrolls and the ram's horn from the little chapel, the shtibl," he advised, "and also some black candles—I think I saw some in the gift shop . . ."

A couple of the old men relayed these requests to the floor—"Eric! Kevin! Kimberly!"—whereupon a gang of eager grandchildren bolted from the room in pursuit of the specified items. One of the doctors petitioned Rabbi Lapidus to put his foot down, but the rabbi was absorbed in the study of his oxblood shoes; and besides, the whole place now seemed galvanized by the sense that something was finally being done. Scarcely believing what he'd set in motion, Saul began to think he might actually be equal to the dreadful responsibility he'd shouldered.

Meanwhile the dybbuk kept up its tireless monologue: "Back in the thirties I'm dating this shikse—you know shikse? a girl who buys retail. So she calls me, says, 'Eddie?'" Shelly held an imaginary receiver to her ear. "'Who is this?'" Eddie waxed falsetto: "'This is Matilda.' 'Matilda?' I say, 'Which Matilda I'm having the pleasure?' 'This is the Matilda which you already had the pleasure.' 'Oh, that Matilda. I remember the wonderful weekend we spent together. Oy, what a weekend! And did I forget to tell you what a good sport you were?' 'That's why I'm calling, Eddie. I'm pregnant and I'm going to kill myself.' 'Say, you *are* a good sport.'" Shelly hung up the receiver. "But seriously . . ."

Shepherded by Milton Graber, the children's crusade returned bearing ritual objects. Further heartened at having been so quickly deferred to, Saul thought he should try and consolidate his authority.

"Irving, David . . ."—waiving the formalities since they were all united in a common cause—"why don't you light the candles and arrange them in a circle under the chupeh."

Clearly of two minds, the groom hung back with Rabbi Lapidus, but Supoznik, having placed his wife in the care of the maids of honor, began dispensing black candles. He kindled them one by one with his mono-grammed Zippo, releasing their incense, as Saul called to the back of the house for someone to turn down the lights. The star-studded ceiling expired and the flames grew brighter, making goatish masks of the old men's faces. There was a crackling of joints as they bent to plant the candles in the puddles of dripping tallow until the bride and minyan were circumscribed and all others banished to the dark periphery.

Skullcaps and prayer shawls having also been issued, the men began putting them on, and Saul followed suit. He pulled a yarmulke over his bald spot, a tallis over his yarmulke like a cowl. Then, though he hadn't asked, Mr. Halevy presented Saul with the scrolls of the Law in their velvet mantle, the silver breastplate mirroring the old gold of the surrounding flames. Cradling the Torah, Saul imagined that in the darkness beyond the candles lay a courtyard instead of a nightclub; and in the courtyard the guests held cocks and hens and garlands of garlic, and were accompanied by the ghosts of ancestors on furlough from paradise.

Filling his lungs with all the righteousness conferred upon him, Saul was more than himself; he was exalted as he hadn't been since his decade mirabilis, back when he was a fine-tuned instrument for the telling of tales. Intoxicated by an energy that cleared his head of any lingering reverence for the dead comedian, he set his sights exclusively on saving the girl. "Spirit," pronounced Saul, "in the name of all that's holy, leave this child!"

Replied the dybbuk: "So this Jewish lady's on the subway when a pervert opens his raincoat. 'Feh,' she says, 'you call that a lining?' Then there was the time I asked my wife, 'How come I never know when you're having an orgasm?'"

"With the power of the Almighty and with the authority of the sacred Torah . . . ," said Saul, taking his text from S. Ansky, who'd taken it from the ancients.

"'Because you're never around,' she tells me," continued the dybbuk.

". . . I, Saul Bozoff son of Belle, do hereby sever the threads that bind you to the world of the living and to the body of the maiden Shelly, daughter of . . ." In a whispered aside to Supoznik: "Ilka?" Supoznik nodded.

". . . daughter of Ilka . . ."

"Not until I get a spot on the Sullivan show," interrupted the dybbuk, Shelly's head having rotated once again toward Saul.

He stopped in midinvocation. "Come again?"

"You heard me, I don't leave the girl till I get a spot on *The Ed Sullivan Show*, which is my deepest regret that I never had in my life."

"Eddie"—Saul was consolatory; he knew that unfinished business was a common reason for a spirit's inability to find eternal rest—"I hate to have to tell you, but Ed Sullivan is dead."

"So give him an enema."

"He's dead over twenty years," said Saul. "It wouldn't help."

"Nu, so it wouldn't hurt."

Realizing he'd walked into that one, Saul attempted to regain lost ground. "What's the matter, Eddie?" he asked. "Didn't anybody say Kaddish for you when you passed away?" Because the old wisdom had it that failure to say the prayer for the dead over a corpse could result in an insomniac soul. To the circle Saul proclaimed, "Let us recite the Mourner's Kaddish."

"V'yish gadol v'yish kadosh sh'may rabo . . ." the men chanted inharmoniously along with Saul, loudly reciting one of the few prayers he had by heart. "May His great name be magnified and sanctified throughout the world . . ."

While Eddie proceeded: "It's Abie and Ethel's wedding night, and Ethel— she's old-fashioned, you know; so the groom goes down to the hotel bar while she gets ready . . ."

". . . Yisborach v'yishtabach v'yispoar v'yisromam v'yis-naseh . . ."

". . . In the bar Abie has a couple of drinks then returns to the room, where he finds his bride in bed with three bellhops . . ."

As the Kaddish seemed to be having no effect, Saul called for Psalm 91, known as the antidemonic psalm. "O thou that dwellest in the covert of the Most High and abidest in the shadow of the Almighty . . . ," which was all he could remember, though he mumbled along as others carried the tune.

". . . 'Ethel,' says Abie, 'how could you!' Ethel's got a little something in every orifice, see, so she lets loose a bellhop from her mouth mit a—" Shelly stuck her thumb in her mouth to make a popping sound, then said via Eddie as Ethel, "'Well, you know I've always been a flirt.' But seriously . . ."

Rather than discouraged, Saul welcomed the opportunity to employ yet another item from the repertoire. "All right," he bellowed, "let's take off the gloves. Blow the ram's horn!"

With the help of his son, the elder Supoznik raised the spiral horn (double-twisted and as long as he was tall) to his bearded lips, but could make only the feeblest farting noise. He passed the horn to one of his brethren, whose lungs proved no stronger than his own. It was then that Rabbi Lapidus began to come around. Apparently offended by the out-of-key bleating and tired of his supernumerary role, he shook off his funk; he picked up his trouser legs to step over the candles, borrowed a tallis to cover his head, and prized the shofar from crooked fingers. Lifting the horn, he ballooned his cheeks and brought forth a long unbroken note that ended abruptly. Then he sounded the note again.

This was tekiah, whose echoes Saul could trace back to his childhood: the first chilling blast of the shofar sounded during the Days of Awe, it was guaranteed to chase demonic intruders back to the other side.

"Which reminds me of the lady," said the dybbuk, "who during the Yom Kippur penance, the al chet, she beats herself below the pipik instead of on the chest. 'Why do you beat yourself there?' I ask her. 'Dezookst mir vi ich hob gezindikt,' she tells me. 'That's where I sinned.'"

"Give it up already, Eddie," demanded Saul, doubly reinforced now that the rabbi had come onboard. "Don't you know you're dead?"

"So it wouldn't be the first time—but give me a minute, I'll warm this bunch up."

Again the ram's horn, and Eddie adopted a minstrel dialect: "Dem Jewrish folk got curious customs; on dey holidays de head ob de household, he blow de chauffeur . . ."

"Rabbi," said Saul, still feeling his oats, "blow shevarim," and Rabbi Lapidus, wielding the horn like a virtuoso, trumpeted a short series of three unbroken notes. Then Saul pressed the dybbuk in a voice so withering he hardly recognized it as his own: "Face it, Eddie, you're just not funny," notwithstanding those maverick members of the audience in stitches. "Don't you know when you're not wanted anymore?"

Once again the shofar, and Eddie: "Ach, didn't nobody ever want me. I couldn't get booked for love or money, and then I dropped dead. Sometimes I wish I was never born—but tell me, who should be so lucky? Not one in a hundred."

Saul wondered if it was his imagination, or had the dybbuk's voice grown more subdued? Had the hectoring perhaps struck a nerve? Then girding himself against pity, he seized the advantage: "Teruah!" Saul clamored for the traditional climactic flourish, a succession of bloodcurdling staccato blasts alternating with eldritch trills.

A slightly winded quality was now detectable in the dybbuk's locution: "Guy goes to the doctor, tells him, 'Doc, I got five penises.' Doctor says, 'How do your pants fit?'"

"Like a glove," answered Saul, still the bully. "I heard it already, your material's stale."

"Gay avek, go away from me why don't you?" said Eddie Romaine in exasperation. "I got my memoirs yet to write." And attempting to bargain, "You could be my whatsit, my ghostwriter; we'd split the royalties. I'd call it *The Catskills and Beyond*."

"Memoirs?" scoffed Saul, satisfied that of the two of them his own will was the stronger. "You've got no memories, Eddie, only stale jokes. You're a cheap, two-bit Borscht Belt tummler, which is what you are for all eternity, so die already and let live. Leave the girl!"

"What do you expect from what I got to work with?" complained the dybbuk, its anger mocked by a throaty delivery. "By which I don't mean the shtik but the shtiff. Look at me, or rather her—a shaineh maidl? This is a beautiful girl? Look at her eyes, like railroad tracks they cross." Shelly tossed her hair to reveal crossed eyes. "This is not Miss America but Meis America. Lips like petals? Like bicycle pedals, gib a keek."

Here, as if to defend the honor of his bride, David Shapiro stumbled into the circle, then in lieu of throttling his frail intended, lowered his fists and donned a yarmulke.

"Beautiful teeth? A kolyerah, such buckteeth she's got, she could eat watermelon through a picket fence." The girl manufactured an overbite. "Body like a treasure?" Shelly slumped, allowing the gown to slip to her waist, exposing lace-cupped breasts and the creamy hollow of her abdomen. "It should have been buried already five hundred years. Let me be, a nechtiker tog—this totsie's no great loss."

Such rancor toward the vessel it occupied was a fair enough sign to Saul that the dybbuk was on the ropes. And oddly, the more abuse Eddie heaped on the head of his host, the more comely appeared the girl in Saul's eyes. All that was left was for him to deliver a swift coup de grâce, and then to hell with Eddie Romaine!

"Leave the body of the maiden Shelly," he commanded, the borrowed lines become his own in the saying, "or be cut off forever from the community of Israel!"

Another, more violent reprise of the ram's horn.

Although reduced to mere curses, the dybbuk fought back: "You should wear out an iron shiva stool, you should fall into an outhouse just as a regiment of Cossacks finishes their prune stew and twelve barrels of beer . . . ," its voice losing volume with every syllable.

"In the name of the most holy, submit to the will of this congregation!" cried Saul.

"May your son meet a nice Jewish doctor."

"Dybbuk, submit!"

"What do you call it"—Eddie's utterance was profoundly weary—"when a Jew has got only one arm?"

Student of exotic lore, Saul reckoned himself no stranger to the popular. "A speech impediment!" he crowed, tearing the mike from the girl's hand to speak into it himself: "Now do you submit?" Electronic feedback rivaled the wail of the horn.

The dybbuk was barely audible: "Why do Jewish women do it with their eyes closed?"

"Because God forbid they should see their husbands having a good time," replied Saul, who—inspired—ordered his minyan to "Snuff out the candles!"

One by one the flames were extinguished, permitting the throng of gawking faces to become discernible once more in the dim cabaret.

So faintly was the dybbuk speaking that Saul muffled the mouth of the shofar with his hand; he leaned near enough for Shelly's lips to brush his ear. "What happens," peeped Eddie, his words souring the girl's ragged breath, "when a Jew walks into a wall . . . with a hard-on?"

"He breaks his nose!" Saul shouted triumphantly, as the last candle was put out.

"In alle shvartz yor," moaned the dybbuk, "my time has come. Ach un vey, what a world, what a world!" Then the bride crumpled to her knees.

Her father and David, along with several old men, lurched forward to take hold of her arms. For a moment the girl sagged between them like washing on a line, her loose gown pooling at her feet. But as they started to lift her, her knees went rigid, her limp body snapped back to attention, and flapping her arms to rid herself of would-be samaritans, she spoke again through the medium of the deceased. "Had you going there, didn't I?" Eddie's voice was restored to its caustic vitality. "So where was I? Oh yeah, this swinger walks into a barroom . . ."

Saul trembled from a rage that made the room swim before him as in the eyes of a drowning man. He wanted to grab hold of something, as for instance the girl's swanlike throat; he wanted to strangle her for the sake of expelling the spirit. But with the candles out, he was once more aware of the size of the assembly onstage, never mind the mob of guests on the cabaret floor. Dumbstruck by the magnitude of the task he'd undertaken, amazed at his own presumption, Saul shrank accordingly.

And deflated, he was his old familiar self, ready to take up the theme of failure again—when he remembered a trump card he'd yet to play.

". . . He's all farputst, the swinger, dressed to the nines," continued the irrepressible Eddie; "he's got the diamond stickpin, the Cuban cigar, the cathouse aftershave; when he sees this kurveh, this whoor sitting on a barstool, her legs crossed high, y'know, the garters showing . . ."

Saul knew the risks involved in what he contemplated, that only perfect masters should attempt so advanced a technique; all others would be in peril of their lives—which, in his case, seemed little enough to lose. Returning the Torah scrolls to Mr. Halevy, the microphone to Rabbi Lapidus, he gazed on the drooping but still luminous Shelly Supoznik.

"So the swinger, call him Marvin—he saunters up to the whoor, asks her, 'What would you say to a little fuck?' Whoor gives him the once-over head to toe, from his single slick strand of hair to his Dr. Scholl's"—at which point Saul took Shelly in his arms—"says mmphm . . . ," and stifled the voice from inside her with a kiss.

He kissed her hard with what the Kabbalists called kavannah, deep intent, and clung to her with the cleaving called devekut. Straightaway a force invaded his body; a black bird seemed to have entered his chest, searing its wings in the heat from his heart till they melted like wax. Hot liquid filled his lungs to overflowing and gathered in his loins, so that his spine became a wick dipped in oil. A spontaneous flame at the base of the wick shot up its length and flared like a Roman candle in his skull. Saul could have wished that the fever was mutual and would fuse them in their embrace; but instead the jolt to his brain pried his lips from the girl's, and with a cry of exquisite pathos— "Hello, little fuck!"—he plummeted into oblivion.

Then I'm hovering just under the wedding canopy. Below me is pandemonium: Irving Supoznik, steadied by his father (himself supported by others), is holding up his swooning daughter, while his wife, Ilka, fans the girl's cheek with the cast-off toupee. A tousled David Shapiro is trying on and rejecting a variety of solicitous expressions to greet his slowly reviving bride. Meanwhile Rabbi Lapidus entreats the still-debating specialists to help the fallen man—who is me, evidently not breathing. A couple of doctors do finally break from their huddle and step onto the stage, where they lean over my horizontal body swapping opinions. Nobody seems to know basic CPR.

But somehow the paramedics have been alerted, because a team of them is lumbering down the aisle with apparatus in tow. Mounting the altar, they push past the indecisive physicians and set straight to work looking for vital signs. Having hoisted their machines onto the stage, they turn switches that start them whirring and blinking, attach wires to various parts of my lifeless form. Like pachyderms come to the aid of a fallen ape-man, they hunker around me, their trousers dipping to show toches cleavage in back.

Fresh from the disbanded minyan, Mr. Halevy is stationed beside my mother, attempting to still her fidgeting with a withered hand. His daughter has left him to join those bending over me under the chupeh, where she practically rides the backs of the paramedicals. "Hooray!" she bawls once the fibrillations have restored a pulse to my body, which the monitors had shown to be technically kaput. A funny thing, though; for while I recognize this as the moment when I ought to be sucked back into my sad sack of bones, it doesn't happen, nor do I feel the least pang of regret. In fact, I don't know when I've been so relieved.

The one I'll hereafter refer to as Saul Bozoff, breathing but still unconscious, is lowered from the stage onto a gurney, which the EMTs, under Myrna's gratuitous direction, begin to wheel up the aisle. Then in another interesting development (though I confess my level of interest is beginning to wane) the suspended marriage ceremony resumes. This is doubtless due to a collective amnesia: since the preceding events have not figured in any rational categories of understanding, they've conveniently dropped from everyone's mind. The rabbi, picking up where he left off, pronounces the final benediction; the groom stomps the goblet and, to salvos of flashbulbs and resounding "Mazel tovs!" kisses the bride. Vacantly she receives the kiss, which does little to rekindle in her cheek the bloom that was never there.

When the stretcher has been rolled as far as the hallway—whose high windows are ablaze with a burnt orange dusk—Saul opens a furtive eye, then closes it. He snakes an arm about the waist of Myrna's rustling pumpkin gown, and abruptly pulls her down on top of him. She screams in a fright that dissolves into giddy laughter, which Saul chokes off with a kiss. This is not the beatific Kiss of Moses, which only I could've inspired him to perform, but judging from Myrna's ardent response it will do. The paramedics, though impressed, remind Saul he's suffered a trauma and should lie back down; he's too weak for such shenanigans. But against their advice, only halfheartedly seconded by Myrna, he rises from the gurney. He agrees that, pending the results of a battery of tests, his discharge will remain unofficial; he promises them in addition a testimonial and a photograph.

By the time Saul and Myrna reenter the Calypso Room, it's been converted yet again. A brigade of waiters have struck the canopy, removed and stacked the folding chairs; they've parted the curtain bisecting the erstwhile altar to reveal a space as large as the original on the other side. In it, laden with steam trays and the centerpiece of a seven-tiered wedding cake, the smorgasbord trestle meanders along a wall. Dining tables surround the parqueted dance floor, and a paunchy, middle-aged orchestra in mambo shirts with ruffled sleeves, dragging fiddles, concertinas, and music stands, have taken over the stage. They are launched into the overture from *Hello, Dolly.*

Posed beside her husband for the ritual cutting of the cake, the new Mrs. David Shapiro, herself a wilted lily, flings her bridal bouquet. It falls short of the assembled maids of honor, who dive for it like scavengers. In the ensuing scuffle the blossoms are so mangled that no single girl emerges with enough to comprise a bouquet. When they sulkily disperse, Mr. Halevy abandons his sentinel post to creep forward; and in an act of unexampled agility, he approximates a deep knee bend to retrieve a sprig of baby's breath from the floor. He returns to Mrs. Bozoff and, bowing from the waist, deposits the stray sprig in her lap; but before he can straighten, she's stuck it in his buttonhole.

Then the band breaks into an obligatory "Hava nagilah," and in a nod to (or parody of?) tradition the bride and groom are lifted in their chairs by spirited youths. Carried in a wild ride around the dance floor, the couple hang on apprehensively to either end of a lace paper napkin.

Following Myrna's lead, Saul loads a platter with potted meat in mango sauce, gefilte fish in honeydew, noodle pudding with smetana, poppy-seed strudel; then he and Myrna approach the table where their parents are seated. Mrs. Bozoff smiles absently at her son to acknowledge the food, then picks up the thread of her discourse. She's relating to Isador the predicament of one Minnie Horowitz—who, during a fit at a Hadassah meeting, began to speak in the voice of a girl kidnapped from a Russian shtetl three centuries ago.

"We were gonna try and give her a whaddayacallit?" says Mrs. B.

. Suggests Saul, "An enema?"

"No," replies his mother, who wasn't supposed to have heard, "one of those things like what you did with the Supoznik girl—only the dybbuk was better company than Minnie."

Saul knits his brow, rummaging his brain for a memory that won't come. (Because it's my memory, though I hereby relinquish it forever.) Giving up the search with a shrug, he inquires of his mother, "Would that be Minnie Ha-Ha-Horowitz, the Indian maidele, to whom you refer?" Then he tenderly assures her, "Mama, you're a stitch, I'm gonna put you in a book one of these days." He stoops to kiss her forehead—he's a regular kissing fool tonight—and Mrs. Bozoff, absorbed again in her story, touches the spot as if to dab a drop of rain.

The orchestra has begun playing a bubbly version of "Never My Love," to which the bride and her father are waltzing, somewhat shakily, alone in the limelight. Having stepped to the edge of the dance floor, Saul watches the ethereal Shelly Supoznik Shapiro with a philosophical appreciation, as if he rather than her father had given the bride away. Then a hand tugs at his sleeve and he turns to face a barrel-shaped matron wearing what looks like a vintage prom gown, who introduces herself as his aunt, or cousin, Rosalie.

"I was just talking with your mama, she's such a love," she informs him, "and I wanted to meet her son, the author."

"Ah, my mama, God bless her," sighs Saul. "Y'know, we may be here next year for her nuptials. Can you believe this is the same woman who last week went to the doctor? Doc says, 'How do you feel, Mrs. B., sort of sluggish?' 'If I felt that good,' says Mama, 'I wouldn't be here.'"

There's a moment when the woman's broad face seems perplexed, her eyes closed as if in pain, just before she gives way to a loud, braying laughter. Some of her intimates bustle over to see what's so funny.

"She's got three sets of dentures, my mama," Saul persists, "one for milchik, one for fleishik, and one for Chinese."

His little circle of admirers cackles like a henhouse, attracting a larger audience.

"She's a card all right—what am I saying, she's the whole fershlogener pack. She gives me a pair of neckties, and when I wear one she asks me, 'What's a matter, you don't like the other?' A shnorrer comes up and complains to her he hasn't eaten for days. 'You should try and force yourself,' she tells him. I ask her how's the champagne and caviar. 'The ginger ale was fine,' she says, 'but the huckleberries tasted from herring.' She says she feels chilly, so I tell her, 'Close the window, it's cold outside,' 'Nu,' she replies, 'if I close the window, will it be warm outside?'"

He's surrounded now by a knot of hee-hawing wedding guests, including Myrna Halevy, who's sidled up next to him. In a motion that appears to be second nature, Saul hooks an arm about her shoulders and pulls her close; he leans toward her to accept her nibbling at his earlobe, and continues talking.

"When my father was dying, I asked him if he had any last wishes. 'All I want is you should fetch me a nice piece of your mother's coffee cake from the sideboard downstairs.' Then I have to tell him what my mama tells me, that it's for after . . ."

As you see, he was never a serious person, Saul Bozoff; I was the only thing that kept him in line. I tried my best to restrain his high spirits lest he squander them in the pursuit of happiness, and for a while it worked: the lost cause of his sorry self was found. But it didn't last; it wasn't enough he had me and the run of a Yid Neverland. He got lonely just the same.

Well, no hard feelings: may he be as at home in his shambling body as I am to be out of it. Anyway, I've stuck around long enough. A vagabond now, I'm content to let the winds of fancy blow me north or south, forward or backward in time. It's all the same to me. And if I sound a little wistful, I can assure you it'll pass; I've already as good as forgotten the container I came in. Still I suppose I ought to look for another—a worthier that can manage, with grace, to live in two worlds at once; though I'm in no hurry, savoring as I do the life (so to speak) of a solitary wanderer. Of course, you couldn't exactly call this flying solo; I'm not really in any immediate need of companions, since the air is as full of souls as falling leaves.

Glossary

beit midrash—Literally, "house of study"; a place for religious services and study, a small synagogue

belfer—Assistant to the melammed (teacher), often in charge of escorting small children to cheder (school)

bendl—The red thread worn on the left hand by the superstitious to ward off the evil eye

beytsim—Testicles

bisl—Bit; a little, a bit; a few

cheder—Literally, "room"; the traditional elementary school teaching the basics of Judaism and the Hebrew language

daven—To pray, used only in reference to Jewish prayer

draikop—Literally, "turn-head"; scatterbrain, numbskull

farkokte—Shitty

farmisht—Mixed up, befuddled

Gehinnom/Gehenna—Hell; the place where the souls of the wicked are punished and purified

geshmat—A Jew who has converted to the Christian faith

HaShem—Literally, "the Name"; God

Hasidism—A branch of Orthodox Judaism founded in the eighteenth century by Rabbi Israel Baal Shem Tov, who promoted spirituality and mysticism in reaction to the overly legalistic Judaism that had become the norm

khapper—Literally, "grabber"; men paid to kidnap Jewish boys (sometimes as young as eight) to fill the quota of Jews required to enter the cantonist schools in preparation for service in the Russian army

kiddush—Blessing over a cup of wine sanctifying the Sabbath or a holiday

kittl—A white garment worn by the pious at festive occasions; also worn by grooms at their wedding and male corpses at their burial

luftmensch—Literally, "airman"; a man without a steady occupation, often without a fixed abode, who makes his living from improvised sources; a man who starves by his wits

melammed—Literally, "teacher"; an elementary-school teacher

meshuggeh—Crazy

meshuggener—Mad, crazy; a madman; an eccentric

mikveh—Pool for ritual purification; ritual bath

minyan—Quorum of ten males required for public religious services

mishegoss—Madness

mitzvot—Literally, "commandments," as in those handed down by Moses from God but commonly used to describe good deeds

narishkeit—Foolishness, nonsense

pilpul—Literally, "pepper"; interpreting rabbinical texts through extreme disputation and casuistic hairsplitting

Rekrutshina Edict (Recruitment Decree)—Decree calling for conscription of Jewish boys between the ages of twelve and twenty-five; conscripts under the age of eighteen were to live in preparatory institutions until they were old enough to formally join the army; the twenty-five years of army service required of these recruits were to be counted from age eighteen.

shaigetz—A gentile boy; a wild Jewish boy

Shekhinah—Literally, "dwelling" or "settling"; used to denote the dwelling or settling of the divine presence of God; held by some to represent the feminine attributes of the divine presence, often viewed in Jewish mysticism as the Sabbath Bride

shmattes—Rags; worthless objects

shmendrick—Fool, dope, simpleton, nincompoop

shnorrer—A beggar, sponger, moocher, usually one with pretensions to respectability

shpilkes—Literally, "pins"; pins and needles; anxiousness

shreklikheit—Terror, frightfulness

shukeling—Literally, "shaking"; the ritual swaying during Jewish prayer

shul—Synagogue

stuss parlor—A place reserved for playing stuss, a variant of the card game faro

talis koton—A tasseled ritual undervest worn by pious Jews

tallis—A prayer shawl

tefillin (phylacteries)—Small leather boxes containing parchment inscribed with Torah verses, worn by pious Jews during weekday morning prayers

Tetragrammaton—Literally, "a word having four letters"; the four-letter name of God

tikkun olam—A Hebrew phrase meaning "repairing the world," accomplished according to Kabbalah through prayer and mitzvoth (good deeds)

yeshiva bocher—A student of a rabbinical academy

yitzkor—Literally, "remembrance"; memorial service recited four times a year by the congregation during Jewish holidays

Acknowledgments

"The Ballad of Mushie Momzer" first appeared in *Prairie Schooner*, volume 84, number 1, spring 2010, and was reprinted in *The Pushcart Prize XXXV: Best of the Small Presses*.

"Avigdor of the Apes" first appeared on JewishFiction.net and was reprinted in *Promised Lands: New Jewish American Fiction on Longing and Belonging*, ed. Derek Rubin (Lebanon, NH: University Press of New England, 2010).

"On Jacob's Ladder" first appeared in *Epoch*, 2009.

"Heaven Is Full of Windows" first appeared on narrativemagazine.com, 2009.

"Legend of the Lost" first appeared in *Ninth Letter*, volume 3, number 1, spring/summer 2006.

"The Man Who Would Be Kafka" first appeared in *Salmagundi*, number 126–127, spring/summer 2000.

"Lazar Malkin Enters Heaven," "The Lord and Morton Gruber," "Shimmele Fly-By-Night," "Moishe the Just," and "Aaron Makes a Match" appeared in *Lazar Malkin Enters Heaven* (New York: Viking, 1986).

"Zelik Rifkin and the Tree of Dreams" appeared in *A Plague of Dreamers* (New York: Scribner, 1994).

"The Sin of Elijah," "Romance," "Yiddish Twilight," and "The Wedding Jester" appeared in *The Wedding Jester* (Saint Paul, MN: Graywolf Press, 1999).

The author wishes to thank his steadfast agent, Liz Darhansoff, and Fiona McCrae and the gracious people at Graywolf Press for giving these stories another chance.

Also Steve Epstein for the flight of fancy on pages 167–168.

STEVE STERN, winner of the National Jewish Book award, is the author of several previous novels and collections of stories. He teaches at Skidmore College in upstate New York.

Book design by Connie Kuhnz. Composition by BookMobile Design and Publishing Services, Minneapolis, Minnesota. Manufactured by Friesens on acid-free 100 percent postconsumer wastepaper.